High praise for Mercedes Lackey's *Valdemar:*

"Leaves us simultaneously satisfied—and longing for more. Not an easy feat. . . . Once you jump into this world, you'll find yourself immediately involved, surrounded by new friends, and glad you made the trip."
—*Realms of Fantasy*

"Fast-moving action and intriguing characters. I can't wait to see what the final volume in this trilogy will bring forth."
—*The Book Net*

"Lackey's back doing what she does best, and the result is affecting and compulsive reading."
—*Locus*

"Lackey is a spellbinding storyteller who keeps your heart in your mouth as she spins her intricate webs of magical adventure."
—*Rave Reviews*

"A strong, suspenseful plot and well developed characters . . . will satisfy the most avid fantasy fan."
—*VOYA*

"Ms Lackey's Valdemar series is already a fantasy classic, and these newest adventures will generate even more acclaim for this fantasy superstar."
—*Romantic Times*

SUN IN GLORY

and Other Tales of Valdemar

Edited by

Mercedes Lackey

DAW BOOKS, INC.
DONALD A. WOLLHEIM, FOUNDER
375 Hudson Street, New York, NY 10014

ELIZABETH R. WOLLHEIM
SHEILA E. GILBERT
PUBLISHERS
http://www.dawbooks.com

First Printing, December 2003
1 2 3 4 5 6 7 8 9

ACKNOWLEDGMENTS

"Introduction" © 2002 *by Mercedes Lackey.*

"Errold's Journey" *by Catherine S. McMullen.* © 2003 by Catherine S. McMullen.

"The Cat Who Came to Dinner" *by Nancy Asire.* © 2003 by Nancy Asire.

"Winter Death" *by Michelle West.* © 2003 by Michelle West.

"A Herald's Rescue" *by Miriam S. Zucker.* © 2003 by Mickey Zucker Reichert.

"In the Eye of the Beholder" *by Josepha Sherman.* © 2003 by Josepha Sherman.

"Trance Tower Garrison" *by Fiona Patton.* © 2003 by Fiona Patton.

"Starhaven" *by Stephanie Shaver.* © 2003 by Stephanie Shaver.

"Rebirth" *by Judith Tarr.* © 2003 by Judith Tarr.

"Brock" *by Tanya Huff.* © 2003 by Tanya Huff.

"True Colors" *by Michael Longcor.* © 2003 by Michael Longcor.

"Touches the Earth" *by Brenda Cooper.* © 2003 by Brenda Cooper.

"Icebreaker" *by Rosemary Edghill.* © 2003 by eluki bes shahar.

"Sun in Glory" *by Mercedes Lackey.* © 2003 by Mercedes Lackey.

Contents

SUN IN GLORY
and Other Tales of Valdemar

Errold's Journey
by *Catherine S. McMullen*

Catherine S. McMullen was just twelve years old at the time of the writing of this story. She wrote her first story when she was seven, but that one is still buried in a drawer somewhere. She has had six stories published professionally or sold, starting with "Teddy Cat" in the August 1999 Interzone. She has been involved in the writing community since she was two, and is constantly reminded that many people used to know her when she was "just a kid." She loves to write, and is fascinated by the peculiarities of the English language. She is also an avid reader and has read as many as one thousand books in one year. Her work has appeared in such venues as Interzone, A Drop of Imagination, Spinouts, and Thrillogies.

Ma'ar was closing in, and while everyone was to be evacuated from the Tower area eventually, the non-combatants were leaving first. Urthro didn't want anyone nearby who would panic and cause disruption. Some large groups had already been sent to places far enough away to be safe from Ma'ar. Everyone was being spread out so thinly that Ma'ar would never have a large group close to him. It was true that the precautions might not be necessary. Ma'ar might eventually be defeated, but unfortunately it was unlikely to happen now, if ever.

I looked at the organized chaos and turned to Master Thomas. I had not counted on being part of the evacuation. I was apprenticed to a great war mage! Surely we would be needed?

"If we're packing our tent, we are going to be evacuated, Master Thomas. I am right in assuming this?"

"You are correct, Errold. You and I are going to go with a large group, about three hundred people, who are to be Gated to safety. The requirements of precisely where are not very rigid, the place just has to be fairly safe: that is, not a swamp or a lava pit, and very, very far away. It will be a one-way Gate; once we are gone, we will be cut off from Urtho's camp permanently. Ahhh, and I can see another question in your eyes. Why are we going with this particular group? They need us as mages: to heal, to defend, and to lead. The group was most reassured when they were told that we were to come with them. They asked for a mage because where they are to be Gated is the farthest away of all. We don't even know what animals live there, what the land is like, or even if there are any other humans there. This group is a special case, and you and I fit the requirements. More people have been watching your development as a healer than you realize. My leadership experience, and probably my reputation, help keep the group together."

"But what about the war here? Don't they need you to help defeat Ma'ar?"

"I am known as a very powerful war mage, I'll grant you that. But what about the people who are being scattered? Who will teach them our skills? Besides, I want to have a place to settle down, where I can live . . . with challenges to cope with, but none of them named Ma'ar. I am heartily sick of that name, and all the troubles that go with it."

"Well . . . I can understand why the group would

need a leader, but why not have a professional healer with the group? I mean, I am not really qualified as a mage or even a herbalist, let alone a healer yet. And a group of this size will need a proper healer, won't they?"

"Have you listened to anything I've been saying? You are known to be a dedicated student, and are well versed in herbal techniques. You would be able to cope with any injuries that occur on the journey, without a doubt. It would be perfect for both of us to go with them. Are you prepared to go? You do have a choice, you know. If you don't want to go, you don't have to. I would understand."

"When are we leaving, Master Thomas?"

Master Thomas smiled.

"That's the spirit. We are leaving soon. Very soon. Our group is ready, and we are only waiting until our Gate gets set up."

"About how long will that be? I haven't finished packing."

"About a half a day, but you'd better hurry. I've already almost finished getting my own things together."

"You just wanted to get a head start on me so the master wouldn't be shamed by his student's fast progress. Hah! I'll show you."

And with Master Thomas' laughter ringing in my ears, I left to pack for the journey of my life.

I had a list of what I needed to pack and how I needed to pack it. I had decided, after many shorter trips where I had been badly equipped, that I would not make a single mistake. It would be faster to pack everything slowly but correctly the first time, instead of throwing everything together and having to repack a hundred times. First in were some of my softer clothes, with no metal buckles or straps in them, placed against the back of the pack so that I had padding against my skin. I had made the mistake of putting a belt buckle at my back once before, on one of my short journeys into the forest. Needless to say, after a day of it rubbing against me, that was a mistake I intended never to repeat.

Next the seeds went in, a vital component of my supplies. When we reached a place where we could settle down, the seeds would be needed to grow crops, and for my herbs. I placed the seeds in specially prepared bags that were proof against water and fire, and woven through with protective spells. The spells had been done by me, not Master Thomas. Master Thomas was an expert on war magics, but he recognized that I knew more about the smaller, more useful spells for daily chores. It wasn't something that was likely to get me recognition as a great mage, but I had a knack for it. After I had learned all the simple spells that Master Thomas could teach me, and after that had become apparent that I would never master the really powerful ones, I started turning to books.

I had had to learn most of what I knew by myself, deciphering the spells alone. I still hadn't learned even half of what I wanted to know, so I was taking some books with me. It had been hard to decide what books to take and which ones to give away, but it came down to what I would really need and, eventually, what a village would need. I carefully packed five spell books into my pack, wrapping them in more clothes. I had also prepared a whole range of herbal remedies, but only a little of each. Someone in the group was sure to need them as we traveled, and I didn't want to be caught unprepared.

Lastly, I packed the food, water, and metal tools that Master Thomas had given me to carry for the group. These all went at the top because they would be needed most often. I did one last check of the list, making sure I hadn't left anything out, then I struggled into the straps and heaved the pack onto my shoulders. I had been confident that I could cope with the weight, or that I would get used to it in time, but it turned out that I had a previously undiscovered ability to underestimate weight. Well, I would have to adapt or die . . . guess which one I thought was more likely at that stage!

I took a last look at my bare tent. It was a sobering sight, seeing the emptiness of it, when only a couple of days ago it had been full of furniture, books, clothes, and other paraphernalia. Everything had either been packed to be taken with us, or given away. There was no point asking people to save things for us, as we would never be coming back. There were some very happy mages as a result of the grand book handout that Master Thomas and I conducted. So many loved, well-used books, now in so many different hands. Oh well, at least they would be appreciated. I sighed and staggered off to find Master Thomas. I hoped that he wasn't moving around, as I didn't want the camp's last memory of me being me hyperventilating as the pack became too much. Probably a forlorn hope, unfortunately.

Our Gate was finally ready. A place sufficiently far away had been found: a forest, with really huge trees. It was so remote that nobody even recognized the types of trees. We all lined up, all loaded down with our carefully prepared and very heavy packs. Have I already mentioned heavy? Anything that couldn't be carried just wasn't taken. When people complained about their packs being too heavy, Master Thomas just took out the really useless things—like jewelry, coins, and so on—and showed them the differences in weight. It worked every time. As soon as everyone was ready, the Gate was activated, showing the forest on the other side. When the last person was through the Gate, it closed. The light from the camp on the other side disappeared, and we were left in the half-light under towering tree giants. We were a long way away from home, with no chance of ever returning.

Master Thomas clapped his hands for everyone's attention.

"We have one long-term problem and a lot of short-term problems," he began. "The long-term problem is finding a place with suitable resources to settle down and build a village. The short-term problems are who will cook, who will hunt, who shares tents with whom, what the rotations of lookouts are to be—in other words our organization for traveling and getting along together. Before we start moving, we must have a meeting to sort everything out. Anyone who has anything to contribute, or who thinks they can do something particularly well, should speak up. This meeting is essential to the group's well-being, so everyone must come along."

The meeting had a really long agenda, and it lasted until after dark. Master Thomas was quickly confirmed as the leader of our group, because he was already experienced with organizing large numbers of people. After that was established he ran everything efficiently, but it still took a long time and a lot of talking. Everyone had to do something, but he arranged duties so that people did what they were good at or enjoyed. The only people who did not have mundane tasks assigned to them were Master Thomas and myself. Master Thomas actually had the hardest task of all: running things, making decisions, sorting out disputes, and shouldering the heavy burden of responsibility. My trouble was that quite a few people didn't realize that I was his student. After a few complaints along the lines of "What about 'im, he don't have to do no dishwashing!" everyone was treated to a lecture from Master Thomas, about who had heated the water, driven the insects away, made the tents waterproof, and many other things. It then became established that for the little spells, you came to me, not him. After that, I not only didn't have to do chores, but I was called on to do a lot of spells that I had never tried before. I knew I would have to study my books a lot more, and find new possibilities in some previously useless spells.

I did some reading by the campfire's light, then returned to the tent that Master Thomas and I shared. He was outside, staring up at the sky through a break in the trees' canopy. He stood up and asked me to walk with him. We had only gone a short distance when there was a flash of light in the east, but it was the sort of flash that blazed out but just kept getting stronger and stronger for a few seconds. Slowly it began to fade. Everyone had stopped talking by then, and they were all looking across at us. I had to turn away, so that I did not show the worry that I was feeling for the people nearer to the blast. Many of my friends had been very much closer.

"That must have been the magical weapon of Urtho's combined with the Tower being annihilated," said Master Thomas. "Hurry, we don't have much time." I had to start to run to keep up with him.

"Why are you running? What's the threat to us?"

"Think. We are at least an ocean away from all that magic, yet we still saw the flash! We must shield the campsite from the magical blast which will follow. If we shield the group, the effects on us might not be too bad. We can only hope."

We gathered everyone together and began putting up the shields. A lot of people were scared, but Master Thomas reassured them by explaining what the flash of light had meant, just as he had explained it to me. Once the shields were up, we just settled down to wait. People began to relax and make themselves comfortable. It had been lucky that nobody had put up their tents too far away from anyone else. A smaller area meant a tougher shield. Master Thomas and I walked back the short distance to our tent and went inside. I was worried, but I hadn't wanted to ask any questions in front of the rest of the group. It would only have scared them.

"Master Thomas, if you think the magic will be dangerous for us, all the way over here, what would it be like over there?" I asked. "Will anyone have survived?"

"I think Urtho's remaining people will have survived. They have experienced mages who are experts at coping with the unexpected. But I don't think the land or the animals on it will ever be the same again." He looked into the distance and seemed thoughtful.

"This means the changing of magic as we know it forever. The people like you, who can ration their magic, will be the ones who prosper and survive. It is highly likely that I will never be able to perform really powerful spells ever again. We have never seen anything like this before, this kind of magical situation. You have just become part of an event that will be remembered forever as the day magic changed."

* * *

Half an hour later the mage storm hit the shields with deadly force. I soon began to worry more about us than the people closer to the blast. Master Thomas and I were the only mages here, whereas they had many skilled mages to put up shields and protective spells. We really had our hands full, considering what lay outside of our shields. Out there, the forest seemed to be in chaos. Magic was swirling everywhere, and when I looked outside of the shields for too long, my eyes hurt. Just as I thought we could hold the storm back up for no longer, it abated. The assault had only lasted for a day, but to me it seemed like it had lasted for weeks. When we lowered the shields, the forest around us seemed fairly normal. But then, when night would normally have fallen, there was only an eerie half-light. There were places where piles of ash and soot were all that was left of great tree giants. Flickering lights in the trees had everyone scared, and the few children in our group had to stay with their parents all the time. I made an observation to Master Thomas about something that worried me a lot.

"Master Thomas, I have noticed something and I want to know whether it is just me. Weren't the leaves green and healthy before the mage storm hit, and not brown and falling from the trees?"

"I think you're right about that, Errold. But what is your point? There have been much worse things done by the mage storm than simply changing the state of the leaves."

"That's just it! All the other effects of the mage storm have been obvious. But what if there are effects that are even more subtle? If the state of the leaves could be changed, couldn't berries we know are safe to eat have become poisonous?"

"That is a very intelligent observation to make, Errold. I will alert the rest of the group to this new danger. They might not react very well, but I think it is necessary. Thank you. I wouldn't want to lose anyone from the group, and your observation may have stopped that from happening because of foolish mistakes."

As I sat in our tent, I continued to worry, and turned similar thoughts over in my head. This forest had been changed dramatically by what Master Thomas now called the "mage storm." But could we survive in it? Or was even the water no longer safe to drink? And what about the animals that hadn't been within our shields? What about them?

We began traveling again the second morning after the storm. All seemed well until one of the scouts saw huge animal footprints. We reported back to Master Thomas, as he didn't recognize what he had seen. Everyone was told to be especially careful until we learned what the animal ate, and more importantly, whether its diet might include us!

The next day, while the group was resting and eating, I wandered off in search of any recognizable wild herbs. I had no luck in finding any, and decided that when we settled down I would experiment to see what those that were new to me were useful for. I was walking back to where the group was resting when I came upon the type of animal that must have made the footprints. It was large and woolly, but seemed to be fairly harmless. I had never seen anything like it in the forests I had traveled before. I herded it back to the group, and Master Thomas proposed that it be taken with us. We had no other livestock for when we founded the village, and besides, it could carry packs.

I thought that the thing probably wasn't safe to eat, because of the magic that had obviously affected it. Master Thomas called a meeting to discuss possible problems from changed animals.

"As we all know, the mage storm has obviously affected the land, and the plants and animals on it. We have one of the results of the storm in our camp now, the animal we have named Carpet. Carpet will be very helpful to us when we settle down, but although she is apparently safe, we do have to look at the wider range of our worries. I personally have noticed that Carpet is unusually intelligent, and other people have also commented on this. Forest animals are often cunning, but never intelligent. We will have to be exceptionably wary, and closely observe all animals that we encounter. From now on our scouts will be carrying magical sensors that Errold will make. These will detect any large animals nearby, and by night I will erect shields around the camp to protect us when we are sleeping. Does anyone have anything else to suggest, or does anyone disagree with our plan?"

Now that people knew the facts, the meeting went well. People who wanted to be taken off scout duty were reassigned, but generally everybody was fairly happy with what our leader had proposed. After everyone had dispersed, I went over to Master Thomas.

"Master Thomas? I have an idea." I said.

"What is it?"

"Master, consider the level of intelligence in our friend Carpet. Herbivores are usually a bit dim, they don't seem to need that much intelligence, but Carpet is as bright as a dog. If a herbivore is now that smart, what will the carnivores be like? They may be extremely intelligent now, possibly even sentient—and all that being sentient implies."

"This is true, Errold. What are you proposing?"

"Making the sensors for the scouts won't be hard. At most, it will take a couple of hours. I must do some scouting myself, though. While you are shielding the camp, I will set up scanning spells to sweep the forest for a hundred yards all around. If some of predators in this forest are as intelligent as we think, they will come at night to observe us. If I detect something, I will go out and make sure it is harmless or try to disable it."

"That's very good proposition, Errold. But I don't want you outside of my protection like that. I am tempted to go instead of you, but I am used to working with huge amounts of magic and I would not be as good as you would be against a single animal. You use the smallest spells to the best advantage. I give you permission for this plan. Do you really think that the predators will be so intelligent?"

"Yes, I do. Even before the storm, it was thought that some predators in the known world were remarkably cunning, if only in pursuit of their prey. I think that any new 'smart' predators will be a real threat to us, if not now, then when we settle down. It is vital for us to establish that we are not prey and should be avoided."

Master Thomas nodded his head but still looked doubtful.

"Better figure out how you are to disable predators, though. They will be fast, deadly, and intelligent, while you are just intelligent. You need a spell that can tell if something really is intelligent."

In all my studies, I had not come across anything like that.

"It'll be tricky, but I'm sure I'll think of something,

Master Thomas," I said, not at all sure if I could actually do it.

I lay in my tent that night, furiously studying the spell books I had brought. I had an idea that would use a really simple spell. Predators are curious, and did a lot of patient stalking. Thus, my trap worked on curiosity and would certainly disable anything watching me. It was the sensing of large animals that I needed to work on. I stayed up most of the night, figuring out how to combine shields together, how to get the right range, and the search requirements. I got it together eventually, then crawled gratefully to my bed roll. I needed all the sleep I could get, because I knew that some night soon we would have company.

The following day everything seemed to go fairly normally. We noticed no large shapes in the distance, and saw no unusual tracks. I still felt as if we were being watched, though. Any truly smart animal would stay on rocky ground or the trunks of fallen trees. It was nightfall that I was waiting for. That was when we were not moving and the shields would be up. It would be then that I would be prowling—just like a predator.

After we had found a suitable spot to camp, I immediately cast my sensing spell, but it wasn't till halfway though the night that it alerted me. I sneaked out of camp, using a simple camouflage enchantment on my clothes and carrying a rope. The magical sensor that I carried told me when I was fairly close to the animal, and it "felt" only one animal in a hundred-yard radius. This made everything a lot easier for me. I sat down a few yards from the bushes where my sensor amulet had shown the animal was. Now I prepared the spell that I had thought of using the night before. I took my time. Anything nearby that was curious would be watching intently as I waved my hands and conjured energies. Then closed my eyes and set it off.

Even with my eyes shut, the blinding flash of light still hurt. Judging from the thrashing noises and growls from the bushes, whatever had been lurking there had been staring at what I had been doing with intense interest. I conjured a globe of light and set it hanging in midair. It showed a huge cat with a high forehead. Its fur was a very deep shade of green.

Using my rope, I ensnared the thrashing limbs and tied up the cat before it could see again. Then I sat down in front of it, weaving a rather delicate and tricky translation spell. Soon I could hear that the animal's noises were not really just yowling, but some very nasty swear words.

After it had blinked a few times, and seemed to be able to see a bit, it focused its gaze on me.

"Speak, I can understand," I told it.

For a moment it just stared in surprise.

"Well? Why haven't you killed me?" it asked.

"I could ask why you have not attacked our other scouts," I replied. "But I already know why. You are intelligent, and you were being sensible and cautious. Because of that, I caught you with a spell that would have worked with any truly intelligent species. A more stupid predator would have just attacked me because I am smaller and look defenseless."

"I do not care to risk injury by attacking dangerous prey. If I am not fast, fit, and strong, I will starve."

"To answer your first question, I haven't killed you, because we, too, are an intelligent species."

"That is obvious. I was sent to watch your camp for three nights, then report to the rest of the pack. You puzzled us: you do not hunt, yet you do not graze either. You are soft and defenseless, like grazers, yet bright and cunning . . ."

"Like hunters."

"Yes. We would have attacked your camp already, otherwise."

"That would have been very, very silly. Our weapons are not claws and teeth, but they are still deadly."

"Now I know that your species is truly sentient, not like the mrran."

"Mrran? What is that?" I asked

"A mrran is the animal that you have adopted into your herd—or should I say pack? It puzzled me greatly when you did not kill and eat the mrran. The others could hardly believe me when I told them."

"We have other uses for the mrran. It provides wool to cover us. Unlike you, we have little fur of our own. Do you understand that?"

"Yes. In a way I pity you for not having a naturally warm, glossy, thick coat." At this it preened a bit. "What are the other reasons?"

"Do you remember what happened a couple of days ago?"

"Vaguely. There was a storm . . . and before the storm I was something else. As smart as the mrran, perhaps. Maybe even less smart. During the storm, I changed. All those of my pack changed."

"In a way, the storm created us as well," I explained. "We make our own food, we are neither hunters nor hunted. But we are very, very dangerous. Spread the message to your pack: leave us alone. Soon we shall stop and make a thing called a village. Stay away from it. You are most dangerous when you pounce, but we are even more deadly when we stop moving."

"I have seen that."

I slipped the knots on its bonds and it shook itself free in a moment. It stood and looked at me. After a moment it spoke.

'Something in me says I shouldn't respect anything without fur. But I respect your kind if they are all as smart as you. Is this the right thing to feel, I wonder?"

"I respect your kind." I replied. "But I do not fear them."

"Then we are equal. And because we are equal, I don't think that our peoples should be enemies."

"Spoken like a true and intelligent predator. If my villagers and your pack can stay friendly, then when one of you is sick or injured and needs care, I can help."

"Help the injured? Why?"

"Because it benefits everyone. Are you intelligent enough to see that?"

If cats could frown, it did.

"Fighting would bring the pack no benefit," it said eventually. "I assume that you need clear land and nearby water for your village?"

"Yes, we do. That is why we have not settled down yet. There are too many trees."

"If you continue on for about a day, and then turn east, you will come to the edge of the forest, where the grasslands begin. There is a stream running close by. We don't like water or open land. You are welcome to it."

"Thank you, I think we shall like it a lot."

I picked up my pack, but it did not move.

"Just one last question before I go to my pack. Do you know what we were before the storm?"

'You were cats," I guessed. "All that has been changed is your coloring, your intelligence, and your size. You weren't dark green before the storm, and you didn't have language and reasoning. You certainly weren't four yards long."

I hoped that I had guessed correctly, but soon it nodded its head and padded for the trees. Then it stopped and looked back.

"Perhaps, sometime, we should talk again," it suggested. "It could prevent misunderstandings in the future. If you need to speak to me, just ask one of my people for me. My name is Proouw."

"A good suggestion, Proouw. My name is Errold." I said.

Proouw turned and glided away into the shadows of the forest without another word.

After I had had the meeting with Proouw, I went back to the camp and called a meeting. I explained what had happened, what he had told us, and what I had arranged. Everyone was very happy that we would not be hunted by anything so big and intelligent, and that there was a site nearby to build the village on. It was felt that looking after Proouw and his pack medically was a fair exchange. After the meeting was over, I just sat and thought. I wondered whether the shields hadn't somehow leaked during the storm, and changed me like it had changed the cats. The old Errold would have never even thought of that plan, let alone have insisted that he be the one to carry it out! And the old Errold wouldn't have negotiated like that with Proouw. But I eventually decided that it was just me doing what everyone did, adapting as new things happened to me.

After a day of traveling, and after we turned east, we found the spot Proouw had mentioned. It was perfect for our needs, and everyone immediately started talking about what we would do, and how the village would be organized and laid out. There was also discussion about what the village would be called. They eventually decided on a name . . . Errolds Grove!

It was a big surprise to me, but as they explained, I had done the most in regard to founding it. The stream was named Master Thomas' stream, which was just as important, as without water there could be no village. I was happy, and the arrangement with the cats worked out well, with Proouw and I meeting like ambassadors, and the pack chasing mrran in our direction to keep in our flock. I had a feeling that the village would last for a long time, two thousand years . . . or maybe more.

The Cat Who Came to Dinner

by *Nancy Asire*

Nancy Asire is the author of four novels, Twilight's Kingdoms, Tears Of Time, To Fall Like Stars *and* Wizard Spawn. *She also has written short stories for the series anthologies* Heroes in Hell *and* Merovingen Nights, *and a short story for Mercedes Lackey's* Flights of Fantasy. *She has lived in Africa and traveled the world, but now resides in Missouri with her cats and two vintage Corvairs.*

The last rays of the setting sun struck the multiple small circular windows of the chapel, fracturing the light into a myriad of sparks dancing on the warm wooden walls and on the altar. Reulan stood for a long moment caught in the glittering manifestation of God's greatest gift to mankind—light. Several village women had finished their task of caring for the interior of the sanctuary only a candlemark ago, and the pungent scent of wood polish filled the chapel.

Reulan held a taper in both hands as he stood facing the altar of Vkandis Sunlord. Where in colder weather a fire burned on the altar, summertime warmth dictated a profusion of red flowers. Reulan briefly bowed his head in contemplation—Vkandis, source of all comfort, light and warmth, protector and sustainer of mankind.

The light faded fractionally. Reulan stepped close to the altar and, as the chapel grew dim with the setting of the sun, he lit the large, thick candle that stood at the center of the altar. Darkness should never touch the chapel, with some form of light needed at all times to honor the Sunlord.

Flickering shadows danced on the chimney altar, then steadied as the candleflame stabilized. The gold image of Vkandis on the chimney glittered in that candlelight, the features of the image inscrutable but hinting of both power and love. Reulan bowed his head again in homage to the God, made the sign of the Holy Disk, and left the chapel through the door to one side of the altar.

Only a step lay between the chapel and Reulan's room, but the distance might as well have been leagues. Closing the door, he removed the heavy gold chain of a Sun-priest and then his vestments, finally standing clad in simple black robes. He sighed quietly, standing silent for a few long breaths, mentally moving from his attitude of worship into the mundane world. With the Night Candle lit, the chapel secure until the rising sun celebration, he could now turn to supper.

The height of summer was nearly on the village of Sweetwater. Two windows and a door stood open to catch the breeze. Just enough light lingered for Reulan to strike flame to the candles on the table, dresser, kitchen cupboard and the smaller table that stood beside his narrow cot. He gathered up the greens he had picked from his garden, added them to the plate where his sausage sat next to a roasted potato, and filled a cup with water from the village well—water so pure and sweet it had given this village its name. Sitting down at the table, he blessed the food he was about to eat, and looked up.

A pair of eyes looked back, the candlelight flaming in their depths like golden fire.

"Vkandis preserve me!" he murmured, staring at the sight. It was a cat, a very large and furry cat, sitting in the chair opposite as if specifically invited to dinner. "Where in the God's green earth did *you* come from?"

The cat, as was typical of all members of the species, gazed back expressionless as a statue. Having recovered from his surprise, Reulan examined the cat closely. Large was a understatement: this was possibly the biggest cat he had ever seen, and the village of Sweetwater was no stranger to champion mousers. But here sat an interloper. The cats of Sweetwater were, by and large, brown or gray tabbies, while his "guest" sported a coat of light cream. A thick mane surrounded the cat's face and, even without seeing it, Reulan knew the creature's tail most likely would be a plume.

"You *are* a big one," he observed. The cat yawned and resumed its staring. "Begging for dinner, are you? I don't think I have any mice and I doubt you can while away the evening with a tale or two. However, the God has been generous this summer and I'm more than willing to share."

He cut off a hunk of his sausage and extended it. With a delicacy belying its size, the cat took the offered meat gently, jumped to the floor, and settled down to its dinner. Reulan chewed his own meal thoughtfully. The low rumble of a purr filled the room and, for an instant, Reulan was transported back to his father's barn, where he had sometimes sat surrounded by the resident cats, all of whom seemed content to lie purring in the sun until night and the hunt were upon them.

Darkness hovered not far away, the long summertime dusk deepening outside. Reulan cleaned his dish, put it away, and blew out the candle on the cupboard. He expected his visitor to be gone when he turned back, but, no, the cat was now busy cleaning his face and whiskers.

"Time to go," Reulan said, and reached down to push his guest toward the open door. "Dawn comes early, and I must be in bed."

The cat protested with a deep meow, standing stiff-legged, but finally allowed Reulan to escort him out the door. He stood facing Reulan for a moment, a half-accusing expression on his face and then sat down, wrapping his thickly-furred tail around his front paws. The young priest felt a slight twinge of guilt as he closed the door and turned toward his bed. Tomorrow he would ask around the village to see if anyone knew who might own the cat. Tonight, however, with all of Sweetwater's barns available, the feline could easily find any number of places to hunt and sleep.

The first light of dawn woke Reulan from a deep sleep. Something heavy lay next to his feet and, when he looked down to the end of his bed, he was amazed to find the cream-colored tabby curled up in a comfortable ball, still sleeping deeply. *The window,* he thought absently, *the cat must have come in through the window last night. We'll see how long he stays.*

But all that day, through the numerous chores Reulan completed, the day after and the next, the cat never stayed far away. No matter what he did—whether weeding his garden, repairing a few shingles on the chapel (and it took some doing to scale the tree nearby to jump across to the roof), or taking meditative walks through the fields or forest—the cat kept close to his side. No one Reulan spoke with could remember seeing such a magnificent beast or one of that particular color. He finally admitted the cat had adopted him and felt oddly grateful for the company.

One evening as he and the cat sat down to supper together, Reulan heard the distant rumble of thunder. He had been expecting a storm, for the air had been close and heavy all day, and its coming promised some relief from the heat. Finished with both dinner and toilet, the cat disappeared into the night. He never stayed away long . . . no chasing down sausages in the night for this fellow. Far better to wait politely and let the human provide the meal.

Reulan closed the shutters to his room as the wind rose and the temperature started to drop. Distant lighting became more vivid now and foretold a good soaking overnight rain. Reulan still didn't see the cat and called out to his companion, but saw nothing. A faint pang of anxiety tightened his heart—he didn't want the poor fellow to be caught in a downpour. Another rumble of thunder and one last call. *Cat's been out in the rain before,* he thought, *and likely will be again. Trust to the Goddess to keep him safe.*

Shutting the door, Reulan slipped into bed, blessed himself with thoughts of the god he served, and blew out the candle. One last prayer for the safety of the cat crossed his mind, and then he fell asleep, the thunder now overhead and the rain beating down on his roof.

Long years of training and practice woke Reulan the next morning before dawn, though with his windows shuttered the interior of his room was dark as night. He reached for the candle on his bedside table and froze in place. A light purr sounded from the end of his bed and the by now familiar weight of the cat shifted ever so slightly beside Reulan's feet. A chill ran up Reulan's spine as he lit the candle and discovered the cat busily engrossed in his morning bath. A quick glance to both windows revealed that the wind had not blown them open during the night, and that the door remained securely shut. How, in the name of Vkandis Sunlord, had the cat managed to get inside?

"You're the oddest fellow I've ever had the occasion to meet," Reulan said, reaching down to scratch his bedmate behind the ears, the sound of his own voice helping dispel the strangeness of the situation. "You must have run in between my feet last night without my knowing it, no?" The cat merely yawned, showing sharp white teeth and pink tongue.

Reulan stretched, rose from bed, and opened his windows and door. The storm had indeed cleared the air and, this high in the hills, even in summer the morning was bracingly cool. The cat rubbed up against his ankles, meowed pitifully as if he had not eaten in days, and planted himself in the chair he had claimed for his own. Reulan washed his face from the bucket on the cupboard, dried off, and donned his vestments. The rising sun celebration was close at hand; he left his room, crossed the small chapel, and threw open the doors at its west end. Then, standing before the altar, he closed his eyes, opened his mind to the glory of the god, and waited for first light to strike the windows above his head.

He felt a bump against his leg and quickly opened his eyes. The cat sat beside him, facing the altar, proper as any worshiping villager. At first, this had somehow bothered Reulan, but he believed that Vkandis cared for all creatures, that any who wished to worship the God should be welcome at his altar. Reulan heard the village farmers arriving and sensed them standing in silent meditation as the first rays of sun struck the windows above. Lifting his hands, Reulan spoke the words of Morning Greeting.

"Vkandis Sunlord, Giver of Life and Light, be with us today. We praise you, we honor you, we keep you in our hearts and minds. What is good and true, help us to do and become. What is hateful and cruel, aid us in denying. We offer this day to you, Sunlord, and seek your blessings on all that we do."

"May it be so," responded the voices behind him.

Reulan extinguished the candle that had lit the chapel during the night and turned to face his congregation. "Go forth to daylight, knowing the god is by your side."

The farmers bowed their heads briefly, smiled at Reulan, and silently filed out of the chapel to their various fields and gardens. Once again, the cat rubbed up against his legs, meowing pitifully.

"Breakfast, eh? What would you like this morning, sir cat? I have only what I've given you in the past—sausage. I'd think you'd grow tired of it."

The cat looked up and, for a brief moment, Reulan could have sworn he heard a voice saying, "Well, if you *must* ask, I'd really rather have fish."

He laughed quietly, amused that he had assigned spoken words to an animal, and returned to his room and his morning meal, the cat following close behind.

Being a Sun-priest in a small village required not only knowledge of the ways of Vkandis Sunlord but also of teaching, mending (both physical and metaphysical), gardening and, to a certain extent, more than a passing proficiency in healing. But one of the most pleasant duties of a priest to Reulan's mind was the time he spent in silent meditation, fixing his mind on the glory of love of the god he served. It had become his habit, not long after arriving in Sweetwater and becoming old Beckor's assistant priest, to spend this time outdoors, preferably at high noon when Vkandis' power was the greatest. The place he set aside for communion with the god was a small clearing in the forest east of the village. It was there that Reulan turned his footsteps this day, his morning chores done and the villagers about their daily tasks. He strode along the pathway, his mind stilled, already slipping into light meditation. The cat, as usual, came along, periodically darting off into the bushes, then back again.

The day was especially fine, blue sky above the sunlight slanting through the trees. Reulan rejoiced and marveled at the power of the god that protected the land and its people. Though apprenticed at an early age to Beckor, which made his parents proud and additionally relieved them of a mouth to feed, he had always felt close to the god. Somehow he sensed he had been born to this . . . that he had been chosen from an early age. Now with Beckor gone to the god and Reulan no longer apprenticed, his life seemed to have become all it was meant to be.

The clearing lay just over a rocky rise in the ground. Reulan could see the sunlight pooling ahead and quickened his pace, eager to arrive at his goal.

:Reulan! Snake! Don't move!:

For a moment, Reulan thought his heart had stopped. He certainly did, for anyone who had been born and raised in this area of Karse knew the peril of snakes. Frozen into immobility, he looked down to see a large rock snake stretched out on the path in a patch of sunlight, only two steps away. A cold sweat broke out on Reulan's forehead: the bite of a rock snake was often fatal. Very carefully and ever so slowly, he backed away, never taking his eyes from the reptile.

Halfway down the path now and far enough away that the snake posed no immediate danger, he started shaking, aware just how close to death he had come. But who had called out his name? Who had warned him?

The cat rubbed up against his leg and sat down.

:Well,: a voice said inside his head. *:The least you could do is thank me.:*

Reulan stared at the cat, feeling his mouth drop open.

:And close your mouth before you catch flies,: the cat advised, cocking his head and twitching his tail around his front paws.

A *talking* cat! Knees suddenly weak, Reulan glanced around, very carefully this time, for a place to sit that was not already occupied by a snake. Sinking down on a small boulder, he stared at the cat, his pulse racing. He had heard old grandmother's tales about talking beasts—birds, horses, cats—creatures larger than normal that could speak mind-to-mind, but he had always considered these tales a fine way to while away the long hours of a winter night, not truth. But now . . .

Reulan swallowed heavily. "You talk!" he finally got out when he had gained control of his voice.

:It's fortunate for you that I do,: the cat retorted, but Reulan sensed a smile. *:And since we're now on speaking terms, you may call me Khar.:*

Khar? Certainly no name of any cat he had ever known—certainly not Boots, Patches, Puss, or any of the other descriptive appellations people gave their cats.

"But . . . how . . . I mean, you're speaking to me like . . . like . . ."

:A person?: And this time Reulan was certain he heard a laugh. *:We all have our burdens to bear. And yours, Sun-priest, is rudeness. You* still *haven't thanked me.:*

Reulan licked his lips and swallowed again. "Thank you, Khar. I could be dead if you hadn't been with me! But why—"

:If you'd be so kind,: Khar interrupted, busy now smoothing down his abundant whiskers, *:I'd appreciate a small reward. I would suggest a fish . . . a large, fat fish.:*

How catlike. Despite his confusion and awe, Reulan smiled. Trust a feline to always be looking out for itself. "I'm sorry, Khar," he said, feeling slightly foolish to be talking to a cat. "Sweetwater has no fish. And if we wanted fish, which most of us don't, we'd have to depend on traders or go to Sunhame itself."

:Well, now, that's *an idea. Let's go to Sunhame, you and I, and you can get me a fish.:*

Reulan stared at the cat, unsure if he was being mocked or not. Sunhame was more than four days' walk away, not an arduous journey, but one he had not particularly contemplated. A sudden thought passed through his mind. Sunhame. He hadn't been in the capital city since the final six-month period of his training as Sun-priest and that had been over three years ago. The Holy Writ required that every person, once in his or her lifetime, should visit Sunhame. The most propitious of times to make that journey was at midsummer, to be present at the high holy day of Summer Solstice, when the sun stood longest in the sky. Naturally, the journey was even more important for Sun-priests, who were expected to serve as examples to the populace. He mentally figured out the calendar: Summer Solstice was only six days away. He could easily make Sunhame by then.

He snorted. What was he thinking? Why should he suddenly leave his village to make a journey to Sunhame? Certainly not for a fish, though he knew he owed Khar more than a simple meal for saving his life. On the other hand, the village was as prosperous as a village its size could be, its people were healthy, and no babies were due. Besides, the village midwife could handle *that* far better than he.

A strange, fey mood swept over him. Sunhame. Why not?

"Do you think," he asked, reaching down to scratch Khar under the chin, "that you could wait a bit to collect your reward? Long enough for me to set things right in the village and to pack my supplies? Or do you suggest we leave this very day?"

If feline expressions could be said to duplicate those of human beings, Khar looked positively disgusted. :*Cats, Reulan,*: he said with monumental dignity, :*are known for their patience. A few more days certainly won't kill me.*:

And so it had been decided. Reulan had sought out Santon, the village headman, and explained that he would be making a pilgrimage to Sunhame to fulfill his obligation to be present at the Temple of Vkandis Sunlord at the Summer Solstice. Santon, understandably, was somewhat taken aback by the suddenness of this decision, but Reulan had mollified the big farmer by pointing out that the villagers could walk to Two Trees, the closest village, for their own midsummer celebration at that chapel. And if anyone was injured or needed medical care, Two Trees was large enough to have its own healer.

Truth be told, another reason surfaced in Reulan's mind for the journey, and that was simple curiosity. When traders had come through Sweetwater a month ago, they had told the villagers that the tragic and untimely death of the Son of the Sun, along with the inability of the seniormost priests of the Temple to choose his successor, had thrown Sunhame into confused anticipation. From what the traders said, infighting among various factions of the senior priesthood had broken out. Time and again they had sought a consensus, put forward various candidates, but had reached no agreement. It seemed as if something was blocking a decision that would make everyone happy.

Reulan looked on the infighting among his superiors with a certain amount of disdain. Politics! God, he *hated* politics! As a priest, it was his duty to worship Vkandis and to look after the god's people, not to find ways to increase his own standing. But if there was any time to journey to Sunhame, to see the Temple again, and possibly to be present at the elevation of the new Son of the Sun, this was it.

And so, the following morning Reulan set forth, carrying a light pack filled with provisions enough to see him there and back. The villagers had wished him a good journey and smiled to see their priest and his always-present cat set off down the dusty road to the south. Long accustomed to physical activity, Reulan soon settled into his walking stride, an easy gait that would carry him to his stopping place for the night without leaving him exhausted. He glanced down at Khar who trotted alongside, and shook his head. If he hadn't thought his eyes were deceiving him, he would have sworn that Khar had grown overnight. The biggest cat he had ever seen now appeared even bigger.

"Well, Khar," he said conversationally, "are you happy now? We're off to Sunhame and your fish."

:*And possibly more than that,*: was the cat's reply.

Reulan waited for Khar to continue, but the cat fell silent. Reulan shook his head. Cats. Some of the most secretive creatures ever born, it ill served a human to attempt to pry information from them. Even ones who spoke.

The setting sun to his right, Reulan and Khar entered the next village south of Sweetwater. His black robes and gold chain of office would grant him food and rest wherever he chose to stop, but he aimed for the chapel, knowing that Faroaks' own priest would welcome him for the night. And he was correct, for as he approached the chapel to attend its own sunset service, Dhadi stood at the doors, waiting for the villagers who chose to attend the service.

"Reulan!" the priest said, extending his hand in greeting. "What brings you to Faroaks?" His eyes fell on the cat, who sat at Reulan's side, breathing a bit heavily from the long walk. "God of Light, Reulan! Where in the world did you find that cat? It's absolutely huge!"

Reulan glanced at Khar and started. If possible, Khar had grown even more during the walk from Sweetwater. "He adopted me," he explained lamely, feeling as if he had blundered into some story. And Dhadi only knew the half of it. Reulan smiled what he hoped was his most disarming smile. "I'm on my way to Sunhame for the Summer Solstice and if I could spend the night with you, I'd be most appreciative."

"Of course," Dhadi said. "'Come in, Reulan. The sun's nearly set and I must light the Night Candle."

He looked slightly askance at Khar. "Does he follow you even to services?"

"He's one of the god's creatures," Reulan responded. "If you don't mind, he'll come with me."

For a moment, Reulan thought Dhadi would refuse, but his fellow priest merely shook his head and gestured inside. 'Stranger things have happened," he murmured. "You and your cat are welcome, Reulan. The god's blessing be on both of you."

After assisting Dhadi in celebrating the rising sun and sharing a wholesome breakfast with his fellow priest, Reulan set out on the road again. He had not even reached the fields when he noticed several villagers following after. With the breeze at his back, he overheard snatches of conversation, not a bit of which was devoted to him. No, it was Khar they spoke about. Finally, curiosity triumphed and one of the men trotted up to Reulan's side.

"Begging your pardon, Sun's-ray," he said, dipping his head in an abbreviated bow. "Me and my friends, well, we've never seen such a cat as the one you've got. He's near big as my dog."

Reulan shrugged uncomfortably. "You think *he's* big? You should see the mice in Sweetwater!"

The farmer simply stared, oblivious to Reulan's attempted humor. "Maybe so, Sun's-ray, but he's one blessed big cat." He dipped his head again. "Sunlord guard you on your journey."

"And bless you and your endeavors," Reulan replied automatically, sketching the Holy Disk symbol to include them all.

He turned away and set out on the road again, Khar trotting along at his side. Once he was out of hearing range, he glanced down at the cat. "You've grown again," he accused, shifting his pack on his shoulders to a more comfortable position. "And don't try to deny it."

:*Perhaps,* Khar replied. *But maybe you're only seeing better.*:

Reulan made a face. "Inscrutable as always, sir cat. I must admit you're beginning to make me nervous."

If a cat could snort derisively, Khar did just that. :*Spoken by a man who for days now has been conversing with a "dumb" animal.*:

A faint blush heated Reulan's cheeks. "Maybe so, Khar, but something's going on here that I don't understand. Why did you 'adopt' *me?* And, for the love of the Lord of Light, how is it that you talk?"

Khar flicked his tail in high good humor. :*You've been initiated into mysteries, Priest Reulan. And aside from your initial shock, you've adapted very well. Who better to ask for fish?*:

Three days into his journey, Reulan found the road becoming more crowded. No longer did he simply meet farmers going out to their fields, or the occasional horse-drawn cart filled with vegetables headed off to market somewhere. Now he shared the road with well-dressed folk who rode horseback, or those who walked in groups, all seemingly headed to Sunhame for the Summer Solstice. As the riders passed, bowing in their saddles to a Sun-priest, he had to endure their comments about the size and beauty of the cat at his side. A few even made offers of purchase, proposing sums that made Reulan's head spin.

As for Khar, despite his dissembling, he *had* continued to grow. The farmers outside Faroaks should see him now, Reulan thought. Though he had become somewhat accustomed (if that word fairly described his state of mind) to Khar's company and to sharing conversations with what everyone else deemed a speechless animal, he felt he somehow skirted the edge of mystery.

That evening, stopping in a large village, he once again sought out the local Sun-priest, arriving just in time for the lighting of the Night Candle. He knew the priest here very well; his former master Beckor had apprenticed Jaskhi at one time, before Ruelan's entry into the priesthood. Reulan and Jaskhi had become close friends after Beckor had died, the young priest turning to the older man for wisdom and support.

"So, Reulan," Jaskhi said, dinner over and the two of them sitting for a moment in the well-lit room behind Jaskhi's chapel. Khar had curled up at Reulan's feet, purring like approaching thunder. "You're making your pilgrimage, eh? Better early than late, I say. You've timed your journey well, my friend. You should arrive in Sunhame the morning of the Summer Solstice. All the inns will be full, but you can always find a place to sleep at the Temple."

"Unless it's too full of quarreling priests," Reulan murmured.

"Ah, that!" Jaskhi waved a dismissive hand. "'When Vkandis wills, they'll find their choice obvious. And what better day for that to happen than Summer Solstice? I envy you, Reulan. To be present at such an event is something no one would ever forget." He ran a hand through his hair. "Now, tell me about your cat."

Reulan sighed. If one more person asked him about Khar, he thought he would choke. By this time, however, he had come up with a story of how Khar had "adopted" him he could recite without even thinking about it.

"There's still something strange about that cat," Jaskhi said, unconvinced, "and I think you know more than you're letting on."

"What do you mean?"

"Aside from his size, which is enough in itself to set anyone back, there's a touch of mystery about him, as if he's a gateway into somewhere we can't go."

Reulan stared. "What are you talking about?"

"I really don't know," Jaskhi admitted. "But, I'll tell you right now . . . this is no ordinary, if simply oversized, cat. Cats don't grow this big, and I've never heard of one walking beside a human all the way to Sunhame." He held up a hand. "No, don't say anything. I'm sure I'm not the first to comment on your cat. Just remember this, Reulan . . . there are more things in this world than even we Sun-priests can see. And I think you've walked straight into one of them."

When Reulan set out on the last day of his journey, he was only hours away from Sunhame. By now the road had grown congested with people from all walks of life. As had become the case yesterday, Reulan was surrounded by a crowd of people who, for all their deference to a Sun-priest, couldn't refrain from making comments about Khar. Reulan set his face in a proper priestly expression, refusing to acknowledge the remarks supposedly made out of his hearing. Khar, of course, remained oblivious to the commotion he caused.

The outskirts of Sunhame came into view around a bend in the road, a road that was now broad and paved with large flat cobbles. As had been the case

when Reulan had seen it first, the capital of Karse
seemed overwhelming. Born and raised in the country,
Reulan had found it hard to believe so many people
could live in one place. The six months he had spent
in his final studies before being elevated to the priesthood had not lessened that feeling. Today was no different. The buildings were huge. The press of people
amazing. The noise, the confusion, the smells . . .

And now, people were pointing in his direction. The
crowds created so much noise that Reulan could not
hear what was being said. From the expressions on
people's faces, some great lord and his escort had been
caught up by the press of people behind him. But
when he looked over his shoulder, all he saw was a sea
of faces, and each one of them seemed to be staring at
him.

Or, he admitted uncomfortably, at the cat.

He glanced down at Khar, who walked very close
to him now to avoid being stepped on by the unwary
person or horse. The cat's appearance was slightly
different . . . his tail, face and legs appeared a darker
shade of cream. But that plume of a tail was held
straight up and there was a spring to Khar's step that
Reulan had not seen before. Fish. It had to be fish.
Close as Sunhame lay to a broad, slow moving river,
and to both Ruby Lake and its smaller companion,
Lake Mist, fish would be readily at hand.

The buildings loomed taller now, over three, sometimes four, stories. The closer one drew to the center
of Sunhame, the more impressive the architecture.
The capital was laid out in the shape of a wheel, or a
Sun Disk, with the Temple holding the center and
twelve main roads leading out from that center. Reulan glanced up and saw faces looking down from many
of those windows. The noise of the crowd grew even

louder and people leaned out from those windows, pointing downward. Vkandis Sunlord! What was going on? Once more, he glanced over his shoulder, certain he would find a procession or something of the sort that could be causing all the commotion. Again, he saw nothing but wide-eyed faces staring at him and the cat that walked at his side.

There are more things in this world than even we Sun-priests can see, his friend Jaskhi had said. *And I think you've walked straight into one of them.*

Reulan quickened his pace. The sun was near its zenith and he wanted to be standing with the rest of the people at the Temple when the Solstice occurred. He knew from past experience he was too late to attend the service inside the Temple. And with no Son of the Sun to lead the ceremonies, the great sanctuary would be packed by senior priests and those who had staked their claims on the best spots to see and be seen.

He heard someone cry out, but couldn't distinguish the words. Nervous now, he kept his eyes straight forward and concentrated on ignoring the growing noise of the crowd. Though he walked down a clogged street, no one bumped into him or, for that matter, even came close. He and Khar walked in a small circle of emptiness and that fact alone made Reulan more jittery than ever.

Vkandis Sunlord, he prayed. *Protect me!* He didn't include Khar in that prayer, quite certain the cat could more than take care of himself.

More shouting broke out, but Reulan couldn't see far enough ahead to tell what was happening. But when the road rose upward toward the Temple at the highest point in the city, he began to see what was going on. A crowd of Black-robes, Red-robes and

White-robes plowed through the crowd, swimming up-
stream as it were against the tide of travelers headed
toward the Temple. Reulan swallowed heavily. Something was happening here . . . something of great im-
portance. And he didn't have a clue as to what it was.

I'm a simple country priest, I'm no one important,
he pleaded inwardly. *Don't look at me as if I were.*

One of the Black-robes, a senior fellow if his gorgeous robes and gold accouterments meant anything,
turned and all but sprinted toward the Temple, his
fellow priests falling back to let him through. The
noise of the crowd intensified, blending into an excited
roar. Reulan could see the Temple now. White marble
caught and held the sunlight and shone like a flame at
nighttime. The many steps leading up to the sanctuary
gleamed in the sunlight and the gold on the cornices
seemed blindingly bright.

He approached the steps, more determined than
ever to ignore the uproar. The crowd had drawn back
from the main entrance to the Temple, leaving the
plaza around it shockingly empty. Reulan stopped, unsure what to do next. Then something bumped into
his leg above the knee, the familiar head-butt of his
cat. But above knee height?

Reulan looked down and his heart gave an absurd
little leap in his chest. Knees trembling, feeling faint,
he stared at his feline companion.

In place of the cat who had journeyed with him
from Sweetwater stood a creature straight out of legend, one every child had heard about in tale after tale.
The cream-colored body was still there, but no tabby
markings marred its hue. Now a brick-red mask, legs,
and tail graced the cream. And the eyes. *O Vkandis
Sunlord!* The eyes were blue, the blue of a cloudless

sky, a blue so deep he felt he could have fallen into their depths and kept falling forever.

A Firecat!

"Khar?" he breathed, knowing the cat would hear. "O Lord of Light . . . Khar, is that you?"

:Steady, Reulan,: Khar said, rubbing his cheek against Reulan's legs. *:Take a few deep breaths, and everything will be fine.:*

The noise of the crowd shut off as if someone had taken a knife to it, separating one moment of clamor from the next instant of total silence. Reulan stood rooted in place, lifting his eyes to the steps leading up to the sanctuary. A procession had formed at the top of those steps that consisted of the seniormost priests of the land, who were now slowly headed down toward where Reulan stood. Though every muscle in his body quivered, screaming at him to turn and run, he could not move. His mouth grew dry and he feared he would choke on the avalanche of emotions that gripped his heart.

The procession stopped a few steps from where he stood, the expressions on the faces of the priests one of uniform awe. It had become so quiet now, he could hear Khar's rumbling purr.

As one, every priest facing him bowed low.

Two of them approached: one removed Reulan's pack and the other fastened a cloak about his shoulders, a cloak heavily encrusted with gold and Sun gems. Reulan could hardly breathe at this point, his mind whirling out of control and his heart beating so loud he was sure the entire plaza could hear it.

Then from the center of the procession stepped the seniormost priest of all who had gathered here, a man his master Beckor had acknowledged as one of the purest souls in the capital. An old man, white hair gleaming in the sunlight and eyes wide with awe, the priest bore in his hands the great golden crown of the Son of the Sun.

Reulan briefly closed his eyes. This couldn't be happening! It was utterly impossible! He had never had any desire to do more than minister to his people and—

"Vkandis has chosen!" the old man called out, his voice surprisingly clear and more than loud enough to be heard by those who had gathered in the plaza. He lifted the crown and set it on Reulan's head at the very moment the sun reached its zenith in the sky.

For an instant, Reulan forgot to breathe.

And then the glory descended.

Light, golden light, light that filled him like water poured into an empty vessel. Light that lifted him out of himself into a place where no darkness could ever come. He was enfolded by light, consumed by light, cradled by light. He was the fiery wick on a brilliant candle the size of the universe. He cried out voicelessly in the presence of that light, protesting that he could not be worthy.

And the light responded, not in words but in something far beyond words. Comfort came with those "words," along with a feeling of subtle good humor. Could he question the will of Vkandis? Could he possibly know more than the god? And what if Vkandis *required* a "simple country priest" to lead his people?

The light, if possible, intensified and coursed through his veins like fire. His heart expanded, accepting the love and wisdom of the god who touched him. He bowed before that Presence, accepting the choice of the god he loved.

And, suddenly, he saw again with the eyes of flesh. The silence in the plaza beat at his ears with the same intensity that the roar of the crowd had possessed not long ago . . . a lifetime ago. He felt Khar's shoulder snug against his leg, heard the Firecat's soothing purr. The crown on his head should have weighed enough to bend his neck, but he felt nothing heavier than the touch of a gentle hand.

He stared at the crowd that stood in a circle around him. No one moved or spoke. He turned slowly, looking from person to person. And his heart quivered in his chest at what he saw.

Behind those who faced him stretched their shadows, as if he were a lamp lit in the darkness and they had turned toward his light.

Khar butted his head against Reulan's leg again. He glanced down at the Firecat, seeing true affection dancing in those very blue eyes.

:Well, Reulan. We're here at last. Now can I have my fish?:

Winter Death
by *Michelle West*

Michelle West is the author of numerous novels, including the Sacred Hunter *duology and the* Sun Sword *series, which will be concluded with the publication of* The Sun Sword *in January 2004. She reviews books for the online column* First Contacts, *and less frequently for* The Magazine of Fantasy & Science Fiction. *Other short fiction by her has appeared in dozens of anthologies, most recently in* The Sorcerer's Academy, Apprentice Fantastic, Once Upon A Galaxy, Familiars *and* Vengeance Fantastic.

Kayla was born in the harsh winter of life in the mining town of Riverend. Her father had been born there, and her mother had come from the flats of Valdemar's most fertile lands. An outsider, she had learned to face the winter with the same respect, and the same dread, that the rest of the villagers showed. She had come to be accepted by the villagers in the same way, slowly and grudgingly at first, but with a healthy respect that in the end outlasted all of their earlier superstitious fear of the different.

Margaret Merton, called Magda for reasons that Kayla never quite understood, *was* different. She could walk into a room and it would grow warmer; she could smile and her smile would spread like fire; her joy could dim the sharpest and bitterest of winter tempers, when cabin fever ran high. How could they not learn to love her?

Even in her absence, that memory remained, and when her daughter showed some of the same strange life, she was loved for it. More, for the fact that she was born to the village.

The Heralds came through the village of Riverend in the spring, when the snows had receded and the passes, in the steep roads and treacherous flats of the mountains, were opened. Heralds seldom stopped in the village, although they rode through it from time to time.

When they did, Kayla took the little ones from the hold and made her way down to the village center to watch them ride through. She would bundle them one at a time in the sweaters and shawls that kept the bite of spring air at bay, and gently remind them of foreign things—manners, behavior, the language children *should* use in the presence of their elders.

She would remind them of the purpose of Heralds, and promise them a story or two *if* they behaved themselves, and then she would pick up the children whose toddling led them to cracks in the dirt, sprigs of new green, sodden puddles—in fact, anything that caught their eye from the moment the hold's great doors were opened—and hurry them along; in that way, she managed to keep them from missing the Heralds altogether.

This spring was the same, but it was also different; every gesture was muted, and if she smiled at all, it was so slight an expression that the children could be forgiven for missing it. It had been a harsh winter.

A terrible winter.

And the winter had taken the joy out of Kayla so completely the villagers mourned its passing and wondered if it was buried with those who had passed away in the cold.

On this spring day, the Heralds stopped as the children gathered in as orderly a group as children could who had been cooped up all winter.

There were two, a man and the woman who rode astride the Companions that set them apart from any other riders in the kingdom of Valdemar.

"Well met," the woman said, nudging her Companion forward at a slow walk. Kayla heard the whisper that started at one end of the small group and traveled to the other. She almost smiled.

Almost.

Mitchell and Evan began to shove each other out of the way in an attempt to be at the front of the group. Kayla set Tess down and separated them, grabbing an elbow in either hand. She didn't need to speak; her expression said everything.

Bells caught light and made of sound a musical cacophony, which was not in fact dissimilar to the sound it evoked from the children, whose quarrels fell away in the wake of shared wonder.

Well, almost all of the quarrels at any rate; there was still some scuffling for position, with its attendant shoving and hissed accusation. Given everything, this was almost angelic behavior; it wouldn't be good enough for the old aunts, but it was good enough for Kayla. Two years ago, she would have asked for more—and gotten it, too—but two years ago, behavior had seemed so much more important than it was now.

These children were the children of winter, and the winter was harsh; she knew that if half of them lived to be eight, the village would count itself lucky; if half of those lived to be fifteen, it would count itself more than that.

The Herald, an older woman with broad hips and an easy smile, watched the children from the safe distance of her Companion's back; her Companion, on the other hand, had no difficulty wandering among the many outstretched—and upstretched—hands. The second Companion seemed to have a more obvious sense of personal dignity—or at least a healthy caution when it came to children; it was hard to say which. Her rider was a handful of years older than Kayla, if at all, but his face was smooth and unblemished by either time or war, and he seemed both grave and dignified in a way that reminded her of her dead. Riverend was a harsh, Northern town; the dead were many.

"Youngling," the older Herald barked, her voice loud but not unfriendly.

Mitchell leaped up about six feet, straining to look much older than his handful of years. "Yes, ma'am!"

The young man who rode at her side laughed. "Ma'am, is it?" His glance belied the gravity of his expression; Kayla liked the sound of his voice.

"Obviously I don't look as young as I'd like to think I do. Ah well, time is cruel." Her smile showed no disappointment at that cruelty as she looked down at Mitchell. "You know the people of the village by name?"

He nodded.

"Good. I'm wondering where Kayla Grayson lives."

Mitchell lifted a hand and pointed toward the large hold.

"Will she be down at the mines, or up at the hold?"

He frowned. "Neither."

Kayla said nothing.

But she felt it: a change in the older woman's mood and intent; there were currents in it now that were deeper than they should have been. She snuck a glance at the man, and listened carefully. There, too, she felt a determination that was out of place. It put her on her guard.

"Why are you looking for Kayla?" she asked.

"We've heard a bit about her, and we—well, I at least—thought it would be nice to meet her on our way through Riverend. We don't often get much call to travel this way."

"What have you heard?"

"Well, for one, that she's Magda Merton's daughter, the last of four, and the one most like her mother."

Kayla hesitated a moment, and hid that hesitation in the action of lifting a child to the wide, wide nostrils of a very patient Companion. She had the grace to wince and pull back when the child's first act was to attempt to shove his whole hand up the left one.

"That's true," she said at last. "At least, that she's the last of her daughters. You'll have to judge for yourself how much alike they actually are." She straightened her shoulders, shifting her burden again with an ease that spoke of practice. "Because I'm guessing you knew my mother."

The Herald's expression shifted; it didn't matter. Kayla already knew what the woman was feeling. Surprise. Concern. Hope. "So you're Kayla."

"And you?"

"Anne," the woman replied. She reached out with a hand, and after only a slight hesitation, Kayla shifted the boy to one hip, freeing one of hers. She shook the Herald's hand and then turned to face the quieter young man. "If you want to join us, there's food, but I'll warn you, it's spare; we can offer you news, or trade, or water—but we barter for most of our food, and only Widow Davis has stores enough to entertain important guests."

The Heralds exchanged a look, and then the young man smiled. "We're well provisioned. We'd be happy to offer food for our discussion or news."

"He means—and is too polite to say it—gossip."

But Kayla felt the twinge of guilt that hid beneath the surface of those cheerful words, and her eyes fell to the saddlebags that his Companion bore without complaint. It occurred to her that the Companions and their Heralds seldom carried much food with them, for the villages who fed and housed them were reimbursed for their troubles, and at a rate that made it especially appealing for the poorer towns.

But when the man dismounted and unstrapped the bags from the side of his Companion, she knew, she just *knew* that they had been brought solely to be offered to Riverend. And she didn't like it, although she couldn't say why.

"Your pardon," he said, dipping his head slightly, "for my manners. My name is Carris."

"And her name?" She asked, staring at his Companion.

The Herald smiled. "Her name is Arana. She is a queen among Companions. And knows it," he added ruefully.

Kayla nodded quietly and turned away. "The hold is dark, even at this time of day; there is only one room with good windows. Shall I send for the mayor?"

"No. No, that isn't necessary. It's really an informal visit." Anne frowned. "And yes, I did know your mother. She was a very, very stubborn woman."

"You know that she died."

Anne nodded, and there was a very real weariness

in the movement. "Aye, I know it." But she added no more. Instead, she turned to her Companion and began to unstrap her saddlebags as well. They were equally heavy.

"I won't lie to you, Kayla," Anne said, as she took a seat while Kayla set to boiling water for the tea and herbal infusions that the Southerners often found too thin or too bitter. "I did not know your mother well. This has been my circuit for a number of years, and although we're often sent out on different routes, we become familiar with the villages along the King's roads.

"Your mother wasn't the mayor, but she was the center of Riverend. I never met a woman with a cannier sense of the dangers of living in such an isolated place—and I grew up a few towns off the Holderkin, so I'm aware of just how dangerous those fringes can be.

"But your mother had a great love for your father, and for the lands that produced him. And she had a gift, as well, a . . . . clear understanding of people." She hesitated, and Kayla felt it again, that low current beneath the words that seemed to move in a different direction from their surface. "A clearer understanding than perhaps most of us have." She waited.

Carris said nothing, but he did clear his throat.

"We've brought a few things that the village will find useful," he said at last, looking to just one side of her face, as if his dark and graceful gaze had become suddenly awkward. "Magda often asked for aid for the rough times, and—and—she made it clear what was needed. There are medical herbs and unguents here, there are potions as well; there are bandages and cleansing herbs, as well as honest tea. There's salted, dried meat in the second bag; a lot of it, which might help. The harvest in the mainland has been . . . poor this year. There's also some money in the last bag."

"You shouldn't be telling me this," Kayla said quietly. "You should talk to Widow Davis; she's the mayor hereabouts, or what passes for one. She'll know what to do, and she'll be very grateful to you both."

They exchanged another glance.

"Well, then, maybe you'd better call for the Widow Davis after all."

Kayla smiled politely. "If you think she isn't already on her way, you don't know Riverend all that well."

But Kayla knew something was wrong.

The Widow Davis did, indeed, arrive; she scattered the children with a sharp inquiry about the current state of their chores, and an even sharper glance at the children who had the temerity to tell her they wanted to stay with the Companions, and then eyed the saddlebags the Heralds carried with an obvious, and deep, suspicion.

"Kayla, go mind the children. If you can't teach them to heed their duties, no one can. I'll deal with the strangers."

Kayla felt her jaw go slack, but she hid the surprise that had caused it as she nodded to the widow and retreated. These were *Heralds,* not medicants, and she had never heard the Widow Davis be rude to a Herald before. She was glad that the children had been sent back to their work.

She did not see the Heralds leave, but when she had time to glance outside again, they were gone, the

white of their uniforms, and the white of Companion
coats, little glimpses into the heart of winter, a hint of
the future.

And when she at last tucked in for bed, she fought
sleep with a kind of dread that she hadn't felt since
she had slept in the arms of her own mother, at a
time of life so far removed it seemed centuries must
have passed. The nightmares had been strong then;
they were strong now.

Many of the village children dreamed. They found
a place in her lap when they wished to make sense of
all the things that occurred only after they closed their
eyes, and she had spent years listening, with both wonder and envy, to the hundreds of broken stories that
occupied their dreamscapes.

Not so her own.

She had two dreams.

There was a black dream and a white dream, set
against the mountain's winter.

As a child, the black dreams were frightening, be-
wildering; she would wake from sleep to search for
her mother; it never took long. Her mother would
come, precious candle burning, and sit by the side of
her bed.

"What did you dream of, Kayla?"

"The dragon."

She had never seen a dragon; the stories that the
old wives told described them as terrible, ancient
beasts who had long since vanished from the face of
the free lands. Books in the hold were so rare they
were seldom seen, and books with pictures tipped in
were rarer still.

But there was something in the shape of shadow
that reminded her of those pictures.

"What was he doing?"

"Crying."

"Ah. Try not to listen to carefully, Kayla. Dragon tears are a terrible thing."

"I think . . . he's lonely."

Her mother's smile was shallow, even by candle-light. "Dragons are lonely; they sit on their cold, cold gold, their hard jewels, and they never come out to play."

"He would," she would tell her mother, "if he could find us."

"I think it best that he never find us, Kayla. River-end is no place for such a creature."

The white dreams were different.

The snows were clearer and cleaner, and the pines that guarded the pass stretched beyond them to cut moonlight and hide it. But the light was strong enough to see by, and she always saw the same thing: the white horse.

He was the color of snow, of light on snow. And in the hold, in this place just one edge of rock and mountain, where spring came and went so quickly and summer's stretch was measured in weeks, snow was the color of death. Even as a child, she had understood that.

He did not speak to her until her father died.

"You can talk?"

Yes. A little. It is difficult now. But . . . :*I heard your voice, little one. I heard your singing.*:

"Singing?"

:*Aye, song, a dirge, I think, to break the heart for its softness. I heard you sing years ago, and your song was so light and so joyful, I waned all of my compatriots to stand, to listen, to feel. There was such love in that song. And in this one. In this one, too.:*

She knew what he spoke of, and said nothing, but looked down at the back of her hands. They were child's hands; smooth and unblemished by calluses and dirt. Because it was a dream, she did not ask him how he had come to hear her heart's song.

:If I asked you to come with me, what would you do?:

And because she understood something of the nature of dreaming, she allowed herself to be honest. "If you had asked me as a child, I would have tendered a child's answer. But I have children now, and they need me greatly, and you are not a creature to be confined to a place like Riverend."

He had met her eyes with eyes, she thought, that saw whole lives as if they were the course rivers ran, beginning to end, and he might map them out, might remark on where the rapids lay, and where the oceans, at last, waited, for the movements of rivers to cease. And he said, *:Tonight then, dear heart, I will not ask.:*

But she knew that the time was coming when he would, and she was afraid of it.

Because Riverend was her home, and she wanted to leave.

He came to her often in her dreams after that, and she spoke with him, he with her. But his was not the only dream which changed.

For one night, huddled alone in the cold, she dreamed the black dream, and it was different: The dragon took flight. It searched; it searched for her. She could hear it roar when it opened its lips, and its voice was a song of death and desire.

And when it sang, she head other voices as well,

thin and terrible, the wailing of children, of grown
men reduced to that earlier state, of women whose
losses were so profound that silence—even the silence
of the grave— seemed to offer mercy. They were lost,
these voices; she knew it. They were lost to the devourer, the shadow, the dragon.

And if she were not careful, if she were not silent
as mouse, and hidden in the darkness of a hold's small
room, it would find her, it would consume her, and it
would add her voice to its song.

She woke, sweating, her voice raw; the walls of the
hold were solid, but she could hear footsteps in the
halls beyond her room. They paused a moment outside her door, but no one knocked; no one entered.
Her mother was gone.

After that, she dreamed of the darkness often. It
grew stronger and stronger, and she, weaker.

On the morning of the worst of these dreams, the
Heralds had come with their ominous gifts, and she
had left them with Widow Davis.

Tonight, the darkness had not yet fallen across the
field of her vision. He was waiting for her, cold beauty.

She felt the howl of winter wind through passes
closed by snow and storm; memory of spring and summer faded until only the cold remained, essential and
eternal. The ice glittered from the heights of the
mountains' peaks; caught light in a skirt around the
fringes of the evergreens that stretched a hundred feet
in height to the edge of her vision.

The snow did not swallow him; is weight did not
bear him down, down through the thin crust of snow.
Silent, he waited for her.

As he always waited.

But it was different, tonight, and she knew it.

She said, "You cannot carry an Oathbreaker."

He met her gaze and held it, but she heard no voice, and she found the absence unsettling, for in dreams like these, she had spoken to him for much of her life.

"Did you send the Heralds? Did they bring gifts that were meant to take my place?"

He offered no reply.

And she was afraid. Her arms were cold; the day was fading. Night in the mountains was bright, if not brighter, by moonlight, but the colors—winter colors, to be sure—were leached from the landscape until only shades of gray remained beneath the black and white of sky and star.

"This is no dream," she said quietly, the question a shadow across the words.

He nodded.

She did not know what to feel; the winter had settled deep within her.

In the morning, he came. He came after breakfast had been prepared, but before the miners had gathered in the hold; the sun cut crisp, long shadows against the sparse growth.

The children carried word of his presence from one end of the village to the other, but they came in numbers to where Kayla cleaned the heavy ceramics that held the morning porridge. Kayla quietly washed and dried her hands, while smaller hands tugged at her apron's hem and strings.

"There's a Companion in Riverend!" Tess said, her dark eyes wide and round.

"I know," Kayla told her softly, bending and gathering her in shaking arms.

"It's got no Herald!" Evan added. "It's got no rider!"

"I know," Kayla replied. She straightened.

"Everyone wants to see it. Do you think it's come searching?"

"Aye, little, I think it's come searching."

"For who?" Tess asked, insistent, and unaware of the stillness of Kayla's expression. "Do you think he'll take Evan away?"

Evan was her older brother, by about four years.

"Not yet."

'Too bad."

She laughed. "I'm sure Evan thinks so, too."

"But do you think he's lost his Herald? Do you think he needs help? Do you think—"

"I think," she said, "that he'll have died of old age before I can see him if I answer *all* your questions first."

"Just one more?"

"One more."

"Do you think he'll let me ride?"

"No, little, I think you'll fall off his back, and Companions aren't in the business of visiting villages just to injure the dearest of their people." She kissed the girl's forehead, just as she would have once kissed the forehead of her youngest.

Tess wrapped her arms around Kayla's neck. "But what do you think he wants?"

"I think," she said quietly, "that we'll find out soon. Now hush."

Widow Davis was there, in the clearing by river's side. The river itself, cold and loud, was a thin one, but it was clear and the water, fresh. She looked up when Kayla approached, her eyes narrowed and wrinkled by exposure to wind, to cold, and yes, to the scant sun. "Well, then," she said, "You've heard."

"I've . . . heard."

"Your mother told me," the widow said, turning back to her bucket.

"Told you?"

"To be careful of the Companions."

"They're not evil, Widow Davis."

"No, I'm certain of it. All of our stories say so, and they've come to the aid of the village at least three times in my living memory." She was silent a moment. "But this will be the first time they take more than they offer."

"Widow Davis—"

The old woman's look stopped her flat. "Come on, then. You're here, and we might as well have it out." She offered Kayla an arm; Kayla shifted Tess to one side and took it.

Together they crossed the uneven ground that led from stream to the shadows cast by the tall, white Companion, caparisoned in livery of blue and sliver, belled so his movements might evoke a sense of music, a sense of play. But his eyes were dark, and large as the palms of a child's hand, and he did not blink when he turned his massive head toward the two women Children dogged their steps, crossed their shadows, whispered eagerly and quickly amongst themselves. Not even the dour expression of the Widow Davis could silence them completely.

The widow's hand tightened; Kayla's arm began to tingle. She did not, however, ask the old woman to let go.

"He's here for you, girl," the woman said, pulling her arm free

Kayla looked up at the Companion, and then she reached out with her free hand. Her fingers stopped inches from his nose, and she let that hand fall. She said, quietly, "Do I have to go with you?"

He looked into her eyes and said, in a voice that made all song seem flat and thin, *:The choice is yours.*

:I have waited long for this day. I have waited, bright heart, and promised myself that I would let you lead the life the mountain would give you.

:But I have heard your cries from across the continent; I have been with you when you buried your dead, when you cradled the living that you knew you could not hold on to.:

She looked up at his eyes; his gaze never wavered. "You know that this choice is no choice."

He was silent a moment; she thought he would offer no answer. And then, quietly, he said, *:Better than you would understand.:*

"Because the choice has always been yours to make."

:Because the Companions Choose, yes.:

"And the Heralds?"

:They are Chosen. But they feel the bond, and they desire it, and they accept it for all that it is; all that it can be.:

"And my oath?" she asked him, voice steady, arm now drawing on an young child for support.

:There are oaths that are made that cannot be kept in the manner that their maker envisioned. If a child promises to love you, and only you, for all of forever, could you hold him to that vow? Would you desire it?:

"I was no child when I made that vow."

:Dear heart,: he said gently, *:you are barely an adult now, and you made that vow when your older brother moved away, long before you had husband or children.:* He stepped forward, and she shied away.

Because she wanted what he offered.

Because she had never wanted anything so badly.

:I choose you, Kayla.:

She heard the song of his name, although she had never asked it of him, and he had never offered it— as if they both understood, in the dreams of her youth, that his name was a binding they had avoided by careful dance until this moment.

"Darius."

Widow David coughed. The old woman's face was set in its harshest lines. In the distance, children that had been silent until that moment surged forward as Kayla did; they came in a press of small bodies, eager and excited.

But she knew that they would understand it truly later.

For now, all they said was, "You're to be Chosen, Kayla? You're going to be a Herald? Will you wear white? Will you have a sword? Will you have a bow?"

She answered all questions gravely, until one lone boy spoke. Evan.

"Will you come back?"

"Yes," she said, fiercely. "Often. I will come back with a saddlebag full of Northern toys and treats and books, and I will come at the edge of winter, just before they close the passes, like some foolish, green merchant."

Darius had saddlebags. She knew, without looking, that they were full; full enough for a long journey.

"Widow Davis," she said softly. "Can you do without me?"

The old woman had some mercy. "Aye," she said gruffly. "We did before your mother came. We managed." She started to say something else, and then stopped. "They must need you, Kayla, They must need you even more than we do."

Kayla said nothing.

Because she knew a lie when she heard it. What could they need from her that a hundred other girls couldn't give them? They had Heralds, full-trained; they had soldiers, they had lords, ladies, Kings. They had so much.

And Riverend had so little.

"I'll be back," she whispered.

Widow Davis met her eyes, without blinking, and then to Kayla's astonishment, the old woman stepped forward and wrapped arms around her shoulders. "Come back, child," she said, although it had been years since she had called Kayla a child. "Come back whole."

Kayla flinched. She felt her eyes sting. "Widow Davis—"

"You've not come back to us with the spring. We missed your song in the winter. It may be that you need what it is he offers; it may be he'll help you to sing for us again."

Kayla buried her face in the old woman's shoulders.

Before lunch that day, she was on the road. Her neck was cramped; she'd done nothing but gaze backward, over her shoulder, until not even the hills that were home to Riverend could be seen in the distance. All of her life lay in that village, or beneath it; all of the things she valued.

Promise me, Kayla, that you'll stay. Promise me that you'll take care of Riverend when I'm gone.

I promise, Mother. But you won't be gone for a long time, will you?

Not if I have anything to say about it.
Of course, she hadn't.

Riding was nothing like it had been in her dreams. It was hard work. And painful.

She could feel Darius' rueful smile. She could not see his face, of course.

"They need me, you know," she told him, the accusation soft.

:I am sorry, dear heart, but so do we.:

"Why?"

:That I cannot tell you yet. But you will understand, I fear, as we approach the city.:

"What city?"

:The King's city,: he told her quietly. *:The capital. Or what's left of it.:*

"What do you mean, Darius?"

Darius didn't answer.

"Are we at war?"

:We are always at war, Kayla. But the battlefields shift and change with time.:

He had to tell her what to do for him when they stopped by the Waystations left for Herald use. She did not know how to brush him, water him, blanket him; was not familiar with the food that he ate. Everything about the life beyond Riverend was strange and unexpected.

But sleep was bad. Every night she spent away from the hold, she spent beneath the great, unfurled wings of the shadow beast, the devourer. She knew that she would never have the white dreams again.

Darius would nudge her out of sleep, and she would cry out, reach for him, and then stop, letting her hands fall away.

"I don't see you in my dreams anymore." The words shook as much as her hands did.

:I know.:

"Will I ever?"

:Yes, Kayla. But . . . it was never easy to reach through your dreams to you. It takes gift. Talent:

"But you—when I dreamed of you, I didn't dream of the—of the—other."

:I would claim that as my action, but there will be too much between us to endure a lie. If you found peace and haven from the—from your dreams, it was not a haven I could create. Not then. Not now.

:If I not been meant for you, if I had not known of you when you were a child, I would never have been able to breach the barriers set by—

He fell silent, and after an awkward pause she asked, "How did you know of me?"

:I heard you.:

"You traveled through Riverend?"

:No. But I heard you. I heard your fear and your terror. I heard your sorrow. I heard your song. Your song is powerful.:

"My mother used to tell me song was my Gift."

:Did she? Interesting. Song is the only way that I have seen you use your Gift. You sing, and others listen. You listen, and you hear the harmonies and disharmonies that are hidden in a speaker's voice. But that is not your gift, Kayla.:

"What is?"

His mane flew as he shook his head. *:The dreams are worse, yes?:*

She knew that that was as much an answer that he would offer, and it made her uneasy. She said, simply, "My mother told me I was safe as long as I was in Riverend."

:You were safe there. But others are not.: He was silent while she gathered her things. Only when she was safe upon the height of his back did he continue. *:What you dream of . . . it is true in a fashion. We are closer to it. We will draw closer still. I am . . . sorry.:*

On the fourth day, she woke from dreaming with Darius' muzzle in the side of her neck. She was sweating, although it was cold, and he caught the edge of her rough woolen blankets in his perfect teeth and pulled the more tightly around her.

His eyes were dark, his gaze somber.

"Darius," she whispered, when she could speak past the rawness in the throat, "I heard bells."

He was silent.

"Not bells like yours, not bells like the ones you're decorated. with. But . . . bells. Loud and low."

:I know.:

"There are no bells here, are there?"

:No. Not on these roads; the next village is half a day's hard riding away.:

"What are they?"

:You know, Kayla.:

And she did, although she did not know how. Death bells. "Tell me?"

He shook his head. *:It is forbidden for me to tell you what they are; you will know. We will reach the capital in the next two days.:*

As he spoke, the hairs on the back of her neck rose. She thought of Riverend. Of Tessa and Evan, of Mitchell, of the Widow Davis. For no reason at all, she wanted to weep.

The first large town that Kayla entered seemed so vast she assumed it was the capital. Darius laughed, but his laughter was gentle enough that it reminded her of her father's amusement at her younglings antics a lifetime ago.

"But it's so—so—*big!*"

:It is big, yes. But . . . it is not a city. The town is large. That building, there? That houses the mayor and his family. And that, that is as close to a cathedral as you will find. But this is a tenth, a twentieth, of the size of the city you will enter when we—Kayla?:

She sat frozen across his bare back, her legs locked so tightly her body was shuddering.

:Kayla!:

She could not even shake her head. Her mouth, when it opened, was too dry to form words. *Darius . . .*

:Kayla, what is wrong?:

The screaming. Can't you hear it? The screaming.

:Kayla! KAYLA!:

She was on her feet. Not his back, not his feet. She could not remember sliding from the complicated bits and pieces of baubles that announced his presence and his station so eloquently.

The cobbled streets passed beneath her; she noticed them only because they felt so strange to her feet, so unnatural beneath open sky. The screaming was so loud she could hear no other words, although she thought she could glimpse, from the corners of her eyes, the opened mouths and shocked faces of the strangers she hurtled past, pushed through.

She was through the doors and into the light before she realized that she had entered the cathedral; that she stood in the slanting rays of colors such as she had never seen captured in glass. A man, ghostly and regal, illuminated her and the ground upon which she stood.

She stopped only a moment because given a choice between beauty and terror, beauty could not hold her. She knew what she heard. She knew it.

The cathedral was an open, empty place of light and space, with benches and an altar at the end of the apse. She ran down it, boots pounding the ground, footsteps echoing in heights she would never have dreamed possible in Riverend. And she forgot to feel small, to feel humble; she knew she had to read the person whose screams were so terrible, and soon, or it would be too late.

And she never once stopped to wonder what too late meant.

She found him.

It wasn't easy; there were doors secreted in the vast stone walls, beautifully oiled and tended, that nonetheless seemed like prison doors, they opened into a room so small. Curled against wall and floor, huddling in the corner, was a man. A stranger.

In Riverend, strangers were always eyed with suspicion, greeted with hearty hospitality and an implacable distance. She had shed both of those the moment she had heard his terrible cry.

And she heard it still, although she could see—with wide eyes—that his lips were still. But his eyes were wider than eyes should be, and they stared ahead, to her, sightless, as if he had gone blind.

:Kayla! Be careful!:

Darius' voice.

She realized then what was so wrong, so cutting, about this man's cry of terror: it reached her the same way that Darius' words did, in a silence that spoke of knowledge and intimacy. Without thought, she bent to the man huddled against the floor, and without thought, she tried to lift him.

Realized that lifting him would strain the muscles she had built in the hold, lifting even the largest of the children; he was not a small man.

And she was a small woman. But determination had always counted for something. Always.

She caught him in her arms. Caught his face in her hands as his head sought the cradle of arms and breasts.

His screaming was terrible.

But hers was louder, longer, as insistent as his own. *Look at me!*

He whimpered, but the sound was a real sound, a thing of throat and breath and lips. His eyes, glassy, brown, deep, shifted and jerked, upward now, seeking her face.

"The darkness," he whispered. "The darkness. The emptiness. I've lost them. I've failed them all." For a large man, his voice was small, tiny. She should have been terrified, then.

But as he spoke, she felt what he felt, and she knew, *knew,* that she had passed through it herself.

Her own children were gone.

And she was young enough that the visiting merchants never realized that she had had a husband—gone, too—and a family; that she had had everything she had desired in her youth.

And what was the point of that desire, but pain? In the end, what was the point? Her children had not disappeared in the mining accidents that killed the men, when the men did die; they had not gone missing in the terrible snows that could strand a person feet away from the doors of the hold, and bury them there, as a taunt, a winter cruelty.

No. She had held them.

She had held them, just as she had held this man, in this dark, cramped room, in this empty place that had no words of comfort to offer her.

The cabin in which she had lived was hallowed by the terrible silence of their absence; she might walk from room to room—for there were only three—and listen furtively to catch their ghostly voices. This was the way she evoked memory, and memory, in this dark place, this gloom of log and burning wood and little light—for light let in cold—was unkind. It led her into darkness.

And that darkness might have devoured her, if her mother had not held her, held on to her, filled the emptiness with her words and the blessed sound of her voice. Mother's pain, always.

She spoke to this stranger.

She spoke to this man who understood, who was somehow—at this instant—a part of all the losses she had faced.

And as she did, she opened her eyes to a dream.

Heard the voice of the devourer, all his voices, the cries of terror and emptiness.

Promise me, Kayla. Promise me you will stay and protect Riverend. Promise me.

I promise. I promise, Mother. I promise.

She forgot the cathedral, then. Forgot the lines of this stranger's face. She held him, as if a storm raged just beyond her bent shoulders, her bowed back. She found voice; she sang. She sang to him.

And the singing did what the words she had spoken—for she was aware that words had left her lips, aware that they were a failure before she had finished speaking them—could not.

Dark eyes turned to her; dark eyes saw her; the agony written and etched in terrible lines across a gray face shifted as eyes she would have sworn couldn't grow any wider, did.

He clung to her; his face made her breasts ache, her spine curved in until it was almost painful just to sit, but she sat. She sat.

And the priest came.

She heard his voice at a distance. She heard his words as if they were spoken from within her. He was praying. After a moment, she joined him, although she didn't know the words that he spoke. Hers were as heartfelt, and they were all she had to offer.

"Come home," she whispered, kissing the sweaty, damp strands of this stranger's hair, stroking his face as if it were the fevered face of her eldest. "Come home."

Darius was waiting for her. Companions, it seemed, were not considered beasts of burden in even the grandest of venues; he stood in the light of the windows as if he were a dream. He walked forward slowly as the priest helped the man to his feet.

:Kayla,: he said gravely. *:What you did here was bravely done.:*

"What did I do?" she whispered softly.

:What you were born to do.:

The priest was staring at her. She turned to him and bowed. "I–I'm sorry," she stammered. "But—I–I—"

He shook his head. "He came to this place seeking help. And you came to this place offering aid that we could not offer. Do not apologize, child. But—"

She shook her head. "I don't know. I don't know what—what I did."

"You saved him," the priest whispered. "I was so certain—" He closed his eyes a moment; she thought he might retreat into prayer again. But he shook him-

self free of the words, and when he stood, she saw
that he was over six feet tall, his shoulders wide and
broad. As her father's had once been, before the
mines.

"There are others," he said after a moment. He
turned and bowed to her Companion. "She is your
Chosen?"

The Companion nickered softly.

"But she wears no white, no gray. Child, can it be
that you have not yet made your journey to the
Collegium?"

"I—no. I think we're on the way there."

"Might I ask—if it's not too much—that you come
to the infirmary?"

She looked at Darius. Darius was absolutely silent,
as if he were adornment to the statues, the windows,
the altar of this place.

Her decision, then. She nodded.

He led her through the cloisters; she realized later
that this was a courtesy to Darius. Darius was comfortable in the apse, but once the halls narrowed, movement would be restricted, and it was clear what the
Companion—no, *her* Companion—thought of that.

She even smiled, felt a moment of almost gentle
amusement, until she glanced at the older man's face.
Care had worn lines from his eyes to his lips, and she
thought that no matter what happened in future, they
were there to stay.

They grew deeper as he left the cloister; deeper still
as he walked down a hall and stopped in front of a
door that was slightly ajar. "Here," he said quietly.

She nodded and opened the door.

And stopped there, beneath the lintel, staring.

There was more than one room; she could see that
clearly in the streaming light of day. And there were
beds, bedrolls, makeshift cots, with only barely enough
room between them to allow a man passage. Each of
the beds was occupied.

Darius.

:Kayla.: The word was urgent, but real.

She was afraid.

"I can't—I can't go in there," she whispered.

:Kayla.:

But the door was no protection; it was open. She
could hear weeping, whimpering, screaming. Her hand
caught the frame of the door and her fingers grew
white as she held it.

:Bright heart.: Darius said firmly, *:see with your eyes.
Hear with your ears; hear only with your ears.:*

She drew a deep breath, squaring her shoulders.
See, she thought, with your eyes.

She could do that. She could look.

Men lay abed. Women. There were children as well,
although they were mercifully few. They gazed up at
the ceiling of the room, or at the walls, their eyes
unblinking. They did not move; their lips were still.
She shook her head to clear it of the sounds of despair, and as she did, the priest gently pushed his way
past her.

"They have been this way," he said softly, "for
weeks. They will eat what we feed them, and drink
when we offer them water; we can clean them, wash
them, bathe them. But they will not rise or move on
their own; they do not speak. Some of them have families in this town, but—but most of their families can
only bear to visit for the first few days." He walked
over to one of the beds and set upon its edge, heavily.

"More and more of my people are brought here every day. And throughout the town there are others whose families can afford the cost of their care."

"They—they have no fever?"

"None. No rash, no bleeding, no outward sign of illness. But they are gone from us." He looked up; met her eyes.

"The man that you—you found, today, would have joined them by evening at the latest."

"How do you know?"

"I've seen it. I know the signs. All of us do."

"But—"

"We have no doctors who can aid us; no healers who can reach them." He closed his eyes. Opened them again. "What did you do, Herald?"

She shook her head. "N–nothing. And—and I'm not—not a Herald." She walked into the room, to shed the weight of the bleak hope in his eyes.

And as she did, she passed a small cot and stopped before it, frozen.

It held a young child, eyes wide, hair damp against his forehead. Were it not for the slack emptiness of his features, he would have been beautiful. She forgot Darius; forgot his words.

She listened with her *heart.*

And her heart shuddered, and nearly broke, from the weight of what it heard. She had once been near the mines when a shaft had collapsed. The roar of falling rock had deafened her; the shouts of fear, of terror, the commands for action, had done the same. And through it all, one guilty thought had kept her still: she should not have come here. Children were not allowed by the mines. But she had wanted to see her father.

Standing in this room, at the foot of this anonymous

cot, she felt the same deafness and the same guilt. Some part of her urged her to turn, to run, but she ignored it because she had heard it for most of her adult life.

What loss could she suffer that she had not suffered?

She took a step, and then another, pushing her way forward as if through a gale, until she stood by the child's side. And then she reached for him.

He was not large; she did not know if he had once been chubby, as children his age often were; he was not that now; he weighed almost nothing. She lifted him, as she had lifted one other sick child, almost two years ago.

He was screaming now, in the silence behind her silence, and she joined him because it was the only way she knew to answer the memories that even now threatened to break her.

Her son.

Mommmmmmmeeeeeee

Her child.

MOMMMMMEEEEEE

Her own son had not wept or cried or struggled. The fever had spared him terror, and he understood, in the height of its grip, that she held him in the safety of her arms.

Almost unconsciously, she shifted her grip on this stranger until it was the same embrace; her shoulders were curved forward, her spine rounded at the top, as if, hunched over him, she might hide from the death that was waiting, waiting, in the winter's depths. She placed her lips against his forehead, and tasted salt.

She was crying.

He was screaming, but she knew how to comfort terror by now. Her arms tightened and she began to rock him, gently, back and forth, whispering his name, her son's name, as if they were the same.

It happened suddenly: His arms jerked and trembled as he tried to lift them. She did not know how long he had lain in that cot, inactive, but his hands were so weak they were like butterfly wings against her neck.

"The dragon," he whispered, his voice a rasp, a creak. "The dragon will eat us."

"No," she told him firmly. "The dragon can't land. He can only fly, making night wherever he goes. He can roar. He can scream. But he can't land."

"He hates us."

"Aye," she replied. She had never lied to her children; she felt no need to lie to this one. "He hates all living things. All *happy* things." And as she said those words, she felt the truth of them, although she had never thought to speak them before. The boy's hands touched her cheeks. "You were scared," he whispered.

"No."

"But you were. You have tears on your face."

She could not dry them; both of her hands were occupied with his scant weight. But she turned to the priest who was watching in utter silence.

"You can breathe now," she said.

The priest's eyes were wide. "Herald," he said again, and this time she did not correct him, "can you reach the others?"

"I—"

:No.:

She frowned. It was Darius' voice. :Darius—why?:

:You are exhausted, Kayla. You are light-headed. You—you will put yourself at grave risk if you attempt to proceed. These people have lain immobile for some weeks, and the townspeople are decent; they will care for them.

:But if we do not reach the capital before he finds you, they will have no way back.:

:Before who finds me?:

Darius was silent.

She drew the boy up in her arms, into a hug; her arms were as gentle as she could make them in a grip so tight. She felt his bony chin in the hollow between her neck and her shoulder, and the weight of it, resting there, was everything she desired for that moment.

But this is how she had quieted her sorrow; she had filled it with life, small life, the immediacy of children.

"Where are his parents?" She asked the Priest.

"He has no parents. I am sorry. They passed away a year and a half ago in the summer crippling plague."

"His family?"

"He was their only child. They were newly married. His grandmother is in the town to the east. She is his only living relation; it is why he was here—when it happened."

She pulled the boy away from her chest and her neck; held him out so that she could meet his serious, brown eyes. He was *so* damn thin. "Daniel," she said softly, "my name is Kayla."

"I know."

"I am going to the capital. I am going to learn how to become a—a Herald."

He was too tired to look awed, and she loved him for it. Was afraid of that emotion, because she knew it should not have come so quickly, so easily, for a stranger.

"But I don't want to leave you here, alone. I dream of the dragon. I have always dreamed of the dragon; he hunts me in my sleep. But he has never caught me, never once. If you want—if you would like—you can come with me."

:Kayla, that is not allowed—:

:I don't give a damn.:

The boy slid his arms around her neck and held her tightly, and that was his entire answer. She turned to the priest, a mixture of defiance and possessiveness lending strength to the soft lines of her face. "I cannot help them all," she said quietly. "Not yet. But I promise, if it is in my power, that I will."

And wondered what the word of an Oathbreaker was worth.

Looked at the child's head, his messy hair, the wax in his ears that hadn't been cleaned out by whoever had been attending him.

And knew that the word was everything. *Mother, forgive me. Forgive me. I will return to Riverend when I am done.*

"I am taking this child with me," she told the priest. She almost lied. She almost told him that if she didn't, he would lapse back into his state of wide-eyed immobility. But she didn't believe it.

"Will you take him into safety, Herald—"

"Call me Kayla. Kayla Grayson."

"Will you take him into safety, Kayla? Or into danger? If you ride toward the capital, you will find this . . . disease . . . is far more prevalent as you approach the palace. We have had care of him for two weeks, and we are prepared to care for him until—"

"Until he falls victim to the terrors once again? No. If I take him into danger, I take him with me, and I know—I *know* how to comfort a child."

"You will have your duties."

"What duty is more important than this? I will protect him. But—"

And a head appeared in the doorway; a white, large

head, with deep blue eyes the size of palms and a long, straight muzzle wearing a silver-and-blue strap and bells. Companions had no words to offer anyone but each other—and their Heralds—if the stories were true, but Darius did not need words; he butted the priest gently in the chest, and met his eyes, unblinking.

It was the priest who looked away.

"I won't abandon you," she said softly, and hesitantly, as Riverend flashed before her eyes. "But . . . but I think I understand now why I was called."

"What are you, child?"

"I don't know."

:Tell him your Gift is Empathy.:

"Darius says my Gift is Empathy."

The priest closed his eyes. "Then he is taking you to an unkind fate, Kayla."

"Why do you say that?"

"The Empaths, the greatest of the Empaths, were the first to fall."

The town's many inns offered food and wine and water when Darius entered their courtyards. But they were silent as they made their offers, and the fear that she had sensed in the infirmary had extended outward in an echo that was terrible to witness. On impulse, she said, "I have with me one of the children who was in the cathedral infirmary. He's not very talkative," she added, as the boy shyly turned his face into her shoulder, "but he's recovering. I know it's been bad on the town, but as an outsider, I'm amazed at the way the town has come together to help the fallen, even when they don't understand the disease.

"There's hope," she added softly.

And the innkeepers, their wives, their guests, leaped

at the words that she had spoken aloud, a clear indication that eavesdropping was a way of life in any place, be it small hold or large town.

They might have called her a liar, but she was astride a Companion, and the Heralds *did not* lie.

So they breathed a sigh of relief instead. "We've been pleading for help," the innkeeper's wife said, as she added four extra pies to their load. "But the only help the King sent lies in the infirmary with the others. We didn't know—" She ran the back of her hand across her eyes. "My brother's in back, same as them that you saw. Thank you, Herald." Kayla had given up telling people that she wasn't. The woman composed herself, although the redness of her eyes spoke of unshed tears. "You'll want a blanket for the boy; it's chilly on the hills in these parts."

The boy ate like a pig. Which is to say, he ate everything they put in front of him, and he ate it in a way calculated to leave the most food on his clothes. The innkeeper's wife—a woman, and a mother, who therefore thought of these things—had seen fit to pack him extra clothing; Kayla was grateful for it.

She did not let the boy leave her, and he did not wander farther than her hand could reach. But his ordeal had left him easily tired, and he slept frequently, his back against her chest, her arms on either side of his upright body to stop him from plunging the distance between Darius' back and the forest floor.

"Is it true, Darius?"

:Yes. In the capital, where there are so many more people, many have died from the . . . ailment. They cannot feed themselves, and if they fall in the streets before the Heralds or the Kings' men find them, they're often robbed and left for dead.:

"How long has this been happening?"

Darius was silent.

"Darius, I think I've figured out why you came to Riverend by now. How does my ignorance serve your purpose? Tell me. If I'm to help, I need to know."

:I would tell you everything in a minute, but there are oaths you must swear, and vows you must undertake, before you become Herald; and if you are Herald, there is no information with which you cannot be trusted.:

She knew when she heard his words that she suddenly didn't want that much trust.

Daniel chattered as they rode. And he helped with the food that was meant for Darius; helped with the blankets that were meant to keep him warm in the night. But he helped in a way that he didn't understand, for he would not sleep without Kayla's arms around him. She held him.

When the nightmares came that night, they were subtly different. The beast that roared with the voice of a thousand—tens of thousands—of screams, had eyes that were focused. Its flight was lazy, the circles it drew in the night sky slow and deliberate.

He was searching, Kayla realized. For her. For the child she had taken from him.

She did not scream. She wanted to, but she knew what it would cost the boy, and she kept it to herself.

And because of that, she reached the capital, and the Herald's Collegium, before sun's full height the next day.

The Kings' guards bowed quietly as Darius approached the main gates, and although it was evident that they were curious, they merely welcomed him home.

:They are usually more friendly,: Darius said apologetically, *:but things in the Collegium have been dark for many months. I— Come, Kayla. Here is a woman you must see.:*

A Herald?

:Yes. She is the King's Own, second only to the King in authority, and she is beloved of the Heralds. I should warn you, though that it is not for the quickness or sharpness of her tongue that she is loved.:

Kayla learned this almost instantly. A Herald met her at the front doors to the dauntingly huge building; he bowed to Darius. "So you've brought her," he said. "Finally."

"Yes," Kayla replied, although the words had clearly not been directed at her. "He did. And I guess he didn't tell you that I'm not used to being talked about as if I'm not here."

The man raised a brow. "I see that you have more in common with Magda Merton than it seems." His frown, edged with weariness, deepened. "Darius—you did not choose someone with a child that young?"

"No," she said flatly. "He waited until all mine were dead."

The Herald had the grace to look shocked, and she regretted the words almost instantly. Such a grief, such a loss, was never meant to be used as a weapon; it was wrong. It was just wrong. She slid off the back of her Companion, gently extricating herself from Daniel's arms. "My pardon, Herald," she said, to the chest of the man in Whites. "I woke the child from a . . . from a deep sleep. It was safest to bring him here."

"There is no safety here, if the child was affected by the—" He grimaced. "The Kings' Own has been waiting for you, if you are Kayla; please, follow me."

She hesitated a moment, and then Daniel said, "It's all right, Kayla." His words were thin and shaky; she could see the fear in his eyes. But he drew himself up to his full height, as if he were adult; as if he could bear the weight of her absence. "Darius says that he'll take care of me."

"Darius says—" Her eyes widened. "You can *hear* him?"

"Sometimes. When he's talking to me."

She pondered that as she followed the Herald. He led her down the hall into a very finely appointed room—a room that was the size of the gathering hall in the Hold of Riverend. There, a woman was standing by the great window that ran from floor to ceiling, an ostentatious display of glass.

Kayla had the ridiculous urge to kneel; she fought it carefully, although she did bow deeply.

"I am Gisel," the woman said.

"I'm Kayla."

"Kayla Grayson, Margaret Merton's daughter."

"Her youngest, yes."

"Arlen says that you've been through Evandale."

"Arlen?"

"Ah. My Companion. She has been speaking with Darius. It appears that you . . . met with . . . the victims of the shadow plague. And that you saved two."

Kayla nodded hesitantly.

"I guess that means that Magda took it upon herself to teach you."

"T–teach me?"

Gisel frowned. "Yes, teach you. Your Gift." When silence prevailed, the unpleasant frown deepened. "You must understand your Gift?"

"W–what Gift would that be?"

Gisel raised a hand to her gray hair and yanked it out of her face. "I wish I had time, child. I don't. Your mother was one of the most gifted Empaths the kingdom of Valdemar has ever known."

"E–empath?"

"I really do not have the patience for this."

It was true. Kayla could feel the older woman's anger, but it was mixed with a terrible sorrow and a deep guilt. Guilt, in her experience, had always been a double-edged sword; it could drive men mad. In the hold, it had.

"Empathy is a Gift that is deeper than words, and more subtle. You have that Gift. And if your mother didn't teach you how to use it, and you've survived the passage through Evandale . . . than you are more than just her daughter." Gisel walked away from the window and the light in the room grew. It was a cold light. "There are people who are born with other talents; you must have heard their stories. Some can summon fire; some can work great magic; some can heal with a touch; some can hear the words that men don't speak aloud. Any of these, untrained, are a danger to themselves, or to others. But Empaths can exist without such training; they are often sympathetic, or perhaps skittish, because of what they can sense. Feelings often run deeper than words; most men and women never really learn how to adequately speak of what they feel.

"I have wine here, and water; would you care for either?"

Kayla shook her head.

"As you wish. I intend to have a great deal of the former before this is over." True to her word, she poured herself a glass of a liquid that was a deep crimson, and stared at its surface as if she could glean information from it.

"An Empath can do these things. It is why empaths have often made better diplomats than those whose Gift it is to read the thoughts, the unspoken words of others."

Kayla had only barely heard of people like that, and she had always feared them. She said nothing.

"You'll be given your grays, and settled in, but you won't have the chance to train and learn with the newest of the Chosen. Your work is already waiting, and—I'm sorry child—but we don't have the time it would take to prepare you.

"This is a risk. I apologize for forcing you to take it. You know that the King has three sons, yes?"

"And two daughters. Which is more children than—"

"Yes, yes."

"And they've all survived," Kayla added, unable to keep the bitterness out of the words.

"It depends. The youngest of his sons was a . . . difficult lad. He doted on his mother, the Queen. When she passed away, he drifted, and his father was not a sensitive man; the running of the Kingdom during the border skirmishes kept him away from the capital for much of the year.

"But Gregori was Chosen, in spite of his black moods and his despondency. His Companion—" and here, she did flinch, "was Rodri. Rodri was as sensitive as Gregori, and gentle in a way Gregori was not, and when Rodri did Choose him, we rejoiced." Again the words were bitter.

'We rejoiced anew when we discovered that Gregori was Gifted; that he was an Empath of exceptional power. It was part of the reason he was so withdrawn and so moody as a child; he could not bear the constant anger, fear, and hatred that he felt around him.

The court . . . is not a suitable place for a child of such sensitivity."

"It's not just those things."

"What isn't?"

"That you feel. That I feel. There's more. There's joy. There's silliness."

"Magda did teach you, even if she didn't tell you what it was she was teaching."

"Rodri did teach Gregori to listen to those things, and Gregori—flourished. We were grateful. The King was grateful."

She knew that the story was going someplace bad, and she almost raised a hand to stem the flow of this autocratic woman's words. But she knew that would be a mistake.

"Rodri died, didn't he?"

Gisel raised a brow. Lifted her glass. "Yes. He died."

"And Gregori?"

Gisel closed her eyes. Set the glass down and filled it again. "There are Empaths among the Heralds," she said, when she chose to speak again. "I am not one of them.

"If I were, I would not be here to speak to you now."

And Kayla knew, as the words left the lips of the King's Own, that she was angry; that had it been up to this woman, Gregori would be dead.

She took a step back, a step away, and lifted her hand.

Gisel's dark eyes became narrowed edges into a harsh expression. "Yes, Kayla, you're right. If it had been up to me, I would have killed the boy. If it were up to me, he would be dead now."

"But the King—"

"Yes. The King feels guilt. Even though he sees the cost of Gregori's continued . . . existence, he feels that if he had somehow been present, he could have prevented what did happen. What is happening even as we speak. And he has summoned every Healer in the kingdom to the side of his son's bed in an attempt to revive him, to bring him back.

"They have failed, all of them."

"And the Empaths?"

"Two of them were my closest friends," Gisel said. She walked back to the tall window and stood in its frame, looking out. "The bells have tolled for the youngest."

"But—"

"But?"

"I don't understand."

"That much is clear. Ask, and ask quickly."

"If the Empaths couldn't help him, why have you been waiting for me?"

"I don't know."

"P–pardon?"

Gisel turned; the light was harsh; it made her face look like broken stone. "I don't know. I don't know what it was that Magda—that Margaret—Merton might have done to save him. I was there when Sasha fell. I was there when Michael joined her. I've been all over the city looking at the sleepers who are just waiting to join the dead. And I can *hear* what they think, when their terror has any words at all. It's my belief that if Gregori died, they would wake."

Kayla listened as Gisel spoke.

:Darius.:

:Kayla?:

:It is—the King's son—he is—:

:Yes.:

:The dragon.:

"You're wrong," she heard herself say.

Gisel raised a brow.

"If you killed him, he'd take them all with him when he went. All of them."

Gisel closed her eyes. Her turn. But she snapped them open quickly enough. "And you know this how?"

Helpless, Kayla shrugged. "I don't know. But . . . I'd bet my life on it."

"Well that's good, because you will be. Go and get a bath, get food, settle into your room. We'll come for you."

Kayla nodded. "Can I have—"

"What?"

"Darius. Can I have Darius with me?"

Gisel hesitated. It was a cold hesitation. "It would be . . . better . . . if you did not."

In her room—and it really was a single room—she found Daniel perched on the edge of her bed. He started when he saw her, and leaped up from the bed's edge, shortening the distance with his flight of steps. She caught him in her arms and held him tightly, seeing another child in his stead.

"You need a bath," she told him gently.

He said very little, but she managed to ask for water, hot and cold, and she tended him first. She had spent most of her life taking care of the children of Riverend, and this one was no different.

Or so she told herself.

:Darius,: she said, as she worked, soap adding to tangles of hair and the murk of what had been clear water, *:What was Gregori doing when Rodri died?:*

:He was at the Border,: Darius replied.

It was strange, that she could speak to him from such a distance, and that it could feel so natural. :*During the skirmishing?*:

:*Yes.*:

:*Why?*:

:*He was a Herald.*:

:*That's not enough of an answer. If he was so sensitive . . . Gisel spoke of training. Was he trained?*:

:*He had better teachers than you, if that's what you meant.*:

:*But he—*:

:*He was very, very powerful, Kayla.*:

:*Then why did it take so long to figure out what he was?*:

:*He let no one know. No one but Rodri.*:

:*He was in the middle of battle.*:

:*Yes.*:

:*Constantly?*:

:*Not . . . physically. But there is evidence that he was aware of it. He could sense the movement of our enemies well before any others could. War breeds fear and hatred.*:

She pulled her son—no, this child, this stranger's son—from the bath water and set him in the towel in her lap.

:*Darius. I need the truth.*:

:*I have not lied to you, Bright Heart. Between us, there can be no lie.*:

:*Could he use his Gift as a weapon?*:

Darius did not answer.

Answer enough.

She did not sleep that night. She knew that sleep, in this place, was death. Close her eyes, and she could see the black spread of dragon wings, the lift and curl of air be-

neath their span. Close her eyes, and she could hear those
borne aloft by that terrible flight; the screaming and the
terror of those who had not yet realized they were dead.

Kayla, her mother said, from the distance of years,
from the safety of death, *people make weapons out of
anything. It's important that you understand this.*

Her mother's voice, sad but firm, was all that remained her. She could not see her face in the darkness. *In the hands of the wrong men, guilt is a weapon.
Love is a weapon. Hope is a weapon.*

*You have the ability to make weapons far sharper,
far harsher, than others can. And the only person who
can choose how those weapons are wielded is you.*

She hadn't understood what her mother meant,
then. She had been younger.

*Young Caroline makes a weapon of desire every time
she wanders past the boys at the mine. She understands
this, but she wants only the power of their adoration.*

Others are not so kind.

You cannot be Caroline.

I'm not beautiful enough.

*Hush. You are far, far more beautiful. To me. But
that's not the point, and I won't let you distract me
tonight. There is a difference between manipulation and
motivation. Sometimes desire is good, sometimes it is
bad; she will discover that in her time.*

*You must understand it now. You understand love
as a young girl does, and not as an old woman, like
me. You must let it come to you; you must never force
it upon another.*

But—

*I've seen you. I've seen you make Caroline cry be-
cause you're jealous of her. I've stopped you from
doing it myself, but I will not always be here to stop
it. She will grow, child. She will change. Let her. In-*

stead of forcing others to respond to you, become
something worthy of the response you desire.

Kayla was silent. In the present, with a child cradled
against her, she lay open-eyed in the dark, hearing his
heartbeat as if it were her own. Her mother's words
continued, the past seeping into the present in a way
that Kayla would never have foreseen.

Why do you think I came to Riverend?

Because of Father.

*Yes. And no. Why do you think I tell you this, now,
when I could keep it hidden?*

I don't know.

Because I killed a man, Kayla.

She felt the harsh shock she had felt upon first hearing the words; felt the panic as she had attempted to
deny the truth of them by finding the lie in her mother's mood. It wasn't there.

B–but why? How?

*I forced him to feel my despair, my self-loathing, as
if it were his own. He was not trained; not aware that
what he felt came from outside of his core; he could
not cope with what it was I placed there. I did not lift
a hand, of course, but the end was the same as if I had.*

And worse.

*I look at my hands now, and I see a killer's hands.
I look at my hands, and I see worse: I taught this Gift.
I passed it on.*

But—but what does that have to do with Riverend?

Nothing. Everything.

*The Holds are so dark and so isolated people can
go mad in the winters. And do. But . . . with my Gift,
here, among these people, I can remind them, without
words, of the spring and the summer; I can give them
hope. They take hope, and they make of it what they
will, and we survive until the passes open.*

But is that so different? If you make them feel what they don't feel—

Is there a difference between watering a plant and drowning it? Here, in Riverend, there are few. The ore the mines produce is needed by the King. I have chosen to help these people, as I can, because I have grown to love them.

She had been silent, then.

Promise me, Kayla.

I promise, Mother.

In the end, she slept.

And the great beast was waiting for her, eyes red with fire, wings a maelstrom of emotion. He was despair, anger, loathing, but worse: He made mockery of the transience of the things Kayla valued: Love. Loyalty. Hope.

And who better to know of transience than she? She had buried a husband, a mother, a father. But worse, so much worse.

The dreams had always been her terror and her salvation.

When she lost her oldest child, Darius, unnamed and unnamable, had come to her in the untouched winter of a Riverend that was barren of life, and she clung to his back and wept, and wept, and wept.

Her youngest was old enough to walk, not old enough to speak, and he was also feverish, and she prayed to every god that might have conceivably lived, and in the end, weak and almost weightless, her second child's fever had broken.

But he never recovered, and although he seemed to take delight in the coming of spring, in the warmth and color of summer, the weight he had lost did not return. And she had wept then, at the start of winter, because she knew what it would mean. But at least, with her second, she had time. She told him stories. She sang him songs. She held him in the cradle of aching arms, and she comforted him, and herself, until she was at last alone.

But she was considered young enough in the village, if her heart was scarred; she was twenty-two. Her oldest son had survived six years, which was better than many, and the oldwives gathered to discuss her fate, and to ask her to marry again.

She had almost forgotten her mother's words, that day, and the promise she had made to her mother—for her mother was dead, and that death was so less painful than this terrible intrusion of the living.

She had had nothing, nothing at all. She had carried the blackness and the emptiness within her until it had almost hollowed her out completely. She felt it now; it was a visceral, terrible longing.

A desire for an end. An ending.

And she knew it for her own.

The dragon nodded, wordless; swept back huge wings, opened its terrible jaws. They were kin, she thought. He offered nothing but truth.

Two things saved her.

The first was the flash of white in the darkness: Darius, the Companion of winter in Riverend. And the second, more real, more painful, the small fingers that bruised her arms, the whimpering that reached her ears, that pierced the fabric of a dream she could not escape, tearing a hole in the wall between sleep and the waking world.

The child was weeping. She held him, and the ache in her arms subsided. *This* was what she was. *This* was what her mother had taught her to be: comfort. Hope.

But when he called for his mother in the darkened

room, she answered; she could not deprive herself of that one lie.

In the morning, grim, she rose. The child was sleeping, and his peace was fitful, but it was there. She dressed in the odd, gray uniform she'd been given, admiring the quality of its workmanship, if not the choice of its colors. Then she lifted him, waking him. He was disoriented, but only for a moment; she let him throw his arms around her neck until she could almost not breathe for the tightness of the grip. She loved that breathlessness.

"Daniel," she told him gently, "I need you to talk with Darius. I need you to stay with him."

The boy's smile was shy, but it was genuine.

"I—I have work to do today. Darius is not really allowed inside."

"But he's not a *horse!*"

"No . . . he's not a horse. He's better than that, and I'm sure he'll let you ride him if you want. Come. Let's find him."

The halls were bustling; there were more people in the Collegium than she had ever seen in the Hold, and she found their presence almost overwhelming. But she discovered two important things from the young—the very young—man who stopped to talk to her. The first, where breakfast was served—and when, that being important—and the second, where the Companions were stabled.

She knew breakfast was important, and stopped for just long enough to feed Daniel. Then she carried him to where she knew Darius was waiting.

He met her eyes, his own dark and unblinking.

Without preamble, Kayla set Daniel upon his back. He accepted the burden.

:*You made a weapon out of him.*:

:*No, Kayla. He made a weapon out of himself. He thought that that was the best way of proving his worth to a distant father.*:

:*But his father—*:

:*His father loved him, yes. Loves him still.*:

:*If he was truly an Empath, he would have* known that:

:*The Kings,*: Darius said sadly, :*are taught to shield themselves. Against all intrusion, all influence. They must be strong.*:

:*And his youngest son was so insecure that he couldn't infer that love.*:

Darius was silent.

:*My mother knew him.*:

:*Your mother . . . knew him, yes. Your mother could have reached him, had she lived; your mother was the one who discovered his Gift, the strength of his Gift. Your mother was the woman who insisted that he be moved from the court and taken to a place without the politics of power.*:

:*But she must have known—the dreams, the dreams I had—she must have had them:*

:*I . . . do not know. She could have reached him. The Heralds who have some hint of your Gift . . . could not. He made a weapon out of himself, and the forging was completed with the death of his Companion.*:

She knew, then.

:*He . . . he killed his Companion?*:

:*No! No. But the loss broke something in him. No other Companion can reach him now, and believe me,*

Kayla, we have tried. He is one of the Gifted; he can hear us all, if he so chooses.:

:But this must have happened years ago—:

:Yes, but few.:

:That's not possible. I felt him years ago. In my dreams. I . . .: But the dreams had been different. She had felt loneliness, isolation, the desperate desire to be loved. Not madness.

:You are powerful, Kayla. What you felt then was true. It is far, far less than what you will feel now. Far less. Kayla, I must warn you—:

:I know.:

:Those who are affected, always, are those who have some hint of the Gift. When the Gift is strong, the effect is not sleep . . .:

:It's death.:

:Yes.:

Gisel summoned her shortly after. Darius informed her of the summons, and she hastened back—with some difficulty, for the building really was a maze of passages compared to the simplicity of the Hold—to the rooms in which they had first met.

"I'm ready to meet him now," she said, before Gisel could speak.

Gisel raised a brow. "There are things you should know about— "

"There is nothing I should know that you will tell me," Kayla replied softly. "But I believe that this— this prince—has been hunting for me for much of my life, and it's about time I stopped running."

"Hunting for you?"

"In my dreams," Kayla replied.

Gisel added nothing. "The Grays will do. Gregori is here, in the Collegium. We've sent all those who might be affected as far away as we can; distance seems to have some affect on his ability to—to reach people."

"But not enough."

"Not enough, no. Understand that we have not explained this to the world at large. It is treason to speak of it. I will have your oath, child, that you will comport yourself as a Herald—as a true servant of the King."

Kayla nodded. And then, quietly, she knelt, her knees gracing the cold stone floor.

The two women traveled; Kayla let Gisel lead, and made no attempt to memorize their journey, to map the long halls, the odd doors, the hanging tapestries and the crystal lamps. She could see other things more clearly. Once or twice she reached out for Darius, and when he replied, she continued.

Until they reached a set of doors.

She froze outside of them, almost literally.

"Do you know why Darius waited?" she asked Gisel softly.

"Waited? To Choose you?"

Kayla nodded.

"No. He told us that he knew where you were to be found, but he refused to tell us how to find you until this spring."

She nodded again. Touched the door. It was *cold*. Winter cold. Death cold. Within these walls, beyond these doors, the dragon lay coiled.

"Will you wait outside?" Kayla asked. It was not possible to give an order to this woman.

Gisel ignored the request; she pulled a ring of keys from her belt and slid one into the door's single lock.

Whatever Kayla expected from the rooms of a prince had come from stories that Widow Davis told the children. She had long since passed the age where stories were necessary, but she wanted them anyway. She gazed, not at a room, but at a small graveyard, one blanketed as if by snow, hidden from sight unless one knew how to look for it.

She knew.

Her dead were here. Her dead . . . and the losses that death inflicted. She faced them now. Swallowed air, shaking.

"It's hard," Kayla whispered. "When they're gone, it's so damned hard."

"What?" Gisel's sharp tone had not softened in the slightest.

"To feel loved. To know that you are loved. I think—I think sometimes it's the hardest thing in the world." She entered the room unaware of the weight of the King's Own's stare.

A young man lay abed.

He was older than Kayla; he had to be older. She knew this because of her mother's words, her mother's memory. But had she not known it, she would not have guessed; he was slender with youth, and he lay curled on his side, shaking slightly, his eyes wide and unseeing. She felt his pain as if it were her own. As if it were exactly her own.

She did not know if she loved Darius.

That was truth. He was part of her in a way that she could not fathom, did not struggle to understand. But she did not know if she loved him.

She could say with certainty that she had loved her husband. Could say—no, could not say, but could feel—with certainty, that she had loved her children, the children that life in Riverend had taken from her one by one.

And she could say with certainty that this man-boy, this terrible dragon, this hunting horror, had loved *his* Companion. Or had felt loved by him.

The loss she felt was profound and terrible. It dwarfed all losses that she had ever suffered but one.

"Leave us," she whispered.

Gisel hesitated for only a minute, but that minute stretched out into forever. And then she was gone.

"All right," Kayla said quietly. "It's time you and I had a talk."

She touched his face; his skin was clammy.

His eyes, wide and unseeing, did not turn toward her, but something beneath them did.

Kayla looked into the red eyes of the dragon.

And trapped within them, she saw a child. Or a mirror.

She had never dreamed of flight, although the other village children often spoke of it. She had never dreamed of wings; the only time her feet left the ground in her dreams was when she rode a Companion who could cross the walls that darkness imposed upon her dreaming.

"Gregori," she whispered.

He did not move.

But the beast did. It knew exactly where she was, and the waking world offered her no protection, no place to hide.

Gregori.
Dragon name. Prince name. Powerful name.
He turned. *You!*
Yes.
I know you.
Yes. I am Kayla.
Despair washed over her. Despair and more: death, images of death. The loss of her home. The loss of her village—of Riverend, the home she had promised

her mother she would protect. But there was more. She felt the death of her husband as the mines collapsed, as oxygen fled, slowly enough that fear and hysteria had time to build. She felt her father's death, the snap of his spine, saw—although not with her eyes—the pale whites of eyes rolled shut when no hands were there to gently drawn lids across them.

Her mother's death followed.

And after that, the deaths of her life: her sons. One by one, in the absence of Healers, in the winter when no one could travel through the pass.

She was alone. Terribly, horribly alone. Everyone that had ever loved her, gone; she was like a ship without anchor.

All that existed was this darkness. She wandered within it, weeping now, her arms so empty she knew they would never be full again.

But she was not terrified. She felt no horror.

How could she? The things she had feared, the things that made fear so visceral, that made her feel truly vulnerable, had already come to pass.

She could not speak; her lips trembled, her jaw; her shoulders shook as if she were caught in the spasms that collapsed whole tunnels dug in rock.

And because these things were truth, she accepted them as she had managed—just barely—to accept them in the village of Riverend.

How? How had she done it? For a moment she could not remember, and then her mother's voice returned, distant and tinny: *Promise me that you will care for Riverend.*

Duty. Just that, only that, hollow and cold.

Despair gave way to anger.

:Is that the worst you can do? she asked the dragon, she so small she was almost insignificant.

:I killed them!: The dragon roared.

She almost believed him, the emotion was so compelling. So much, so very much, like her own. But she said, as she had said to herself over and over again for the last year, *:Life killed them. Winter killed them. Work killed them.:*

:How dare you! Do you not know who I am?:

:Oh, yes, I know you. Despair. Terror. Fear. I have lived with nothing but you for the last several months of my life.:

:I killed them!:

:No.:

:I killed them.: She could no longer feel her feet. She threw her weight forward because she had some hope that she could land on the bed instead of the hardwood floor.

:No, you didn't:

:I killed Rodri.:

:No.:

He laughed, and the laughter was terrible, the most terrible thing she had heard from him. In all of her nightmares, the dragon's voice had been a roar of pain. But this, this mirthless sound, was worse.

It was true.

She could not see for darkness, but sensation returned to her hands, and beneath her hands she felt the clammy warmth of his body, the fever of it; she could count his ribs as her palms traveled the length of his slender chest, child's chest. He was dying. He was dying; the fever-root had done nothing to drive the fires away, and he was burning from within. He—

No. No.

:Tell me,: she said softly, as her hands touched his chin. *:Tell me.:* His hair was a tangle, matted and thin, child's hair. The sensation was almost more than she

could bear, and only the fact that she knew he was too heavy for her to lift kept her from gathering his body to her.

She had carried her son.

She had carried him for three hours, in the cold, while her toddler wailed.

:Mother?:

She could not answer him; could not lie to him. Instead she continued to stroke his hair.

And after a moment, she sang, her voice a little too dry, a little too shaky. Song had been her gift. She had never found a person in Riverend who would not listen to her song, not be gentled by it.

:I wanted to help them. I wanted to help. I couldn't wield a sword. I tried. I tried for so long. I cut my legs, my arms; I cut Rodri's flank. I couldn't do it. And I couldn't pull the bow. I could wind a crossbow. I—:

His hair.

She saw images of a child, thin and awkward, and she knew what that child represented. The Prince. Gregori. She saw the ghostly image of a mother, a specter composed of a child's loss, a child's longing; she saw the gray, distant ice of a father's disappointment and contempt. She felt his isolation and his loneliness so clearly she could not separate it from her own.

Nor did she try.

:Rodri loved me.

:Rodri found me when I was lost. He called me, and I came.

:They gave me Whites. They tried to train me. We were happy here.:

She felt his terror building, and she knew the storm would return. But she had lived life in Riverend, and she had wintered there. There was no storm that she could not weather, not now.

:I could tell where the enemy was. I could tell them by what they were feeling. I—:

They had not made a weapon of the boy. She saw that; he had made a weapon of himself.

She saw her mother.

She saw an assassin. She knew, then, when her mother had killed, and why: to save this boy.

He had begged her to teach him this Gift, and her mother had fled, taking her love—yes, even her mother—with her to the farthest reaches of the Kingdom's border.

That desertion had hurt him; she could feel the pain clearly. But she could also feel the determination that followed as he dismissed Magda Merton for a selfish, powermongering woman, like all the other women in court.

In silence, she let his story unfold. It was not neatly told; it was broken by storm and rage, by fear, by self-loathing.

He had taught himself. He had used his power, his full power, for the first time; it had been a surprise. A Gift. A thing to give his father, a way to prove to his friends that he, too, could help save the Kingdom from invasion. He had turned his Gift outward, reflecting emotion, magnifying it. It worked. It struck the enemy, scattering them, breaking their lines.

But the bond between Companion and Herald was strong; the creature most affected by the sudden outward blow was Rodri. Would have to be Rodri.

Gregori screamed. He screamed, not with his Gift, but with his voice. And she, seeing her own graveyard, and knowing what lay beneath the earth, screamed with him.

And then, soundless, he turned, dragon wings wide. He listened for the sound of singing, for the songs of joy or hope or love that he had heard for almost all of Kayla's life. She knew: It was her song.

And what he found was her pain, her despair, her endless rage at fate and winter and people who still had children to love.

She continued to stroke his hair.

Darius woke her.

She rose at the sound of her name, and found that she could see the room clearly; the storm had passed for the moment. She turned to look at the man who lay in the bed; saw that his eyes were closed. His lashes were long, like boys' lashes so often are; his skin was winter-pale.

On impulse, she bent and kissed his forehead.

"He isn't doing it on purpose," she said quietly, her arm around Darius' neck.

Darius said nothing.

"The King had little patience for him, and no affection."

:He loves his children.:

"Gregori felt what the King felt, Darius. He wasn't just guessing."

:He felt part of it; some people remember best the things which wound them.:

She thought of her children. After a moment, she said, "He would have killed himself."

:Why didn't he?:

"I don't know." But she was beginning to. She said, instead, "You lied to me. He did kill Rodri."

:He did not. The enemy shot Rodri.:

"Rodri was mad with terror and fear, and it was Gregori's."

Darius said nothing.

Kayla let her arm slide away from his shoulder. "I have to speak with Gisel," she said softly. Just that.

Gisel was waiting for her, tense and pale. She looked old, Kayla thought, bent with Gregori's weight. But she smiled a moment when she saw Kayla enter the room.

And looked surprised.

"He can't stop," Kayla told her.

"You don't believe in idle chatter, do you?"

"I'm from the Holds," Kayla replied tartly.

"But you survived him. You . . . touched him, and you survived."

Kayla nodded. "I know why Darius waited," she told the King's Own. "And I know that what you thought he waited for can't happen. Not here."

"You can't reach him?"

"I can. But—" She shook her head. Stared at her hands for a moment.

"But?"

"Not here."

Gisel rose, mistaking her meaning.

"Not in the capital," Kayla told her gently, almost as if she were speaking to a child.

"What do you mean?"

"Let me take him home."

"This is his home."

Kayla rose. Rose and walked to a window whose splendor she had never seen in Riverend. Light broke upon the river that ran through the city; the river was murky and slow. She thought it must be warm, as warm as the air in this almost endless spring. Without turning, she said, "I have to take him to Riverend."

"You can't. Here, the Healers and the Empaths have worked to contain him."

"And they're failing. One by one, they're failing. He

speaks to sorrow and loss, and speaks so strongly that that's all that's left to those who can hear his voice."

"You hear him."

"Yes."

"Magda—Margaret Merton—was the only Empath to equal Gregori in the Kingdom. You—and I mean no offense, child—are untested."

"Yes. And I will remain untested. For now. I am safe in Riverend. Do you know why I can hear him, feel him, listen to him, and walk away?"

"No, child, although I am certain there are those within the Collegium who would love to know it."

"Because I have felt everything he offers, and I have learned to . . . walk . . . away from it. Let me take him home."

Gisel hesitated. And then, after a moment, she nodded. "I will need to speak with the King. Wait outside."

But Kayla did not wait.

Instead, she went to her room, and found Daniel. He smiled when he saw her.

"Daniel," she said quietly, "I have to leave the Collegium. I come from the North, near the mountains, and I have to return there."

"Can I come with you?"

"Yes." She held out her arms and he ran into them; she lifted him easily, catching most of his weight with her right hip. "But first, I want you to come with me."

"Where?"

"To meet a Prince."

The door was open slightly. No one, Kayla realized, had touched it since she'd walked away. She took a deep breath. "No matter what you feel or hear here, remember that I'm with you. That I will always be with you."

Daniel nodded.

She nudged the door open with her foot and took a step inside. The Prince was sleeping.

"Is that a Prince? Really?"

'Yes, Daniel."

"He doesn't look like much of a Prince."

"No, he doesn't."

"Is he sick?"

"Yes."

"Can you make him better?"

"Maybe." She walked to the side of the bed and sat on it.

The eyes of the Prince opened. She felt Daniel's sudden terror, and she held him tightly, pressing her chin into the top of his head and rocking him. This sensation was as real as any sensation, an echo of another time. She'd been happy, then.

She remembered it.

Drew on it, calling her ghosts. This boy was her son. this boy was her child.

She loved her children, and for her children, she could sing. She remembered the sweet, gentle nature of her oldest, and the stubborn fury of her youngest, and for the first time since she had bid them farewell, she laughed in delight at their antics.

The man in the bed stirred.

She had survived their loss because of her vows, and she had found that sorrow, in the end, could not keep her from the other children in the Hold. They needed her. Their parents needed her. In the worst of winter, she could soothe temper, displace boredom, still fury; she could invoke the love her mother invoked.

Even after the deaths.

Even then.

"Gregori."

The sound of his name drained the room of light. But Daniel was safe; she felt his fear struggle a moment with her love. And lose.

Such a small thing, that fear.

She reached out to touch Gregori's forehead; his eyes widened in terror and he backed away. But he had been abed many, many months; he was slow. And she, mountain girl, miner's daughter, was fast. She ran her fingers through his hair and let go of all thought.

What remained was feeling.

Love.

Loss.

Gently, gently now, she brushed his hair from his face. She felt the raging fury, the emptiness, the guilt, and the horror that he could not let go. Not on his own.

But surely, surely she had felt this before?

A child's emotions were always raw, always a totality. They existed in the *now,* as if the past and the future were severed neatly by the strength of what they felt in the present.

:Don't touch me! Don't touch me! I'll kill you!:

But she continued to touch his face, the fine line of his nose, the thin, thin stretch of his lips.

"You need my song," she whispered, "and I had forgotten how to sing. I am sorry. I am sorry, Gregori."

She did not question; did not think. To do either was death. Instead, she gave in to her Gift.

To her mother's Gift. What she felt, she *made* him feel, just as he had made his enemies feel.

:Don't—don't touch me

:Don't touch
:I'll kill you
:I'll kill you, too
:I don't want to kill you, too

She sat in the room with her younger child in her lap and her older child in his bed. *:Hush, hush.:*

And when the older child began to weep, she held him.

Darius was a patient Companion. And a large one.

He did not complain at the weight of three passengers, and had he, Kayla would have kicked him. After all, she was no giant, Daniel was less than half her weight, and the Prince, tall and skeletal, probably weighed less than the saddlebags.

The King had agreed to let his son go, but with misgivings; it was therefore decided, by Royal Decree, that a Healer, and three attendants, would accompany them.

She was grateful for that; the spring in Riverend had already passed into summer, and in the winter, with a Healer, there might be *no* deaths. A winter without death.

"Kayla?" Gregori said, as the Hold came into view.

She felt his anxiety.

"Daniel's fallen asleep and my arm's gone numb. I don't want him to fall—"

"You won't let him fall," she told the Prince gently. "And I won't let you fall."

"Will it be all right? Will they accept me?"

"I was so lonely here," she answered. "I was so lonely. I don't think they'll begrudge us each other." She smiled, and the smile was genuine. "Do you think you've learned the dawnsong well enough to sing it with me?"

A Herald's Rescue
by *Mickey Zucker Reichert*

*Mickey Zucker Reichert is a pediatrician whose sci-
ence fiction and fantasy novels include* The Legend
of Nightfall, The Unknown Soldier, *and several books
and trilogies about the Renshai. Her short fiction has
appeared in numerous anthologies, including* Battle
Magic, Zodiac Fantastic, *and* Wizard Fantastic. *Her
claims to fame: she has performed brain surgery, and
her parents really are rocket scientists.*

Dust motes swirled through the sunbeam glaring into
the barn. By its light, Santar trapped the upturned
right front hoof of the salt merchant's gelding between
his muscular calves. "Hand me the pick." Blindly, he
held out his right hand.

Santar's younger brother, Hosfin, slapped the tool
into the proffered palm. "Do you see something?" He
crowded in for a closer look, his tunic tickling Santar's
bare arm, his shadow falling over the hoof.

"Think so," Santar grunted. "Got to get past all the
crap first." Flipping the pick in a well-practiced motion, he gingerly hooked out chunks of road grime and
straw. The sharp odor of manure rose momentarily
over the sweet musk of horse. "Here." He touched
the pick to a gray cobble shard lodged in the groove
between forehoof and frog. He dug under the hard,
sharp stone. The horse jerked its foot from his grasp,
just as the pick lodged into position, and the move-

ment sent the fragment flying. It struck the wooden
wall with a ping, then tumbled to join the rest of the
debris on the stable's earthen floor. Still clutching the
pick, Santar scooped the hoof back upward to examine
the damage. He discovered a light bruise but nothing
that suggested serious swelling or infection. He
stroked the injury with a gentle finger, and the horse
calmed.

Hosfin's head obscured the hoof. "No wonder he
was hopping and snorting."

"Yeah." Santar released the hoof and patted the
horse's sticky flank. "Could have been a lot worse.
Lucky beast."

"Lucky *man*," Hosfin corrected. He stepped back,
skinny arms smeared with grime, sandy hair swept
back and tied with a scrap of leather. "Don't think he
could afford another horse by the look of him. Needs
to learn to take better care of his valuables."

Santar's brown hair hung in shaggy disarray, in need
of a cut. Horse work had honed his muscles: lugging
grain bags and hay bales, exercising his charges, cleaning and grooming. He also had an almost inexplicable
way with afflicted creatures that made his father's stables an exceptionally logical place for any traveler to
board. They might find stables nearer their lodgings
or destination, ones larger or with more modern con-
struction, ones with fancier names or décor. But Santar's father prided himself on service, mostly provided
by his seven sons and one daughter. Travelers who
cared as much for their animals' comfort as their own
tended to seek them out, including the occasional Herald from Valdemar. Santar especially loved their huge
white mounts with their impeccable coats and strange,
soft blue eyes. They seemed so docile and intelligent,
their conformations so perfect, their intensity of

attachment to their riders so mythically intense. The Heralds tended them so vigilantly, Santar rarely had the opportunity to do anything for them but stare.

A sharp whinny from the yard sent Santar's head jerking up so suddenly he nearly brained his brother. "Who's that?"

Hosfin's thin shoulders lifted, and he slouched from the stall. As Santar watched him move, he marveled at how his brother had grown just in the last few months, gaining the gawky, spindly proportions of an adolescent. Santar wondered if their eldest brother had looked at him the same way when he had turned fourteen three yeas ago.

Santar caught up to his brother at the door of the stable. The younger man stood as if frozen, the door wedged against him. Alarmed, Santar pushed past Hosfin. "What is it?"

A handsome white stallion stood in the yard, coat shimmering silver in the late afternoon sunlight. Against his fine, pink hooves, the grass looked like crystalline emerald; and blue sky reflected from eyes full of wisdom. Santar shook his head to clear it, shocked to find the creature of his reverie come so abruptly to life. "It's . . . it's a Companion."

Hosfin finally spoke, but only to force out a single syllable. "Yes."

The Companion let out another trumpeting cry, this one seeming ten times louder without the sheltering walls of the stable. It cocked its head, one pale eye focusing directly on Santar.

Hosfin managed more words. "I've never seen one without a Herald on it."

Santar had, but only after the rider had negotiated its board. "Very odd." He held out a hand toward the animal and advanced with shy caution. If it wanted, the huge stallion could stomp him to a smear.

Head still tipped, the Companion watched Santar's approach. He had almost drawn near enough to touch it, when the stallion raised his muzzle in a blasting whinny.

Ears ringing, Santar jerked back, watching the animal prance a wild circle, then stop to snort and stare at him again. Cursing himself for his own sudden movement, he spoke softly and soothingly as he would to any horse, "What's wrong, boy?"

Still at the entrance to the stables, Hosfin said, "Maybe he's lost his Herald."

It seemed unlikely. Santar believed the Companions chose the best and brightest, and the Herald/Companion bond was unbreakable. Needing something to say to the horse, however, Santar repeated, "Have you lost your Herald, boy?"

The horse bobbed his head savagely and pawed the ground. He whirled, stepped, then looked back at Santar over his shoulder.

The gesture was unmistakable.

Hosfin explained the obvious. "He wants you to follow him."

"Yes." Santar studied the horse. Only one scenario made sense to him. "Is your Herald . . . in need . . . of help?"

The Companion's head whipped up and down so hard he had to make himself dizzy. He pranced forward and back, still staring at Santar.

Terror shocked through Santar. He wiped his grimy hands on his tunic. "All right. Let me just gather a search party." He considered aloud. "We'll need a doctor, a few strong men, a—"

The Companion spun suddenly and charged at Santar.

"Hey!" Santar ran toward the barn. Hosfin ducked behind the door.

Santar had barely managed two steps when the stallion's head slammed his side, bowling him to the ground. "Hey!" he shouted again, throwing up his hands to protect his head from the heavy hooves. Huge, flat teeth closed over his tunic, hefting him into the air.

Santar bit back a scream, which would only further upset the horse. Instead, he launched into a steady patter in a calm voice meant to compose both of them. "Easy now, boy. Nothing to get riled about." He hid fear behind a tone deliberately pitched to rescue self and animal from panic. He felt himself lifted, tossed. Air sang through his ears, then he landed on his belly across the horse's withers. It did not wait for him to settle before galloping away from the village.

For an instant, horror overwhelmed logic. Stunned silent, Santar could only feel each wild hooffall jar through his body. Instinct awakened first, and he scrambled to a sitting position, grasping a hold on the streaming, white mane. The smooth precision of the Companion's run thrilled through him. He had ridden many horses in his day but none with the silken grace of this stallion. Every stride seemed to flow into the next, and his body cycled like liquid through every movement. Finally, the last of Santar's fear slipped away, replaced by exhilaration.

Hesitantly, Santar stroked a neck as soft as velvet, glazed with sweat. The familiar perfume of horse musk filled his nose, and the mane striped his knuckles like bleached twine. "All right, boy. I get it. Your Herald is in immediate trouble."

The Companion nickered, a clear indication that Santar had properly interpreted his actions.

"What good's my getting there fast if I don't have any supplies or expertise to help him?"

This time, the horse gave no reply, the road through the surrounding farmland unscrolling beneath his hooves. Apparently, the horse found Santar adequate enough to save his Herald. The stable boy hoped Hosfin would have the sense to call for help. Perhaps they could mass a group to follow him, hopefully one that included men with healing knowledge and strength.

As the Companion's long strides ate up a mile, Santar caught sight of farmers too far away to hear his call. Suddenly, it occurred to him where the Companion was headed. *Not toward the river.* Recent rains had swollen the waters past their banks and well over the ford. Santar glanced around the stallion's neck. They approached the river at breakneck speed, and Santar knew it had surged to well above his head. "Stop!" he shouted.

To Santar's surprise, the horse obeyed. It drew up with a suddenness that should have sent him flying, but that motion proved as fluid as every other. Instead, they came to an effortless halt just a few steps in front of the flooded fording. Uncertain of his next chance, Santar dismounted.

The Companion made a mournful sound deep in his throat. He plunged toward the water, then looked longingly at Santar. He lunged forward again, this time splashing at the edges of the pool.

Though it was against his better judgment, Santar approached the Companion. "I know you're intelligent, and you can understand me."

The horse pawed the ground furiously, attention beyond the water where the road continued eastward through the Tangled Forest. Santar had only gone this far a few times, and then only in the company of his father and brothers. The sun already lay well behind him. Unless the Herald lay just past the ford, they would wind up in the woods at night, never a pleasant prospect even in broad daylight on the well-traveled path. Demons owned the forest nights, ready to steal the soul of any man foolish enough to wander into their realm.

Santar continued, "It might take a few more seconds to gather a party, but it'll be well worth the trouble to save your—"

The Companion bellowed out an impatient sound, then slammed a hoof into the river, splashing muddy droplets in all directions.

Santar bit his lip, trusting the Companion's judgment. He knew the bond between Companion and Herald surpassed anything he would ever understand. *This horse came to me for help, and I'm going to give it. I'm not going to let another man die for my fear.* "All right. Let's go." Catching a handful of mane, he dragged himself to the stallion's withers again.

Without a moment's hesitation, the Companion sprang into the ford.

Cold pinpoints of water splashed Santar's face and arms, and his legs seemed suddenly plunged in ice. He wound his hands into the Companion's mane, gripping desperately, as the water surged and sucked around them, threatening to drag him from the stallion's back. He watched a massive branch swirling wildly in the current, lost to his sight in moments. The understanding of true danger finally reached him. Having thought only of the bare possibility of demons, he had not considered how much the horse would struggle in the current, how dire the swim, that the churning current could pluck him like a twig from the animal's back and send him helplessly spinning to his doom. Though an able swimmer, he could never win against such a force.

Apparently immersed in the swim, the Companion paid the man on his back no notice, though Santar's death grip on his neck had to have become burdensome. The water slapped and tugged at Santar's sodden clothing, threatening a hold that he gradually winched tighter. Focused on his grip, Santar put his trust wholly in the Companion, blindly depending on him to bring them safely ashore and never once considering that the stallion's strength, too, might fail. It was a Companion, the most clever and competent animal alive and used to having a human wholly reliant upon it. *Not wholly reliant,* Santar reminded himself. *We're talking about Heralds here, plenty capable and talented in their own right.* Only then, Santar thought to worry that his own puny normalness might disrupt the tenuous balance, that the horse might count on him to perform with the ability of a Herald. *We're dead!* By the time the idea materialized, the Companion gave a mighty surge that hauled both of them from the water.

Glad to find himself on dry land, Santar leaped from the horse and wrapped his arms around the nearest tree. *We made it!* Gradually, the doubts raised by his earlier thoughts intruded. The torrent had carried them far enough downstream that he could no longer find the road. The horizon cut a crescent from the lowest edge of sun, giving the woods a gray-orange cast that seemed supernatural. Over the bubble of water, he could hear a softly rising chorus of bugs

punctuated by other, unidentifiable sounds. *Demons.*
Santar shivered in his soaked clothing and looked to
the Companion.

The horse pawed the ground, clearly anxious. He
nudged Santar toward the woods.

Santar swallowed his fear. *A Herald's life depends
on me. On us.* He appreciated the company, though
it had dragged him here in the first place. He remembered how the stallion had given him the chance to
back out at the fording. He had chosen to continue to
save a man's life. To trust the horse's instincts meant
believing time of the essence. For the Companion to
opt for sped, over preparation and skill, had to mean
the Herald lay close to death. The horse, he felt certain, would know.

Though the urge to remount prodded strongly, Santar resisted. In the dark forest, he could see and lead
safely better than any horse. He only wished he had
had time to grab a lantern, or even just a tinderbox
as the forest supplied plenty of torches and kindling.
He pushed through the underbrush, tense as an over-
wound lute string, the horse moving quietly at his
heels. The woods smelled of damp moss and pungent
berries, close and green. Branches swept across his
face, stinging; and he tried to hold them aside for his
larger companion. A whirring sound appeared and disappeared at intervals, grinding at his nerves. An owl
cut loose above his head, sending him skittering forward in a rush. *Stop it. Stay calm.* Accustomed to regular horses, Santar tried to maintain the appearance of
self-control. The animal might sense his fear, and a
panicked horse became a deadly and unpredictable
weapon.

Forcing himself to appear calm gradually resulted
in a true inner peace. Santar surrendered himself to

the mission. For whatever reason, the Companion had chosen him to rescue the Herald, an enormous responsibility. At first, he had believed it sheer coincidence, but he discarded that thought. Companions had a good people sense. It could have approached anyone else in the town, or his brother, but had selected him. Whether Santar saw the quality in himself or not, the Companion had; and he would not betray the stallion's trust nor the life of its Herald.

The animal's nose poked Santar's right side, steering him leftward. The moist nostrils tickled the inner part of Santar's elbow, and he could not help smiling through his fear. He allowed the horse to steer him in this manner, blazing a trail through the Tangled Forest that anticipated deadfalls, brush too thick to penetrate, and trees packed too closely for a large horse to squeeze around. A gray glaze descended around them, deepening the forest shadows to unsettling darkness. The black flies and mosquitoes swarmed in a biting cloud that followed their every movement. Chilled, Santar wished his tunic at least had sleeves.

As the night wore on, Santar battled exhaustion. He had worked a full day in the stables since sunrise, hauling bags and bales, cleaning stalls, wrangling horses; and he had missed the evening meal. The bugs and the cold seemed to drain his vitality along with his blood. Yet, the Companion steered him ever onward with delicate nudges that displayed need but forced nothing. Santar wished for supplies but refused to bemoan them. Somewhere out there, an injured man needed him. *Or woman,* Santar reminded himself. *The Heralds,* he remembered, *come in both varieties.*

The journey continued as fatigue became a leaden weight across Santar's shoulders. He longed to sit for just a few moments. His eyes glided shut, and he forced them open in time to avoid walking into a towering oak. Worries about demons receded, replaced by a solid fight against the sleep that threatened to overwhelm him. Just putting one foot ahead of the other became an all-encompassing battle. Only the realization of a life dependent on his own kept him going. He found himself blundering into dead-ends and copses, uncertain how he had gotten there. He forced himself onward, every step a victory, and hoped he would catch a second wind when he finally reached the ailing Herald.

Suddenly, the stallion gave Santar a hard nudge that drove him to his knees. Moonlight glared into his eyes, blindingly bright after the vast expanse of dark forest. In front of him lay a craggy mountain that seemed to touch the very sky. Santar closed and opened his eyes, but the towering monstrosity remained, a dozen others beyond it. Groaning, Santar staggered to his feet and willed himself forward, preparing to climb.

The Companion gave Santar another abrupt nudge that, once again, dropped him to his knees. Rocks stabbed into flesh, and a trickle of blood stained his britches. Pained, tired, irritated, he turned on the horse. "I'm going, already. I'm going!"

The Companion nickered, pawing up divots of muddy weeds. He tossed his head.

Santar glanced ahead, only then noticing the dark mouth of a cave etched against the rocky cliffs. Suddenly the horse's intention became clear. "He's in there?"

The horse whinnied, head bobbing.

Santar felt a warm wash of relief that he would not have to fight his way up the mountains, tempered by the realization that he would have to enter a dark cave alone and without a light. The stallion could never fit inside, which made sense. If he could, he would have scooped up the Herald and assisted or carried him to safety rather than dragged some stable boy through demon-infested forest and high water to the Herald. Santar sucked in a deep breath, releasing it in a slow hiss. "All right. I'm going in." He rose and picked his way to the entrance, staring into the black interior. "Any chance you could help me find my way around inside?"

The Companion nickered.

"Didn't think so," Santar mumbled. He returned his gaze to the cave, seeing only as far as the moonlight could penetrate. It did not show him much. "Let me gather some weeds or pebbles, first. Something to drop and follow back out."

The Companion shook his head wildly, silver mane flying.

A stranger's voice touched Santar's mind then: :I *will guide you.:*

Startled, Santar whirled. "Who? Who. . . ?"

:*Come. I'll guide you.:*

The Herald. Santar had heard that Heralds had unusual powers, but it still took him inordinately long to figure out the obvious. "Can you hear me as well?"

No response. The voice gained a touch of urgency. :*Please come. Quickly.:*

"I'm coming," Santar promised. If this Herald was like those he had met, he would maintain grace under pressure, which meant he probably needed help a lot more than he would admit. Santar secretly wondered if he could do anything worthwhile to assist. He did have a way with horses and their wounds, but he had never tried his skills on humans. Nevertheless, he plunged into the cave.

The leathery flap of wings filled Santar's hearing, and the air became pungent with guano. A clotted mass of bats hurtled from the cave, wings beating furiously. Startled, Santar dropped to the floor, ears filled with the smack and cut of their wild flight. Silence followed, eerie with menace. Though glad the bats had gone, Santar could not help filling the intensity of the quiet darkness with unseen demons.

:Take your first left,: the voice ordered.

Shocked from his own thoughts, Santar obeyed gratefully. He hoped the Herald would stay with him in spirit. He felt so much braver with a companion, even a disembodied, faceless one. *:All right.:* Santar concentrated on the thought, though the other gave no indication he received the message.

Santar veered leftward, keeping a hand lightly against each damp, musty wall. Better to glide his fingers through something disgusting than to risk losing his way.

:Skip the next opening to the left, then the one to the right.:

Santar obeyed, passing up both opportunities to turn.

:Now go right.:

Santar did as the other suggested, still scraping the stone with his fingers. Though worried to interrupt the concentration of the one he sought, he tried tentatively, *:Can you understand me, too?:*

:Yes,: the other sent. *:Go right again.:*

Santar did so. *:My name is Santar.:*

:Orrin. Skip the next right, then go right again. Careful, it's a tight fit.:

Orrin was not kidding. Santar found himself suddenly entering a narrowing that seemed impassable. If he became wedged, they would both die in the dark, dank interior. *:Orrin, I can't fit.:*

:You'll fit. Trust me.:

Santar had to keep reminding himself that he spoke with a Herald, one who desperately needed his help for survival. The idea that he might become stuck fast grew into obsession. Santar realized he alone could make that judgment; the Herald could not know the size of the man who had come for him. *:I can't make it, Orrin. I'm sorry.:*

:Do what you must.: Simple words, brave words, from one who had just condemned himself to death.

Santar knew he had to try. He could not banish his fear, but he could choose to ignore it. He sucked in a deep breath, then let it out fully, tightening his muscles and huddling into the smallest area he could manage. Then, he forced himself into the opening.

The rock crushed in on him, tearing furrows of skin from his chest and arms. He closed his eyes, trying to trick his senses into believing this deliberate act was the source of the darkness. He felt pinched, squeezed in all directions. Crushed empty, his lungs spasmed, seeking air. Panic trickled through him, sending his wits scattering. He forced himself onward, gathering his thoughts and binding them together into one solid goal—the rescue of a stranger for whom he had already risked so much.

Then, suddenly, the pressure disappeared. Santar popped into a cavern that seemed enormous after the constriction that had nearly held him fast. *:I'm coming,:* he sent. *:You were right. I made it through.:* His tunic had torn and now hung in two rags from his shoulders. Though irritating, he did not remove them. He might need the fabric to cushion some other movement or to use as bandages. For a moment he wondered how he would get back, especially towing another man. He brushed the thought side. First, he had to find that injured Herald.

When Orrin made no reply, Santar forced conversation. He had once seen a Healer do the same thing, keep his patient talking to assure he did not lose consciousness. Obliged to respond, the wounded man had had little choice but to attend the questions, no matter how silly or obvious the answers, which kept his mind working, awake, and focused. *:Your Companion brought me here.:*

The Herald did not seem impressed. *:I'd guessed that. Next right, please.:*

Undeterred, Santar continued. *:A remarkably handsome creature, in addition to being loyal and intelligent.:*

:Best there is.: Orrin's voice itself seemed to smile, distracted from the pain. *:I'm very lucky.:*

:What's his name?: Santar took the indicated right and suddenly found himself bathed in moonlight. Though still night, the contrast with the depthless cave interior seemed blinding. He blinked several times, gradually taking in the spray of stars across the blue-gray sky, the skeletal hulks of trees waving in the wind, and the snarl of weeds and bushes that defined the Tangled Forest.

The Companion lifted his head and looked worriedly in Santar's direction.

"Oh, no!" Filled with a tense mixture of alarm and despair, Santar dropped to a crouch. *:I messed up. I lost you.:* Santar whirled, rushing back into the cave. *:I've gone in a circle. I'm sorry. You'll have to start over.:*

:The Companion's name . . . is Orrin.:

Santar froze. *:Orrin. But that's your—:* Shoulders drawn up to his ears, he turned slowly to confront the stallion. *:You?:*

The horse nodded. *:Yes.:*

Santar could only stare incredulously. "Why?"

:I needed to know you were up to the job, someone who can push himself to his limits, who will do so for the good of a sick or injured stranger.:

:Why?: Even as he asked the question, Santar understood the answer. *:Your Herald—:*

:My Herald,: Orrin repeated, then added, *:is you. I Choose you.:*

"Me?" The reply was startled from Santar. *:Me.:* he repeated internally. *:Herald Santar?:* He shook his head to awaken himself from what had to be a dream, then looked into the blue eyes of the very real, dazzingly gorgeous white stallion in front of him. He had aspired to owning a horse half this fine, and now he had a Companion as a lifelong friend, so much more than a possession or a mount.

"Thank you," Santar breathed. "Thank you for Choosing me."

Orrin lunged like a striking snake, caught Santar's britches, and hurled him into the air. Santar barely managed to twist before he found himself, once again, unceremoniously dumped, belly first, astride the Companion. *:Come on,:* the horse sent. *:Let's go home.:* Turning toward Valdemar, he trotted into the forest.

Mounted on "the best there is," Santar scrambled onto the stallion's withers and forgot to worry about demons.

In The Eye Of The Beholder

by Josepha Sherman

*Josepha Sherman is a fantasy novelist and folklorist,
whose latest titles include: Son of Darkness; The Cap-
tive Soul; Xena: All I Need to Know I learned from the
Warrior Princess, by Gabrielle, as translated by Josepha
Sherman; the folklore title Merlin's Kin; and, together
with Susan Shwartz, two Star Trek novels, Vulcan's
Forge and Vulcan's Heart. She is also a fan of the New
York Mets, horses, aviation, and space science. Visit
her at www.sff.net/people/Josepha.Sherman.*

Toward the end of the second day of struggling her
way through the forest, Marra was certain she was
being followed.

The question was, by what?

I don't need this. Really, I don't.

Marra was not exactly young anymore, not exactly
slim and heroic in shape or manner. Just an ordinary
woman, she thought wearily, not anyone to be followed by, well, whatever. A four-legged predator
would already have tried an attack, and a two-legged
one, the bandit sort, would have had no reason not to
have done the same. As for Lord Darick's men . . .

Marra bit her lip. That was done and over. She was
the last survivor of what had been a peaceful village,
and if she hadn't collapsed after burying . . . what she
could . . . she wasn't going to break down now. She
couldn't afford to collapse. Someone had to deliver

the story of that unprovoked raid to whatever authorities she could reach, even if it did mean pushing on through she had no idea how much wilderness.

Marra was doing her best to keep heading in the right direction. If she could only reach the shore of Lake Evandim, she could, hopefully, follow it along to civilization, or at least a real road. At least, Marra thought, she knew woodcraft and could forage for food easily enough. And at least Darick had had the . . . good taste to attack in warmer weather, so she didn't have to worry about freezing to death.

Damn him. Damn him and his men and his idea of—of burning down a village over an accidental insult—ha, no, he burned it down for fun!

For a minute she had a flash of imagined satisfaction, seeing white-clad Heralds declaring Darick's guilt, hearing him proclaimed a criminal and punished as a murderer. . . .

Might as well imagine herself a Herald while she was at it, with one of those snowy-bright Companions, or maybe—

Marra whirled, hands clenched on the branch she was using for a walking staff. "All right, whoever you are, I know you're there. So stop being childish and either step forward where I can see you, or get the hell away from me!"

Oh, smart. You've just announced where you are to anyone in earshot.

She waited, heart pounding. The forest had gone utterly still, shocked into silence by her shout.

Then a male voice, low but so musical it gave her a little shiver of delight said, "Your pardon. I shall bother you no longer."

"Who—what—"

No answer. Marra waited, but whoever had been

following her really must be gone now, because the birds were resuming their cheerful noise. Warily, wondering, Marra moved on.

But night fell swiftly in the forest, and even though a glance upward told her that the sky was still bright with sunlight, down here it was already twilight. She'd better start thinking about stopping for the night.

Another glance upward, and Marra froze, wonderstruck. Far overhead, two gryphons were sporting in the air, so high in the dazzling blue that they looked small as birds. The sunlight glinted off their golden coats and wings, and for a moment more, she stood motionless, holding her breath.

Then they were gone, soaring down the wind, and with a sigh, she began hunting for a place to camp till morning. It really was growing dark, and in a hurry, too—

Suddenly, a . . . thing was on her with a roar, hurling her to the ground under a mass of dark fur. Fangs glinted, and Marra, gasping, managed to get the staff up in time to have them clash together on the branch, splintering it, as she struggled to get free before sharp talons could rake her or—

Suddenly the thing roared again, in pain this time, and the suffocating weight was gone from her. Marra caught a glimpse of a man—no, not a man, not with those curling horns, or those clawed hands. But whatever he as, he was fighting the creature, saving her, and Marra looked wildly about for some way to help him. Pebbles, twigs, nothing like a good solid rock.

She grabbed the largest branch she could find, and whaled the creature over the head with it. The branch broke, and the thing whirled to her, snarling. Marra thought wildly, *Wonderful, now it's* really *mad!*

But she'd given the—the man the chance he needed.

He had other weapons than claws, evidently, because a blade glinted, then stopped glinting, red with the thing's blood. The creature lunged, the man—whatever he was—cried out in pain—

Then the creature fell, twitching, and then lay still. Over the crumpled mound of dark fur, eyes golden as a gryphon's stared at her for an instant.

Then the man, too, had crumpled.

Oh, no, you don't! Marra thought, and hurried to his side. *I've seen enough death lately.*

But then she froze, looking down at him. His face was finely drawn, almost thin, handsome in its own way, but rimmed with russet . . . fur. The tips of sharp fangs showed between human lips, and the tips of pointed animal ears poked through the tangled russet . . . hair? The horns she'd noted rising from his forehead were elegant, like twin spirals of ivory maybe a hand's breadth long, definitely not what one expected to see on a human head.

Marra swallowed dryly. His hands were such normal hands—but they ended in powerful, curving claws. Yet the rest of him seemed utterly human, clad in tunic and trousers that were tattered but clearly of fine weave. And he—

And he was going to bleed to death if she didn't stop maundering and did something to help him. A slash crossed his chest, and as Marra pulled the torn tunic aside to get at the wound . . . it was no longer bleeding. In fact, it was no longer there.

A clawed hand caught her own. Before Marra could pull away, the man's eyes shot open. They were that brilliant gold, wild and confused, and Marra said hastily, "It's all right. You killed the—the thing."

The wildness faded, and suddenly those were purely human eyes despite the odd color, the eyes of someone who has lived with despair so long that it has become a companion.

"Yes," he said. "I remember now."

Releasing her, he sat up in one fluid movement.

That voice! That musical voice— "You were the one following me! Why?"

"I wanted to be sure you came to no harm."

"Oh, please. I'm not some fine lady with a noble protector." Marra closed a hand about a rock, just in case. "Why were you following me?"

The . . . man sighed. "If you must know, I was lonely. I . . . don't get to see too many of my kind these days."

"Your kind?" she echoed warily.

"Human, lady! I am—was a human, even as you!"

"Of . . . course."

He stood, shuddering. "The night is almost here. Come, I'll lead you to a safer place to camp."

Marra glanced about, wrapping her arms about herself. Forest, forest, and more forest, and all of it growing dark. With a sigh, she followed him since there didn't seem to be much of a choice. Besides, he *had* saved her life . . . for whatever reason.

"Who are you?" Marra asked suddenly.

"No one."

"Oh, don't be cute! If you really are as human as you claim, you have a name."

Was that a reluctant chuckle? "I can see that you have scant patience for fools. I am Albain Tandarek," a slight, ironic bow, "at your service."

"Ah." That was clearly a noble's name. "I'm Marra."

He glanced back at her, as though about to ask what a village woman was doing wandering in the wilderness by herself, but said nothing.

They walked on through the growing darkness in

silence. But then he—Albain—whatever he was, stopped suddenly. 'This looks like a good place for you to camp."

With that, he vanished into the gloom.

"Hey! You can't leave me like that! *Hey!*"

Albain returned in only a few moments, his arms full of wood. "Surely you wish a fire?"

"Surely I wish to know what's going on. Who are you? I mean, really, not just a name. And *why were you following me?*"

He sighed and squatted down, making a big show of arranging the firewood just so, clawed fingers neatly snagging stray tinder and putting each bit in place. "The second part I already told you: I was lonely. Besides, I didn't like the idea of a woman alone, not here."

He clearly didn't mean in an ordinary forest. "The, uh, thing?" Marra paused in the middle of lighting the fire. "The one you killed?" She heard her voice rise. "There are more of those?"

"Very possibly."

"But then, but then," Marra stammered in a rush of sudden, desperate hope, "officials, warriors, Heralds, *someone's* bound to be coming to investigate!" *And I won't have to go so far to tell them about Darick!*

"How would they know?"

"Wouldn't you send word that . . . oh." They'd think him a monster, too, and probably slay him before he could convince them otherwise. "They would. Magic, or . . ."

Marra clicked flint and steel together once more in fierce determination. The fire burst into life, tinder first, then branches. As the light blazed up, Albain shrank back into the shadows, an eerie figure in the night.

That was the final strain on Marra's already over-worked nerves. "You enjoy being mysterious, don't you?" she snapped. "Or is it that you're busy feeling sorry for yourself?"

He lunged forward with a snarl, fanged face clear in the firelight. "Shouldn't I be?"

Marra refused to flinch. "Look, I just lost my whole village to a bastard who thought it would be fun to wipe us out."

"Oh. I didn't realize . . ." He sat back, staring. "I am sorry, truly."

"I wasn't married, or anything like that, but, but . . ." Marra fiercely wiped her eyes. "I don't know what happened to you, but I don't think you have the corner on self-pity."

"It's not self-pity to mourn for others." But then his voice hardened. "Who was it? Who led the attack?"

Surprised, Marra said, "Lord Darick." *Damn him.* "Why, do you know him?"

She saw the faintest of flinches before he caught himself. "No," Albain said, a second too late to be convincing. "But then, I've been alone in this forest long enough to be doubtful about a good many things."

"You do know him!"

He sighed. "Put down the rock. I'm not his ally. The very opposite, in fact. Much to my disgust, he and I are related. And yes," Albain added sharply, "I meant disgust. When I last saw him, he was a sadistic boy."

"And now he's a sadistic man."

"Ironic that he's the one who's human."

"Self-pity," Marra prodded.

"Don't I have the right? I don't belittle your loss, truly. But at least you are not a monster."

She sniffed. "And you are?"

"What do you call this?" A fierce sweep of clawed hands took in fangs, pointed ears, horns. "Just a few blemishes?"

"Look, whatever happened to you, you clearly started out human." She paused. "Which brings us back to my first question: What *did* happen?" When he looked at her in what might have been annoyance or surprise, Marra added honestly, "I know I'm prying. It's none of my business. But, well, you're not the only one who's been alone and lonely."

"Ah. understandable." Albain shrugged, not meeting her gaze. "The worst of it is that what happened was my own damned mistake. I'm not a wizard or a sorcerer, or anything so grand, but I do have some tiny powers. I . . . well, when the creatures started to appear, the result of a greater mage's battle or experiment gone wrong, I thought I could be a hero. I thought I could take on some monstrous powers that would help me defeat the things.

"As you see, I succeeded far too well."

"You can't change back."

He snorted. "I can't even kill myself. You saw how quickly my wounds heal."

"You didn't answer me. There's no way for you to change back?"

Albain gave a sharp little laugh. "Oh, there's one. Someone has to *want* to take on this appearance. Not very likely, is it? Never mind, Marra. On my word, which at least is still wholly mine, I'll see you safely through the forest, and that's the end of it."

No, it's not, Marra thought with a touch of pity. *You're not the first man to make a mistake while trying to do the right thing. And I've never yet seen a mistake that couldn't be corrected.*

One way or another.

It was startling to realize that she cared. It was even more startling to realize that she still *could* care.

Albain caught them dinner—rabbit, which Marra was secretly relieved to see he ate cooked. After that, well, after that, she was just too tired to stay up all night worrying about what he might or might not do. Curling up, she slept.

She woke with a start in the first dim light of morning, a clawed hand over her mouth. Before Marra could struggle, she saw Albain frantically gesture with his free hand. Silence! She relaxed ever so slightly, and he removed the hand from her mouth, whispering, "We're not alone."

"Monster?"

"Humans. We're near a trail."

She sat bolt upright, mouthing, Darick? At his nod, Marra scrambled to her feet, suddenly so overwhelmed with rage that she was blind and deaf to all reason. She rushed forward, hardly aware of Albain trying frantically to stop her. They crashed out of the underbrush together, out onto the trail, right in front of men on horseback—Darick's men, who were fighting horses gone mad with terror at Albain's nonhuman scent.

Good! Get them out of the way!

It was only when she was looking up at Darick, who had managed to stay on his horse, that the truth penetrated Marra's mad rage—she was trying to attack an armed man with nothing but her bare hands. He couldn't have recognized her as one of the villagers, just as a madwoman trying to tear him apart, and Marra saw the glint of the sword that was about to cut her down—

"Oh, hell," said a voice.

Clawed hands pushed her out of he way. Albain lunged at Darick, Darick's horse decided enough was enough, and suddenly Albain, Darick, and Marra were on the ground. She grabbed the first weapon that came to hand, another rock, and started beating at Darick with it. His flailing arm caught her a sharp blow to the head, and she lost her grip on the rock. She heard Albain . . . roar, no other word for it, and saw those clawed hands rake at Darick.

Yes, but his men—if they have bows—

Only a few had managed to stay on their panicked horses, but those few did, indeed, have bows. Marra struggled to her feet, shouting wildly, "Shoot and your lord dies!"

"The monster's already slain him!" one of them shouted back.

Marra whirled. Albain had drawn back, shaking, clearly horrified at his own brutality. No, Darick wasn't dead . . . yet. But Albain's claws had done some ugly work on his throat and chest.

He won't be in that body much longer.

And then the idea hit her with a force that nearly staggered her. Marra threw herself down beside Darick, snapping, "Do you want to live? Well? Do you want to live?"

A pain-filled, terrified glance flicked her way. Darick managed a nod.

"Would you be invulnerable? Would you be immortal? Wait, watch this!"

Marra clawed the startled Albain's hands, drawing a few beads of blood. Darick gave a choked cry of wonder as the scratch neatly sealed and disappeared. Then the wonder turned to a frantic gasping, as his lacerated throat couldn't get in enough air.

"Choose!" Marra cried. "Take this immortality, or

die! Which? Life or death—and the ghosts of the villagers you slew? Choice!"

" 'mortl'ty. Chos'n."

The words were barely understandable. But—

—it was enough and—

—there was mist everywhere and—

Suddenly the mist was gone. Marra heard the men gasp and stared at Albain, terrified that she might have done something wrong. But he . . . he was human, fully, normally human.

The monster that had been Darick snarled its shock, clenching its clawed hands, then scrambled up and raced off into the forest.

"Did you see?" Marra cried to the men. "Did you see your lord? He is a monster!"

They couldn't argue with her, not after what they'd just seen. With shouts of horror, they crashed off through the forest after him.

Albain . . . stood. Just stood.

"Are you all right?" Marra asked carefully.

He looked down at his human hands, flexing them in wonder, then turned to give her an equally wonderstruck look. "You—he—Powers, oh Powers, lady, I would never want to be on the wrong side of your anger. But thank you, thank you, and thank you."

"You're welcome," Marra said, and to her utter embarrassment, burst into tears. She felt Albain's arms go about her, and thought, *A village woman and a lord?*

Well, stranger things had happened.

Indeed they have, Marra thought, and shifted position so that Albain could kiss her more easily.

Trance Tower Garrison
by Fiona Patton

Fiona Patton was born in Calgary Alberta in 1962 and grew up in the United States. In 1975 she returned to Canada, and after several jobs which had nothing to do with each other, including carnival ride operator and electrician, moved to 75 acres of scrub land in rural Ontario with her partner, four—now six—cats of various sizes and one tiny little dog. Her first book, The Stone Prince, *was published by DAW Books in 1997. This was followed by* The Painter Knight *in 1998,* The Granite Shield *in 1999, and* The Golden Sword *in 2001, also by DAW. She is currently working on her next novel.*

The Ice Wall Mountains were ablaze with color. The pink-and-orange glow of the setting sun crowned the tops of the pine trees and feathered across the foothills and plains like wisps of fire. It settled over the slate roofs of Trance Tower Garrison, the northernmost outpost of King Valdemar's young realm, and gleamed off the pikes and helmets of the surrounding force which had poured through the mountain passes at the first hint of spring.

Standing on the eastern ramparts, Corporal Norma Anzie of Gray Squad, one of Trance Tower's senior sentinels, spat toward the ground.

"That's one big friggin' army," she noted sourly.

The gray-haired man standing beside her gave a brief nod. "Yep."

"And it looks like they're plannin' to stay."

"Yep."

"A long time."

"Me'be."

She glared over at him. "Don't be strainin' your voice box now, Ernie."

H shrugged. "Me'be not so long," he elaborated after a moment.

"How do you figure?"

"The King'll send help."

"Only if he gets word."

"Bessie got through."

"You don't know that."

His eyes narrowed. "She got through," he growled.

Raising her hands, Norma dropped the subject. After the first trickle of soldiers had come over the mountains, the garrison commander had sent his lieutenant galloping for the capital. As the trickle'd become a flood, he'd sent half a dozen more. All but one, Ernie's niece, Bess Taws, had been returned to them as a headless corpse thrown down before the gate—including the lieutenant. Bess was their only hope but, after nearly a month with no sign of aid, only Ernie still believed she'd made it through. Her expression grim, Norma squinted southward.

"How long do you figure it takes to get to Haven?" she asked.

Ernie shrugged. "Ridin' hard, eight, me'be nine days."

"Less if she could get a boat down the Terilee River."

"Yep."

"How long to raise a relief force?"

"Dunno. Depends."

"A couple of weeks?"

"More like a couple of months, me'be."

With a scowl, Norma peered up at the tiny line of enemy troops bringing supplies over the mountains. With the harsh northern winter just past, Trance Tower's own stores were low. If it took another month, it wouldn't matter if Bess had gotten through or not. The garrison would be out of food.

"You'd think there'd have been a paymaster or a supply wagon or somethin' come from Haven before now, anyway," she snarled.

"Me'be there has been," Ernie answered in an ominous voice.

As one, they glanced toward the main gate. Neither could se the dark, fly-covered bloodstains from where they stood but that didn't stop them from looking.

"How long before they'd be due back do you figure someone might go lookin' for them?"

"Dunno. A while, I guess."

Returning her attention to the force below, Norma shook her head. "With a friggin' army that big," she muttered, "you'd think somebody would've noticed it by now."

Ernie just shrugged.

The sound of shouting pulled their attention back inside the garrison.

"What the. . . ?"

From their vantage point they could see a knot of people behind the west barracks, shouting at—cheering on—Norma amended, two struggling figures. There was a glint of golden hair as one had his head knocked back from a well-placed blow, and Ernie swore.

"Garet!"

"Blast! You know that means Andy."

Ernie was already halfway to the stairs.

"Little . . . I told him . . . come on," he puffed angrily.

Andy ducked a wild swing, drove his fists into the other youth's unprotected right side in a quick flurry of blows, then danced back with a tight smile. Although Garet was older and larger than he, no one at Trance Tower was faster. Around him, the growing crowd began to chant his name, and the smile snapped off. Time to finish this before the noise drew the wrath of the sergeant-at-arms down on them. He pressed forward.

Sixteen-year-old Ander Harrow had been born in the garrison. His mother had died in childbirth and his father and three others had been caught in a rockslide when he was nine. Jem and Karl Harrow's remaining squad-mates had raised the boy together, bringing him into the Guard at twelve, protecting him, teaching him, but mostly just trying to keep him out of trouble.

Garet Barns had joined the garrison two years before, and although they were not friends, at eighteen he was the closest to Andy's own age, which meant that when Andy was bored or just itching to cause mischief he either sought Garet out to manipulate him into some scheme, or goad him into a fight. Garet had a quick temper that could always be counted on to flare up with the right words and Andy always knew the right words.

Now, his blue eyes narrowed, Garet watched the other youth weave back and forth in a parody of feints and counter feints, then struck out. His fist connected right where he planned. Andy went flying into the crowd.

The blood on his face gleaming as brightly as his

dark eyes, Andy showed his teeth to his opponent in recognition of the blow, then leaped up, only to be jerked off his feet once again.

"What the blue blazes do you think you're playin' at!"

Her fist wrapped in the back of his shirt, Norma shook him like a dog with a rat in its teeth.

"Haven't we told you half a hundred times, no more fightin'?"

Behind them, Ernie stepped in front of Garet, who simply wiped the blood from his nose with an even expression. Andy gave Norma a disarming smile.

"It was just a boxing match.'

"Bollocks!"

"Really. Something to pass the time and keep fit, right Garet?"

Andy turned his wide-eyed gaze on the other youth who just shrugged. "Sure, whatever."

"I'll show you fit, I'll toss you off the north wall. Then we'll see how bloody fit you are with half them bastards out there chasin' you."

"Now there's an idea."

All eyes turned to see the sergeant-at-arms leaning against the barracks, his expression dark. "Don't you lot have somewhere else to be?" he asked with dangerous politeness.

The area was suddenly empty of spectators.

He turned back to the two combatants. "Barns, K.P. Harrow, latrines. Don't," he held up one thick finger as Andy made to protest, "even think about speakin', just git."

When the two youths were out of earshot, Norma gave the sergeant a sideways glance.

"That was kinda lenient for you, wasn't it, Lorn?"

He shrugged. "There's little enough to keep up

morale these days, might as well make use of what distractions we've got. Keep him outta my sight for a while, though, I might have a change of heart."

"We'll put him on night watch," Ernie answered. "That should tire him out some."

"Good idea. Barns can take a turn as well."

That night Andy stood on the north wall staring out at the nearly full moon. The afternoon had been a partial success, he'd blown off some steam, satisfied himself that Garet was no better a fighter than he, and stirred up everyone's blood a bit. Since the enemy had bottled up Trance Tower, the entire garrison was walking around like they'd already lost. The air of doom and gloom was getting thick enough to cut with a knife. Eyes narrowed, he glared down at the surrounding campfires. So they were temporarily cut off from the rest of Valdemar, so supplies were tight. Bessie would be back any day with an army at her back and then they'd send this lot packing back over the mountains double quick.

His stomach growled, and he rubbed it in rueful acknowledgment of its point. All right, so they were in a tight spot—the quartermaster already had them down to half rations— but they weren't beat yet, not by a long shot. The enemy wasn't so tough. If they were, they'd have taken Trance Tower already instead of just sitting out there with their thumbs up . . . a movement below the wall made him stiffen. He stared into the darkness for a long time, but eventually relaxed. It was probably just a night-bird. He returned his attention to the enemy.

Nobody knew who they were. The standards and banners they carried were unfamiliar and the language their single envoy had spoken was gibberish even to the commander; although the body he'd brought with him had spoken his message clearly enough: surrender Trance Tower.

Andy spat over the wall in unconscious imitation of Norma. Not in this lifetime or any other, he swore silently. His parents had died for this garrison and no bunch of pike-wielding sons of whoevers were going to defile their memories. They could sit out there until moss grew over them. Trance Tower would never surrender no matter how hungry they got.

His stomach rumbled mournfully.

"Aw, shut up."

Leaning against the parapet, he stared out past the dark bulk of the surrounding army. The moon was low in the sky, shining down on the lightly wooded foothills. He'd hunted rabbits in those hills with Phen Royn and Harn Anzie every year since he was ten years old. They should have been out half a dozen times already this spring instead of standing on the walls watching the enemy move about like they owned the place. Andy grimaced. Their hunters had probably already stripped the hills of rabbits. They were probably sitting around their campfires right now eating roast rabbit and rabbit stew and rabbit pie and . . .

Something white flashed in the distant trees.

He frowned.

Ground lightning?

It flashed again and, risking arrow-shot from below, he leaned forward. Something was moving in the hills beyond the enemy, moving fast.

He saw it again some twenty yards west of where he'd spotted it the first time. Then again a few moments later farther still. It sparkled in the moonlight for just an instant., its half hidden form vaguely familiar, then it disappeared again.

"What'cha you doin', boy?"

He jumped. Spinning about, he shot a glare at Phen, who held out his canteen with a chuckle.

"Lookin' at somethin'," he growled back.

"What? Someone takin' a piss?" Phen risked a glance over the edge.

"No. Somethin' strange. There." He pointed.

"Where?"

"Past the troops to the west. Somethin's movin' out there like it's circlin' around us."

Phen peered into the darkness.

"I don't see nothin'." He turned with a grin. "You imaginin' mountain cats again?"

Three years ago Andy had been certain there'd been a mountain cat stalking the garrison flocks. He'd even found tracks, but they'd turned out to belong to a particularly big jackrabbit. Phen had never let him forget it. Of course, now the enemy had the flocks as well.

"This was no mountain cat," Andy replied hotly. "It was white."

"Late snow drift."

"Snow drifts don't move. There, in the underbrush. Tell me you didn't see that?"

Phen leaned forward again. "Maybe." He shook his head. "It was probably just an owl or somethin'. Anyway you're relieved, go get some sleep."

"Shouldn't I report it?"

Phen shrugged. "Go ahead, if you want everyone to say you're seein' giant, sheep killin', jackrabbit mountain cats again."

"Drop dead."

"Just givin' you a friendly warning."

"Yeah, sure." With some reluctance, Andy turned away but, as he did, the flash of white caught his eyes again, another twenty yards to the west. Something was out there, it was circling them, and it wasn't no owl.

He spotted it again the next night, this time to the east. Throughout his shift he watched it wink in and out of the trees, moving incredibly quickly, east to west and back again. Then, just before Phen relieved him, it crested the top of a small hill, rose up, and pawed the air with its forelegs, silver hooves gleaming in the moonlight.

"It's a horse."

Andy made his announcement to Phen as they lined up for chow the next morning.

"Not a mountain cat, then."

"I said it's a horse."

"Probably one of theirs set out on a hobble to eat grass."

"It wasn't hobbled."

"Maybe it escaped, then."

"I don't think so."

"Then I guess it musta been a ghost horse."

"Aw, shut up, Phen."

Ernie was no more help when he told him that afternoon.

"Mountain pony," he pronounced.

"Aren't they usually brown?"

"Yep."

"Have you ever seen a white mountain pony?"

"Nope."

"Then it can't be a mountain pony."

"Must be a ghost horse, then. Or me'be a mountain cat, eh?"

Andy gave up.

*   *   *

He watched the horse pace back and forth from west to east for another full shift, then finally reported it to the sergeant-at-arms.

The older man frowned thoughtfully.

"How long you been seein' it?"

"Three nights now."

"And you're sure it's a horse?"

Andy clamped his mouth closed on an imprudent reply. "Yes, Sarge."

"Hm. Garet Barns thought he saw somethin' white to the east last night as well."

"Garet?"

"Yeah. Your fightin' partner's been on the south wall these last three nights now." He stood. "Well, there's nothin' for it. I'd better go see for myself. You're sure it's not a mountain cat this time?"

Andy snapped his teeth together. "No, Sarge."

That night the sergeant stood watch beside him as the white horse flashed between the trees. Finally it crested the hill again, pawing the air in agitation before disappearing once again.

"It's so fast," Andy whispered in awe. "I've never seen anything move so fast."

"Hm. Funny how the enemy hasn't spotted it," the older man mused.

"You don't figure it's really a ghost horse, do you, Sarge?" Andy asked, trying to mask the uneasiness in his voice.

"No."

"So, it wouldn't be there to . . ." He trailed off.

"To what?"

"Well . . . my da, he died in the mountains. Maybe it . . . you know."

"Maybe it's come to take you off to join him?"

"Maybe."

"No." The sergeant gave him what amounted to a reassuring show of teeth. "Your da was a good man and a brave soldier, but he'd have rather faced that lot down there single-handed than get up on the back of a horse, ghost or otherwise. And he sure wouldn't have sent one for you. No, that there's something else altogether."

"What?"

"Well, that remains to be seen." He turned. "Keep your eyes on the enemy," he ordered tersely. "They're a lot more dangerous than . . . whatever that is out there. You understand?"

"Yes, Sarge."

His jaw tight, the sergeant headed for the south ramparts.

By the next morning everyone wanted to hear about "Andy's latest mountain cat." Finally he'd taken a swing at Mac Rellden and they'd backed off a little. Leaving him in the tender care of Norma and Ernie, Phen took their bowls to the chow line.

"So, what's this slop s'posed to be?"

Norma's brother Harn glared at his bowl. The garrison cook shot him a resentful look back.

"It's beans, mister, and you should be glad to get 'em. Stores are running low. Pretty soon you'll be looking at yer boots and wondering how to I can cook 'em up."

Phen laughed. "That would break the siege double quick. We all die from the fumes."

Harn glared at him as everyone about them laughed.

"Hey, heads up, the Commander."

There was a hushed silence over the chow line as Commander Dravin strode across the parade ground. Those seated made to stand, but he waved them down again.

A tall man in his late twenties, Dravin had been the late Commander Beckwin's lieutenant for four years before an infected tooth had taken the old man to his reward. He was not an imposing officer, but rather one who carried an air of practical confidence that inspired the same confidence in others. Today his eyes were shadowed with fine worry lines, but he smiled easily as Phen and Harn saluted.

"How's the food?"

"The same, sir," Phen replied. "Have some?"

"No thank you, Mister Royn, I've already eaten. The last of the turnips I'm afraid, privilege of rank. But ask me again tomorrow."

"No sign of relief column yet, sir?" Harn asked bluntly.

"None as yet, Corporal, but Bess Taws got through. King Valdemar will be here any day now. And then there'll be roast lamb and fresh bread instead of beans and turnips," he said loudly his voice pitched to take in the gathered soldiers. They grinned back at him, raising their spoons in salute. "Have you seen Ander Harrow?" he asked in a quieter tone.

Phen nodded. "Yes, sir. Andy!"

When the youth came forward, the commander indicated the north wall with a turn of his head. "Walk with me."

"It's a Companion."

"Sir?"

"A Companion, Mister Harrow. One of the Saviors of Valdemar who came in answer to the prayers of the King himself."

Andy squinted up at his commander. "I've heard stories of 'em, sir, but don't they always travel with Heralds?"

"They do."

"I didn't see no Herald, sir."

"No."

"Do you think . . . they killed its Herald?"

"No. If its Herald had been killed, it wouldn't be pacing the garrison. It would have returned to the Companion's Field if it hadn't died as well. No, I believe it's here to choose a Herald, Mister Harrow. It just can't get close enough to do it." The Commander stared into space for a moment. "Did you get any kind of feeling when you first saw it?" he asked finally.

"Sir?"

"A feeling, like it was calling to you or trying to draw you away from the garrison?"

Andy glanced up at him in alarm. "No, sir."

"No sense of familiarity or purpose?"

"No, sir."

"Hm." His gray eyes cleared. "Never mind. I'm sure we'll find out who it's come for soon enough. Thank you, Mister Harrow."

"Sir."

"Well, if it's come to choose a Herald out of this garrison its got bloody poor timing," Norma pronounced a few minutes later.

"And bloody poor taste if it wants Andy here," Phen added with a laugh.

"No one said it wanted me," Andy snapped back with unusual vehemence. "It could want anyone."

"They usually Choose the young," Harn answered thoughtfully, digging a grubby bit of wood from behind his ear. After a moment's scrutiny, he began to pick his back teeth with it. "And you're the youngest we've got," he finished.

"There's Garet. He's even seen it. And Tara's only two years older'n him."

'None of them have your sparkling personality, though."

"Shut up, Phen."

"Hey, really. It'll look into your eyes, then carry you away from all of this to Haven with its soft beds and clean sheets and you'll forget all about us."

"I said, shut up!"

Ernie shot him a curious glance but Norma just shook her head. "Don't you wanna be a Herald, boy?"

Andy jerked to his feet. "Want's got nuthin' to do with it," he almost shouted. "It's not me, all right!"

Norma made to answer, but Ernie laid his hand on her arm.

"Sure, lad. It's all right."

He sought him out an hour later. Andy was sitting with his back against the west barracks, stropping his dagger hard enough to raise sparks. Hitching up his pants, the older man squatted down beside him.

"So, what's what?"

"Nuthin'."

"Bollocks."

"Really, nuthin'. I just don't want everyone on my back when it turns out it wants someone else."

"Why would it want someone else?"

"Because there's dozens it could want: Garet, Tara,

Mac, maybe even you." His tone was challenging, but
Ernie just snorted.

"Doubt that, somehow."

"Still. For all we know it might even want one of
them." He jerked his head past the wall.

"None of them's from Valdemar."

"So?"

"So, it matters. No boy, it's one of us. An' if it's
you, it's you, and you go."

"Why?"

"Because that's what your folks'd want. Neither one
of them ever shrank from their duty, and you'll not
either. We'll miss you and you'll miss us, but you'll
go."

Andy glared at him resentfully but didn't debate the
unusually long speech. He just dove the dagger into
its sheath and stood up.

"Doesn't matter anyway, does it? I can't get to it
and it can't get to me."

Ernie gave him a neutral look.

"Me'be."

The next night everyone wanted to see "Andy's
Companion." They crowded the walls and betting was
brisk with two to one odds on Andy, three to one on
Garet, five to one on Tara, and ten to one on Mac.
Someone even placed a bet on the garrison cook with
the hope he'd be taken away. Finally, the sergeant
chased them off. Betting continued in the barracks
and across the parade ground and discussion was
heated on how to bring the Companion and its new
Herald together. Most favored a break-out fight with
the four hopefuls in the middle, some wanted to sneak
out in the middle of the night, and Phen suggested

building a catapult and throwing first Andy, then the other three, over the walls, one at a time. Both Tara and Mac took the teasing well, and even Garet unbent long enough to reply, that as long as Andy went first, it was all right with him. Andy, however, refused to be drawn into the joke.

He'd been quiet and withdrawn all day, spending much of his time alone. At supper he answered Norma's questions with grunts and ignored Phen completely. When it came time for his shift, he took the stairs like he was climbing to the gallows. As the moon rose, he watched the illusive creature that might turn his life upside down flit back and forth through the trees, then turned away.

The next morning, Norma and Ernie went to see the commander.

"It's about that Companion, sir," Norma began.

"Yes?"

"Well, sir, we was wondering . . ." She glanced at Ernie who widened his eyes expectantly at her.

"The thing is, sir," she continued, "the sergeant-at-arms, he says they, the Companions, are smart, that they can talk to each other and to their Heralds like."

"Yes."

"So we was wondering why, if it is a Companion and all, and if it's so smart, how come it's been pacing around the garrison for four days instead of high-tailing itself off to get help. We could sure use the help and that would bring it to its Chosen a lot faster."

Commander Dravin leaned back thoughtfully. "As I understand it, Corporal, the Companions are extremely . . . single-minded when they search for their Chosen. It would likely be totally abhorrent to it to leave once it had located that Chosen, even to get help."

"Right, sir, that's what we figured. Also, the sergeant-at-arms, he says that they're magical, that they know things, so maybe, it knows something about us."

"Meaning?"

"That maybe it knows we're gonna bring its Chosen to it."

The Commander's eyes narrowed.

"Go on."

"Well, sir, the thing is, we know it's here for one of us, and most of us figure it's Andy, him or one of the other three under twenty-five. Also . . ." she glanced at Ernie.

"Also?" the Commander prodded.

"Also," Ernie answered, "though I'd like nuthin' more than to believe my Bessie got through, the truth is she'd have reached Haven long before now, and the King would have got word back to us somehow, if only to keep our spirits up."

"Don't you think, sir?" Norma prodded.

The commander looked away for just a moment, then back, his expression weary. "Yes."

"And we're running out of food, sir. This time a month from now, we'll be in a desperate place, and they'll be that much stronger. So," Norma's eyes brightened. 'We had a thought, see. The garrison's at full strength now, decently fed and itchin' for a fight. You won't ever find us more determined than right now. We've got it into our heads, all of us, to see this Companion and one of our own matched up. So, we take the fight outside, all of us, in one mad rush, and we bring that Companion its Chosen. The enemy'll never know what hit 'em."

The commander smiled faintly. "You realize they outnumber us at least five to one, Corporal? That most of us would never survive this mad rush?"

"At least we'd go down fightin', sir, and we know, too, that even if we do beat 'em this time, they'll be back with reinforcements. That's why it's so important to get word to King Valdemar. We figured a Companion'd have the best chance of anyone to get through, I mean It's been dancin' about their perimeter for nearly a week now and they ain't noticed it yet."

"True."

"And besides," Ernie added, "a Herald'd be a fine legacy for Trance Tower, don't you think, sir?"

Commander Dravin glanced from one old veteran to the other, then nodded slowly.

"Yes, I do."

The Commander sent for Andy, Garet, Tara, and Mac an hour later. He came straight to the point.

"We're going to attack the enemy at dawn tomorrow," he said bluntly. "With everything we've got. Once outside, the four of you have one objective only, regardless of who might fall around you, to find that Companion. When you do, I don't care which of you is Chosen, you're to make for Haven at once, all of you. Obviously the one riding will quickly outstrip the others, but I want you all heading south at double time, is that clear?"

The four glanced hesitantly at each other.

"But shouldn't the others join the fight after one of us is Chosen, sir?" Andy asked. "You'll need all the swords you can get."

"Maybe so, but those are my orders, Mister Harrow."

"But . . . sir, what if it doesn't choose any of us," Tara asked.

"Then it's up to the Companion to find its Chosen on its own. We can't line up for it, can we?"

"No, sir."

"Whatever happens, the four of you are to make for Haven, period. Someone has to get through."

"Yes, sir."

That night the five remaining members of Gray Squad stood on the north wall together, watching the future of Trance Tower flit gracefully between the trees. Is movements were blindingly fast, one minute appearing to the east, the next to the west, but somehow it seemed less agitated tonight, as if it knew the decision they'd made.

Word of the morning's attack had spread quickly and all along the walls, the garrison watched the Companion move in reverent silence. Finally Phen stirred faintly.

"Is it my imagination or has it come closer than it was?"

Ernie nodded. "It has."

"It sure is pretty."

"Yep."

"Think we should give Andy here a bath first thing tomorrow? We can't hardly have a grubby little scrub like him representin' Trance Tower like that, now can we?"

"Leave him be, Phen," Norma admonished. "Tonight's not the time for teasin'." She turned. "You got the drink, Harn?"

"Yeah."

"Get it out, then."

Harn pulled a dark, brown bottle from his pack. He

uncorked it in one swift motion, then passed it over. Norma held it up and the smell of brandy wafted out on the breeze to tickle against their nostrils.

"Compliments of the commander," she said. "Now, to us, eh? For years of loyal service, every one of us, and to Jem and Karl. They'd have been proud of the job we did on their boy whatever happens in the mornin'." She took a deep drink, then passed it to Ernie.

"To duty. Harn?"

"To Ander Harrow. Phen?"

The younger man smiled. "To mountain cats, and to Companions."

Finally the bottle passed to Andy. He held it cradled in his hands for a log time until Norma nudged him.

"C'mon, boy, finish the toast."

Andy held the bottle up, feeling the liquid inside slosh about inside. "To Trance Tower Garrison," he said thickly. "I never thought I'd . . ." he stopped, his jaw working, "I never thought I'd have to leave it, but if I do, I will." He took an abrupt drink, then turned away so the others couldn't see his face.

"Good enough," Ernie answered.

The next day dawned cool and damp. The cook doled out the last of the potatoes fried up with the last of the mutton, then the garrison lined up, weapons ready, facing the main gate. Commander Dravin sat on his horse before them, his swords drawn. He didn't speak, just cast his gaze across the faces of his soldiers as if memorizing their features, then nodded once. The sergeant-at-arms gave the order, the gate was flung open, and Trance Tower Garrison attacked.

*   *   *

The enemy was surprised, but not for long. It rallied quickly and then it was hand-to-hand combat on the northern plain.

Protected at the center of the Gray Squad, Andy moved as fast as he could for the foothills. Somewhere out there he knew the others were doing the same, ringed by a circle of swords and spears. They made three hundred yards, then four, then five, before by sheer weight of numbers the enemy penetrated their defenses. Harn was the first to fall. Then Phen. When Norma went down, Andy leaped forward, but a great ax-wielding man jumped between them and, with a scream, Andy closed with him. He never saw Ernie take the blow aimed for his back, but he heard him fall.

The battle raged unabated throughout the morning. Trance Tower had something to fight for now and they broke wave after wave of enemy troops sent against them. In the face of their ferocity, the enemy began to falter, and when a white flash entered the fray, kicking and slashing with hooves like silver lightning, they broke and ran.

The cry went up, "For the Herald!" as Commander Dravin led Trance Tower Garrison after them.

Two hundred yards from the foothills, Andy sank to his knees in relief.

It seemed like hours later than he managed to struggle to his feet and survey the damage though it was really only a few moments. Harn was dead, Ernie was dying, and Phen was so badly wounded that he probably wouldn't last the day, but what was probably worse, Tara and Mac lay together on the northernmost edge of the battlefield. They'd almost made it to the hills. Almost.

Breathing hard, Andy knelt beside Norma. Taking her hand in his, he squeezed her bloodied fingers until her eyelids fluttered open.

"Did we beat 'em?" she asked hoarsely.

He nodded, his gaze blurred by tears. "Yeah."

"Then . . . what are you waitin' for? Git."

"I can't leave you like this."

"I'll mend. Takes more than the likes . . . of them to put an Anzie in her grave. I said, git."

There was a whicker behind them and Andy turned slowly.

Twenty paces away the Companion stood, staring at him with its brilliant blue eyes. This close, it was dazzlingly white in the sunlight and he could barely look at it without squinting. He moved forward.

The Companion and the Guardsman looked into each other's eyes for a long time, and then Andy's mouth quirked up.

"I told them it wasn't me," he whispered, his tone a combination of relief and disappointment.

The Companion turned its attention away, sweeping its bight gaze over the battlefield, clearly searching, then turned back to stare into Andy's face once again.

He nodded his understanding. "Yes," he said, laying one weary hand on its back. "I'll help you find that Herald of yours."

They reached Garet Barns a few moments later. He was lying on his back, his eyes wide with shock, his hands pressed tight against his side. Blood seeped through his uniform tunic to pool darkly beneath him. His face was ashen, but when he looked up into the Companion's eyes, a bit of the color returned.

Andy shook his head. "Shoulda known." He knelt. "C'mon, lemme see it."

His gaze still locked on the Companion's eyes, Garet allowed the other youth to examine the wound.

"It's not terrible," Andy pronounced after a minute. Taking off his own tunic, he used his knife to cut his shirt into strips, then bound up the wound. "All right, let's get you up. That lot won't keep runnin' all day." Arms wrapped about the other's chest, he drew Garet to his feet. The Companion knelt and somehow Andy managed to get him onto its back. It stood carefully. Then, one hand holding the other youth by the belt, Andy nodded.

"Let's go."

They made their way slowly across the battlefield, careful not to step on any of the wounded. Friend and foe alike watched them go in silence, and the ones that could, saluted as they passed.

They reached the south road without incident. Still shocky, Garet rode without speaking and, deep in his own thoughts, Andy hardly noticed his surroundings until a white blur flashed between them and a stand of pine trees. Looking up, Andy stared straight into a pair of brilliant sapphire eyes. The world fell away beneath the intensity of its gaze and all he could think to say was, "Oh. There were two of you."

The second Companion whickered softly. After a few moments it nudged him gently. Then it nudged him harder.

:Chosen?:

The fist Companion pawed the ground and Garet stirred. "Andy? The garrison? We have to keep moving."

"Right."

Shaking himself out of his stupor, Andy carefully mounted up. They had miles to travel before he could pause to wonder at the sudden change in his life. They had to get to the capital, warn King Valdemar, and come back with an army to save what was left of Trance Tower, but suddenly it all seemed possible. Smiling down at . . . Lillia, he nodded.

"All right. I'm ready to go now."

Together, they headed down the south road toward Haven.

Starhaven
by *Stephanie D. Shaver*

Stephanie Shaver is a single twenty-something living in St. Louis, Missouri, where she works as a web-master for an online games company. She's been published in various anthologies and magazines over the years, and was one of the resident writers at Marion Zimmer Bradley's home in Berkeley in the early Nineties. When she's not making soap, studying aikido, or working on websites, she's writing a book about a girl who misplaced her soul. Her official website is at www.sdshaver.com.

She was dying, blood trickling down her side and legs into the grass. The mage's body was a crumpled, charred mess at her feet. But—his soul—

At the instant she had killed him—the moment when she'd poured everything she had left at him—he had done the unexpected. He was tangled with her soul somehow—buried like a jagged black seed.

She was too weak to think clearly enough to destroy him. And even if she could have gotten back to the Vale—

The seed inside her. Who would it bury itself in next?

She fell to her knees, her vision dimming as she fought death with the scraped-up dredges of her strength. Her teachers had always told her she threw herself too far into what she did—but how could he *not? The mage killed her daughter—and her husband—*

In more ways than one, she had nothing left.

With the last of her strength she slipped the moorings of her body and plunged deep into the earth, dropping like an offering into the burning node of power beneath her—

Vess writhed in his bed, screaming.

His body was on fire—his body *was* fire—locked in the process of agonized immolation. He arched in pain and horror as his skin and bones melted—

And it was gone.

Vess sat up, soaked in sweat and breathing heavily. He was in a Waystation inside the village of Solmark. It was morning. He was not a woman dying alone in a forest; he was a Herald, here on business for the Crown.

That wasn't just a nightmare, he thought. *That was— what the hells* was *that?*

He was shaking as he dragged himself out of bed and dressed. He felt a curious emptiness within, as if someone had cracked open his chest and scooped out his insides.

As if a part of me just died, he thought, unsure of where the thought came from.

:Chosen?:

He paused, momentarily disoriented by Kestric's voice in his mind. *:Yes?:*

:Are you all right?:

He nodded. *:I'm fine.:*

:I felt something—a nightmare?:

:Something like one. I'll be okay. I need some air.: He straightened his collar, brushing out the front. *:I need to do what I came here for.:* He sucked in a deep breath, relaxing his shoulders on exhale.

:Right. After all those days of riding—to get so little

rest. Are you sure you don't want to try to go back to sleep?:

:I'm sure. I don't think it'll get better with more sleep.: He rubbed the back of his neck. *:It's the damn Pelagirs. I never have good dreams, this close to them.:*

Vess had no illusions of being the next Windrider—his Mage-Gift, in comparison to some of the other, *real* Herald-Mages, was pretty pitiful—but the sliver of active Mage-Gift he *did* have made him sensitive to local magic. It was more a bane than a boon—it was distinctly unpleasant to be able to simultaneously *see* magic and be completely helpless to affect it.

His other Gifts more than made up for where the supposedly superior Mage-Gift had failed him. He was one of the strongest Mindspeakers in the Heraldic Circle—strong enough to use it as a weapon. A touch of Empathy coupled with a noble upbringing had also made him a viable member of the King's inner circle.

Viable enough that, for the last six months, he'd effectively *been* the King's Own, sans the title, the senseless attacks on his reputation, and Jastev, the Grove-born stallion. He'd been in that uncomfortable, ill-defined position of King's closest adviser ever since the *real* King's Own, Nadja, had stopped being able to get out of bed in the mornings.

Nadja . . . I hope you're not hurting, though I know you probably are.

:Chosen, are you dwelling?:

Vess shook his head, trying to disperse his brooding thoughts. *:I am,:* he said. *:I should stop.:* He opened the door, the cool hand of early dawn caressing his face. *:Want to come along with me on my walk?:*

He felt a pleasant surge of affection from Kestric—the closest the Companion could come to a hug. *:As if you had to ask.:*

*   *   *

The gate to the stockade was pushed up for the day, and in the light of the new morning Vess could see now why they'd needed to gather up five men last night to get it open. It was composed of entire tree trunks planed, caulked, and lashed together to form a formidable barrier that could be dropped at a moment's notice.

The Waystation was built inside the stockade—to put it outside amid the unpredictable dangers of the Pelagirs would have been suicide. Not to mention a constant hassle. Pelagir plants grew with preternatural quickness. The Waystation would have been overcome by greenery within a few short years.

. . . much the way Starhaven is, he thought.

They passed out from under the cool shadow of the gate and down the road leading away from Solmark. There weren't many people about—just one girl, who waved to them as they passed by, her smock pockets stuffed with herbs—and the weather was pleasant and cool.

The quiet was as pleasant as the weather. Vess had become accustomed to living in Haven, with the daily pressure of hundreds of minds pressing on his shields. He didn't usually notice it, but out in the hinterland it was strange to not have that sense of others around him.

Just me and Kestric, he thought as he and his Companion headed down a thin, overgrown trail. *What a change.*

Of course, the Pelagirs had a presence all their own; something akin to a ghostly hand brushing the back of his neck. He had felt it even as a child, when his mother had sent him to Solmark to be fostered for a summer.

It had not been pleasant. And if Solmark was enough to give him nightmares, Starhaven was even worse.

As if cued—or possibly listening in on his surface thoughts— Kestric said, :*So, where are you taking us? I assume you have a location in mind.*:

:*Starhaven,*: he replied. :*Or what used to be Starhaven. It was Solmark's sister town fifty years ago.*:

:*. . . was?*:

:*Was until everyone in it died. I've mentioned this before, haven't I?*:

:*You've mentioned being fostered in Solmark, but not Starhaven.*: Patterns of sunlight and shadow dappled Kestric's pure white coat as they passed under the forest's canopy. The trail, for all that it surely wasn't used regularly by anyone anymore, was in remarkably good shape, easy to discern and unbroken.

:*There isn't a lot to say about Starhaven,*: he said. :*Even without Mage-Gift, it's disturbing to visit a place if you know over a hundred people all died at once there. One night, no signs of struggle or violence. And I would imagine that's why the adults told us* not *to go there. . . . .* :

:*And exactly why you did.*:

:*Of course.*: He smiled. :*Boys will be boys. And something was waiting for us there, in fact.*:

:*"Something"?*:

:*As a child I thought it was a ghost, but my adult reason says it was probably just a wandering mage.*: He shrugged. :*He seemed amused—though I didn't realize it till* months *later, when I wasn't so terrified of the memory. All white robes, bleached hair with what I think were crow feathers in it—looked as much like a bird as a person.*:

:*Hunh.*:

Kestric nodded, leaning forward in the saddle. *:I think it might have been an outKingdom mage—some of them wear some strange costumes.:*

:What's so strange about all white?:

Vess laughed aloud. *:Aside from making me a walking target—nothing, really. Ah . . . the marker stone—: He looked down to where a crumbling stone lay to one side of the road, imprinted with the letters for STARHAVEN. :Here it is.:*

The road emptied out into a clearing the size of Solmark. Green hulks that had once been houses shared space with saplings and tender bushes. The place was disarmingly cheery—birds sang in the trees, and there was ample sunlight.

Kestric stopped three steps "in" and turned his head about as he surveyed the scene. Vess considered dismounting, but decided against it. He didn't think they'd be staying long.

:I don't know why I picked coming here,: he said after a while. *:It always struck me—the mystery and the sadness—so many people gone, without any reason, overnight.:*

:You're infinitely silly, you know that?:

Vess blinked in surprise at the lighthearted tone in Kestric's mind-voice.

:I am?: he said.

:Sure you are. Vess, you're a Herald! *Of course you want to know what happened here! Not that I think you'll ever know—these are the Pelagirs. Strange things happen all the time.:*

He nodded. *:They do, indeed. Like girls who people think are goddesses . . . :*

:Speaking of which, we ought to go find her.: Kestric tossed his head toward the road. *:Neh?:*

Vess was about to give his nonverbal agreement when something pale caught the edge of his vision.

He turned his head, and there, off to one side amongst the trees that bordered the clearing, stood a pale figure in white.

For a moment Vess forgot to breathe as the vertigo-sensation of having *seen* this person before swept him. It was the figure from his childhood—the strange, pale man with feathers in his hair.

In the next moment, his training took over, and he unconsciously reinforced his shields while simultaneously slipping open his inner eye to look at the man with Mage-sight—

Nothing.

Not the power pulses that signaled an illusion, nor the seamless invisibility that someone with very strong and specific shields would have—just wisps of gray must sprinkled with pinpricks of light.

:What the hells *is that?:* he yelled in panic, throwing down the mental image of the man's seeming.

Kestric swung around and backed up. In the instant he brought his head about, the figure raised a hand and waved—

And vanished.

The birds had not stopped singing, and the sun had not gone behind a cloud, but Vess could feel the bumps rise on his arms and a chill rise up his spine. He felt much less safe than he had a few moments ago.

:Gone?: he heard Kestric say.

:Damn,: Vess said. *:Maybe Starhaven is haunted after all.:* He took a deep breath. *:And I have exactly enough Mage-Gift to be completely useless toward doing any good, if a Herald of any sort can even help— might be better to find a competent priest.:*

:Might be better to get back to Solmark.:

:Good idea.: Vess looked around, reassuring himself that—to his eyes—they were still alone. *:The sooner, the better.:*

"Heyla—Herald—"

The voice came from off to the left of Vess as he walked around from the stable toward the Waystation. Looking over, Vess saw an elderly man crossing over to him, a girl in tow—

The same girl we passed this morning, he thought. *What irony, if she turns out to be the one who was the whole reason for my leaving off vacation to come out here.*

"Greetings, sir," Vess said, bowing slightly. "How can I help you?"

"I heard you were looking for my granddaughter," the man said, coming to a stop with his hands on his hips and a grin on his face. "I'm Sevastan, and this is my famous Juni. You need Healing?"

Well, at least he's congenial, Vess thought.

"No, actually, I don't." He smiled. "I heard about your granddaughter while I was visiting my mother and—to be honest, I admit to being a bit concerned."

"Heh! Came all the way out to this backwater town out of concern? Now that's something, isn't it, Juni?" Sevastan looked down at his granddaughter, who was smiling slightly.

"Sir, if you'd like to talk in private with me?" Vess asked.

"Well," Sevastan said, "If you prefer. Juni?"

"It's all right," she said. "I have work to do." She stood up on her toes and kissed her grandfather on the cheek, then bowed to Vess before strolling off and disappearing behind a house.

Vess turned back toward Sevastan to find that the man's outward congeniality had vanished, replaced by a firmly set mouth and cold eyes.

This is a switch, Vess thought. "Would you like to adjourn to the Waystation?" he asked.

"No, actually, I want to make something clear," Sevastan said, all remnants of cheerfulness erased from his tone. "My wife is dead. My daughter died when Juni was only a few months old and my son-in-law died when she was five. I don't have any family—most of them got killed in Starhaven. Now, I know about you Heralds. You like to take children away from their homes and families. Juni isn't going with you. She isn't anything you'd want, and she doesn't want to leave anyway."

The faint smile on Vess's face felt forced, but he maintained it anyway. He could point out that it was the Companions, not the Heralds, who took away children—and he could point out that Healers weren't Heralds—but neither point would matter or help. Sevastan didn't want his granddaughter leaving him, and that was the real issue.

"You are assuming," Vess said, "that I have a choice in this matter."

"You could choose to leave."

"Only if I was assured she wasn't a danger to herself or those around her. Forgive me for not asking," Vess said sharply, "but am I perhaps mistaken? Has your daughter been trained by a Healer?"

"I taught her what I know about herbs," Sevastan said. "Setting bones, splints, wrapping wounds—"

"I'm sorry," Vess said. "That's not what I mean when I say *Healer*. What I have heard of your daughter's skills sounds like she is Healing with a *Gift*. It's not the same as applying bandages or ointments."

Vess firmed his mouth. "If it goes untrained, it could wind up killing someone. Wild Gifts inevitably twist in on themselves—they must be schooled. And since he is using hers—"

"Assuming," Sevastan interrupted, an edge of annoyance in his voice, 'that she is using a 'Gift.' "

Vess resisted the urge to sigh. On one hand, he sympathized with the man over his lack of family—but on the other—

I think the Crown would not approve of me smacking him upside the head, he thought with bland amusement. *Though I'm sure the King would understand. . . .*

"You're right," Vess said. "I *am* assuming—because I *haven't* seen her Heal anyone yet. And when I do, I'll know. Which is why I'm here. Sir—" Vess crammed as much sincere compassion as he could into his voice, "—I don't want to take your granddaughter away from you. That's the last thing I seek. But you have to understand that this is for her own good. And I wager that once her training is done, the Healer's Circle would be happy to send her back here—especially since she seems to be needed."

"And if she does not have a 'Gift' at all?" Sevastan asked, one brow raised. "What if the gods have touched her and are working through her? Hm? Will the priests then be taking her away?"

"If that is the case—" *And it's bloody unlikely,* Vess thought, *but I'll let you have your wishful thinking* "—then it's a matter I will leave to the priests. I have no jurisdiction when it comes to religion."

"Very well, then." Sevastan nodded his head to Vess. "Come by my house at sunset. Marsi is bringing her son Garth by for Juni to attend to."

"I'll see you then," Vess said.

Sevastan snapped about, moving off with a stiff, unhurried gate. Vess waited till he was out of sight, then slumped against the Waystation door, pinching his nose with his thumb and forefinger.

:I'm sure you heard it all.:

:Oh, yes,: Kestric said with a mental sigh that gusted loudly through Vess' mind. *:I think you did your best, considering that he wasn't here to listen. And he's not going to be happy when you confirm what we already know. . . . :*

:That's his *problem,:* Vess thought. *:If he loves her so damned much, he should move to Haven to be with her.:* He straightened. *:I'm going to go take a bath.:*

His anger faded as he stalked off toward the public house, giving his mind room to ponder what he was going to do after this evening to get Juni out of Solmark.

Because just then, that whole idea of Heralds kidnapping children sounded *damned* attractive. . . .

"It really is a shame you're the only one who can hear me," the woman's voice said, "because you're the first person in decades to show up who can, and you aren't listening."

Vess blinked. Nothing but darkness and mist surrounded him and he realized peripherally that he must be asleep. "Hunh?"

"You still *don't understand?" A sigh. "It seems this sort of naïvete runs rampant with your people. Perhaps you should find one of your so-called Herald-Mages and call them here? The danger you are flirting with is not a normal one. I failed—with disastrous consequences. You cannot—"*

Vess sat up in bed, his heart fluttering rapidly against his ribcage and his mind full of strange dreams. He was, thank the gods, not sweating too badly—so

while he was a trifle jarred, at least he didn't smell
like old socks.

:*How was the nap?*: Kestric asked.

:*Lousy,*: Vess replied, sticking out his tongue. :*Another weird dream.*: He grasped at the fraying ends of
the dream's memory, but it melted away. :*Eh—it's
gone. How are the apples?*:

:*You mean how* were *the apples? Excellent. The
slightly mushy ones taste gooooood. Tell the publican
next time you see him that I really appreciate it.*:

:*My Companion, rotten apple eater.*:

:*I prefer* well-ripened *to rotten. And this from a man
who likes tripe stew.*:

:*Just the one from that inn at Kettlesmith,*: Vess said
with a smirk. :*And no other!*:

:*Did I mention it's nearly sunset, tripe-eater?*:

:*Crumbs. And I was so looking forward to a graphic
description of rotten apples. Thanks for the reminder.*:
Vess rose from the bed. :*Let's see what we see.*:

He got back to the Waystation sometime after sunset and immediately walked into the stable—built for
Companions, so it was wide enough for him and Kestric to stand in together—and sat down on the stool
in one corner of the stall.

Vess put his head in his hands and curled the tips
of his fingers in his hair.

:*Are you going to talk now?*: Kestric asked.

Vess took a deep breath, inhaling the dusty scent
of hay and leather. :*This day couldn't have been
stranger if the gods themselves had tried.* :

:*What's wrong?*:

:*She's not a Healer.*: Vess looked up at Kestric,
meeting the faintly luminescent blue eyes of his Com-

panion. *:I looked at her while she was Healing the boy—and it's not Healing Gift she's using.:*

:That doesn't make any sense.:

:Maybe this will help,: Vess said, drawing up the mental image of what he'd seen and tossing it down the bond. Juni—eyes shut, hand out and glowing faintly red to Vess's Mage-Sight. The edges of her patient's lacerations drawing together and sealing up, the trickles of sweat dripping down the sides of her face.

He followed up the wordless report with the "signature" of the power she had been using, exercising his limited Empathy to give Kestric the full experience.

Then he waited.

:That's . . .: Vess Felt Kestric recoil in disgust as the Companion took a step back in the stall. *:That's blood-magic! She's using it to reshape the flesh!:*

Vess nodded. *:I wasn't sure of it, but if you think so, too . . .:*

:But she's not a blood-mage! We would have felt it!:

:She has the Mage-Gift—and it is *active,:* he said soberly. *:She also has Empathy and Mindspeech—gods, she's just like* me. *Except her other two Gifts are dormant. She doesn't even have Healer potential, Kes. And worse . . . something happened to the boy after she "Healed" him. It's like a bloodstain on his soul, and his mother's just the same. I took a look around the village before I came back. Just about* everyone here *has the same marking.:*

:Oh, hellfires.: The Companion flared his nostrils. *:We need a Herald-Mage.:*

:I know.: Vess rubbed his nose. *:It just doesn't seem to make sense, though. I don't pick up the least bit of malevolence from her. Something doesn't fit. How is*

she doing this? Why is she doing it? Is it possible to do blood-magic without knowing you're doing it? Or does she just have one hell of a shield around her?:

:*That,*: Kestric said, :*is what I'd like to know.*:

Vess opened his eyes, staring at the ceiling.

Something was floating there, hovering above his head—

And then he *really* woke up, and realized that his mind was once again playing tricks on him. There was nothing on the ceiling but shadows, and no one in the room but him. He was alone.

And maybe that's my problem, he thought suddenly. *Too many goddamn years in the court with an empty bed and fewer friends than a mean drunk. Just working day in and day out, waiting for the next crisis to strike.*

And wasn't that the whole point of taking leave in the first place? I could have told Herald Becka to find another person with Mage-Gift to investigate Solmark, but no . . . I went instead. If it's not trouble finding me, it's me finding trouble. He grimaced. *I'm pitiful.*

He pulled himself out of bed and into his clothes. A brush to Kestric's mind found him to be sleeping, and Vess didn't see a reason to wake him. In the distance, he could hear the sound of the Solmark gate raising. He waned to walk, and think, and for once really, truly be alone. No people, no Companions— just him and the forest.

It wasn't healthy to go walking in the Pelagirs alone, but the same could be said for parts of Haven, as well. Picking up his sword from the table where it lay, Vess stuck it into his belt, and set off to be by himself.

It took longer to get to Starhaven on foot, and this time he approached it with the caution it deserved. He stood silently at the entrance, peering about once with his regular pair of eyes, then again with Mage-sight. When he was certain things were safe, he walked into the center, pulled the sheathed sword out of his belt, and sat down.

If I'm going to go looking for trouble, he thought, *I might as well go all out.*

But after a while, when the birds kept singing and the sunlight grew warmer, he found himself relaxing. He lay down in the grass, the sword on his chest, and stared at the one cloud in the sky above him, shaped like a fist.

How long, he thought, *since I've just watched clouds?*

The answer came easily: *Since Nadja got sick. Since I started worrying the Companions might make me the next King's Own. Oh, gods—if there's one thing I don't want . . . I don't care if I'd be good at it, I don't want that job!*

He sighed. *But if I had to, I'd do it. And we all know it.*

"Herald?"

He hadn't heard her walk up, but he knew the voice, and he recognized that it was close. Sitting up and letting the sword fall into the crook of his left arm, Vess looked over to see Juni walking toward him.

"Good morning," he said with a smile. He had acted as if nothing unusual had happened last night—making the (true) excuse that he needed to think about what he had discovered. He was pretty sure that she didn't suspect anything.

"What are you doing here?" he asked.

"I visit here a lot," she said. "Especially early." She paused, her mouth half open, then took a step forward, saying, "You seem . . . troubled."

He smiled. "A lot of things on my mind."

"About me?"

He shook his head. "No, not you."

She cocked her head. "What about?"

"The court. The King. My duty."

She widened he eyes. "You know the King?"

He nodded. "Sure. I'm one of his counselors—I know quite a bit about court life." He winked. "That's my curse."

She smiled. "Is the Palace nice?"

"It can be."

She nodded. "This place must be strange to someone like you."

"It would be, except that I was raised not far from here. My mother is Lady Baireschild."

She widened he eyes again. "My Lord—"

"No." He raised a hand. "Dropped the titles when I got Chosen." He grinned. "Never liked them much, anyway." He felt the smile fade. "You're a very nice young lady, Juni."

She bowed her head, blushing a little. "Thank you."

"You're welcome." He stood, stretching, and brushed grass out of his hair and off his shirt. Then, dwelling on that last comment to her, he opened his inner eye and reached out to her—

—*Maybe I was wrong*—

The red-black energy he had witnessed around her just last night was gone. He pressed further, delicately snaking past her natural defenses. Her three Gifts were still there, but now he saw that there was something more—something like the "bloodstain" he had seen on the people of Solmark—only deeper—

That's odd. Why would she have marked herself with her own stain?

Something slammed into him, an unseen force that lifted him into the air and threw him back down to the ground in a pain-stricken sprawl. He blinked stars out of his eyes and tasted blood in his mouth—before he'd been hit, though, he'd Felt a surge of magic coming from nearby.

:Chosen!: he heard Kestric's panicked call.

:I'm not dead—yet,: he thought dazedly. *:Get out here, quick. Something's not right.:*

He rolled over, shaking his head to clear it, and for a moment all he saw was a pale, frightened Juni—

And then he saw Sevastan. Sevastan—but not Sevastan. Even when the man had been curt yesterday, he hadn't looked this—malevolent. The set of his mouth, the shape of his eyes, the way he held himself—little pieces that amounted to a startling, sinister change.

A different person was standing before Vess. One look in his eyes revealed that.

"It is unfortunate," Sevastan said, "but necessary. I meant it when I said I can't have you taking her away."

The blow had thrown off Vess' internal balance—he was seeing double, the physical world layered under his Mage-sight. Sinuous red tendrils wrapped Sevastan's arms, gathering in pools in his hands. A cord of red power, like a leash, dripped out of his left hand and connected to Juni, and from Juni spun out hundreds of thin red threads, pulsing in time with a heartbeat of their own.

Everything fell into place with painful clarity.

He's *the blood-mage,* Vess thought in shock. *Not her. She has Mage-Gift—he's working* through *her and disguising it as a "Gift"—good gods!*

Sevastan raised his arm and shouted something, and a black levin bolt cracked through the air toward Vess, who threw up his arms in a pitiful mockery of defense.

Inches away from him, it disintegrated in a shower of sparks as it hit invisible shields.

Vess blinked in surprise, then blinked again as a pale white form faded into sight beside him.

:I can't keep this up,: a vaguely familiar female voice said into his mind. *:If you have a plan, use it.:*

"Well," Sevastan said, his attention shifted off Vess. "This is unexpected. Didn't I kill you?"

Vess heard the female voice answer with flat emotion, *:By your own hand we are entangled, mage. I do not die if you do not die.:*

Sevastan laughed. "A complication I will swiftly amend," he said, raising his hands again—

Vess didn't give him a chance.

Dragging up his mental energies, he split open his shields, threw his mind at Sevastan—

And *screamed* inside his head.

Years of anger, frustration, and disgust broke out of Vess, his Empathy fueling the raw violence of his attack. Months of watching Nadja die by inches in her bed—months of sitting with the King as he quietly went to pieces with the agonized guilt of the latest Herald he'd had to send off to possible death or worse. Years of court deception, petty politics and subterfuge—deceivers and backstabbers with smiling faces and no concept of the pain they caused.

Tragedies. Sorrows. Pain. The struggle to keep from being beaten down by the very people he tried to help.

And past that, the certainty that the *thing* he was fighting was the same *thing* that had killed Starhaven, the thief of life.

The mind-blast broadened and changed to incoherent rage. Lost in the blinding power he had given himself over to, Vess's world dissolved into a solid sheet of fury, and evaporated.

* * *

"Herald."

Vess blinked, finding himself elsewhere. Not Starhaven, not Solmark—not the Palace or his mother's manor. He was somewhere where his Whites seemed to glow with their own light, and everything was the gray of twilight.

"Herald," the voice said again, "I want to thank you."

Vess sat up, and saw a man standing over him, his face in shadows but his hand extended out to him.

"All my life, I've been that wizard's puppet," the man said. "He used me to destroy Starhaven, and when he realized that I wasn't a suitable vessel for his power, he worked through my daughter and grandchild for the same. I'm sorry, Herald. Please know that anything I said to you—the mouth and the voice were mine, but the words were his."

"Sevastan?" Vess said, reaching up to take the man's hand. "What—"

"Take care of my granddaughter, Herald," Sevastan said as his warm, dry fingers closed around Vess' hand. "Please let her know that even with that bastard's hand on my mind, I tried my best to love her."

:Chosen!:

Vess came around to too-bright sunlight. The aura of a reaction headache was building behind his eyes, and he tasted copper in his mouth.

:Chosen! Wake up!:

"I'm alive," Vess said, his voice feeble. "And sweet Kernos, how I wish I weren't."

A sob cut the air and, grimacing, Vess climbed to his knees, fighting nausea and dizziness. His hands were shaking and his skin felt clammy. He had definitely overextended himself.

Juni had thrown herself over her grandfather and was crying hysterically. Vess' mind was still painfully open to thoughts—Juni's grief-stricken regrets and stunned questioning of what had just transpired, and the telling silence coming from the body of Sevastan.

I killed him, he thought, reaching out to pull the veils of his shields around his mind.

:No,: said the woman's voice in his mind. *:I killed him. You broke his concentration long enough to give me the opportunity to throw the bastard into the node— which, thank the god of my fathers, actually* worked *this time.:* A sad sigh. *:Unfortunately—the trauma was too much for Sevastan himself—damnit.:*

Vess turned slightly, looking in the direction of the ghostly mage, her arms folded across her chest and one slender eyebrow raised.

"What's a node?" he asked.

She rolled her eyes. *:Naïve outlanders. Never mind. He's gone.:* Her face softened. *:And you have done me a great service.:* She smiled. *:I knew, that first time I saw you, that you'd be something special. Farewell, Herald. I'm off to the place I should have been long, long ago. . . .:*

She dissolved before his eyes, reforming into a broad-winged white crow that launched itself upward, flying up toward the sun. He tried to watch her go, but the impending headache and his own physical weakness dissuaded the notion.

"Good-bye," he said. "Good rest."

And then there was just the matter of Juni.

Vess heard the muffled bell-tone of Companion hooves behind him. Kestric, no doubt—though Vess wasn't sure how he'd gotten *behind* him. The Companion came up alongside, and Vess grabbed hold of the saddle to pull himself up—

Wait a moment. How did he get his gear on?

Vess really *looked* at the Companion now, and it gazed back at him with what seemed to be faint amusement—

Hellfires, Vess thought, stunned. *That's—the Grove stallion!*

:Greetings, Herald,: he heard the contrabass voice of Jastev boom in his mind. *:I Choose—Bright Havens, certainly not you! You've* got *a Companion!:*

Vess lost his fine grip on upward mobility. He fell over and landed in a sprawl on the grass—bowled over not only by the fact that another Companion had just spoken to him, but had done so *in order to tell a joke.*

:He's got quite a sense of humor, doesn't he?: Kestric said dryly in Vess' mind. From the overgrown trail that led to Starhaven, the Companion galloped into view, slowing to a trot as he came up to Vess and stood before him.

"He's a bloody *sadist,*" Vess gasped—and hen the surprise faded, and he realized what was going unsaid. "Has Nadja—did she finally—?"

:Right after you left. I didn't want to tell you, but— yes. Peacefully, in her sleep.:

Vess nodded, tears building up in his eyes and trickling down his cheeks.

:Poor Chosen. You've been through so much. Are you going to be all right?:

"It's a sadness," he said, watching dazedly as Jastev walked with exaggerated dignity over to the dead man and Juni. "I wish I could say it was a relief. It is— and it isn't. It is what it is."

He still wasn't completely all there, because he was still trying to figure out why Jastev was *here* and not looking for a new King's Own when the Companion bent his head down, touching the girl's forehead with his muzzle.

Juni raised eyes bright red from crying, and Vess felt a momentary shock as her eyes widened and her face brightened with amazement.

"Oh, thank the god!" Vess moaned.

Much later, when he'd done his best to explain the Sevastan situation to the people of Solmark—when he'd made sure they understood that Juni was neither demon or Healer—when he'd quaffed enough willowbark tea to stop an army—when he'd arranged for a Herald-Mage to visit Solmark and ensure it was free of blood-magic's taint—and when he was sure that Jastev was tending to Juni, newly Chosen but still in mourning—

Only then did he find himself lying in bed, listening to the crickets and the crows at sunset—aching but alive.

:Juni will be a compassionate King's Own,: he thought drowsily to Kestric.

:And a good trainee for you to teach,: his Companion responded.

:I do know more about the job than anyone else.:

He subsided into silence then, finding comfort in the crows as they sang their harsh song to the sunset. He thought of the last glimpse of the white crow spiraling up to the sun, and he smiled.

He slept all through the night: dreamless and at peace.

Rebirth
by Judith Tarr

Judith Tarr is the author of a number of historical and fantasy novels and stories. Her most recent novels include House of War *and* Queen of the Amazons, *as well as the* Epona *Sequence:* Lady of Horses, White Mare's Daughter, *and* Daughter of Lir. *She was a World Fantasy Award nominee for* Lord of the Two Lands. *She lives near Tucson, Arizona, where she breeds and trains Lipizzan horses, of whom she says, "They're white, they're magical, they bond for life to a single human, they don't think or act like horses— when I was asked to write a story about Valdemar, of course I had to write about Companions. That's called 'writing what you know.' "*

Lord Dashant's forces had drawn off the battlefield, marching backward in ordered retreat. A ragged cheer ran down the line of what had, only moments ago, been a beleaguered army.

Mathias the Herald-Mage, from his place at the rightful Heir's right hand, found he could not share the army's celebration. Something smelled wrong. In point of fact, something stank.

His Companion raised her head and fleered her upper lip in a strikingly horselike gesture. She smelled it, too, although there was nothing earthly about it. As far as his nose knew, this was a battlefield like any other: reeking of blood and loosed bowels, rank fear-sweat, and the incongruous sweetness of crushed grass.

Beside him, Vera's own Companion shook his heavy neck and snorted. Vera stroked him absently with a gauntleted hand. The visor of her helmet was up; her eyes narrowed, studying the enemy's retreat.

He was the bitterest of all enemies that a royal Heir could have: her own half-brother, who had killed their father the King and claimed the throne of Valdemar. Dashant was a murderer and a traitor, but one thing he had never been, and that was a coward. It was not like him to abandon a battle before he was well and resoundingly defeated.

"It's a feint," she said. "He's laid a trap. But I can't see—"

Neither could Mathias, and that was not reassuring at all. Mathias had the gift of seeing through any wall or veil, and piercing any illusion. His wards were intact. His protection spells were undisturbed. There was no magical threat anywhere, nothing, except that infernal stink.

He glanced to either side, down along the ranks that were beginning to waver. The commanders were doing nothing to stop them. One or two had had the sense to send parties in pursuit of the enemy, but the rest were acting as if the battle was over. None of them paid any attention to Vera at all. Even her personal guard, her squires who adored her, the messengers and pages who had stayed by her through exile and civil war, had turned away from her. As if they had forgotten her existence. As if—

The spell was as strong as it was subtle. Mathias felt it creeping around the edges of his wards, seeking out chinks and weaknesses. It blurred his sight, so that when he looked at Vera, she seemed to shimmer like a reflection in a pool. But in his heart where she had been since the first day he saw her, long ago when he was a callow boy, new-Chosen, and she a curly-headed child, she was as clear and strong a presence as ever. He had never even asked if she loved him as he did her. It made no difference. She was the Heir and would be Queen. He was her servant—her Herald and her Mage.

He strengthened the wards, giving her all that he was, for her protection. She was not a mage of any kind, but she was a sensitive; she felt some at least of what he did for her. Her hand reached across the small space between them and clasped his, as warmly trusting as if they were both still children.

The earth boiled up with an army three, four, five times as large as the one that they had faced and, they thought, defeated. It swarmed over the Heir's weary forces. Its hordes of warriors were fresh and well-fed, with unscarred weapons and bright new armor. The spell that had concealed them was shredded and tattered, but still fuddled the minds and hearts of Vera's army.

They had forgotten why they fought, or whom they fought for. Swords dangled from slack hands. Spears struck without force. Arrows flew wide of the mark.

It was all Mathias could do to hold off that mind-blurring magic from himself while sustaining the wards about Vera. The guards were useless; each of them was fighting for his own skin.

The enemy could see the Heir. The heart of her own forces' blindness was clear to Dashant's troops. They converged on her.

Mathias was beyond desperation. Lytha, his Companion, fought with every weapon and wile at her disposal. He dropped his sword and bow and raised his hands. The spell that rose up in him was a spell for the other side of hope. It would kill him, but it would break the spell on Vera's army and weaken and befuddle Dashant's horde, and maybe—just maybe—give Vera enough cover to run for safety.

There was no time to explain. He had to hope against hope that both his Companion and his Queen would understand; that their hearts were close enough to let them see the sacrifice he had made—and that Vera, at least, would save herself.

He was not afraid. Fear was lost somewhere in the life that he was leaving. The spell was whole inside him. It was beautiful, a structure as intricate as a snowflake and as deadly as the track of a viper in the sand. It stirred and shimmered, tugging at the edges of his control, drawing power from the roots of his earthly self.

The horde was almost upon them. Vera held her sword in both hands, raised above her head, ready to fight to the last.

No grief. No hesitation. One more instant and the spell would be cast, and his life and magic with it.

He let it go.

The world shattered. All spells broke—every one, except those which guarded Vera. Mathias' body was gone, and so was every enemy within a furlong of it. Vera's forces reeled, stumbling over the sudden dead.

He clung to the reality of them, and most of all to Vera. But the world was whirling him away. He looked down into her white, shocked face—and if he had still had throat or tongue, he would have cried aloud. He knew—he understood—he foresaw—so clear, so terribly, appallingly clear—

Long waves sighed upon a shining shore. The foam on their breasts was the color of moonlight and snow. The sand on which they rolled was dust of jewels, opal and moonstone, lapis, malachite, chalcedony. The sky was silver, and the sun was gold, fixed it in forever, never shifting, never changing. Somewhere, in another heaven, were moon and stars, but not in this place. Here, it was morning for all eternity.

Luminous spirits walked in the jeweled sand or on grass the color of emeralds. Some wore the forms of men or women; others chose the shapes of moon-white horses, blue-eyed, silver-hooved, mystical and magical. They grazed on the eternal grass, or ate the fruits of paradise, or drank from springs that flowed supernally pure. Everywhere was a dream of peace.

The soul that had been Mathias stood on the edge between the sea and the sand. He still wore his human shape: a tallish man in Herald's whites, broad-shouldered, with curling brown hair, and green eyes more fit for laughter than for sorrow. But they had not laughed since well before he died. Here in the land of laughter, they knew no mirth at all.

A slender woman stood beside him. Her eyes were blue; her hair was long and silver-white, drawn back in a straight and shining tail that swung to her haunches. "My dear," she said, "you can't grieve here."

He kept his eyes fixed obstinately on the place where the horizon would have been if this had been an earthly isle. "Why can't I grieve? Is there a law against it?"

"Well," she said, "no. But—"

"Then I will grieve," he said.

"But why?" she asked him. "Your sacrifice ended the war. Your beloved is safe. The traitor's army is broken; she has marched in triumph to the capital, and taken her throne. She is Queen—and by your doing. You should be rejoicing."

"Yes," he said dully. "I should."

"Dear one," said the woman who in mortal life had been his Companion, "is it that you can't be with her? Your two souls are bound, you know that. In the fullness of time, you will both be reborn, and be together again. If I know the laws that constrain the gods, in your next life you will have her, and you will reap the reward of your sacrifice."

He shook his head. "No. That's not what it is. I know how the gods parcel out their favors. It's . . . I can't speak of it. Please, by the gods, don't make me try!"

She was relentless. She was a blessed spirit, he reminded himself, but she was not omniscient. She was not a god, or even a mage with a deathbed gift of prescience. She had not seen what he had seen. "Tell me," she said. "Tell me why you grieve."

But he would not. After a moment or an age, she went away. Her sadness stung him with guilt, but he could not tell her the horror that he had seen. They were all the blessed dead here. They were all ended, done with, rewarded. Anything that they had left behind, was left forever.

Some would go back to the mortal world, yes, but never soon enough. Not within the lifetime of anyone they had known.

That was his grief, and the core of his terror. By the laws of the cycle of death and rebirth, he had withdrawn from earthly cares. He would return to them, of that he had no doubt, but the life he had given up was gone. He could never get it back again.

Yet what he had seen in the moment of dying, the vision that he had had, tormented him even in these blessed Havens. He spoke it aloud, though only for his own ears to hear, soft beneath the sighing of

waves. "If I don't do something—if I don't take some
action—she will never come back. There will be nothing left of her. Her self, her soul—gone. Never again.
Never—"

He sank down in the sand, sobbing like a child. He
did not even care that the blessed souls stared, or that
the more compassionate or the more curious gathered
to wonder and whisper.

One of them came to stand over him. It was not
Lytha. This one he did not know: it wore Companion's shape, with some quality about it that made him
want to bow low before it. The blue eyes were mild,
the brush of its mind as soft, as gentle as sleep. *:Little
one,:* it said, *:what troubles you?:*

"I can't tell you," he said, though the core of his
resolve was crumbling fast.

The Companion bent its beautiful head. *:Come to
us,:* it said, *:in the Hidden Country.:*

"The Hidden—but where—"

But the great one was gone. Only then did Mathias
realize how very strange it had been: it had been neither male nor female, nor known any distress for its
lack of gender.

He straightened slowly. The semicircle of the curi-
ous drew back. He looked from face to shining face.
"Where is the Hidden Country?" he asked them.
"What did the great one mean?"

No one knew, or would admit to knowing. Only one
of them came forward to say, "Go inland. Follow the
light." She would not explain herself; perhaps she
could not.

It was as good advice as he was likely to get. He
would not have said that he had hope, but his despair
was a little lighter. He was doing something. He had
a place to go, a riddle to ponder. Maybe it was mere

distraction. Or maybe it would show him the way to save Vera's soul—and with it the soul of Valdemar.

If he had still been in mortal flesh, he would have found this journey tedious, if not particularly exhausting. Inland away from the sea was a sea of grass, greener than any earthly meadow, rolling monotonously into the luminous distance. He began to think that he had been deceived, that this was a punishment for bringing grief into the blessed land: to be condemned to wander forever in the featureless green. Not a soul stirred there, not single sentient thing, living or blessed dead.

Then he realized that without knowing it, he had been following the light. Little by little as he went onward, the sun was brighter, the grass more vivid. He was never blinded, but he was inundated in light.

He came at last to a wall of living fire, pure white, without heat, rising up into infinity. Standing there, contemplating it, he realized that it was not a barrier. He walked toward it.

It took it to itself. It was somewhat like passing a veil of fire, and somewhat like ascending a mountain of living coals. The dead knew no earthly weariness, but certainly they knew pain. It scoured away all that was impure in him, and all that was of earth—save only those memories which he clung to with implacable persistence. That was the price of passage. He paid it as freely as he had paid with his life to save Vera— but in so doing, he had doomed her soul.

With this, the Powers willing, he would save her. He pressed on. It was more like a mountain and less like a veil, the farther he traveled; and little by little the pain faded. In time, it dwindled to nothing. He trod stones underfoot, following a path up a steep slope, rising into a bank of luminous cloud.

There were trees, impossible if this had been an earthly peak, but all things were possible here. These were slender and tall. Their leaves were deep green; blossoms opened on the branches, pure white enfolding a spark of gold.

The scent that drifted from those branches was ineffably sweet. It tempted Mathias to delay, to slow, to drift and dream in this hall of trees. But he was armored in memory and armed with terror. He climbed onward and ever onward.

The heart of the wood was a space of light. The grass there was so dark a green as to be almost black. The flowers in it were stars.

The Companion was waiting for him. As he approached it, the circle widened immeasurably, expanding into infinite space. He stood in a field of stars, beneath the orb of a sun.

The great one was not alone here. There were others like him, legions of them, as numerous as the stars. All revolved around the sun, singing a song of pure praise.

Mathias' voice was a lone small dissonance. "Can you help me save my world?"

"Your world is safe," the great one said.

He shook his head. "Even you can't see. Before I died, I saw. Dashant works a spell to win back what he lost. That spell will destroy the Queen and enslave every soul in Valdemar. But her soul—her soul will be gone. Unless I do something. Unless I find some help, some hope for her."

"That is no longer your world," the great one said. "There is nothing you can do to save it."

He clenched his fists. "There must be! Where is the quality of divine mercy? Where is the care the light takes for its children?"

"It is where it has always been," said the great one. "All that is, is meant. Yes, child: even this."

"Then why did you bring me here?" he cried. "Why did you let me hope? What use is there in any of you?"

His outcry died into the silence of eternity. The stars shone undimmed. The sun's light burned as bright as ever. It was not mortal, to know pity, nor human, to know sorrow. It knew nothing but the glory of itself.

The great one said, "There is nothing that you can do."

"That is not the truth," said Mathias, almost spitting the words. "There are stories, memories, tales of powers—Avatars—"

"There is nothing *you* can do," the great one repeated. "This is ordained. You are forbidden."

"If I am forbidden, why was I allowed to see? Why, except to torment me?"

"Sometimes," said the great one, "in extremity, a mortal can see where no mortal eyes should ever see. That vision was not meant for you."

"Yet it came to me," he said. "I will save her. I must."

"Even if it costs you your soul?"

"If it saves hers," he said, "yes."

The great one bent its glimmering head. The field of stars shrank to a field of grass and flowers under a silver sky. Mathias stood in it with a creature like a Companion, surrounded by blossoming trees.

"You are forbidden," the great one said. But in its eyes as another word.

He held that stare for a long moment, lost in an

infinity of blue. "What will they do to you," he asked, "if—"

The great one shook its head infinitesimally. "Peace is yonder," it said, "on the shores of the Havens."

But Mathias was listening to what it did not say. He looked around him and recognized this place, this circle of trees, this grass; this spring that bubbled forth from the great one's feet, just as it must have done in the morning of the world.

"Do not drink from this spring," said the great one. "Mortals who drink of it are doomed. The hounds of heaven will hunt them, and the Powers will condemn their souls."

"But you," he said. "You children of heaven who drink of it, what dos it do? What powers does it give you?"

"That is forbidden," the great one said. "Go, seek peace. Forget this place."

Even as it spoke, it turned its back. The spring had bubbled into a pool. It seemed perfectly harmless, a pool of clear water, reflecting the sky. Mortal sky— blue as a Companion's eye, and mortal sun in it, looking down on living earth.

The great one's tail switched. Another instant and it would return to its guardianship. Mathias bent quickly and cupped water in his hands. It was cold, as spring water should be; it numbed his fingers. He did not pause to marvel at so earthly a sensation in this unearthly place. He lifted it to his lips and drank.

It was like liquid ice, like living fire. It was the wine of angels. His mortal spirit was not made to imbibe such potency. It rocked him with agony. It tore him, twisted him, rent him asunder. Darkness took him even here, in this land of perpetual light.

*   *   *

Mathias lay winded on bruised grass. But, he thought, grass did not bruise here. The dead did not breathe. He was not—

He staggered up. His body moved strangely. His head was too heavy, his neck, his hands and feet—

He had no hands. When he scrabbled at the grass, long white legs responded, and silver hooves. His neck twisted about, impossibly long. White mane flew as he whirled; white body spun. When he cried out, a shrill whinny pierced his ears.

His forefeet tangled; he fell to his knees. It hurt. Earth was hard. He heaved himself erect. Through the whirl of confusion, still he recognized this place. He was in the Companions' Grove. He wore that all-too-familiar shape, and it was not that of a newborn foal either. He, though mortal, had drunk from the well of the Powers. It had done to him what it must do to the great ones, the shining spirits: it had given him Companion's form.

Such a thing was forbidden to mortal soul— impossible, he would have said. He had defied the will of heaven. He wore flesh again, with full capacity of the body, and full memory of the life that he had lived before. And it was still—gods, it must still be the time in which he had lived.

As he paused to will his gratitude toward the one who had shown him the way, a shudder ran across his skin. Something was rising in the Grove, some force of wrath.

The hounds of heaven were coming to hunt him down. He must run with all his magical strength, and find her before they found him. Then it did not matter; the hounds could rip him into nothingness, he did not care. But first he must save her soul.

His body knew how to run. He had only to let it

go. There was glory in speed, and joy—he had thought
never to know joy again. Behind him the earth heaved
and the spring boiled. He heard, faint but drawing
nearer, the baying of hounds.

He ran for Vera's life. Companion's Field was full
of white almost-horses and their Heralds in white, and
the usual scattering of attendants, gawkers, and
hangers-on. They were all gaping at him. He hardly
needed to hear the word that ran even faster than he:
"Grove-born! There's not been a Grove-born since—"

Since before his human life began. Intentionally or
otherwise, they were gathering, clotting, blocking his
way. He darted around and through them, and sometimes over them.

'But,' said someone, who sounded young, "his eyes
are green!"

That checked his stride and nearly sent him sprawl-
ing. He got his legs under control again. The road
from the Field was not so crowded. The sight of a
Companion at full gallop parted the stream of pas-
sersby and left them murmuring in his wake.

She was not in the palace. He had known it before
he came there, in his heart that was like a needle
quivering toward the lodestone. Yet he had to go, had
to see—had to prove to himself that those halls,
though full of people, were empty of her.

It was a long and desperate while before he found
someone who could hear when he Mindspoke. His
throat would not produce a human voice, nor would
his lips or tongue shape even the few words he needed
to say. *:Where is she? Where is the queen?:*

The child in the servant's smock blinked hard. He
was frightening her with his intensity. He tried to control it a little, but he did not succeed very well: she

was very young and he was desperate. Thank the Powers, she mustered her courage and said steadily enough, "She's gone out riding, sir. With—with the Consort. The one who's to be, I mean. After the wedding."

:Consort?:

She blinked even harder. "Yes, sir. Lord Terrell. Don't you know—you aren't—are you new here, sir?"

:Newer than the morning,: he said with a sudden wry twist. *:Here, get on my back. Show me where they went.:*

Her eyes went wide. "I? Ride a Companion?"

For answer he folded his long legs and knelt, pressing lightly against her, so that she had to swing her leg over his back and cling to his mane. He rose as smoothly as he could. She squeaked a little in alarm, but the fear was fading fast before incredulous delight.

Her weight was negligible, and she balanced well enough once he was upright. She knew how to ride. She guided him as if he had been a horse—odd sensation to be on the receiving end of it.

His mind was racing down too many tracks at once. He focused in on two: the child's guidance, and the news that she had given him. Vera and Terrell? If he could put aside the stab of pure, green, and completely unreasonable jealousy, he could see it, even force himself to approve of it. Terrell was not too young but not too old, his family connections were impeccable, and much more to the point, Mathias had known him to be an honorable man. He was both warrior and mage, and equally accomplished in both. He had been loyal to Vera during Dashant's war; he had served her well. He would make a more than adequate Consort.

Mathias' young rider guided him out of the Palace

and into the city. She held on tighter there, tensing when people stared. He soothed her as he could, and thought calm at her. Her gratitude was like a warm hand slipping into his.

The crowds of the city made their own joyous mortal noise, but he heard that other sound beneath, the baying that would pursue him until he was caught and made to pay for what he had done. He was tiring, a little; even the body of a Grove-born Companion was mortal, and its strength was finite. He slowed his pace a fraction. He was almost through the city. The gate was ahead, and open country beyond it.

"They can't be far," said the child on his back. "They only left a little while ago."

He resisted the urge to quicken his stride. The sun shone blandly down upon him. The road was level underfoot, until at his rider's urging he turned to follow a narrower track.

This had been Vera's favorite way when she was younger. It led up a long hillside to a stretch of wood, where there was fine hunting in autumn, and where in spring the ladies liked to go a-Maying. It was a pleasant ride on a warm afternoon, ending in a little lake beyond the wood, where a rider could stop to rest and water her horse, and swim if she were minded.

He left the child by the road, with such blessing on her as he had to give, and a word of warding that would bring her back safe to Haven. She did not want to be left behind. There was no time to explain; he bucked her off as gently as he could, pausing to see that she was unharmed, before he went on alone.

As he ran through the wood, his nostrils twitched. That scent beneath the scents of living greenery—he knew it from another life. In this body the senses were keener; the scent was stronger. It was cold, like the breath of graves, and all around it was woven the sick-sweet stench of death.

Dashant.

Mathias could not hold himself in. Not now. Vera was ahead, dismounted by the lake. He could see her in his mind's eye, walking along the shore, hand-in-hand with a tall, dark-haired young man. Her face had grown somber since Mathias had died, but it was as beautiful as ever. Lord Terrell bent his head to hear what she said. His smile was so warm, his glance so tender, that Mathias need have no doubt of it: this man loved this woman with all his heart.

Behind them, unseen and unnoticed, the waters of the lake had begun to stir. Darkness was rising. The spell was keyed to this place, where her heart was. It would set hooks in her soul and draw her down into itself, and swallow her.

His lungs were burning. His legs were beyond pain. And still there was the last ascent to face, and the steep twisting track down to the lake. He would never come there in time. The thing in the lake, Dashant's conjuring, would rise and devour her.

Deep within, he found a last surge of strength. He sprang to the top of the ridge and skidded down the track to the lake. Its waters were heaving. The dark thing was close to the surface. The two on the shore were still oblivious, lost in one another.

There should have been an escort. Mathias could detect no sign of them. It was eerily like the battle in which he had died: the same cloud of deception, and the same utter abandonment.

This time Vera was warded. To his eyes it was like armor of light. But even that would no be proof against what rose to take her. Dashant had awakened something very, very old and very, very black. It loathed the light; living flesh, to it, was abomination.

The wards warned her—too damnably late. She turned in her lover's arms. Her eyes went wide.

It was like a towering wave. It was darkness absolute. It reached for her.

She did not cower—not Vera. Her only weapon was a dagger, but she drew it and set herself between the darkness and her consort. He was a fraction slower to understand, but his wits were quick enough once he saw what fell upon them. He summoned up a spell, a bolt of light against the dark.

It guttered and went out like a candle in a whirlwind, nearly taking Terrell with it. The darkness took no notice of him at all.

Mathias' whole heart and soul screamed at him to leap between his lady and the thing that would destroy her. But it only had volition through the one who commanded it. Dashant was near—he had to be. Power of this magnitude needed a mage's fullest strength and focus.

There. On the far side of the lake, in a ruin from the older days. Legend had it that had been a sorcerer's tower during the Mage Wars. Mathias in this incarnation knew that for truth. Dashant was drawing up the dregs of power that had gathered there, feeding his own strength.

He had paid a high price for his ambition. He was skeletally gaunt; his face was twisted with scars. One hand was a claw. His own spellmongering had done it to him, but in the darkness of his bartered soul, he held Vera to blame.

Mathias had no magic to match his, and next to no strength. He had only the weight of his body, driven at the speed of desperation. He hurtled over the broken wall.

There were wards, protections. His flesh charred and crackled at the touch of them. He ignored the pain, ignored the barriers, ignored the slow and excruciating dissolution of his mortal substance. He fell on Dashant.

Bones snapped like dry sticks. His own, the sorcerer's—it did not matter. Dashant screamed. Mathias had no breath left for such a thing. Silver hooves battered the writhing body. His nostrils filled with the iron scent of blood.

On the edge of awareness, he knew that the darkness had collapsed upon itself. Terrell drove it back with a barrage of fire-spells.

This world would believe that Terrell had saved his queen from Dashant's last assault. That was fitting. She would never know who had broken the laws of heaven for her—would never suffer that guilt.

Mathias' knees buckled. He was dying, again. He made certain that when he fell, he crushed the sorcerer's remains beneath him.

The last of his sight saw the blue of the mortal sky, and the brightness of the sun, and a pack of pale gleaming shapes drawing in. The baying of hounds was painfully loud. They were almost upon him.

He let go. The world whirled away, sky and sun and Companions, all of it—even the hounds of heaven.

He knelt on grass that never faded, under a sun that never set. His form was a man's again. He was rather surprised to feel no pain; no broken bones, no bruises.

Not that it would have mattered if he had. His heart was as light as air. The grief was gone from it. He knew, at last, the peace of this blessed country.

He knew also that he had no right to any such thing. Three judges stood over him. They seemed to be Companions: white horse-shapes, supernally beautiful. Their eyes were not blue but dark, like the night full of stars.

Their hounds lay at their feet, panting like mortal dogs. None seemed to bear him any malice for outrunning them. He was caught, after all. He had come to face his judgment.

"Whatever you do to me," he said to his judges, "let it be enough. No one else should pay for what I've done."

"No?" said the judge in the center, who was perhaps the chief of them. Its eyes flickered toward one who stood not far from Mathias: the great one, now much shrunken and its light greatly dimmed. It could have been a mortal horse, standing with head low, ears slack as if exhausted.

His heart went out to it. He rounded on the judges. "If that one has any guilt, let it be on my head. Let me pay for whatever sins it has committed."

"You would pay a doubled and trebled price?" the judge asked him. "Even if that price should be the dissolution of your very self?"

"Even so," Mathias said without hesitation.

The judge stood motionless. There was no breath here, and no heartbeat to mark the passage of time; only the stillness of eternity. Mathias existed in it in perfect peace, without fear, without apprehension. Whatever sentence was laid on him, he would accept it. He had done what he was set in the world to do. The rest, as the singers sang, was silence.

After a moment or an eon, the judge spoke. "All things are possible under the eyes of heaven. What you did, you were permitted to do by the One who is above the gods; and you did it for love of another. That mitigates your sentence. Yet sentence there must be, for you broke the laws that divide mortal from immortal, and did violence to the barriers between life and death."

Mathias bowed his head. "That is true," he murmured.

"You did it knowingly," said the judge, "and in full knowledge of the consequences. Therefore we grant you justice. Since the world of the flesh is so dear to you, we condemn you to return, and to live life after life in human form, each time anew, each time without memory of the life before—save only once in each life, in utmost extremity, when you will know what you are and why you have come into that life. And because you would have surrendered your very soul for the Queen and the Kingdom of Valdemar, we charge you to serve it forever, in life after life, until with the passing of time you shall have atoned for your transgression."

Mathias sank down under the weight of that sentence, on his face in the undying grass. And yet his heart was incorrigibly light. To live for her—to live for Valdemar. He dared to speak, though it might damn him even further. "And she? Will I stand beside her in life after life?"

"In every life," said the judge, "you two shall be bound. You shall never have her as mate or consort, nor shall your love ever be requited."

"But we will be together," Mathias said. "That is enough."

The judge was silent.

Mathias did not care what any creature or Power might think. It truly was enough. His soul knew it, deep within itself, where joy was rising like a lark in the morning.

"Go," said that dreadful and merciful judge. "Live out your sentence, man of Valdemar. Serve it forever as you served it in these lives of yours, both that to which you were entitled and that which you stole in her name."

Mathias rose. He kept his head bowed in respect, but he could not keep the smile from his lips. Maybe the judge saw it. If that was so, it said nothing—and that was divine mercy.

Already Mathias felt the pull of the living world. It drew him down out of the land of peace. It enfolded him in a scrap of flesh, the barest beginnings of a human being. Memory was too expansive a thing for this mote in eternity. All that was left was a spark of joy. It would grow as he grew, and fill him always, however dark the world about him.

The Queen of Valdemar bent over the cradle in which her son lay burbling softly to himself. She smiled—she could not help it; there was something so light about him, so irresistibly joyous. "Look," she said to her consort. "his eyes are changing color already. I think they'll be green."

Lord Terrell took her hand and kissed it. "Have you decided yet what you'll call him?"

She did not answer at once. Even as besotted with new motherhood as she was, she knew that this was an ordinary enough baby; he ate, slept, and filled his diaper as monotonously as any other of his kind. And yet sometimes she could have sworn that someone she knew and had loved before was watching her out of those blurred infant eyes.

She held her finger in front of them. His hand

reached up to clasp it. Yes, those eyes would be green. "Mathias," she said. "His name is Mathias."

Terrell shot her an odd look, but he did not object. Not for the first time, Vera was glad of her choice of consort. She stood with him, looking down at this new Mathias, and knew in her heart that she had chosen the name well. And maybe . . . who knew? Maybe it was her dearest friend come back again, to be Heir and eventual King of Valdemar.

That was justice, she thought, and mercy, too. It seemed that he agreed. The nurses all said that he was much too young to smile, but a smile that certainly was, curving his lips as he slid contentedly into sleep.

Brock
by *Tanya Huff*

Tanya Huff lives and writes in rural Ontario with her partner, six cats, and a chihuahua who refuses to acknowledge her existence. Her latest book, out for DAW in May of 2003, was the third in the Keeper Chronicles called Long Hot Summoning *and she's currently working on the first of three books spinning the character Tony off from her Blood series (DAW spring 2004). In her spare time she gardens and complains about the weather.*

"Id's just a code."

Trying not to smile at the same protest he'd heard for the last two days, Jors set the empty mug on a small table. "Healer Lorrin says it's more, Isabel. She says you're spending the next two days in bed."

The older Herald tried to snort, but her nose had filled past the point it was possible, and she had to settle for an avalanche of coughing instead. "she cud heal me," she muttered when she could finally breathe again.

"She seems to think that a couple of days in bed and a couple of hundred cups of tea will heal you just fine."

"Gibbing children their Greens . . ."

That was half a protest at best and, as Jors watched, Isabel's eyes closed, the lines exhaustion had etched around them beginning to ease. Leaning forward, he blew out the lamp, then quietly slipped from the room.

"Oh, she's sick," the Healer assured him, exasperation edging her voice. "What could have possessed her to ride courier at her age, at this time of the year? Yes, the package and information she brought from the Healer's Collegium will save lives this winter, but *surely* there had to have been younger Heralds around to deliver it?"

Jors opened his mouth to answer.

Lorrin gave him no chance. "If she hadn't run into your riding sector, she might not have made it this far. She needs rest and I'm keeping her in bed until I think she's had enough of it."

Jors didn't argue. He wouldn't have minded an actual conversation—Lorrin was young and pretty—but unfortunately, she seemed too determined to run this new House of Healing the way she felt a House of Healing *should* be run to waste time in dalliance with the healthy.

"Have you good as new. You see. Good as new. Soft and clean."

Jors stopped just inside the stable door and stared in astonishment at the young man grooming his Companion. The stubby fingers that held the brush, the bulky body, the round face, angled eyes, and full mouth told the Herald that this unexpected groom was one of those the country people called Moonlings. He wore patched homespun; the pants too large, the shirt too small, both washed out to a grimy gray. His boots had seen at least one other pair of feet.

He'd already groomed the chirras and Isabel's Companion, Calida—the sleeping mare all but glowed in the dim stable light.

:Gervis?:

:His name is Brock.: The stallion's mental voice sounded sleepy and sated. *:Can we take him with us?:*

:No. And how do you know what his name is?:

:He talks to us and he knows exactly—oh, yes— where to rub.:

Companions were not in the habit of allowing themselves to be groomed by other than Heralds' hands. Jors found it hard to believe that they'd not only allowed Brock's ministrations but were actually reveling in them. He stepped forward and, at the sound of his footfall, Brock turned.

His face broke into a broad smile radiating welcome. Arms spread, he rushed at the Herald and wrapped him in a tight hug. Staring up at Jors, their faces barely inches apart, he joyfully repeated "Brother Herald!" over and over while a large gray dog leaped around them barking.

:Gervis?:

:The dog's name is Rock. He's harmless.:

:Glad to hear that.:

"Brock . . . I can't breathe . . ."

"Sorry! Sorry." Releasing him so quickly Jors stumbled and had to grab the edge of a hay rack, Brock shuffled back, still smiling. "Sorry. I brushed." One short-fingered hand gestured back at the Companions. "Good as new. Soft and clean."

"You did a very good job." Jors stepped around the dog, now lying panting on the floor and ran his fingers down Gervis' side. There wasn't a bit of straw, a speck of dust, a hair out of place on either Companion.

:Better than very good,: Gervis sighed.

Jors smiled and repeated the compliment. *:Did you say thank you, you fuzzy hedonist?:*

In answer, the Companion stretched out his neck

and gently nuzzled Brock's cheek, receiving a loud, smacking kiss in return.

"Okay. We go now." Brock bent and picked a ragged, gray sweater out of the straw and wrestled it over his head. "We go *now*," he repeated, placing both hands in the small of Jors' back and pushing him toward the stable door. "Or we come late and Mister Mayor is mad and yells."

"Late for. . . ?"

:The petitions.: Gervis' mental voice sounded more than a little amused and Jors remembered he'd intended to merely look in on the Companions on his way to the town hall.

Heading out into the square, he realized Brock was trotting to keep up, and he shortened his stride. "Does the mayor yell a lot?"

"Yes. A lot."

"Do you know why?"

Brock sighed deeply, one hand dropping to fondle the ears of the dog walking beside him. 'Mister Mayor wears the town," he said very seriously after a moment. "The town swings heavy heavy."

Okay; that made no sense. Maybe we should try something less complex. "Is Rock your dog?"

"He's my friend. They were hurting him. I . . . Wait!"

Uncertain of just who had been told to wait, Jors watched Brock and the dog run across to the town well where a pair of women argued over who'd draw their water first. Ignored in the midst of the argument, Brock began to draw water for them. He had no trouble with the winch, but while pouring from bucket to bucket, he splashed the older woman's skirt. Suddenly united, they turned on him. By the time Jors arrived, Brock had filled another bucket in spite of the shouting—although his shoulders were hunched forward and he didn't look happy.

The older woman saw him first, shoved the other, and the shouting stopped.

"Ladies."

"Herald," they said in ragged unison.

"Let me give you a hand with that, Brock. You bring the water up, and I'll pour."

"Pouring is hard," Brock warned.

"Herald, you don't have to," one of the women protested. "We never asked this . . ." When Jors turned a bland stare in her direction, she reconsidered her next word. ". . . boy to help."

"I know." His tone cut off any further protests and neither woman said anything until all the buckets had been filled, then they thanked him far more than the work he'd done required. He'd turned to go when at the edge of his vision he saw one woman lean forward and pinch Brock on the arm, hissing, "Now that's a *real* Herald."

"HERALD JORS!"

Across the square, the mayor stood on the steps of the town hall, chain of office glinting in the pale autumn sunlight, both hands urging him to hurry. *Well, he'll just have to wait!* Lips pressed into a thin line, Jors turned back toward the well, had his elbow firmly grabbed, and found himself facing the mayor again.

"Mister Mayor is yelling," Brock explained, moving Jors across the square.

"Let him. I saw what happened back there. I saw that woman pinch you."

"Yes." He turned a satisfied smile toward Jors, never lessening their forward motion. "I made them stop fighting. Heralds do that."

"Yes, they do." They'd almost reached the hall and

Jors had a strong suspicion that digging his heels in would have had no effect on their forward motion. "You're stronger than you look."

"Have to be."

I'll bet, Jors thought as he caught sight of the mayor's expression.

"Brock! Get your filthy hands off that Herald!"

"Hands are clean."

"I don't care! He doesn't need you hanging around him!"

"I don't mind." Jors swept through the door, Brock caught up in his wake, both moving too quickly for the mayor to do anything but fall in behind.

"Heralds work together," Brock announced proudly. He clapped his hands as heads began to turn. "Be in a good line now. Heralds are here."

"Heralds?" a male voice jeered from the crowd. "I see only one Herald, Moonling."

"Heralds!" Brock repeated, throwing his arms around Jors' waist in another hug. "Me and him."

Oh, Havens.

:Trouble, Heart-brother?:

:I just realized something that should have been obvious—Brock believes he's a Herald.:

:So? You'd rather he believed he was a pickpocket?:

:That's not the point.:

But he couldn't let the townspeople chase Brock from the hall as they clearly wanted to do and Brock wouldn't leave because it was time for the Heralds to hear petitions, so Jors ended up sitting him at the table and hoping for the best.

He realized his mistake early on. Brock had a loudly expressed opinion on everything, up to and including calling one of the petitioners a big fat liar—which turned out to be true; on all points. Unfortunately, short of having him physically carried out of the hall, Jors could think of no way to get him to leave.

:*Have him check on Isabel.*:

:*How. . . ?*"

:*You're worried. You're projecting. And I'm only across the square. If he wants to be with a Herald, send him to check on Isabel. She's sick and she needs company.*:

:*That's a terrific idea.*:

Gervis' mental voice sounded distinctly smug. :*I know.*:

It worked. Jors only wished the Companion had thought of it sooner. A Herald's office protected him or her from the repercussions of a judgment—no matter how disgruntled the losing petitioner might be, few would risk the grave penalties attached to attacking a Herald. Brock didn't have that protection. *Good thing he's safely tucked away with Isabel.*

"No, Brock's not here." Healer Lorrin continued rolling strips of soft linen. "He left at sunset for the tavern."

"The tavern?"

"He's there every evening. He fills their wood box and they feed him—him and Rock."

"He works there?"

Lorrin nodded. "There, and the blacksmith's whenever there's a nervy horse in to be shoed—animals trust him. I tried to have him deliver teas to patients, but if he's carrying something, there's always troublemakers who try to take it from him."

"I'm surprised." Jors rubbed his elbow at the memory. "He's quite strong."

"Is he?" She set the finished roll with the others and picked up a new strip of cloth. "He's bullied all the time, but I've never seen him defend himself. Did you know that poorer mothers have him watch their infants if they have to leave them? I'll tell you something, Herald. When I came here a year ago, I was amazed to discover this town has almost none of those horrible accidents that happen when a baby just starting to creep is left alone and burns to death or drowns—that's because of Brock."

"Where does he sleep?" This far north, the nights were already cold.

"In various stables when the weather's good. By someone's hearth when it isn't."

"Has he no family?"

"His parents were old when he was born, old and poor. They died about three yeas ago and left him nothing."

"Why doesn't someone take him in?"

"He doesn't want to be taken," the Healer snapped. "He's not a stray cat, and for all he can be childlike, he's not a child. He's a grown man, probably not much younger than you and he has the same right as you do to choose his life."

"But . . ."

She sighed and her tone softened. "'There are those who try to make sure he doesn't suffer for those choices, but that's all anyone has a right to do. Besides . . ." One corner of her mouth quirked up. ". . . he tells me that Heralds never stay in one place so no one thinks they like some people more than others."

Simpler language but pretty much the official reason, Jors allowed. "How long has he believed himself to be a Herald?"

"As long as I've been here. I'm surprised you haven't heard about him from other Heralds. You can't be the first he's latched on to."

"He wasn't in the reports I read and I . . ." About to say he doubted Brock would come up in casual conversation between Heralds, he frowned at a distinct feeling of unease. "I should go now."

"There's no need to go to the Waystation tonight, I've plenty of room." Her smile edged toward invitation. "I doubt anyone will accuse you of favoritism if you stay here."

"No. Thank you. I need to . . ." The feeling was growing stronger. ". . . um, go."

He doubted she'd be smiling that way at him again, but personal problems were unimportant next to his growing certainty that something was wrong. Taking the steps two at a time, he hit the ground floor running and headed for the stables. *:Gervis?:*

:We can feel it, too. Calida says it's close.:

It wasn't in the stables or the corral, but when Jors opened the small door, a pair of huddled figures tumbled inside.

Brock lifted a tear-drenched face up from matted gray fur and wailed, "Heralds don't cry."

"Says who?" Jors demanded, dropping to one knee.

"People. When I cry."

"People are wrong. I'm a Herald and I cry." He stretched out a hand, keeping half his attention on the big dog who watched him warily. Herald's Whites meant nothing to Rock, and he didn't lower his hackles until Gervis whickered a warning of his own. "What happened? Did someone hurt you?"

"Heralds don't tattle!"

His various tormentors had probably been telling him that for years. "If someone does something bad, we do."

"No."

"Yes. If we can't make it right on our own, we tell

someone who can. Bad things should never be hidden. It makes them worse."

Brock drew in a long shuddering breath and slowly held out his arm. Below the ragged cuff of his sweater was a dark bruise where a large hand had gripped his wrist.

"Is that all?"

"Rock came. The man ran away."

"Who was it?"

"A bad man."

No argument there. "Do you know his name?"

"A bad man," Brock repeated, wiping his nose against the dog's shoulder.

:You catch him and I'll kick him.: The Companion's mental voice was a near growl. *:Calida says she'll help.:*

"It's a bad bruise, but it is just a bruise. Healer Lorrin wrapped it in an herb pack and she says he'll be fine. He won't stay, says he's not sick enough, but I can't just let him wander off into the night."

"Coors you cand."

"And I can't take him to the Waystation and I can't stay with him because that would be seen as losing impartiality. So, do you mind if he spends the night with Calida?"

Isabel managed a truncated snort. "Fine wid me, bud you'd bezd ask her."

Leading Gervis and the chirras out of the stable, Jors turned for one last look at Brock curled up against Calida's side. The elderly mare had been pleased to have the company and had positioned herself in such a way that Brock could pillow his head against her flank. Rock had snuggled up on the young man's other side and although his face was still blotchy, Jors had never seen anyone look so completely at peace.

:Why do you two care about him so much?: he asked as he mounted.

:He believes he is a Herald.:

:Yes, but . . .:

:And he acts accordingly.:

The next day during petitions, the mayor tripped over Rock sprawled by the table. Jerking his chain of office down into place, he snarled, "That dog is vicious and ought to be destroyed."

Jors pushed Brock back into his chair. "Who says this dog is vicious?"

The mayor's lip curled. "I heard he attacked a man last night."

"I heard that, too, Herald," called out one of the waiting petitioners.

"Brock, show everyone your arm." The bruises were dark and ugly against the pale skin. "The man Rock attacked did that and would have done more had the dog not come to his master's defense. This dog is no more vicious than I am."

"We've only your word on that, Herald. You can't truth-spell a dog."

"No, but I *can* truth-spell the man who made the accusation if he's willing to come forward."

No one was surprised when he didn't.

Mid afternoon, as Jors was returning to the hall after a privy break, the town clerk fell into step beside him and apologized for the mayor's earlier behavior. "It's just he feels responsible for the whole town, and it weighs on him and makes him short-tempered. Believe me, Herald, he's a whole different man when he can take that chain off."

"Mister Mayor wears the town. The town swings heavy heavy."

Brock's explanation suddenly made perfect sense.

* * *

It had been arranged that Brock would spend another night with Calida.

"Companions need Heralds. Lady Herald is sick. *I* am not sick. I am here." He threw his arms around Jors. "I see you tomorrow, Brother Herald."

"No, not tomorrow, Brock. Tomorrow, I'm going to see the tanners." Tanning was a smelly business, tanners set up their pits downwind of towns, far enough away they could work without complaint but not so far they couldn't get skins or find buyers for their hides. These particular tanners had chosen distance over convenience and had settled nearly a full day's travel away. The townspeople he'd spoken to about them had made it quite clear that the animosity was mutual. No one went near the place unless they had to. "I'll stay overnight, then go back to the Waystation the next day. The day after that, I'll be back in town. That's why I brought my chirras in today, so he won't be left alone at the station."

"No."

"It's okay. Gervis travels very fast, I won't be gone long."

"No!" Brock released him, stepping back just far enough to meet Jors' eyes. 'Don't go!" Pulling the hair back off his face with one hand, he grabbed the Herald's wrist with the other. "See?" An old scar ran diagonally from the edge of a thick eyebrow up into his hairline.

"The tanners did that?"

"I bumped mean lady's cart. Don't go." His eyes welled over. "Mean lady is there."

Jors pulled free of Brock's grip and squeezed his shoulder. "I'll be fine. Really. The mean lady won't do anything to me." The sort of people who'd strike a frightened Moonling were unlikely to be the sort who'd strike a healthy young man in Herald's Whites. "But I have to go and check on them. They haven't been into town for a long time and it's almost winter."

"Not alone."

"Don't worry, I'll have Gervis." He gave the trembling shoulder another squeeze, then swung himself up into the saddle. "You stay with Calida, and I'll see you in two days."

He supposed he'd been half expecting it. When Jors came out of the Waystation early the next morning there sat Brock—which was the half he supposed he'd been expecting—on Calida—which was a total surprise. It wasn't often a Companion would choose to bear anyone but her Chosen—and those exceptions were almost always Heralds.

"Good morning, Brother Herald!"

Actual Heralds. "Brock, what are you doing here?" The young man's crestfallen expression insisted on better manners. Jors rubbed a hand over his face and sighed. "Good morning, Brock."

The smile returned. "It's early!"

"Yes, it is. What are you doing here so early?"

"I go with you. To tanners."

"No, you don't."

"Yes, I go with you."

"No."

"Yes."

Jors hated to do it, but . . . "What about the mean lady?" The smile faltered as Brock sucked in his lower lip. "You don't want to see the mean lady."

"Don't want you to see mean lady alone." He took a deep breath and squared his shoulders. "I go with you."

"That's very brave of you." And he meant that. Courage was only courage in the face of fear. "But even though I know you mean well, you can't just *take* a Companion."

Brock's eyes widened indignantly. "Didn't take!"

:Calida says if she hadn't wanted him to ride her, he wouldn't be here.: Gervis scratched his cheek on a post and added thoughtfully. *:He's very bad at it.:*

:At what?:

:Riding.:

:No doubt. What does Isabel say about this?:

:Herald Isabel trusts her Companion.:

:That's not very helpful.:

:It should be.:

One more try. "Brock, by taking her Companion, you've left Herald Isabel alone."

"No." He leaned carefully forward in the saddle and stroked Calida's neck. "Left Rock."

Jors reached for Calida's bridle, but the Companion tossed her head, moving it away from his hand. "Calida, you *have* to take him back."

The mare gave him a flat, uncompromising stare.

:She says, "make me.": Gervis translated helpfully.

:Yeah. I got that. What do you think I should do?:

:Help him down.:

:You think this is funny, don't you?: Jors demanded doing as the Companion suggested.

:I think this is inevitable, Chosen. You might as well make the best of it.:

Even with Jors' help, Brock stumbled as he hit the ground, fell, rolled, and bounced up, declaring, "I'm okay!"

:Now, get ready. : Gervis shoved at Jors' bare shoulder. *:We'll be moving slowly and Calida says it's going to rain.:*

:And won't that *make this a perfect day?:*

:No. She says it's going to rain hard and I don't like to get wet. I want to be there before *it rains.:*

That began to look more and more unlikely as the morning passed and the clouds grew darker. Brock managed to stay in the saddle at a fast walk and Calida refused to go faster. Once or twice, Jors was positive he was going to fall off, but at the last instant he'd shift weight and somehow stay mounted.

:His balance is bad. But Calida's helping.:

:Why is Calida doing this?:

One ear flicked back. *:So he won't fall off.:*

:No, I mean why is Calida allowing any of this? Why is she allowing Brock to ride her? Why is she allowing—insisting—he come along today?:

:She has her reasons.:

Jors sighed. He knew that tone. *:And you're not going to tell me what those reasons are, are you?:*

:He's very happy.:

:I can see that.:

Happy was an understatement. For all he held the pommel in a death grip, Brock looked ecstatic. *This is really not helping his delusion that he's a Herald,* Jors realized. Something would have to be done about that and since the two of them were spending what was likely to be a full day traveling together, now would be the time to do it. Maybe *that* was why Calida had brought him.

There'd be no point in bluntly saying, *"Brock, you're not a Herald."* The townspeople said that all the time, shaded in every possible emotion from amusement to rage, and it had no effect.

"Brock, do you know what makes a person a Herald?"

"Heralds help people. Heralds can cry. Heralds tell

when bad things happen." He beamed proudly. "I remember the new things."

"Yes, all those things make a Herald, but . . ."

"I'm a good Herald."

". . . but there's other things."

Brock twisted in the saddle to look at him and Calida adjusted her gait to prevent a fall. "Heralds wear shiny white."

"Yes . . ."

He looked down at his gray sweater, then looked back at Jors smiling broadly. "Clothes are on the outside."

:And a Herald is on the inside.:

:I get it.:

A sapphire eye rolled back at him, distinctly amused. *:Just trying to help.:*

"Brock, all those things are part of being a Herald, but the most important part is being Chosen by a Companion. You don't have to be a Herald to be a really good person but you *do* have to be Chosen. Do you understand?"

Brock nodded. "Companions have Heralds."

"*You* don't have a Companion."

"Yes!" He bounced indignantly, lost a stirrup, and nearly went off. "Have Calida," he continued when he was secure in the saddle again.

"But she's Herald Isabel's Companion. Herald Isabel is letting you ride her."

"No. Calida is letting."

:He's got you there.:

Jors sighed. "Riding a Companion isn't the point, Brock. You're not Calida's Herald."

"Not her Herald," Brock agreed, his smile lighting up his whole face. "A Herald."

Between the less than successful conversation and

the glowering sky, Jors had picked up a pounding headache. They rode without speaking for a while, Brock humming tunelessly to himself. Finally, more to put an end to the humming than for any real desire to know, Jors turned in the saddle and said, "So, you were going to tell me how you saved Rock."

"Kids were hurting him." Brock's placid expression turned fierce at the memory. "I made them stop." Although he wouldn't defend himself, he seemed quite capable of defending the helpless. "He was hungry. I counted his bones. One, two, three, four . . ."

"Where did he come from?" Jors interrupted, unsure of how high the other man could count and not really wanting to find out.

"Don't know. Now, he is my friend." The broad brow furrowed as he searched for words. "Some mean people aren't mean now because he is my friend."

That was hardly surprising. Rock was a big dog. Probably a hunting dog of some kind who'd gotten separated from his pack and managed to finally find his way back to people. "Why did you call him Rock?"

"So when kids are mean, it doesn't matter."

"I don't understand."

Brock stared down between Calida's ears and chanted, "Brock, Brock, dumb as a rock." Then he grinned and turned just far enough in the saddle to meet Jors' gaze. "Rock isn't dumb. I fooled them."

He looked so proud, Jors found himself grinning in return. "Yes, you did. That was very smart."

"I am a smart Herald."

It was a good thing he didn't need affirmation because Jors had no idea of what to say. :*And now*,: he sighed quietly as large drops of cold water began splashing against his leathers, :*it's raining*.:

:*I know. I'm getting wet.*:

:*So am I.*:

:*I'm bigger. There's more of me, so I'm more wet.*:

In a very short time all four of them were so drenched there was little point in comparisons. Fortunately, as they crested a rise in the trail, the tanners' holding came into sight on the other side of a small valley. Neither Companion needed urging toward the river running through the valley center although they both stopped well back from the bank. The water was brown and running fast, the log bridge nearly awash.

:*What do you think? Is it safe?*:

Gervis stepped cautiously out onto the edge of the logs. :*If we move quickly.*:

But Calida hesitated.

:*What is it?*:

:*Calida says the river's already undermining the bridge supports. That the bridge is going to wash away.*:

:*Tell her that if it does, better we're all on the side with shelter. I'm half drowned and half frozen and Brock's got to be colder still. She's got to get him out of this weather.*:

Eyes wide, the mare stepped up beside Gervis who took her arrival as his cue to leap forward. One stride, two, three. As Jors watched anxiously from the other shore. Calida slowly followed, placing each hoof with care.

Wood screamed a protest as the bridge supports caved.

The huge logs dipped and skewed out from the bank, dragged by the river.

Calida half-reared as her front hooves scrambled for purchase in the mud.

Brock bounced over the cantle and disappeared.

"No!" Jors threw himself to the ground. Stumbling to the Companion's side, he grabbed the mare's saddle and heaved. Step by step, as she managed to work her way forward, he worked his way back until, to his amazement, he saw a very muddy Brock holding on with both hands to Calida's tail, his feet in the river. A heartbeat later, with solid ground, beneath all four of them, he dropped to his knees and gathered Brock up into his arms.

"Are you all right?"

He looked more surprised then frightened and returned the hug with wet enthusiasm. "I fell."

"I know. The bridge broke."

Brock twisted around to look, and clutched at Jors' arm. "I'm sorry!"

"It's okay. It wasn't your fault." His heart slamming painfully against his ribs, Jors grabbed a stirrup and hauled himself onto his feet. "Come on, we're almost there."

The tanners' holding looked deserted as they stumbled up to the buildings. Jors called out a greeting, but the wind and rain whipped the words out of his mouth.

Brock grabbed his arm. "Smoke," he said, pointing to the thin gay line rising reluctantly from a chimney. "I'm cold."

"Me, too."

All thoughts turned to a warm fire as they made their way over to the building, the Companions crowding in close under the wide eaves.

:We'll be right back as soon as we find someone.:

:Hurry, Chosen.: Gervis sounded completely miserable. Covered in mud almost to his withers, his mane

hanging in a tangled, sodden mass, he looked very little like the gleaming creature who'd left the Waystation that morning. Calida, if anything, looked worse.

Jors considered leaving Brock with the Companions, but the other man's breathing sounded unnaturally hoarse so he beckoned him forward as he tried the door. The sooner he got him inside the better.

The door opened easily. It hadn't even been latched.

"Hello?"

Stepping inside wasn't so much a step into warmth as a step into a space less cold. It looked like they'd found the family's main living quarters although the room was so dim, it was difficult to tell for sure. The only light came from a small fire smoldering on the fieldstone hearth and a tallow lamp on the floor close beside a cradle.

"No." Brock charged across the room, trailing a small river in his wake. "No fire beside baby!"

Remembering what Lorrin had told him about Brock and babies, Jors held his position by the door. The younger of two, what he knew about babies could be inscribed on the head of a pin with room left over for the lyrics to *Kerowyn's Ride*.

Squatting, Brock picked up the lamp. "No fire beside baby," he repeated, began to rise, and paused. "Baby?" Leaning forward, he peered into the cradle.

"Is it all right?" The lamp and the fire together threw barely enough light for Jors to see Brock. He couldn't see the baby at all.

Setting the lamp down again, Brock stretched both hands into the cradle. When he stood and turned, he was holding a limp infant across both palms, his broad features twisted in sorrow. "Baby is dead."

:Jors!:

Jors spun around as the door slammed open and five people surged into the room. They froze for an instant, then the man in front howled out a wordless challenge and charged.

Bending, Jors captured his attacker's momentum then he straightened, throwing the other man to the floor hard enough to knock him breathless. The immediate threat removed, he faced the remaining two men and two women. "I am Herald Jors. Who is in charge here?"

"I am," the older woman snarled.

The hate in her eyes nearly drove Jors back a step. He didn't need Brock's whispered "mean lady" to know who she was. It took an effort, but he kept his voice calm and understanding as he said, "The child was dead when we arrived."

"Dory came to say the babe was sick, not *dead*," she spat as the younger woman ran silently forward and snatched the body from Brock's hands. "The Moonling killed him."

"He did not . . ."

"You're here and he's there," she sneered. "You can't see what he did."

Spreading his hands, he added a mild warning to his tone. "And you weren't even in the building. I understand this is a shock . . ."

"You understand nothing, Herald." She placed a hand on the backs of the two remaining men and shoved. "Have the guts to support your brother!"

They sprang forward, looking like nothing so much as a pair of whipped dogs.

"Jors?"

He ducked an awkward blow. "Outside, Brock. Now!" If anything happened to him, the Companions would get Brock to safety.

"There's two of you and one of him, you idiots! Don't let him protect the half-wit!"

:Chosen?:

:It's all right.:

Fortunately, neither man was much of a fighter. Jors could have ended it quickly, but as they'd just suffered a sudden terrible loss and weren't thinking clearly, he didn't want to do any serious damage. After a moment, he realized that had it not been for the old woman goading them on, neither would have been fighting. *Maybe I should have Gervis deal with . . .*

He'd forgotten the first brother. The piece of firewood caught him on the side of the head. As he started to fall, he felt unfriendly hands grab his body.

"No!"

Then the hands were ripped away, and he hit the floor. Two bodies hit the floor after him, closely followed by the third.

"Never hit a Herald!"

"Get up, you cowards! That's a Moonling—not a real man!"

"But, Ma . . ."

He killed *my* grandson!"

Hers. Jors thought muzzily. *Not grief. Anger. Anger at the loss of a possession.*

"You never loved him!"

Apparently, the child's mother agreed.

"You always complained about him! You said if he didn't stop crying you were going to strangle him! If anyone killed him . . ."

"Don't you raise your voice to me, you cow. If you were a better . . ."

"ENOUGH!"

The doors slammed open again. Hooves clattering against the floor boards, the Companions moved to flank Brock. From Jors' position on the floor, it looked as if there were significantly more than a mere eight muddy white legs.

"Don't lie there with your idiot mouths open! They're just horses!"

"They're not *just* horses, you stupid old woman!"

:*Gervis?*:

:*I'm here, Heart-brother.*:

Jors felt better about his chance of recovery. Gervis was angry but not frantic.

"A baby is dead. Is time for crying, not fighting. A Herald is hurt. You hurt a Herald."

:*Is that Brock standing up to the mean lady?*:

:*It is.*:

:*Good for him.*:

"You will cry, and you will make the Herald better!"

"I will *not.*"

No mistaking that hate-filled voice.

"Then *I* will."

Nor the voice of the child's mother.

For the first time, Brock sounded confused. "You will cry?"

"No. I will help the Herald."

:*Out of spite . . .*:

:*You need help, Heart-brother. Your head is bleeding. Spiteful help is still help.*:

Jors got one arm under him and tried to rise. :*If you say . . .*:

:*Chosen!*:

His Companion's cry went with him into darkness.

Jors woke to the familiar and comforting smell of a stable. For a moment he thought he'd dozed off on foal-watch, then he moved and the pain in his head brought everything back. :*Gervis!*:

:I'm here.: A soft nose nuzzled his cheek. *:Just open your eyes.:*

Even moving his eyelids hurt, but he forced them up. Fortunately, the stable was dark, the brightest things in it, the two Companions. He could just barely make out Brock tucked up against Calida's side, wrapped in a blanket and nearly buried in straw. *:How long?:*

:From almost dark to just after moonrise. Long enough I was starting to worry.:

He stretched up a hand and stroked the side of Gervis' face. *:Sorry.:*

:The young female made tea for your head. There's a closed pot buried in the straw by your side.:

The tea was still warm and tasted awful, but Gervis made him drink the whole thing. *:I take it we're in the stable because you and Calida wouldn't leave me?:*

:The old woman said the young woman could do as she pleased but not in her house. I do not want you to be in her house.: The obvious distaste in the young stallion's mental voice was hardly surprising. Even on short acquaintance the old woman was as nasty a piece of work as Jors ever wanted to get close to. *:Brock told two of the young males to carry you here.:*

:He just told them what to do and they did it?:

:They are used to being told what to do.:

:Good point,: Jors acknowledged.

:And,: Gervis continued, *:I think they were frightened when they realized they had struck down a Herald.:*

:They knew *I was a Herald!:*

:Knowing and realizing are often different. Had the blow struck by the child's father been any lower, they would have killed you and that frightened them, too. They were thankful Brock took charge. He saw you

were tended to, he was assured you would live without damage, he groomed us both, and then he cried himself to sleep.:

:Poor guy. Good thing he was there. If he hadn't been, I wouldn't have put it past the mean lady *to have finished the job and buried both our bodies.:*

:The Circle would know.:

:We'd still be dead. Is this why Calida insisted on bringing him?:

:She has told her Chosen we need no assistance and convinced her not to ride to the rescue. The Herald Isabel agreed but only because she felt the townspeople would lay the blame on Brock.:

:That's ridiculous.:

Gervis sighed, blowing sweet, hay-scented breath over Jors' face. *:There is already much talk against him taking a Companion.:*

All of which he needed to know but didn't answer his question. About to ask it again, he stopped short. *:Calida can reach Isabel from here? I couldn't reach you from here!:*

:Nor I you.:

He sounded so put out by it, Jors couldn't prevent a smile. *:Never mind, Heart-brother. Calida and her Chosen have been together for many years; when we've been together for that long, I'll hear you if I'm in Sorrows and you're in Sensholding.:*

:I'd rather we were never that far apart.:

Jors wrapped one hand in Gervis' silken mane. *:Me either.:*

:Sleep now, Chosen. It will be morning soon enough.:

When Jors opened his eyes again, weak autumn sunlight filtered into the stable. An attempt to rise brought Gervis in through the open door. He pulled himself to his feet with a handful of mane and, throwing an arm over his Companion's back, managed to get to where he could relieve himself.

:The old woman made them bury the child this morning.:

:They're only a day's ride from town; they can't wait for a priest?:

:The bridge is gone. The priest cannot come.: He pawed the ground with a front hoof and added. *:I don't think the old woman would send for a priest even if he could come.:*

:Do you know where they are?:

:Yes.:

Jors took a deep breath and, holding it, managed to swing himself up on Gervis' bare back. *:Let's go, then.:*

The tanners had a graveyard in a small clearing cupped by the surrounding oak forest. When Jors arrived, the three men had just finished filling in the tiny hole. As Jors stopped, half hidden by a large sumach, Brock wiped the tears from his face on Calida's mane and stepped up to the grave.

"There is no priest. I will say good-bye to the baby."

"I'm not listening to a half-wit say anything," the old woman snarled. She turned on one heel and started down the hill. "I only came to see the job was done right. Enric, Kern, Simen; back to work, there's hides to be sammied."

Two of the three moved to her side, the third looked toward the young woman and hesitated. "He was my son, Ma."

"He was my son, Ma." She threw it mockingly over her shoulder. "Look around you, Simen. I've buried a son, two daughters, and a husband besides, and it don't make hides tan themselves. Stay and listen to the half-wit if you want."

"Dory?"

She lifted stony eyes to Simen's face. "Better do as your ma says," she sneered. " 'Cause you always do as your ma says."

Scarred hands curled into fists, but they stayed at his side. "Fine. I'll go."

"I don't' care."

"Fine." But when he turned, Brock was in his way.

Jors tensed to urge Gervis forward, but at the last instant, for no clear reason, he changed his mind.

"Stay and say good-bye." A heavy shove rocked him in place but didn't move him. "Stay." And then gently. "Say good-bye to baby."

Simen stared down into Brock's face, then wordlessly turned back to the grave.

Brock returned to his place and rubbed his nose on his sleeve. "Sometimes," he said, "babies die. Mamas and papas love them, and hug them, and kiss them, and feed them, and they die. Nobody did anything bad. Everyone is sorry. The baby wasn't bad. Babies are good. Good-bye, baby."

"His name," Simen said, so quietly Jors almost missed it, "was Tamas."

Brock nodded solemnly. "Good-bye, Tamas. Everyone is sorry." He lifted his head and stared at Tamas' parents standing hunch-shouldered, carefully apart. "Now, you cry."

Dory shook her head. "Crying is for the weak."

"You have tears." Brock tapped his own chest. "In here. Tears not cried go bad. Bad tears make you hurt."

"You heard Aysa. She buried a son and two daughters. She never cried."

"She is the mean lady," Brock said sadly. "You can't be the mean lady." He opened his arms and, before Dory could move, wrapped her in one of his all-encompassing hugs.

Jors knew from experience that when Brock hugged, he held nothing back.

It was a new experience for Dory.

She blinked twice, drew in a long shuddering breath, then clutched at his tattered sweater and began to sob. After a moment, Brock reached out one hand, grabbed Simen and pulled him into the embrace.

"Cry now," he commanded.

"I . . ." Simen shook his head and tried to pull away.

Brock pulled him closer, pushing Dory into his arms and wrapping himself around them both. Simen stiffened then made a sound, very like his son might have made, and gave himself over to grief. All three of them sank to their knees.

:These people need help.:

Gervis shifted his head. *:It seems they're getting it.:*

With the funeral over, Jors pulled himself into something resembling official shape and sought out Aysa.

"Your son attacked a Herald."

"*His* son just died. He was mad with grief."

"You goaded his brothers . . ."

"To stand by him," she sneered triumphantly. "I never told no one to hit you. And now I'm givin' you and that half-wit food and shelter. You can't ask for more, Herald."

Given that he and Brock were trapped on her side of the river, he supposed he'd better not. "About the bridge . . .

Without the bridge, there was no way back. The

river wasn't particularly wide, but the water ran deep and fast.

"You come out here to stick your nose in on us, then you're stuck out here till we head in to town and we ain't headin' nowheres until them hides is done. We wasted time enough with Dory having that baby. You want to leave before that, then you and the half-wit can rebuild the bridge yourself."

"That's fair. I can't expect you to drop everything and assist me." His next words wiped the triumphant sneer from her face. "I'll have them send a crew out from town."

"You can't get word to town."

He smiled, hoping he looked a lot more confident of the conversation's outcome than he felt. "There's a Herald there and I already have. By this time tomorrow, there'll be a dozen people in the valley."

"Liar."

"Heralds can't lie, Ma."

"Shut up!" Aysa half turned and Kern winced away as though he expected to be hit. Lip curled, she turned back to Jors. "I don't want a dozen people in the valley! And it don't take a dozen people anyway. And the water won't be down enough tomorrow."

"Then I'll have them come when the water goes down."

"You won't have no one come. My boys'll rebuild."

"Then the townspeople can help."

"My boys don't need help. They ain't got brains for much, but they can do that. You let them know in town I'm hostin' you *and* the half-wit till then."

It was a grudgingly offered truce, but he'd take it.

Jors wasn't surprised that Aysa'd refused help. The last thing she'd want would be her sons exposed to more people, to people who'd make them realize they were entitled to be treated with kindness. Over the next few days, while they waited for the water to recede, she proved that by keeping him by her side, keeping him from interacting with anyone else at the holding.

Brock, she considered no threat.

Which was a mistake.

Because Brock treated everyone with kindness.

"You call that supple?! I could do better chewin' it! How could you be doin' this all your life and still be no damned good? You're pathetic." Enric and Kern leaped back as she threw the piece of finished leather down at their feet. "Pathetic," she repeated and stomped away.

"Mean lady calls me names, too," Brock sighed, coming out from behind the fleshing beam and picking up the hide.

Enric ripped it out of his hands. "We ain't half-wits."

"Mean lady calls me half-wit. Not you."

"You *are* a half-wit!"

"Are you pathetic?"

Kern jerked forward, face flushed. "You callin us pathetic?"

"No. It hurts when people call names." Brock looked from one to the other. "Doesn't it hurt?"

"If your half-wit falls in a liming pit," Aysa snarled as Jors caught up, "my boys'll stand there and laugh."

"You taught them that."

"I'm all they got."

"They're terrified of you."

"Good."

"Dory isn't."

"You think one of my boys is stupid enough to

pick up a weakling?" Aysa nodded toward the garden where Dory heaped cabbage into a basket. "But she does what I say like the rest. If she doesn't like it, she can leave any time."

While they watched, Dory lifted the basket, gave a little cry and let it fall.

Aysa snorted. " 'Course that baby left her stupidly weak."

Jors took step toward the garden but stopped as Simen came out of the chicken house and hurried across to his wife.

"Simen! You get back to work, you lazy pig."

His mother's voice froze him in his tracks. Then he shook himself, and began retrieving the spilled cabbages.

"Simen!"

He ignored her.

"This is your fault, Herald. Turning a woman's family against her." Muttering under her breath, she strode toward them.

Dory looked up, saw her coming and stood, hands on hips.

"You think you can face me down, girl? Simen, get up!"

He stood.

"Now get back to work."

He took a step forward and put his hands on Dory's shoulders. "When I'm finished here, Ma."

Aysa's mouth worked for a moment, but no sound emerged. Finally, she spun on one heel and stomped away.

The corner of Simen's mouth curled. "You'd best help here, Herald. I wouldn't follow her right now."

The river was low enough the next day.

The bridge took only a day longer to rebuild and

for the most part involved fitting the original pieces back into place.

Jors stared the completed bridge in amazement. "That's incredible."

"Nothin' incredible about it, Herald," Enric snorted. "Damned thing goes out every other season. Easier to build it so it breaks apart clean."

His bare torso red with cold, Kern shrugged into a sheepskin coat. "Supports slip out so they don't shatter, logs end up in the same place, we float 'em back and rebuild. Any idiot can do it."

"Trust me, I've crossed a hundred rivers—or maybe a couple of rivers a hundred times—but I've never seen anything like this."

"Ma says it's not . . ." Simen paused, frowned, and looked up at the Herald. "It's really good?"

"It's really good."

The brothers exchanged confused looks and Jors had the horrible suspicion this was the first time they'd ever been praised for anything.

The next day while Jors was checking Calida's girth strap for the trip back to town, Dory came out of the house with a bundle. "It's for Brock," she said, folding back a corner. "I want you to give it to him for me."

At first Jors thought it was white leather. Made sense; they were tanners after all. Then he realized the leather had been cut and sewn into a fair approximation of Herald's whites. Dory had clearly taken the pattern from his and sized it to fit Brock.

"I saw he didn't have none of his own."

Oh, help. "Dory, you know he's not . . ."

"Brother Herald! We go now? What you got?"

His hands and Dory's together closed the bundle.

"It's a surprise," Dory said, her cheeks crimson. "For later."

"Not for now?"

"No."

"Okay." He took Calida's reins and stood waiting patiently while Jors tied the bundle behind Gervis' saddle.

:You seem upset, Chosen.:

:I can't tell her Brock's not an actual Herald while he's standing there. He'll say he is, I'll say he isn't, and I'm not sure that in this place at this time, I'd win the argument.:

:You shouldn't argue.:

:Oh, that's helpful.:

:Thank you.:

The whole family went with them to the bridge. Jors didn't know why the rest came, but he was certain Aysa just wanted to make sure they were off her land. He wanted to say something, something that would convince them they didn't have to live inside the darkness of an old woman's anger, but before he could think of the right words, Brock hugged Dory. And Simen. And Enric. And Kern.

Then he scrambled up into the saddle and, from the safety of Calida's back, took a deep breath, looked Aysa in the eye, and spoke directly to her for the first time. "Why don't you love your babies?"

Her lip curled. "I buried my babies, half-wit."

He nodded toward the three young men standing to her right. "Not them."

She turned, looked at her sons, looked back at Brock and muttered, "Half-wit." But there was little force behind it.

Jors had no idea he was going to do what he did until he did it.

                              *   *   *

"Jors, you hugged mean lady."

"Yeah. I know." Although he still couldn't believe it. "Everyone else got hugged, I just . . ."

She'd pushed him away with such force that he'd slammed back into Gervis' shoulder.

"You are the bravest Herald. Ever, ever."

"Thank you."

Then she'd snarled something incomprehensible, turned, and stomped away.

He'd probably accomplished nothing at all by it.

The bundle Dory had given him pushed against the small of his back.

The weather remained clear and cool and just as the sun was setting, they stopped outside the village.

"Gate will close when sun is set," Brock warned.

"I know. Brock, I think you should go back to Haven with Isabel."

"Lots of Heralds in Haven?"

"Yes."

Brock sighed and shook his head. "No. I have to stay here. I am the only Herald."

"Brock, you're not . . ." He couldn't say it.

Brock waited patiently for a moment then smiled. "Is it later?"

"Yes . . ."

'What's Dory's surprise?"

"Um . . . it's um . . ."

Both Companions turned their heads to look at him. Their expression said, *this is up to you.*

:He believes he is a Herald.:

:Yes, but . . .:

:And he acts accordingly.:

                              *   *   *

"I couldn't do it, Isabel. They're just clothes and I know that but if I gave Brock those whites, then there'd be fake Heralds showing up all over the place."

"A bad precedent to be sure," the older Herald agreed.

"There has to be a line and that line has to be the Companions. Sometimes it seems like we're barely keeping order in chaos now. I couldn't . . . No matter how much . . ." Jors ran both hands back through his air, he couldn't believe how much the decision, the right decision had felt like betrayal. "It wouldn't make any difference to Brock. He knows who and what he is, but for the others in the village, those who made fun and called him names . . ."

"Come here, I want to show you something." Isabel took his arm and pulled him to the window. "What do you see?"

Jors squinted down into the stable yard. "Brock's grooming Gervis again."

"While you four were gone, I talked to a lot of people. Seems that whenever a Herald comes into this village, the Companion manages to spend time with Brock. Even if it's only a moment or two." They watched as Calida crossed the yard and tried to shoulder Gervis away. Brock laughed and told her to wait her turn. 'You were right not to give him the Whites," Isabel continued, "but you were also right when you said it makes no difference. He couldn't be Chosen because, as Heralds, we have to face dangers he'd never understand, but the Companions know him. All Brock needs from *us* is our love and support. Now, since Healer Lorrin has finally allowed me out of bed, what do you say you and I go down there and give our brother a hand with the fourfoots?"

Jors grinned as Brock gamely tried to brush both tails at once.

Heralds wear shiny white.

Brock wore his Whites on the inside.

True Colors
by Michael Longcor

Michael Longcor is a writer and singer-songwriter who recently wrote a dozen songs for the Mercedes Lackey album, Owflight. *Aside from writing and performing, Michael has also been an insurance investigator, employment counselor, news reporter, fencing instructor, and blacksmith. His more exotic hobbies include donning medieval armor and competing in the bruising tournaments of the Society for Creative Anachronism. He also once placed third in a cricket-spitting contest. He currently shares a 130-year-old farmhouse outside of West Lafayette, Indiana, with a variable number of pets and guitars.*

It had worked again.

The sun was well up as Rin rode out of Goldenoak. Summer light filtered through the trees, dappled the white coat of his mount, and sparked off the hilt of the sword bouncing gently at his side. It also showed the grimy spots on his white tunic and leggings.

It had been a good visit. Good for Rin, that is. The take included four solid meals, road rations, several pots of the local beer, and a few kisses stolen from the hamlet's daughters.

There's something about a man in uniform, he mused. Fine-boned, even features, blond hair, and blue eyes helped, too. *If you can't be big and burly, slight and handsome will have to do. Too bad I couldn't manage some coin.*

But coinage was almost as scarce as Heralds among the tiny settlements scattered along Valdemar's Northern Border. Out here, the forest's dangers combined with distance to isolate the villages. Other than infrequent sweeps for brigands, people this far out never saw much of the Militia, let alone Valdemar's regular Guard, especially since the recent problems in the South. Even less often, they might glimpse a legendary Herald. They and their spooky-white horses were near-mythical heroes. Rin figured folks should get to meet their heroes on occasion, and show a little hero worship. It wasn't his fault if the real Heralds were too busy saving the Kingdom to take time to share a few meals, drinks, and kisses with the salt of Valdemar's earth.

Two months back he'd made his break from Torto's Traveling Show, a ratty handful of slickmen, peep shows, and crack-throated minstrels, ruled by the beefy, sadistic Torto. The show had about as much resemblance to a true traveling troupe of gleemen as a weed does a rose. In Torto's Show, you rarely saw the same town twice. After swindling and stealing everything that wasn't nailed down on one end, they packed up in the night and moved on to fresh marks. Rin ran shell games with the best of them, developed a healthy contempt for the townies, and never stopped hating and fearing Torto. The night he'd made his break they were between towns in western Iftel. Rin hoped he'd truly cracked the drunken Torto's head with that tent stake, but with Torto's thick skull, he doubted it.

Rin had started this Herald game less than a month back after crossing Iftel's border with Valdemar. It wasn't much, but it beat being a cup-and-ball man in the towns. With luck, it would get him somewhere more comfortable, where constables didn't know him and Torto couldn't trail him.

He didn't know a great deal about Heralds, but apparently neither did the locals. His story of being a "Special Auxiliary Herald" worked well enough, and explained why he only talked with them, took mysterious, coded notes, and moved on. Rin was sure his code was unbreakable. His scribblings were just that. As much as he'd wanted, he'd never learned to read or write.

The story also let him get food and other necessities from the villages, rather than the Waystations normally used by Heralds and other servants of the Crown. The Heralds rode regular circuits, and Rin simply made sure he was somewhere else. That wasn't hard, this far out.

He was safe enough, so long as he picked the right villages, and didn't stay too long or take too much. It was simple as games went, but not bad for an eighteen-year-old slickman. It kept him fed, equipped, and admired. Of the three, he liked the admiration best.

The morning warmed as he rode through patches of sunlight and shade. Scarlet flashed as a bird took wing, and a woodlark's song piped through the trees. He remembered the woods like this, out with his family hunting wild berries. It was one of his few memories of a time before brigands hit his village and took him, fourteen years ago this summer. He didn't remember the village's name, even though it had been somewhere in this region. He barely remembered the faces of his parents, but he remembered the look and feel of the woods.

Rin fingered a townchit, given him by Goldenoak's

headman. The small brass plate was stamped with a crude, stylized tree, representing the village's name. He gathered they expected him to turn it in at Haven to get the village a tax break for feeding and sheltering him. Interesting, how trustful folks could be of a government. Maybe it came from not constantly pulling stakes and moving. He shook his head, chuckling softly, and leaned back to slip it into his saddlebag, adding to the pile of townchits already there.

At midday, Rin stopped to rest the mare, watering her at a shaded brook before he took his own drink. He was as good to her as he could manage. She was a good horse and his only real friend in Torto's show; no prince's charger, but not a plug either. Rin thought of unsaddling her and letting her roll, but here he had to move fast if needful, so he only loosened the girth strap. She was white, mostly, but that was just good luck and the graying out of age. She'd been Torto's, but Rin was the one who cared for her. It didn't really bother Rin that he'd stolen her, though a slickman with pride in his craft wouldn't resort to outright theft unless there was no way to swindle for what was needed. Which was also why he'd later stolen the Herald's Whites.

The flashy sword was from Torto's prop box, taken with no thought of this particular game. He just liked having the sword, even though the slim, heavy knife in his boot top was probably a better weapon. A sword made him feel more like a heroic servant of the Crown, and half of any game was feeling the part.

He dug into a saddlebag, and came up with a small cloth sack. Rin peered in, laughed delightedly and popped one of the golden brown slices into his mouth. He rolled his eyes and nearly cried. The taste of the lightly seasoned, dried apple brought back a wave of memory and feeling. For Rin that taste whispered of another time, and a loving mother's special treat for a small boy.

Rin munched road rations while the mare grazed. He drank deeply from the brook and topped up his water bottle. After a half-hour's rest, he cinched the mare's girth strap and set off again.

In late afternoon he rounded a turn and glimpsed two small figures perhaps a hundred paces ahead on the narrow, uphill road. The taller darted into the brush. The shorter seemed frozen, holding something. The taller figure reappeared to drag the other back into the bushes They didn't seem big enough to be a threat, but this region was never entirely free of brigands.

With one hand on the reins and the other on his sword, Rin edged the mare on up the hill. Reaching the spot, he heard voices whispering fiercely. The brush rustled, and a small boy stumbled out onto the path. He was four or five, dressed in homespun tunic and breeches. The boy stared round-eyed up at Rin, clutching a battered toy stick horse. The head of the horse was cut from split wood, and painted white. Its eyes were blue.

"Valon!" the bushes behind the boy hissed. "Get back here!" More rustling, and a girl of about nine years came out on the path. She was dressed in the same material as the boy, with similar features, her hair a darker shade of blonde; sister and brother, probably. She pulled the boy behind her.

"Natli!" piped the boy, peering around her. "He's a Herald!"

"May be," she said, eyeing Rin. "An' may be not. If you're a Herald, what's your name, an' how come your horse's eyes hain't blue?"

Rin gave the girl his warmest smile, feeling as if he were stepping onstage.

"I am Special Auxiliary Herald Rincent, m'lady, at your service." Rin let his voice ring with easy authority. Time for fast answers and distractions. "As for my Companion, the regular Heralds around the big cities have the ones with blue eyes. They don't all have blue eyes, you know. But Serena here can do other things. She can read minds."

"Read minds?" The girl looked less wary and more interested.

"And talk without words."

"Hmf!" the wary look was back in the girl's eyes. But Rin was on familiar ground here. The few tricks he'd taught the mare always came in handy. He cocked his head as if listening, and tickled the mare's neck on the side away from the girl. The horse snorted and shook her head slightly.

"She says, Natli, that you and your brother, Valon, shouldn't be out in the forest, especially with your family worried about you." The girl's eyes widened.

"But we had to run!" Valon had edged out from behind his sister. "We had to! We can't go back to the village!"

"You had to run?"

"That's right . . . Herald Rincent," said Natli. "Mum said to run an' run, an' not stop till the bad men weren't followin' us no more."

"Bad men?" Rin didn't like the sound of this. "What bad men?"

"The ones that came to our village. Mum said they wanted food an' gold an' people. Mum said to run till we found someone to get help."

Brigands; robbers and killers with a taste for slaving. They were hunting these children, if they hadn't given up. The same sort who'd attacked his home, killed his parents, sold him to be "adopted" by that greasebucket Torto. Rin was very sure he wanted nothing to do with these "bad men." He hadn't planned on returning so soon (if ever) to Goldenoak, but it was far better than meeting the outlaws. He hoped the kids could keep up. If not, he could tell the villagers they were on the trail, while he rode on to "get help."

"You'll help us, won't you, Herald Rincent?" Valon's eyes pleaded along with his voice. "Won't you?" Rin had been about this boy's age when the raiders came.

"How far back are these bad men?" asked Rin. A shout snapped his attention up the trail, where the hill crested. A big, broad-shouldered man stood there. He stared at Rin and the children, then turned, shouted again, and waved behind him. It was too far for Rin to make out his face, but Rin could guess who and what he was.

"Not very far." said Natli gravely, pulling Valon back to her. She looked back up at Rin, staring eye to eye. "You have to help us. Now."

Rin looked back up the hill. Two more men appeared, one after the other. The last seemed to be breathing hard, leaning over to rest his hands on his knees. The outlaw catching his breath might give them a few seconds, the sight of the Herald's Whites and horse a few more. But these were hard cases, men marked and hunted by the law. They wouldn't be put off for long by the sight of one "Herald."

The brigands were here to steal him again. A dark, closed part of Rin's mind flashed a bright, jagged series of memories, racing with his panicked thoughts.

Got to get away. Just ride off. He smelled the choking reek of burning thatch.

The brigands will take the kids. They won't bother chasing me. He heard his mother's screams.

The boy and girl won't be killed. He glimpsed his father's bloodied legs sprawled outside the doorway.

They'll just grow up without parents, without lives. Like me. Inside Rin's mind, something broke free, stood up on its hind legs, and snarled.

No, by the Nine Hells, they will not!

"Hand him up!" He told Natli as he reached down. "Then get up behind me. Move!" As Rin hauled Valon up, an arrow hissed past his face. The mare jerked and danced, but Rin kept a taut rein and turned her to face downhill. He glanced back. The slow brigand at the hill's crest fumbled another arrow onto his bowstring. His two ugly partners were running downhill, the first well ahead of the second, closing fast. If Rin could get the girl up quickly, they should make it. Even the three of them would load the horse little more than a large man, and Rin had past experience running from angry people.

He shifted the reins and settled Valon with his right hand, and leaned down to help Natli up with his left. Another arrow whistled past the mare's eyes and nose. Frightened from the first arrow and the smell of fear, the mare's neighing sounded like a child's scream. She reared.

Rin fell with Valon atop him, the toy horse still in the boy's fist. The packed earth of the path was better than rock, but landing still hurt. The mare ran headlong back downhill, away from them all.

Rin had survived enough street fights to know you checked hurts only after getting clear. He untangled himself from Valon and lurched to his feet, cursing himself for choosing now, of all times, to be good and stupid. He put himself between the children and the oncoming brigands and hauled out his sword.

"Run," he said grimly, and faced his attackers.

The first outlaw, a big man with scarred face and matted hair, reached him and swung. Rin ducked a side cut to his head and jumped back to avoid the return slash to his stomach. No, they weren't awed by the uniform. He had to attack before the second thug reached him.

Rin put all his strength and speed into an overhand cut at his opponent's head. The man shifted fast and blocked the blow solidly. Rin's cheap show blade twisted and folded over the outlaw's tarnishcd stccl.

Rin had one dismayed glimpse of the blade's right-angle bend before a kick caught him at the top of his stomach, just under the breastbone. It knocked him back to land butt-first, the air driven from his lungs, feeling like he'd never take another breath. Which was likely correct. He didn't know where his sword was, but it wasn't in his hand.

The second outlaw, a short man in dirty, gaudy clothes, arrived on the scene and looked down on Rin, who was making raspy, squeaking noises that were a poor substitute for breathing. The outlaw grunted, and grinned.

"Huh! I'd heard them Whiteshirts was pretty tough in a fight."

"I always thought these heroes was overrated." The big brigand leered and stepped up to Rin, raising his sword. "G'night, Whiteshirt."

A short figure in homespun rushed in, and the head of Valon's toy horse was a white blur as it swung. The solid wooden horsehead whacked the outlaw's knee, and he bellowed and swore. The blow had to hurt, even if it didn't really injure. The big man spun and caught Valon by the back of his tunic, lifting the boy flailing and kicking. Attention off him for the moment, Rin still gasped vainly for air as he clawed at his boot top.

"Bugger! This one's too much trouble. We ain't takin' *him* back!" The outlaw hefted Valon up as if serving a game of shuttle cock, but the arm he cocked back held a sword instead of a paddle.

Rin's knife flickered silver as it flew and turned. It made a muffled *thack* as it hit the outlaw in the back of his thigh, just above the knee.

He dropped both Valon and his sword and went down, holding his leg and cursing. The second outlaw moved grimly at Rin, his sword raised to strike, his other hand up shielding against the stones Natli threw at him. The first stone had drawn blood on his cheek. The second missed, and then Natli was out of stones. There was still no sign of the third, slower brigand.

"Aughh! Damnit!" The downed outlaw continued cursing from where he lay, gripping his injured leg. "Forget captives! Kill 'em all!"

Rin's lungs still wouldn't cooperate. He tried feebly to get to his feet, but the sword was up and Rin could see his death. He closed his eyes.

There was a hissing, a loud *chunk,* and a louder scream. Rin's eyes flew open to see an arrow standing out of the man's sword arm. He'd dropped his sword, and wasn't looking at Rin. On the downhill trail a rider pelted up toward them on a mount so white it hurt the eye. Behind him, an identically mounted figure fitted another arrow to bowstring.

The outlaw turned and sprinted back up the hill, the arrow still in his bleeding arm. His downed comrade tried to drag himself up and run, cursing and gasping, but fell after two clumsy, limping steps.

The running outlaw sped up the hill, but now men in steel caps and leather armor filled the roadway, seeming to rise up from the hill's crest. Long blue shields locked edge to edge, and spears leveled over the rims. The running brigand turned without breaking stride and plunged into the woods. Muffled commands were shouted as the Militia broke ranks, some chasing the running outlaw, others coming down to seize the other who was still trying to drag himself into the brush. A few mounted Militiamen rode into sight at the hill's crest, holding the horses of their dismounted comrades. The horses, like some of their riders, appeared past their prime.

Rin, on hands and knees, looked back again at the two white-clad figures now riding abreast toward him. *Nice shot,* he thought. His lungs worked, but he was in no shape to run, even after Valon and Natli helped him up. His next thought, after seeing the two riders' mounts close up was, *how could anyone ever mistake them for just horses?* It wasn't just the sheen of their coats, the rippling muscles beneath, or their regal, easy grace. The blue eyes had intelligence behind them, and more.

The Heralds were an older man and a tall, dark-haired young woman. The woman still had an arrow on her bowstring, and a look for Rin that said she knew exactly where she wanted to put it. Rin noted that she and he were about the same size, and had an uneasy suspicion she was the original owner of his stolen Whites. The man was muscular looking, with a close-cropped beard and hair shot with gray. He looked first at the children.

"Are you injured? Did those men hurt you?" His voice was a soothing baritone.

"They wanted to!" blurted Natli. "But we fought 'em!" She looked at Rin, then back up to the Herald. "Well, we helped Herald Rincent fight 'em."

"So we saw, from about the time this young man," a nod to Valon, "ordered that fierce Companion of his to defend . . . uh . . . Herald Rincent. I think you have a solid career if you ever join the Guard, lad."

Valon had retrieved his hobbyhorse. Its ear was broken off.

"Unh-unh." The boy shook his head solemnly as he looked up. "Don't wanna be a soljer . . . I'm gonna be a Herald."

The older Herald grinned broadly. Even the grim-faced young woman smiled.

"That might also be possible," responded the Herald. He turned to the woman. "We'd best split up to help the Militia." The woman nodded, never taking her eyes off Rin. The older Herald dismounted in the usual way, but the woman pulled her left foot free of the stirrup, raised her right leg over saddle pommel and her mount's neck, and slid smoothly to the ground. Her hands never left bow grip or arrow nock.

The Herald's Companion snorted, and both left the road and cantered into the woods, following the sounds of shouting, running men. Rin felt the hair on the back of his neck stand up.

The senior Herald looked grim as he turned back to Rin.

"As for you, Herald Rincent." His eyes flicked over the children, and back to Rin. "We have a great deal to discuss."

They were an odd parade as they came into the children's home village. The Militia officer rode first,

leading a stubby packhorse straddled by the big outlaw with the injured leg. The outlaw was bound and
neck-roped to the other two brigands who walked,
also bandaged and bound, on either side of the horse.
Any escape attempt would likely strangle all three.

Next came Rin, leading his mare. She had been
found wandering in the woods by the Companions,
and the children now rode her, with the two Heralds
and their Companions to either side. The senior Herald, who called himself Terek, had warned Rin to keep
his mouth shut and maintain the game until they could
talk privately. Terek made it plain bad things would
happen if Rin tried to get away. Rin was sure this
was true, even without the too-knowing gaze of the
Companions and the ready bow and hard looks of
Trefina, the other Herald. They were followed by the
Militia, pleased with themselves and riding in smart
order, shields up and spears braced upright, late sunlight catching red gleams off spearheads and bridle
fittings.

At the edge of the village, a young woman with
disarrayed hair and reddened eyes rushed up to the
mare, laughing and weeping at once. The children's
mother pulled the children fiercely to her for a long
moment, and then recovered her composure. She gave
fervent but dignified thanks to the Heralds and Rin.
Rin's feelings were jumbled. He felt proud for his part
in the children's return, but oddly confused about how
to receive thanks and praise he for once partly deserved. He felt happy about the children returning to
their mother and family and profoundly sad that he'd
never had the same chance himself, and probably
never would. Too, it bothered him that he'd so long
regarded people like this with amused contempt, at
best.

The summer night was soft and warm, and the waxing moon cast pale light on the village's cluster of homes and outbuildings, added to by lamps and a fair number of bonfires. The surviving outlaws, both those chasing the children and three others captured that afternoon after the Militia's sudden appearance at the village, were locked in the smokehouse. The stale smell of charred wood carried from the one cottage partly burned by the outlaws before the Militia arrived. Five fresh graves at the edge of the wood held neither villager nor Militia. Wounds of Militia and villagers were bandaged. People were quietly celebrating the end of the brigands, the return of their children, the survival of their friends and families.

After tending his mare, Rin helped Terek bring water to his Companion, whom Terek introduced as Coryandor. The Companion (much more then a horse, Rin now knew), drank deeply, then nodded briefly to Rin as if in thanks. Rin didn't know where the other Companion was, but he was glad it wasn't here. The young woman's mount made it clear she disliked Rin as much as her rider, twice bumping Rin roughly, and looking as if she wanted to do more.

Terek brought out a currycomb and began running it over the Companion's coat, Coryandor closed his eyes and sighed with sheer bliss.

"Time to talk." said Terek. "To be specific, time for me to talk and you to listen as if your life depends on it. Which it does."

Rin nodded. He felt very uncomfortable.

"Impersonating an officer of the Crown is a serious offense, usually a capital crime. Serious enough to drag me from Haven to find you. People must be able to trust their Herald, and impersonating a Herald is unthinkable. Well, almost unthinkable. You obviously thought of it."

Rin thought of running, but gave it up when he saw Coryandor staring at him as if the Companion knew his every thought.

"In your defense, there's your protection of those children. Even after meeting you, the boy *still* wants to be a Herald." From the direction of the houses came the cheerful sound of voices singing with more enthusiasm than skill; something about drunken crows. They sounded much happier than Rin felt.

"We've been following you for three weeks." Terek continued. "Apparently, you never stole anything outright while posing as one of us, and you have no history of violent crimes." Terek straightened up from brushing Coryandor's front leg. "At least none we discovered. Another small point in your favor is that Cory says you took good care of your horse." Rin wondered *how* the Companion told Terek that.

"Because of these factors, you have a choice between two options. One is to go back to Haven with us, where, after unpleasant interrogations, even more unpleasant things will happen to you."

"How unpleasant?" asked Rin, feeling unpleasant already.

"Very." said Terek. "Perhaps hanging if you're lucky. If you're not, well . . . as much as Heralds despise someone posing as a Herald, there's a group with even stronger feelings. You could be turned loose in the exercise yards with a dozen young Companion stallions."

Rin's spine chilled. It got worse as Coryandor turned his head to give Rin a hard, unblinking look, and Rin caught, not words, but a *feeling,* as if pressed into his mind from outside. The feeling said Rin would be much better off hanging.

"I'll take option two." said Rin.

"Better hear it first. Understand that if you don't deliver on any part of option two, option one becomes the *only* option. And never think we can't find you." Coryandor turned slightly so Terek could get to his flank, but the Companion still stared at Rin.

Rin simply nodded. "Go on."

"If yours was a lesser crime, and these less pressing times," continued Terek, "I'd have you go back to each and every village you visited, and work off every morsel of food, every piece of equipment and every courtesy." Terek shifted and curried the Companion's other side. "But these are special times. So, the Crown will honor that pile of townchits in your saddlebags, and give the village their tax credits. In other words, Valdemar will buy your debt from the villages."

"And then?" Rin asked, though he didn't much want an answer.

"You return to Haven with me. That reminds me, change clothes as soon as we get away from here. Wear any combination of tan, or brown, or purple spots, or anything *except* white or gray. If anyone recognizes you as a "Herald" tell them you're on a Philosophical Leave of Absence, developing your humility and service."

"Heralds do that?"

"They do now. At least you do. After we reach Haven, you will go through training. Ethics, for a start, and Weapons, too . . . you can certainly use it. Mathematics, Reading and Writing, too, along with some . . . specialized classes."

Reading and Writing? But Rin still grimaced. "That could take years!"

"Option number one, then," said Terek.

"Um . . . never mind," said Rin quickly, "forget I said anything. So I go to school on the Crown's coin. That's the punishment?"

Terek smiled as nastily as any brigand.

"That's the preparation. Understand that any short-coming, any shirking, any attempt to disappear or go back to your old ways and it's option number one."

Coryandor was looking at him again, with those scary blue eyes. *The man who said there's always a choice was a liar,* thought Rin.

"I, uh, accept." he said. Even with Herald wizardry watching, there was always the chance he could slip away later. "What happens after I get educated?"

Terek smiled like he meant it. "You come to work for me and Valdemar."

"What?! Why me?"

Terek rubbed his Companion's neck. "Because if you don't, you're back to option one," he said cheerily. Coryandor snorted and bared his teeth at Rin. Rin blanched.

"Also, you're reasonably intelligent, if not always smart. Gods know you're lucky. You've traveled around both in and outside Valdemar. You can gain people's trust quickly, and convince them you're something you're not. And if needed, you can think the unthinkable. Any Monarch who cares about Valdemar and her people can use a few knaves fighting and conniving for the Right and the Good. You likely won't be a Herald; that choice is out of my hands, but with time you may equal one in service to Valdemar. It's up to you."

Rin being of service to others, without being forced. The idea was a new one. Still . . .

"You think I can do all this?" he asked.

"With my job you have to be good at reading a person's potential and seeing his true colors." replied Terek. "I'm very good at it. You might even call it a Gift."

Rin's smile grew slowly to a huge grin as he thought about it. Here was a chance to be admired for himself, to learn to read and write and to use a sword, to adventure, to defend a kingdom using a slickman's stock in trade, and maybe most importantly a place to belong.

It might even be worth school.

Valon stuck his blond head in the doorway behind Terek and smiled shyly at Rin. The boy still had his wooden Companion with him. Valon's mother appeared behind the boy, put a hand on his head, and smiled. For the tiniest moment, Rin tasted dried apples.

Rin looked down at his torn, dirty Whites, back at Terek and Valon, grinned crookedly, and spread his arms.

"Looks like it's time to change." He said. Terek's chuckle said he knew Rin wasn't just talking about clothes.

Touches the Earth
by Brenda Cooper

Brenda Cooper has had stories published in *Analog* and *Asimov's* with collaborator Larry Niven, and her own work has appeared in *Analog*. A long-time fan of Valdemar, Brenda loved doing a story for this anthology. She lives in Bellevue, Washington, works in Kirkland city government, and loves to run, read, write, and enjoy family.

"That's right. Locate the energy line below you—good—now draw it up through your feet, through your center, and feed it out slowly." Tim's voice teased the edges of Anya's focus as she drew a mental picture of energy flowing. Floor to flank to fingers, earth becoming light. She fed the tiny flame she had conjured in the bowl in front of her. The fire flared from the size of her thumb to something that would engulf her palm, and she drew in a sharp breath. Her calf muscles quivered, pain shot through the small of her back, and the bright glow winked to nothing.

"You lost it. What happened?" Tim asked.

"I . . . I don't know. All of a sudden my back hurt and then it was gone."

Tim frowned. "And what happened last time?"

"My fingers quivered and didn't point the right way." He'd been there when she caught the edge of a tablecloth on fire. Anya heard the defensiveness in her voice and labored to find another tone. "It . . . it

265

seems like I can only hold so much energy, and then something happens. It's not always the same thing, but it's always something. Physical. In my body. I don't *know* what to change!" Now it sounded to Anya like she'd exchanged defensiveness for despair. "I'm sorry," she mumbled.

"You can hold more energy. I can feel your potential. You aren't even near your capacity." Tim tugged on his graying braid, and frowned. Then he looked intently into Anya's eyes. "You're fighting it. There's a point where you have to surrender. You have to feel it—there are no words, and I've been told it's different for everyone. It's keeping focus, maintaining control, but it's also surrendering. All at once." He was pacing, his words more insistent than usual. Anya knew better than to interrupt him—he could be harsh when frustrated. "Your focus is clear, but I can't feel your surrender. You're trying to be a warrior spouting flame at an enemy, but Healing isn't warrior's work. Surrender, and your body will be able to hold energy much longer. Now, try again."

Anya breathed into her belly, tucked her hips, and refocused on her shielding. Then she started again, conjuring the flame, feeding it to fist-sized, holding it, holding it, and then her forehead flashed with pain and she blinked, opening her eyes to an empty bowl.

Tim didn't comment. Instead, he said, "I'll go catch us some supper. While I'm gone, think about what might be between you and your full abilities. Feeding flame is a small trick, but it's handling the same energy you'll need for any major Healing." Tim stood, glanced at her, and walked out the door.

Grateful for the respite, Anya allowed herself a long sigh as soon as Tim was out of sight. Tim expected her to be good enough to replace him as the troubled village's Healer soon. If only they could have a real Healer from Haven!

She had been studying for two whole years now, and while she'd started out learning fast, the last year had felt like stepping backward. Or, at best, sideways. She'd learned new things, but hadn't made any real progress. At the beginning, Tim had expressed surprise at how quickly she started to cure simple maladies like headaches and sniffles, and to make a tiny flame. Since then, she'd added the ability to form— no, *collect*—balls of light and to lessen stomach cramps. She knew how to shield, to ground and center, to focus. It wasn't enough. Real healing eluded her. Tim had to step in every time.

She'd seen Tim repair multiple burn wounds last year when a half-finished sheep barn had burned, and then have the bad grace to barely look tired. After just two hours of much less difficult work, every muscle along her back was tense, calves to shoulders. She wanted to close her eyes and sleep. Instead she looked around, struggling for alertness.

Tim's home was an ingenious cave. Campfire stories whispered that the mysterious hertasi had built it secretly, when Northend Homestead was only a few families struggling to feed themselves. If so, the hertasi were masters at their craft. Anya had never seen one, but they had been described as lizard-like, with hands that worked more cleverly than human hands, fashioning and shaping and building for the Hawkbrothers.

She'd never spoken to a Hawkbrother, but Anya *had* seen them twice before, riding fast on graceful *dhyeli*, warning Homestead of a storm once, and a dangerous hedge-wizard another time. She wanted the mysterious and beautiful people to stay, to talk to her, but of course they were busy.

Nevertheless, she'd watched for them on woods walks, but they were as elusive as true Healing. All the best magic in the world, except her teacher himself, was hiding from her. Everything bright and positive was hiding, ever since she'd moved here and left her home, searching for work. Tim had identified her Gift. He was a good thing, the best thing, in her life. His regard for her was bright, but she was so far from his expectations she might as well have become the village sheepherder.

Homestead was one of a handful of towns in the far north of Valdemar; land the Hawkbrothers had reclaimed for safe human habitation only a few generations ago. Lately, raids had come with no warning, and the town was now smaller and more indrawn, afraid. Now, townspeople only came to Tim's cave in the light of day, and even then, they often sent Anya to fetch the Healer. In the past three months, ten men had disappeared with no trace. Ten more had left to find them, disappearing as well.

Light spilled in through the door and fell from two clever round openings in the roof, illuminating the large open space with mid-afternoon sun. A few carefully crafted items lined the walls, leaving a large clear area where Tim struggled twice a week to teach her. Anya's gaze fell across the small altar in front of her. A wide burled maple trunk had been sawn flat and polished to a bright surface that glowed when the light—like now—hit it just right. A fine hand-sewn cloth two handspans wide sat in the center. It shimmered when sunlight hit it, somehow twisting from black and gray to purple and blue. The work was so magnificent that Anya couldn't imagine the weaver. In the center of the cloth rested a candle and a drawing of three figures. The drawing showed a woman, a man, and a small boy. Anya was sure Tim had drawn them, although they looked somehow less alive than pictures he drew of wolves and deer and, sometimes, of townspeople.

Anya closed her eyes, pulling her focus inward, trying to release the tight muscles along her spine. Then suddenly, they clenched again. The peal of the town alarm bell screamed for attention, and in two heartbeats Anya had grabbed her backpack and was pelting down the trail toward Northend Homestead.

This time it wasn't a direct raid; there was no noise of fighting staining the town. Nevertheless, Anya's landlady Elena was crying quietly, a group of women gathered around her. Hovering at the edges of the crowd, Anya was able to glean that Elena's oldest, nine-year-old Justine, had left before dawn to deliver eggs and had not returned after half a day. She should have been gone just a candlemark.

Justine's father was one of the men who had followed the raiders ten days ago. Elena and Justine had not seen or heard from him since. After Anya moved to town three yeas ago, Justine had become a frequent visitor to Anya's room. Just last night, Anya had prepared a tea of comforting herbs to ease Justine's bedtime fears. The girl had stammered and thanked her. Then Anya had held her close for almost a full candlemark, while she cried for her father, until Justine fell asleep in a tangle of bedclothes and blonde hair.

Only a handful of candlemarks remained until dark. Teams split up in the four directions, agreeing that the town bell would call them back if anyone succeeded in finding Justine. Tim insisted they go east, the same direction as his underground home. They stopped there to provision, but rather than helping Anya, Tim sat down in front of the small altar and just stared at his drawing.

"Well?" she looked at him.

He didn't respond at all, just picked up the picture of the three people and held it in his hands, his eyes closed.

Anya gathered cheese, bread, and an herb kit into packs. She stared at Tim's unmoving back. After a few moments she said, "We need to hurry. Justine could be hurt."

Tim ignored her and slipped into his bedroom, closing the door.

Anya waited, drumming her fingers, and then pacing.

When he finally emerged, Anya raised her cyebrows at him.

"They're . . . from how I lived once before." A quite serviceable sword was buckled around his waist, and a long knife stuck hilt-up from his boot. In his right hand he held out a short dirk toward her. He looked unfamiliar, different. Somehow he fit the mood he had been in all day: stern and serious

"But . . . but you've always told me you weren't a fighter."

"I didn't say I wasn't one. Just that I'm not one now. So go on, take it. I'll feel better. I made you stop practicing with the young men at guard, but that was to hone your focus on healing skills," Tim said. "I've seen you use a weapon, you'll pass. You may need one today. Go on."

Puzzled and a little alarmed, Anya palmed the blade and stuck it in her waistband. They left, climbing up the rise behind Tim's cave. A stream ran down the hill on the other side, and there they walked with just the water between them, searching for tracks, but close enough to talk. "So, tell me about it," Anya said.

"I used to be a fighter."

"I can see that."

"A mercenary. I thought it was a good thing to be. I loved the action . . . loved being so strong. But then I went too far."

"And?"

"I killed people for money. Sellswords do that." Tim stopped for a minute and bent down to look at the ground. Then he shook his head. "Not Justine's track. Someone bigger, but not necessarily an enemy." He shrugged. "Anyway, I went too far and one day I woke up sick and tired of it all. I had done something . . . wrong . . . terrible the day before. At first, I drank it off. But in the morning, my head became crystal clear, and I got up and walked away."

That wouldn't have made him popular with his troop. "What did you do?"

"We'd been hired to clean out a bunch of thieves from someone's holding."

"That sounds pretty normal," Anya said.

"Yeah. But it turned out *we* were the thieves."

"Does this have anything to do with the pictures on your altar?" Anya asked

"They were the rightful owners." Tim's voice clamped down and he walked a while before he spoke again, "They were defending their home. I killed the man with my own hands. I broke his back and pulled his head back and snapped his neck. I threw the firebrand that caught the house's roof on fire. The woman and the boy burned alive. I did it just because I was told to. I didn't think."

Anya had no response. They walked as quickly as

they could and still watch the ground. At one point they found a bit of red string stuck to a low branch, about waist level. There was no way to know if it was Justine's, but it kept them following the stream. As the sun touched the treetops, the temperature dropped, shadows lengthened, and Anya felt fear building.

"So, when you left, when you walked away from being a mercenary, what did you do?"

"I got lost." Tim stood still and looked around. "We should stop soon, we may spend the night out here."

"I haven't heard the town bells."

"You won't. I'm sure we're going the right way."

"I thought you said FarSeeing wasn't a Gift of yours."

"It's not. But sometimes I just know things. I have ever since I was a kid. I think that's what made me good at fighting in the first place."

Three forest tracks converged near the bottom of the hill. Gold light dappled the paths and a rabbit flashed its white at them as it dove into the safety of the underbrush. Tim pointed out shallow hoofprints. "These look fresh. Probably made today, at least." He gestured at her to stay close to him. "Did you think about what is stopping you?"

Anya bit her lip. "Fear, I guess."

"Of course. But what are you afraid of?"

Anya let the question hang in the air for a bit. She was so absorbed in trying to read the faint tracks that her next words surprised her. "Healers are people in stories and songs—not me. I'm just Anya."

"You don't know how good you are."

Anya smiled. Tim was always saying she was good, and complaining at her for failing, all in the same conversation. "But still I can't do half of what you do. How will I ever take over for you?"

"When you have to, you will."

An owl screeched. It was close to dusk, but still early—owls shouldn't be hunting yet. And the sound was—desperate. Anya looked at Tim.

He was standing completely still. "I think we'll know something pretty soon. Follow." Tim took off to the right, toward the sound. The owl screeched again, sounding at once angry and frightened. They ran.

Two hundred yards farther along, Anya heard the sounds of fighting. Tim gestured to her to stay back, and he kept going, running low, tugging his sword from its scabbard as he went. He disappeared down the edge of a ridge.

Anya's breath tangled in her lungs as she worked her way quickly and silently to the fir trees at the ridge's edge. A shadow passed over her head. She looked up. The bird was impossibly big, twelve feet or more wingtip to wingtip, and it was diving down, silent and deadly. The owl arrowed directly at a man Tim was fighting. The man flinched, stepping back to avoid the wings and talons directed at his face. Tim ran his sword through the attacker, whirling to hold off a second man.

Anya's fingers clenched the dirk's hilt, fear and confusion anchoring her feet. Her eyes swept the scene, trying to make sense of the movement. A wagon sat in the middle of the path, twisting dangerously as two horses danced and kicked with their back legs. The spooked horses were unable to run; leather hobbles bound their front legs. A small figure lay in the wagon, covered by a blanket. Justine?

A dead man lay near the wagon. Another man, no two men, rolled on the ground. One of them was covered with twigs and mud and colored like the forest. It was so hard to see him, Anya had to focus hard to keep him in sight even though he was moving. He must be a Hawkbrother scout. Then the owl was his bondbird!

The scout slashed a knife across the throat of the man he struggled against. Now free, the Hawkbrother stood quickly, running toward Tim.

Anya wanted to move, but couldn't tell where to run. Her eyes found Tim. There was a new slash across his shoulder, and blood ran down his bicep and dripped from his elbow. Still, she had never seen him move with such speed and sureness. Tim circled, using the long knife that was in his boot, keeping his attacker from the sword that now lay gleaming dully on the ground. His challenger came in low, and Tim blocked with his damaged arm, pushing the man off as Tim himself fell. New blood bloomed where the man's knife had gouged his thigh.

A flash of silver light caught the last rays of the sun and the Hawkbrother's knife thudded into the neck of Tim's challenger, who crumpled. Tim waved thanks. He tried to stand and made it to one knee, his right leg dragging. He reached for the sword, holding it out in front of him as blood dripped from his arm and from the edge of the sword as well. No one else moved.

Anya finally leaped into motion, running down the small hill toward the rocking wagon. She was only halfway there when the wagon tipped and rolled over, knocking one of the fractious horses off its feet. The other one planted a solid kick on the wagon's side. Anya scrambled to the front of the wagon, banged her knee, and used the dirk to saw the leather traces loose from the tongue. Hooves sliced the air, one quite near her head. She backed up, talking softly to the frightened animals, trying to calm them enough to see if Justine was under the wagon.

Abruptly, both horses stilled, their attention focused on the Hawkbrother walking carefully toward them. He bent and expertly cut the hobbles. Now free, the big animals stood placidly.

All of the chaos had disappeared from the scene, and the path and forest became silent and still. The owl glided in, landing on a branch at the edge of the clearing, watching with the same quiet that had settled on the rest of the forest.

The Hawkbrother looked directly at Anya, paused, and then simply said, "Well met. I'm Nightsinger."

"Thank you." she replied, then offered, "I'm Anya, and that is Tim."

He grinned. "I know who Tim is. You must be his student."

How could the man grin at a time like this? Nightsinger helped her turn the crumpled and staved wagon over. It *was* Justine under the wagon, legs twisted sideways, both arms splayed wide as if she had tried to break her fall. Blonde hair spilled out from the blanket, dark with blood. Nightsinger ran toward Tim, gesturing that she should stay and tend to the girl.

"Justine!" Anya called out, kneeling by the still form, placing one hand on Justine's chest. She had a heartbeat, but her skin was chalky, her scalp bleeding. As Anya felt along the top of her head, one part felt mushy, as if the business end of a horse's hoof or a board had knocked into her. Anya looked around frantically for Tim.

He was still thirty feet away, and Nightsinger had rolled him onto his back. The new wound on the back of his thigh was bleeding extremely fast, staining the earth around it. She had to go to him! She leaped up and ran to his side. Pain swirled like a live thing in his bright, wet eyes, and he clenched the knife tightly.

"Let me . . ." She began.

"Justine." Tim croaked. "Justine first."

"But . . . but you might die!"

"I'm tougher than I want to be—this won't finish me." Tim's teeth ground into his lip, sweat stood out on his forehead, and Anya could hear noises dying in his throat as he refused to cry out. How could he survive this?

Defiantly, she placed her hands on his thigh near the worst of his wounds.

He raised the knife, made as if to slash at her with it. "Justine first."

Anya felt like she was being severed in two. The little girl clearly needed her, but Tim was the real Healer, not her. Not yet. If she helped Tim, he could help Justine . . . but Justine could die without immediate attention. It was beyond her to save one, and they both needed her. What if Tim died? She felt anchored in place—the way she had been when she was watching the fight, unable to choose a direction because all of the choices needed doing. But Nightsinger was with Tim, and Justine was a child. Turning away from Tim was like spiraling through a physical wall. Her legs shook as she walked away from him.

Anya forced herself to look only at Justine, to hear and taste and sense only things surrounding the little girl.

Justine's head wound was threatening by itself; enough to explain why the girl was out stone cold. Her legs were bound together, badly chafed, the skin deeply raw around the ropes. Anya thought they could be broken. Her arms and torso looked unmarked, except her left hand was gashed and bleeding. Anya cut the ropes around Justine's legs and straightened them.

Now, how could she ground herself? She had always worked in homes or in the main room at Tim's—and always with Tim coaching her. Here, there was no comfortable place to stand rooted to. Justine was in an awkward spot, and Anya didn't think it safe to move her. She chose a kneeling pose and probed for Earth energy, the way Tim had taught her.

It was there, a breath, a stream, and available. She pulled it up into her, setting shielding to keep her focus, to close out the woods and the path and the wounded Healer behind her. Her body gained life, her mind focus, and she began to see things more clearly as she prepared to transfer the energy filling her to the wounded girl.

She needed Tim. It felt like so much, like more than she had ever felt. Tim should do this—she wasn't up to it.

The energy poured away, lost like water over a cliff, and she put her head down and hid her face in her hands. She shivered; cold and frustrated.

A croak rose from far behind her. Tim's voice. "I can see you do this. Start over." A softening of his tone. "Surrender, Anya. Let go."

She looked back. Nightsinger sat quietly next to Tim. The Hawkbrother nodded at her. "Can you help Tim?" she pleaded.

"Only a little. You must help him by doing your work."

Tears stung the corner of her eyes. She touched the earth, tapping the stream of energy again. It was weak and she reached, and reached, and barely gathered a warm trickle. It wasn't enough. She was going to fail.

She let go, started over, ignoring her first touch of darkness. Whether real or not, she heard Tim's voice in her head, saying, "Surrender. Surrender." She touched and reached, and this time the line of power felt focused, less diffuse. She filled herself with each breath, establishing the stream into her as a river, seeing it as light she could channel through her palms. It was more than she could take, and still less than Justine needed. She wanted to scream. Necessity pushed at her until something inside crumpled away, something thin but important. Loss swept into trust, and Anya realized how afraid she had been to . . . trust . . . herself. Power, earth energy, filled the places where fear had been. Now, she was part of it, and it was part of her, and the outcome no longer mattered, just the work.

She placed her hands on Justine's head, directing the energy into the prone form. It was warmth flowing down her arms and through the center of her palms into Justine, overwhelming the cold of her wounds, acting on them like sun on ice, melting pain. Slowly. Ever so slowly. Anya could feel it, almost see it, and it was exquisite, like spring colors and stored sunshine flowing into Justine from the earth. It used Anya, like a vessel and a map, seeking direction and amplification in her focus.

Warmth spread through Anya into the girl's head, burning away pain and harm, healing her broken skull. Warmth began to flow down Justine's shoulders, and Anya felt almost as if the two of them were one being. Then suddenly it was too much, her back was freezing. Anya shuddered, the connection lost. Now it was only her own empty hands on Justine's head. Every muscle in her arms quivered and shook.

Anya's body demanded rest, sleep. She fought for strength to see to Justine. The girl was breathing better, more regularly. Her skin wasn't quite the right color, but it was somehow less white. Anya probed Justine's head gently, and it felt normal. Justine's legs were bleeding where the bonds had been, and still swollen and bruised. So she hadn't finished. But it would be enough. Justine's youth would heal the rest quickly. Anya sighed, and then in a tiny flash of energy, she remembered Tim.

Nightsinger sat immobile by Tim, hands on her teacher's thigh wound. Tim's head was turned away from her, but Nightsinger looked directly at her and said, "You did well, little one. Let go." She wanted to go to Tim, but blackness caught her, and she barely felt the ground slap the side of her head as she surrendered to it.

Anya woke to the sounds of many people. She was bundled in a blanket by the side of the path. Her mouth was fiercely dry. She licked her lips and tried to sit up, but her head was so dizzy and painful she simply fell back again.

She heard the rustle of clothes, and a cup of water appeared in front of her eyes. An arm propped her up, and another held the cup to her lips. She sipped greedily. When the cup was empty, Nightsinger rocked back on his heels and let her sit on her own. Surprisingly, she found she had the strength, if barely. She watched him refill the cup from a water bag he slung over his shoulder, all of her focus on the precious water, on quenching the desert inside of her.

Nightsinger grinned at her as she got partway through a third cup of water, and finally looked up at him. His long hair was down, a signal to her that they were safe. "Now, take it easy, little one. You'll be sick. Let the water in slowly. You used a lot of energy."

Memories flooded back over her. "Justine?"

"Is fine. I had to splint her legs until one of our Healers got here, and sew her up in a place or two. Nothing I don't know how to do. But you saved her life. I'm Healer-trained, but have no Gift like yours. I could not have done what you did. She even woke up this morning and asked for you."

"This morning? How long have I been asleep? How's Tim?"

"You've slept almost two days."

"And Tim?"

"Ahhh, Tim. He's gone back to the vale—to our home—for a while. A brother of mine came to get him. Tim lived with us once before, that's where he learned his healing skill—the things he taught you."

"I've heard stories. He never would talk about his past. At least until . . . until the day we found you. But how is he?"

"He'll be all right." Nightsinger laughed. "Sorry, I should tell you more. Years ago, when he was my age, when we found him, he was—broken. Learning Healing gave him enough purpose to stay alive. And now, well, he swore never to fight again, but you and I just saw how well he does that. This time it was to save people he loves. Maybe, the next time he leaves us, he will be able to both fight and heal."

"Can I see him?"

"He's already gone. He said you should move to the cave. He'll visit." Nightsinger held his hand out for the empty water cup.

"But I . . . I need to learn more," she protested,

handing over the cup. "Tell him he has to come back as soon as he's healed."

"He said he'd visit."

Anya frowned.

"Maybe I'll visit, too—I've never seen this fabled *hertasi*-built house of his—no, yours—before."

"I'd like that," she said.

Nightsinger was smiling companionably. She tried to match his expression and asked, "Hey, is there food?"

Icebreaker
by Rosemary Edghill

Rosemary Edghill is the author of Speak Daggers to
Her, The Book of Moons, *and* Fleeting Fancy. *Her
short fiction has appeared in* Return to Avalon, Chicks
in Chainmail, *and* Tarot Fantastic. *She is a full-time
author who lives in Poughkeepsie, New York.*

It was Midwinter Festival in Talastyre, and the
younger children were gathered in the square to watch
the traditional Midwinter play before heading home
to spiced cider and oranges and the family feast. Elidor stood at the edge of the crowd, unwilling to admit,
at fifteen, that he still liked to watch the play, but this
was a day of rare liberty for him. Elidor was one of
a dozen copyist-apprentices at the great Library of
Talastyre—when other libraries around Valdemar
needed a copy of one of their books, it was copyists
like Elidor who would write out the text in a fair hand.
When he was fully trained, he might seek work at any
library, or in a lord's household, or even at the Collegium in Haven itself.

He had been brought to Talastyre at the age of
six, on a winter's day even colder than this one. He
remembered crying, and clinging to his uncle's coat,
begging and pleading not to be left here among strangers, to be allowed to go home to his parents, to his
brothers and sisters.

He remembered the fire, of course. He had gone into the attic to play at Heralds and Companions—the carved wooden toys had been his Midwinter gift, and when he'd told his brothers that someday a Companion would come to choose him for a Herald, they'd laughed at him, and teased him so badly that he'd decided to find a place to play undisturbed. The attic was cold, but he'd taken his cloak with him, and later it had gotten so warm that he'd taken it off.

He remembered how his eldest sister Marane had come running in. She smelled of smoke, and her face was streaked with tears. He'd started crying, too, because she frightened him, even more when she told him he mustn't cry, he must be brave. He was still clutching the white painted Companion when she pushed him out the tiny attic window, too small for an adult to get through.

He screamed as he fell—such a long way—but the snow was deep that year, and he wasn't badly hurt. He crawled away, through the melting snow, clutching the carved white horse, shouting for his mother, for Marane.

He understood later that the house had burned, and the townsfolk had come to try to put out the fire and see if any of the house's inhabitants might be saved, and found him, the only survivor. At the time, all Elidor knew was that strangers took him away, and would not tell him where his family had gone.

When his uncle finally came, Elidor hoped he would be taken home again. His uncle was a silent and distant man, who rarely came to visit his brother's family, but he was Elidor's closest kin. He had no experience of children, and spoke to Elidor as if he were an equal.

"Simon left his affairs in order, I'll give him that. And I can get a good price for the land, even though there's nothing left of the house. It will all come to you, boy, never fear—no man can say that Jonas Bridewell would cheat his brother's kin. It comes to a tidy sum. I've taken steps to secure your future, and an enviable one it is, too. You need have no fear of toiling in a shop or a mill for the rest of your days. Folk will look up to you, young Elidor."

There was little about this speech that made sense to Elidor, beyond the knowledge that he was not to go home again. His uncle hired a coach, and after a long and tiring journey, they reached Talastyre.

There he discovered he was to be abandoned.

It had been the Master of Boys who dried his tears, who gently explained to him what his uncle had assumed he understood: that his parents were dead, and that Talastyre was to be his home now. In the dark days that followed, Elidor clung to only one hope: that a Companion would come for him, to take him from this terrible place. Every chance he got, he slipped away from his duties and hurried to the woods at the edge of town, watching for the flash of shining white through the trees that would mean a Companion was near.

He told no one of his dream. In his thoughts, the fire and his last Midwinter gift were tangled up together in a way he couldn't explain. At first, he slept with his painted horse beneath his pillow, but he got into such terrible fights with the other boys when they tried to take it away from him that at last the Master of Boys said he would keep the toy safe for Elidor in his own office, where Elidor could visit it whenever he wished.

The weeks passed, then the months, then the years, and no Companion came, and slowly, rebelliously, Elidor settled into the routine of the library and its school. First he worked as a runner, delivering messages between the offices of the great library, then as a page, reshelving books and bringing volumes when they were asked for. Along with the other children sent to Talastyre to learn—to Elidor's astonishment, most of them had families (his uncle had been telling the truth when he said he had secured for Elidor an enviable position)—Elidor was taught to read and write: his first lessons were in the Common Tongue and to scribe a simple fair hand, but they would be followed by courses in other, older languages and the clear difficult copyist's hand. That training would be the work of years, for it took decades to make a fully-trained Scribe. Not everyone completed it. Some lacked the aptitude. Others were there only to learn the basic lessons before returning to their families, or passing on to other training. Elidor hated and envied them, while clinging to his secret hope: that *he* would be Chosen, that *he* would be more special, more loved than all of them, in the end. He made no friends, and wanted none, and the work he could not avoid, he did grudgingly, and only if watched.

Literacy was Elidor's salvation.

"Here is something that might interest you," the Master of Boys said. He sat down beside Elidor—who was being detained, as punishment, while the other boys were sent out to play in the spring sunshine—and set a book upon the desk. It was large, bound in blue leather, stamped in silver.

Elidor hated everything about books—the way they looked, the way they smelled, their weight, their pages filled with incomprehensible symbols. He turned his head away. But the Master of Boys didn't seem to notice. He simply opened the book.

A flash of color drew Elidor's attention, and he looked. There, painted on the page, was a brightly colored painting of a Companion and its Herald. Every detail was clear, and in the spring sunlight, the silver bells on the Companion's harness shone like stars.

Elidor grabbed for it, but the Master of Boys drew it back.

"Are your hands clean?" he asked gently.

Elidor inspected his palms. They were gray with the slate of the pencils the boys had been using to practice their letters.

"Go and wash them, then."

Elidor hurried to the back of the room and rinsed his hands quickly in the basin there, leaving most of the dirt on the towel. But his hands were clean when he returned. He held them out for inspection.

The Master of Boys passed him the book.

Quickly—and carefully, as he had been taught— Elidor turned the pages. But there were not many pictures, though many of the pages had a large bright initial letter, each one in Herald blue, some with a tiny picture of a Companion twined around it.

"It is a great pity you cannot read this," the Master of Boys said thoughtfully, "for it contains many tales of the Companions and their brave Heralds." He gently drew the book away from Elidor and closed it. "There are other such books in our library. Perhaps someday you will be able to read them, if you apply yourself to your lessons."

From that day Elidor worked hard at his lessons, and harder at any task that brought him among the books. Soon he could read as well as many of the older boys, and when two more years had passed, the Master of Boys made good on his promise, and Elidor was given a pass that allowed him free access to any book on the open shelves of the library.

At first he was only interested in works about the Heralds and the Companions, their history and their deeds, but as the years passed and he had run through all of those, his interests broadened until a book's subject hardly mattered. All of Elidor's adventures were lived through books, and most of the time he was resigned to the fact that this was how it would always be. His friends were the books of the Great Library, and his teachers spoke approvingly of his abilities. Elidor, they said, will be a Master Copyist someday, and a great credit to our training.

But deep inside, the unacknowledged spark of resentment at how life had cheated him still burned dully, and the hope remained, grown faint and dim with the passing of years, that a Companion would come to make his life magical.

In the town square, the play was getting to the part that he liked best, and unconsciously Elidor rose up on tiptoes, trying to see better.

There was a jingle of bells onstage, as the actor dressed as the Companion appeared from the wings. The horselike body was woven of light wicker covered with white velvet, and its flashing eyes were made of bright foil-backed blue glass. Slowly the Companion danced forward, pausing in turn before the Raggedy Woodman, the Greedy Tax Collector, and the Karsian Wizard before stopping at last at the feet of Hob the Orphan Boy.

Something soft and moist touched Elidor on the back of the neck.

He turned and stared, only dimly realizing that everyone else was staring, too.

It was a Companion, real and live and in the flesh, no more like a horse than the carved wooden toy of his childhood was. Its coat was white, almost more like duckdown than horsehair, and from its blue eyes shone such a sense of calm majesty that Elidor nearly wanted to weep.

It was so close to the moment he'd dreamed of all his life that it seemed unreal, as if he ought to be reading about it, not living it. A Companion had come for him at last!

But somehow it didn't seem right. All the stories agreed that the candidates *knew* when they'd been Chosen, though the stories never managed to describe the feeling. He reached out a hand to stroke that downy muzzle, and the Companion took a step backward, still watching him with grave, wise eyes.

He wants me to follow, Elidor realized. He nodded, not really sure if the Companion could understand, and took a step forward.

Immediately the Companion turned, and took several steps away, and waited, almost fidgeting. He hadn't known something in the shape of a horse could fidget, but there it was.

"You!" Elidor said to the nearest boy. "Go and tell them at the library that a Companion has come!" He didn't know what else to say, but surely that would be enough? Then he hurried off after the Companion, trotting to keep up with it. He realized he felt no impulse to even try to mount the stallion, and that, too, wasn't as things went in the stories.

Some of the townsfolk followed them—at a prudent distance—as far as the edge of the town, but it became obvious that the Companion's destination lay farther, and Elidor began to wonder if he was going to have to walk all the way to the Collegium. As they left the shelter of the buildings and passed through the town gate that stood open from dawn to sunset, the winter wind struck with renewed chill. He pulled his cloak— dark red, with the arms of the Library of Talastyre sewn in a badge at his left shoulder, as befit a Journeyman such as himself—tighter, and hurried even faster to keep up with the Companion.

"If you'd let me ride, we could get there faster, wherever we're going," Elidor muttered under his breath.

The Companion stopped dead, turning its head to regard him with an affronted expression. Apparently, it had heard him.

It stood so still not even the silver bells on its harness jingled, swishing its tail dangerously.

Hesitantly, Elidor approached. He'd made the suggestion, and it seemed he was to be taken up on it.

The Librarians and Scribes of Talastyre had little need to learn horsemanship, and certainly Elidor had learned no equestrian skills before he came here nine years before. But he could not resist the demand in that arrogant blue gaze any more than he could have tuned back in the first place. Hesitantly, Elidor set his foot into the silver stirrup, and heaved himself ungracefully onto the Companion's back.

It was the moment he'd dreamed of, the dream he'd lived in, and for, so completely that the real world around him had seemed dim and unreal by comparison. But now, when he had it in his grasp, it all seemed wrong, as if he were straining to squeeze his feet into a pair of boots that didn't fit.

The Companion hardly waited for him to settle himself before it took off—at a much faster pace than before. It was the Companion, rather than any skill of his own, that kept the saddle-leather beneath Elidor's rump. The trees whipped past him in a blur, and the wind that had been cold before turned to a thousand needles of ice seeking every opening they could find in his good wool tunic and heavy trousers. He knew better than to reach for the reins, and clutched with one hand at the edge of the saddle, and with the other, at his wildly-flapping cloak. He barely had time to realize how acutely miserable he was—and only think, this was a Herald's job, to ride out in all seasons and all weathers!—before the Companion stopped once more, and again Elidor had that sense of barely-restrained impatience.

He scrambled from the Companion's back without even looking around, and then saw he was in the middle of nowhere.

"What?" he said aloud.

Snow covered the ground, but this was the main road, and usually remained passable unless there was a major blizzard. A few yards down the road he could see one of the huts built for emergency shelter in winter. He frowned. Something about what he saw wasn't right.

The Companion shoved him in the back.

"Ow!" Elidor yelped, staggering forward. He'd thought that in person Companions would be the way they were in books—kind and loving and faithful, but this one seemed a lot more like some of his teachers; firm-minded and impatient.

Then he saw it.

"Something went off the road."

He saw the wheel-ruts in the snow. They stopped short and went to the side of the road—not the inside, where anyone familiar with the countryside would pull off, but the outside of the road, where a screen of trees concealed the sloping hillside that led down to a little stream. With the winter snow, the extent of the drop-off and even the stream were hard to see.

Elidor ran forward to where the tracks stopped. He could see a coach down there, lying on its side—a small one, far too light for the road and the season. There must be something down there, though, some reason a Companion would come all the way into town and lead him back here.

"You stay here," he told the Companion firmly, speaking to it as if it were a large dog. "If you go down there, you'll break your neck. There's ice, and a stream. Understand?"

He didn't stop to see whether he'd insulted it, but plunged down the hillside, moving carefully through the snow. He slipped and slid, holding onto the trees for support, and finally reached the bottom. The snow was deeper here, all the way to his knees, and he moved through it carefully.

There was someone under the coach.

A man in Herald's Whites—that was why Elidor hadn't seen him before. His spotless Whites made him invisible against the snow. Elidor could see now that the coach had landed on a rock, propping it up so that the man beneath hadn't been crushed. Though his eyes were closed, and his cowl pulled up, covering most of his face so Elidor couldn't see him clearly, the Herald might still be alive.

"Herald? Sir?" Elidor said hoarsely.

When he spoke, the Herald opened his eyes and pushed the cowl away from his face. His skin was dark, and his hair and eyes were black.

"Ah," the Herald said. He managed to smile, though Elidor could see it cost him. "You're from the Library."

"Yes, sir, Herald, sir. I'm Elidor. Your, uh, Companion brought me. I told him not to come down here."

"And did he listen? That would be a great marvel. Darrian rarely listens to anyone. But I forget my manners. I'm Jordwen. I am very pleased to make your acquaintance, Librarian Elidor."

"Oh, no, sir, Herald Jordwen, sir. I'm only a Scribe, and a Journeyman anyway. But you must be cold, sir, lying there in the snow."

He was babbling like an idiot, and Elidor's ears flamed with the embarrassment of it, and the shame of having thought, even for a moment, that the Companion had come for him. Of course the Companion was already bonded to a Herald, and of course if any Companion were to come looking for Elidor, it would only be to seek help for its Herald. But in the strangest way, mixed in with his feelings of humiliation and wild embarrassment, was the oddest sort of relief.

"We have to get you out of there."

"Ah, there lies the difficulty," Jordwen said regretfully. "I'm afraid that when the blessed contraption fell on me, it managed to tangle itself up with me in a way I haven't yet unraveled. I'd resigned myself to lying here until spring came and the birds built nests in my hair. There's beauty in a meadow, of course—"

He was rattling on a little breathlessly, and it occurred to Elidor that whatever had happened to him, it must hurt very much. Somehow, that made his own fear and awkwardness go away.

"Look here, Herald sir—"

"Do call me Jordwen. I don't think our discourse can survive many more Heralds and sirs, do you?"

"I'm small, and there's space under the carriage," Elidor said, ignoring his interruption. "I think I can gct under there and see how you're pinned, if you're willing. I might be able to gct you loosc."

"I think you must," Jordwen said, and for all his languor, there was steel beneath his words.

Elidor pulled off his cloak and draped it over the Herald like a blanket. Kneeling down beside him, where the gap beneath the coach was deepest, he began to dig and burrow through the packed snow, tunneling his way beneath the coach alongside Jordwen's body.

He soon saw what was wrong. When the coach had fallen, Jordwen's foot had slipped between the spokes of one of the wheels. It was twisted far to the side, swollen to shapelessness, the white leather of his boot ugly with blood. Elidor gulped, swallowing bile. He couldn't begin to imagine how much that hurt.

He slithered back out again. Jordwen was watching him.

"And will I ever dance again on moonlit nights on green lawns with fair ladies? Ah, for the perfumed air, the gentle music of the harp. . . ."

"Your foot's caught between two of the spokes of one of the cartwheels," Elidor announced, trying not to listen to what either of them was saying. "I think the ankle's broken. I can work it free, and then you can just slide out. But it's really going to hurt."

"Then give me a moment," Jordwen said. "I may seem to sleep, but I assure you, I won't be. Since I may be . . . somewhat incapacitated . . . may I beg a further favor?"

"Yes, of course, Herald si—uh, Jordwen," Elidor stammered.

"There's a shelter by the side of the road—you will have seen it, when Darrian brought you here?"

Elidor nodded.

"The driver and his passenger, and the two coach-horses—Darrian will have brought them there for safekeeping after my disastrous and ill-considered attempt at coach-repair. You will see them safe to Talastyre if I cannot?"

How could Jordwen possibly think he'd be doing anything after Elidor got him out from under the coach? Elidor wondered. Aloud, he said. "Of course I will."

Jordwen smiled. "Then in just a few moments, we will begin."

As Elidor watched, Jordwen seemed to fall into a light sleep. His eyes closed, and his breathing deepened, until once again he was as Elidor had seen him first. Only the ache of cold roused him to his own task, and once more he squirmed beneath the coach.

Desperately careful, not wanting to hurt the Herald any more than he must, he took the leg in both hands and eased it forward, toward the edge of the wheel where the gap between the spokes was widest. He still had to turn it to get it through, though he was as careful and as gentle as he could be in the cramped and awkward space. When at last he could lower the mangled leg gently to the snow, he was trembling and covered in sweat.

Now to get Jordwen out from under the carriage.

When he crawled out from under the carriage again, it was to confront Darrian standing over Jordwen, nuzzling gently at his face. Elidor had the sense he'd somehow intruded on a very private moment, that he was watching something forever beyond his reach.

As if feeling automatically for a broken tooth, he probed for feelings of jealousy and resentment—the same feelings he'd had when hearing the other children at the Talastyre school speak of their families and their futures—but for the first time, they weren't there. But they *ought* to be there, shouldn't they? Because this was a Companion with his Herald. He was looking at what he'd always wanted most.

Wasn't he?

He put those thoughts aside. There was work to be done.

Jordwen was starting to rouse. As his eyes fluttered open, he gasped and grimaced, then set his teeth against the pain.

"Yes, I know," he said, answering a comment Elidor hadn't heard, "but we can't always choose the easiest path, can we?" He turned to Elidor. "Thank you for your help. You were very brave."

"Me?" Elidor shook his head. "We aren't done yet. I need to pull you out of there."

"As to that—" Jordwen's voice was slightly breathless with the pain, "I think it's time for Darrian to start earning his keep. If you can get my hand to his stirrup—"

"Be careful," Elidor said quickly, not sure to which of them he spoke. "There's a stream right behind you, and I don't think it's frozen through."

Darrian shook his head, and all the bells on his harness jingled. He stepped daintily through the snow behind the Herald, onto the frozen stream. The ice groaned beneath his silver-shod hooves, then gave way. The Companion turned and stamped, until he had cleared a safe place to stand on the streambed, then came up the bank again, standing over Jordwen so that his stirrup dangled above the Herald's face.

Carefully, Elidor guided Jordwen's hands to the stirrup, though his own were nearly numb with the cold. "Okay," he said. "Now."

Darrian backed carefully into the stream again, and Elidor pushed, making sure that no part of Jordwen stuck or caught. The Herald's clothing had frozen to the snow, and Elidor winced in sympathy as it tore free.

But then Jordwen was sitting up, his good leg drawn up to his chest, leaning against Darrian, who had come forward to support him.

"Well-served for my vanity," he said shakily, regarding the bloodstained leg. "Here, Journeyman Elidor, your cloak. Winter Whites are much warmer, I assure you, when one is not lying in the snow. You look blue with cold, and only think, if someone had to come and rescue you in turn—why, it would be like the tale of Mistress Masham and the Goosegirl's Daughter: by spring we would have all of Talastyre here, one by one, each coming to rescue the one who had come to rescue the one before."

Elidor grinned at the image as he took his cloak and wrapped it around himself again, but the seriousness of their situation quickly sobered him. He was strong for his age, but he could not carry Jordwen up the slope to the trail-hut, or even lift him to his Companion's back, and there was no way under heaven the man could walk even a step.

"But what now, you may ask? Well, if my good Darrian will consent to humble himself—a great concession, I do assure you—and you will give me some trifling assistance, we shall ride in style back to the road, collect our dependents, and be on our way."

"Yes, of course," Elidor said dubiously.

The Companion regarded him sternly. Elidor slipped his arm around Jordwen's back for support, and the great white stallion moved away, then slowly and carefully knelt in the snow.

"Now, help me to my feet," Jordwen said.

Elidor scrambled around to his other side, where the bad leg was, and squatted beside him. He got an arm beneath Jordwen's shoulders, knowing how this was done and knowing he must do it well. He must not slip. He must not fall. He must not fail.

"Now," Jordwen said softly, and Elidor rose to his feet.

Cold muscles screamed with cramp, but he ignored them. He clutched Jordwen hard against his side, pulling with all his wiry strength, a strength honed by years of working among the heavy volumes of Talastyre. To his surprise, he and the Herald were much of a height.

"Not—much—farther—now—" Jordwen gasped. His bronze skin had an ashy tint.

Elidor shifted his grip to the Herald's belt, and half lifted, half dragged him through the snow to his Companion. The bad leg scraped against the drifts. There was no way to stop it, and Elidor heard Jordwen's breath catch in ragged sobs, starting tears in his own eyes.

When they reached Darrian, it was all Elidor could do to deposit Jordwen sideways upon his back, as if the saddle were a chair.

"This won't do," Jordwen said after a long moment, with a brave attempt at his usual light tones.

"If— If— If he puts his head down," Elidor said, amazed at his own presumption, "I could lift your bad leg over, I think. But—"

"—But it will hurt," Jordwen finished for him, with the ghost of a smile. "Still, I think it will work. What say you, my friend?"

The last remark hadn't been addressed to him, Elidor realized. In reply, Darrian stretched his neck out as far as it would go, and laid his head against the snow. The position looked awkward.

Elidor hurried around to the Companion's other side, and gently reached for Jordwen's leg. He slid his hands beneath it, above and below the knee, and raised it high, flexing it like the joints of a doll, and swiveled it toward him, across Darrian's neck, until Jordwen sat astride the saddle.

Darrian raised his head quickly, with a huff of relief.

"You have good hands," the Herald said. "Gentle and deft."

"Scribes have to have good hands," Elidor said, still holding Jordwen's leg so that the heel didn't have to rest against the snow. He was proud of being a Scribe, he realized. He was good at it, and it wasn't something everyone could do. He put the thought aside for later consideration. "I don't think you should try to put your foot in the stirrup," he said gravely.

That surprised a shaky laugh from Jordwen.

"Bless you, I am through with rash mistakes for today!"

Darrian got carefully to his feet. There was a line of snow melted into the Companion's coat, as even as the waterline of a boat. Elidor stared at it with a scholar's fascination. *They really ARE whiter than snow . . .*

"And now to our charges," Jordwen said.

"'But I can—"

"No. They are my responsibility," Jordwen interrupted sharply.

Again there was that sense of conversation Elidor couldn't hear, and Jordwen shook his head.

"You're right, of course. My apologies, Journeyman Elidor. My incivility is precious little thanks for all your aid."

"If you are Jordwen, then I am Elidor," Elidor said,

trembling at his own amazing boldness at speaking to a Herald so. "I'll meet you at the top," he said, to cover his embarrassment. He turned quickly away, and hurried back along his own tracks up the side of the hill.

Darrian took a longer path, finding a gentler slope, so they reached the hut at the same time. Since Jordwen was manifestly unable to dismount, it was Elidor who pushed open the door.

Two carriage horses stood placidly in one corner, gazing at him incuriously. In the other, sitting on a bench, was a large man in a heavy driving cloak, and beside him, a small child of perhaps four or five, her face red and swollen with tears.

"Are you with the rescue party?" the man demanded truculently. "It's about time. I've been cooped up with this squalling brat for hours!"

"And you are?" Elidor asked.

"Meachum, job-coachman, hired to deliver Mistress Vonarre to the Library at Talastyre, and I've had a time of it, I tell you—first one of the horses went lame, then the coach lost a wheel, and then some fool of a Herald came along and made matters worse—"

You haven't had as bad a time as Mistress Vonarre or that "fool of a Herald" has had. Ignoring the man, he went over to the girl and knelt before her.

"Hello, sweetheart, are you Mistress Vonarre?"

She looked at him, blue eyes made enormous with tears, and nodded, lip trembling.

"I'm Elidor. I live at the library. There are a lot of little girls there who want to be your friend. I'll be your friend, too. And right now, there's a Herald outside. I bet he'll even let you say hello to his Companion, Darrian. Would you like that? And then we'll go to Talastyre."

"What about the rescue party?" Meachum demanded.

"There is no rescue party," Elidor said, over his shoulder, his attention focused on the little girl.

"Got no parents," Vonarre said, hiccuping on a sob. "And it's cold."

"Well, it won't be cold soon," Elidor said. "And do you know what? I haven't got any parents either. But there are wonderful things at the library. Books with beautiful pictures all full of stories. I'll show you. Now come on." He scooped her up into his arms and carried her outside.

Her eyes widened when she saw Darrian again, and she reached out to touch him. Though he'd been standoffish with Elidor, Darrian lowered his muzzle into her hand and allowed her to stroke him. She seemed to forget most of her troubles at the sight of the Companion, and Elidor could understand why. They were wonderful, magical creatures.

But he didn't want one. He wanted the life he had. He was *proud* of the life he had.

He looked up at Jordwen. The Herald smiled, as if he could guess most of Elidor's thoughts. "It's not for everyone, you know," Jordwen said softly.

"I do. Now. Is that why Darrian came for me?" In a different way than a Companion would come for his Chosen, but one that had made just as much of a difference to Elidor.

"Could be. He had to get someone before I froze to death, and oddly enough, not just anyone will go off with one of us. And I assume you sent a message to the library?"

"Sure. It might take a while. It's Midwinter."

"Ah. You lost track of things on the road. Well, give her here. We'd best go and meet them."

"Sweetheart, how would you like to be able to tell your children you rode on a real live Companion?" Elidor asked the girl. "This is Herald Jordwen. Jordwen, here is Mistress Vonarre."

"I am most pleased to make your acquaintance, Mistress Vonarre," Jordwen said, in his most courtly tones. No one would have guessed that the man was freezing and injured. Elidor handed Vonarre up to him, then went back into the shelter. As he did, he heard the faint jingle of silver bells as Darrian started down the road at a slow walk.

"Come if you're coming," Elidor said with determined cheerfulness to the unpleasant coachman as he gathered up the horse's bridle-reins. "It's a long walk to town, and better with company."

"You can't expect me to walk?" the man said in astonishment. "It's freezing out there, and we're miles from town! If that fool of a Herald hadn't put my coach over the cliff, we could ride in comfort. I'll sue the Collegium for damages, you see if I don't!"

Sharp words rose to Elidor's tongue, but he didn't say them. If Jordwen could be kind and forgiving to a Journeyman Scribe while lying cold and injured, Elidor could certainly keep his temper with a blustering fool.

"I'm sorry. Perhaps you can ride one of the horses. They should be sending someone to look for us, but if they don't, at least we'll reach Talastyre by dark."

They had gone less than half a mile when they were met by the Master Librarian's own coach and a dozen outriders, and Elidor, Jordwen, Vonarre, and Meachum finished the journey safe and warm.

Several of the outriders went on ahead, so everything was waiting for them when they reached the city gates. Suddenly shy, Elidor slipped away in the confusion, before anyone could think to speak to him, and hurried to his rooms.

As one of the Journeymen, he had a semiprivate room of his own, and Caleanth was home with his family at Festival time. It was odd to think, now, that he had grudged his fellow journeyman that, when he had all of Talastyre for his own, as much his kingdom as any prince's.

No one is too young to be a fool—or too old either! he thought, thinking of Meachum. But surely the coachman's greatest crime had been only that he had been thinking too much of his own troubles—he had gone quite satisfyingly white when the outriders from the library had lifted Jordwen into the carriage to finish out the journey, his leg in a makeshift brace and bandage, and there had been no more talk of "foolish Heralds."

He stood for a while, gazing out the window at the buildings of the Library and Scriptorium, its stone dark silver in the winter twilight. Imagine being on the road so many days you didn't know it was Midwinter, and then having to spend most of the Festival pinned beneath a broken coach, only to be half-rescued by a wet-eared journeyman with a dream-stuffed head! Elidor smiled ruefully at the thought, then went to the chest at the foot of his bed, opened it, and withdrew his oldest and longest-prized possession.

The white paint was worn away in spots, showing the wood beneath, but the tiny blue eyes were still as bright, as were the tiny beads that stood in for the silver bells on the painted harness of the carved wooden Companion. He kissed the small wooden toy gently on the forehead, saying good-bye to a dream that had served him well, then tucked the toy into a pocket in his cloak and went to do something he should have done long ago.

He walked across the quadrangle to the infirmary. The Herald would be in the hands of the Healers, of course, but Mistress Infirmerer was a reliable source of all gossip at the library, and he hoped to find where little Vonarre had been taken.

But to his surprise, the first person he encountered upon entering the infirmary precincts was the Mistress of Girls, Lady Kendra. As he lingered in an outer room, uncertain of how far to go exploring, she came through a doorway and advanced upon him, heavy skirts swishing.

"So here is our hero," she said, keeping her voice low.

Elidor ducked his head, feeling awkward. It was one thing to do what was needed, he realized, and quite another to hear about it later. "I came to see Mistress Vonarre," he said.

Lady Kendra's expression softened. "Poor mite! To come such a long way, and at this time of year, and sent like a parcel of old clothes to the ragman, her that wasn't to come until spring—you may be sure that yon coachman will have a better care for the next child he must bring such a distance, and pox upon him!" Lady Kendra's eyes flashed, and she took a deep breath. "But a hot bath and a bowl of soup mends much, and I will sit with her until she sleeps. She will soon settle in. Tomorrow we will send someone to the wreck to bring back her things, and the letter that will undoubtedly explain all." From her tone, it was clear the Mistress of Girls doubted the explanation would satisfy her.

"I can go with them. I know where it is," Elidor said. "But I've brought her a present. It's Midwinter. Can I give it to her? I'll stay with her, if you like."

Lady Kendra looked surprised, but the expression passed so quickly that Elidor wasn't quite sure he'd seen it. "Well, then. Do. But mind she drinks her milk. There's a sleeping posset in it."

"I will," Elidor promised.

He went through the door the Mistress of Girls indicated. There was a table with a small lamp burning on it, and a wooden cup beside it. Beside the bed that took up most of the space in the room was a wooden stool. Vonarre was sitting up in bed. She had been scrubbed, and her hair brushed out, and dressed in a thick flannel nightshirt a few sizes too big, just as any traveler whose things had been lost might be. Elidor loosened his cloak and sat down beside her bed. She smiled when she saw him, hopefully, as if—just perhaps—the world was not terrible after all.

The books he'd read spoke of breaking hearts, and of the pain they caused, and its curious joy, but in all their stories, never once had Elidor read of the comforting pain of a heart that mends, though he knew he felt it now. *Thank you, Jordwen. Thank you, Darrian.* He reached into his cloak.

"I've brought you a Midwinter present," he said, offering the carved Companion to the child. "This was mine when I was little. I think you'll like it."

"His name is Darrian," Vonarre said firmly, clutching the wooden horse against her chest.

"Shall I tell you a story?" Elidor said, taking off his cloak. He picked up the wooden mug and held it out. "Drink your milk and I will. Once, long ago—a long, long, time ago, there was a Companion named Darrian, who was the partner of a Herald named Vonarre. . . ."

Sun in Glory
by Mercedes Lackey

Mercedes Lackey is a full-time writer and has published numerous novels, including the best-selling Heralds of Valdemar series. She is also a professional lyricist and a licensed wild bird rehabilitator.

Sunset was long past; the light in his study came from the lanterns high on the wall behind him. The floor-to-ceiling stained-glass window on the other side of the room was a dark panel spiderwebbed with lead channels. It formed a somber backdrop behind the two men seated across from Herald Alberich. The Weaponmaster to the Trainees of all three Collegia at Haven in the Kingdom of Valdemar coughed to punctuate the silence in his quarters. He regarded his second visitor, who was ensconced in one of his austere, but comfortable, wooden chairs, with a skeptical gaze.

His *first* visitor he knew very well, dressed in his robes of office, saffron and cream; mild-mannered, balding Gerichen, the chief Priest of Vkandis Sunlord here in Haven. Not that anyone knew Gerichen's temple, prudently called only "the Temple of the Lord of Light" *was* of Vkandis Sunlord, at least not unless you were a Karsite exile. . . .

Of which there were a surprising number in Valdemar—surprising, at least, to Alberich even now.

Gerichen had been born here, but most of his fellowship had not been, and Karse did not easily let loose its children, even if all it wanted of them was to reduce them to ashes. Yet, year by year, season by season, for decades it seemed, Karse's children had been slipping over the Border into Valdemar, beating down their fear of the "Demon-lovers" because real death bayed hot at their heels and the possibility of demons seemed preferable to the certainty of the Fires of Purification. Some couldn't bear the fear of the things that the Priest-Mages (in the name of the god, of course) sent to howl about their doors of a night. Some came because the Red-robes had taken, or had threatened to take, a child or spouse—either to absorb into the priesthood or to burn as a proto-witch. And amazingly enough to Alberich, some of them came because *he* had dared to, so many years ago.

Alberich had met Gerichen longer ago than he cared to think about, when he was first a Herald-Trainee and Gerichen a mere Novice. Both of them were older than they liked to admit, except over a drink, in front of a cozy fire, late of an evening. Gerichen was one of a very small company of folk who had supported Alberich's presence in Valdemar from the very beginning.

The other visitor, sitting beneath the left eye of the stained-glass image of Vkandis as a Sun In Glory that formed the outer wall of Alberich's study, was someone that Alberich knew not at all, though he knew far more *about* this fellow than the man probably suspected. He was here at Gerichen's request. He was also here, if not illegally, certainly covertly, for *he* was a Priest-Mage of Vkandis Sunlord in Karse. There had not been one of those on Valdemaran soil in centuries.

There had not been one on Valdemaran soil as anything other than an invader in far longer.

Karse—sworn enemy of Valdemar for so long that very few even knew it had once been a peaceful neighbor, had been Alberich's home. Karse was ruled, in fact if not in name, by a theocracy who called the Heralds "Demons" and were pledged to eradicate them. And of that theocracy, the ruling priests, the Priest-Mages and the priests who had clawed their way up through the ranks, were the true aristocracy of Karse, answerable only to one authority, the Son of the Sun.

Who—until very recently, at least—had called Alberich himself "The Great Traitor" for not only deserting his post as captain of a company of Vkandis' Holy Army, but for turning witch and joining the ranks of the Demon-Riders of Valdemar. And worse; rising to a position of such trust that Witch-Queen Selenary counted him among her most valued advisers.

The Priest-Mages were not only the Voices of Vkandis; they had the power to summon and control demons themselves—not that they *called* such creatures "demons," not even among themselves, preferring to refer to them as the "Dark Servants" or "Vkandis' Furies." All in Vkandis' name, of course, or so they said. All at the behest of Vkandis Himself, or so they claimed.

One of those Voices had condemned Alberich to death by burning, and all because he'd had the temerity to make use of a "witch-power" and save the inhabitants of a Karsite Border village from certain slaughter by a band of outlaws. Never mind that he'd had no more control over that so-called "witch-power" than he had over a raging storm, had never *asked* for that power, and would have given it up without a moment of hesitation.

But the current Son of the Sun—the newly chosen Son of the Sun—was not of the same stamp as all of those who had preceded her. And the Voice that sat beneath Vkandis' left eye was not at all like the arrogant, cold priest who had pronounced sentence on Alberich that day. He was young, surprisingly so. It would hardly be politic for him to be clad in the red robes of his office here in the heart of a land that was his enemy's, but in ordinary clothing that would not disgrace a moderately prosperous merchant, he had an aura of calm authority that set him apart, even from Gerichen. He was short, stocky, clean-shaven; his white-blond hair was as close-cropped as that of all Sun-priests, with keen eyes as blue as those of any Companion set in a face whose planes might have been cut by a chisel. And yet—not cold, that face; alive and curiously *accepting*. Beside Alberich, on the other side of the fireplace, sat Herald-Chronicler Myste. She regarded the two priests with a gaze as penetrating as that of the visitors, and perhaps more uncanny, at least to the stranger, since her hazel eyes looked at him through a pair of round glass lenses that magnified what was behind them, giving her an owllike stare. Myste was the official historian of Herald's Collegium, the Herald-Chronicler, and had been since she finished her internship. She had a facility with words that would have suited her to the job had she not had other handicaps that kept her out of the Field.

Myste had been as odd a Herald, in her way, as Alberich. She had always, from the moment she arrived, been shockingly short-sighted, and had never been assigned to Field work on account of it—*not* the best notion to put someone in the Field whose precious glass goggles could be lost or broken, rendering her the next thing to blind. Perhaps that was why she had always been Alberich's friend. "When you can't see what people are like on the outside," she'd once said in her blunt manner, "you stop even considering appearances and concentrate on everything else."

That was, among other reasons, why Myste was here tonight.

Alberich coughed again. "And exactly it is to what that I owe the *honor* of your presence?" he asked, stressing the word "honor" in such a way that implied it was anything but. He spoke Valdemaran, not Karsite.

The stranger cast a mild glance at Myste. "Could one ask why the lady is present?" he replied—in Karsite, not Valdemaran.

"I am the Herald-Chronicler, and I am here to record this meeting, at the request of Herald Alberich," Myste said for herself—in *flawless* Karsite, not Valdemaran. She'd learned it from Alberich, of course, but she owed her accent to her own exacting ear for languages.

To Alberich's surprise, the stranger smiled. "Excellent," he said, with every appearance of approval, "Would it be too much to ask for a copy for myself— and to conduct this discussion in my own tongue? My command of *yours* is in nowise as good as yours clearly is of mine."

His smile was sudden, charming, dazzling even—and apparently genuine. Alberich and Myste exchanged more than a glance.

:I don't sense any falsehood,: Myste Mindspoke. Her unique Gift was a strictly limited ability to Truth-

Sense without the use of a spell. She could only concentrate on one person at a time, and had to be within an arm's-length or two of him, though, which (again) rendered it less than useful in the Field.

:But their so-called Priestly Attributes are no more nor less than our Gifts,: he reminded her. *:What if he can block you?:*

A purely mental shrug. *:Then what I sense is meaningless. On the other hand, how many people know* my *Gift—and of those, how many are outside the Heraldic Circle or would guess I'd be here at your request?:*

Not many; he had to admit that. Surely no matter how good the Karsite spies were, they didn't know *that* about Myste, or would think to warn this man against her. "I think, if only for the purposes of clarity, we should conduct our discussion in Karsite," he replied.

"And I will be pleased to provide a copy," Myste added smoothly.

The visitor smiled again. "Before we begin, then, will you introduce me to the lady, Herald Alberich?"

The word "Herald" sounded strange in the middle of a Karsite sentence. They didn't have a word for "Herald." It sounded even stranger spoken without a curse appended.

"Herald-Chronicler Myste, this is Mage-Priest Hierophant Karchanek," Alberich said solemnly. He couldn't resist a slight smile of his own as Karchanek started just a little, while poor Gerichen's eyes practically bulged out of his head. "I assume I have given your title correctly?"

"Quite correctly," Karchanek replied, recovering. Since *he* hadn't given Alberich his title, and Gerichen didn't know it, he must be wondering how Alberich got it—and from whom.

Your borders are not as secure as you think, Alberich told the man silently.

But of course, one single Karsite priest would not have come here, unescorted, into the heart of the enemy's capital, if he was not the equivalent of a one-man army. Karchanek probably could fight his way out of this room using his own deadly skills, wreaking considerable havoc as he did so, and might even escape if he could outrun the alarm. He definitely could *slip* out of his quarters at Gerichen's temple, be they ever so closely guarded, and make his way past just about anything Alberich could throw at him to get home. Karchanek commanded magic—*real* magic— the magic that Valdemar hadn't seen for centuries until this current war with Hardorn. He might be the most powerful Priest-Mage that Karse had seen in centuries, save only the Son of the Sun.

And the Son of the Sun had sent him here. To speak with Alberich. The Great Traitor.

Karchanek pursed his lips. "I find myself wondering if I can tell you *anything* that you do not already know," he said at last.

Alberich leaned back in his chair. "I am a man of great patience," he replied. "I have no particular objection to hearing something more than once. Begin at the beginning."

"The beginning . . ." mused Karchanek, then smiled again. "Ah, then you will have to have great patience, for the beginning, the *true* beginning, lies with the Son of the Sun, may Vkandis hold her at zenith. Solaris. Who has been and is my friend as well as my superior."

Alberich was very glad of his ability to don an inscrutable card-sharper's face, for he surely needed that mask to hide his eagerness. Solaris! Now *there* was a

person no one knew much about here in Valdemar—
and someone whom they all desperately needed to
know *everything* about.

But he kept his mask in place. "The new Son of
the Sun," he observed dryly. "The—*female* Son of the
Sun." Just to pair "female" with "Son of the Sun"
would have been a blasphemy so profound a few years
ago that the speaker would not only have been
burned, but his ashes mixed with salt, his lands plowed
under, his wife and children sacrificed, his ancestors
dug up and reburied in a potter's field, and every trace
that he had ever lived at all utterly eradicated.

Karchanek's smile broadened, and he spread his
hands wide. "Even so. And so crowned by Vkandis
Sunlord—" he made the sign of the Holy Disk, "—
himself, with His Own hands. Perhaps you had heard
of this?"

"Some," Alberich admitted. "Rumors, tales that
seemed particularly wild."

"Not so. This, I witnessed along with thousands of
others, and do believe me, Herald Alberich, it was
no delusion, no trick of magic or mind, no clever
artifice with a moving statue. Though the statue *did*
move, it was no mere trumpery with a cleverly hinged
arm. The Image arose from His throne, walked lithe
and manlike, and took the crown from His Own head
to place it upon that of Solaris. Which shrank as He
put it there to fit her—exactly. I *saw* it. I have held
that very crown in my two hands, and—" he paused
again. "There is a thing not many would know about,
save the handful of novices sent to polish the Image
entire, one of which I was, and the *only* one among
them to polish the crown. Which task I owe to my
habit of squirreling up the cloister walls, into the
cloister orchard, round about when the plums were

ripe." His eyes twinkled, and Myste hid a grin. "At the back of the crown upon the Image there was a lozenge, no bigger than my palm and *quite* invisible from below, where the sculptor, the gilder, and the jewel smith set their marks. That lozenge and those marks are upon the back of the crown that Solaris now wears."

"Interesting," Alberich began, still skeptical, for a truly clever fraud would have taken that into account and made sure to replicate every oddity and imperfection in the crown worn by the Great Image. And someone who was Solaris' friend as well as her supporter would probably swear that the Sun had stood still in the heavens for a day in order to lend more strength to her claim to the Sun Throne. But Karchanek was not finished.

"Nay, there is more, for has the Sunlord in His wisdom not granted her direct counsel in the form of—a Firecat?" Karchanek's brows arched, and well they might.

"A *Firecat?*" The words were almost forced from him. Alberich had not been a scholarly man, but even children knew all the tales of the miraculous avatars of Vkandis, and most Karsite children played at Reulan and the Firecat the way Valdemaran children played at Heralds and Companions. "But—Firecats are legend, merely—"

Karchanek shook his head emphatically. "No more. One walks by her side and sits at her Council table, and, when he chooses (which is seldom) lets his thoughts be known to those around Solaris as well as to the Son of the Sun herself." Karchanek sat back just a little, a smile of satisfaction playing on his lips. "He has, in fact, deigned to address a word or two to me. It was a remarkable experience, hearing someone speak inside one's head. Although I imagine that *you,* Heralds, are so used to such a thing from your own Companions by now that you take it as common-place."

That was a shrewd shot—telling them that *he* knew not only that Companions weren't horses (or demons), but that they Mindspoke to their Heralds.

:Is he saying this—Firecat—Mindspeaks?: Myste asked incredulously.

Well, if it was a real Firecat, that would be the least of its talents. If? There was no reason to doubt it. Without a Firecat, the living, breathing, and very *present* symbol of Vkandis' favor, Solaris could not have lasted a month. *:Like a Companion, yes. And, presumably, gets its wisdom from the same source.:*

"There have been reforms of late, in the ranks of the Sun-priests," Alberich ventured. "Solaris' reforms, it is said."

Now Karchanek actually laughed. "Reforms—yes. One could call them 'reforms'—in the same way that one could refer to the razing of a robber's stronghold as 'a little housecleaning.' Not even Solaris can root out all the corruption of centuries, but the cleansing has begun." Then he sobered. "The Fires, the summoning of demons, the terrorizing of our own people, all these are no more. And there is something that should die with them. The enmity between Karse and Valdemar."

Well, there it was, the offer that Alberich had been hoping for, but was still not certain he should trust. "We seem to be facing the same enemy," he pointed out. "Ancar of Hardorn—"

"Hardorn can devour us separately: United, we will be too tough a morsel to swallow," agreed the other. "And there is no surety on your part that once he is disposed of, we will not turn back to our old ways and warfares."

"But—"

"But hear the words of the Son of the Sun." Karchanek brought out a thin metal tube from within his sleeve, in diameter no larger than an arrow shaft. He opened it, and removed a sheet of paper so thin that Alberich could see the writing on it from the opposite side.

Greetings to Captain Alberich, now Herald of Valdemar, loyal son of two warring lands," Karchanek read aloud. "*I, Solaris, Son of the Sun by the grace of Vkandis Sunlord, send these words to you and not to the Queen who holds your allegiance because the counsel of the Sunlord is that one with a heart divided will be more like to lend heed to that which promises division will be healed than one who is single-hearted. To you I say this: without Karse, Valdemar may fall, and without Valdemar, Karse may perish. Yet to unite our peoples, more than words on a treaty are needed. All overtures were like to come to naught, or be concluded too late. So I brought my prayers to the Sunlord, and the Sunlord has said this unto me. 'Bring Me a Herald of Valdemar, that I may make of her a Priest of My Order in the sight of all, that none may doubt or dare to prosecute a war which is abomination in My sight.'*"

Alberich suddenly found it hard to breathe, and Myste gasped openly. With Karchanek's eyes on him, he forced himself to take a breath, forced himself to think, *think* about this offer, so strange, and so unexpected.

And when he managed to get his mind focused, one thing leaped out at him.

"You read Solaris' words exactly?" he demanded, his voice harsher than he intended.

"Exactly," Karchanek averred. "And there is just a little more." He cleared his throat, and went on. *"And when the Sunlord had said this to me, I bowed before His will. "I shall send my trusted envoy with all speed,"* I pledged, but He had not finished. 'Not any Herald for so great a trust, not any Herald can bridge this gap between our peoples,' *He said unto me.* 'Send thou to the one they call the Great Traitor, for only his tongue will be trusted, and say that I require they send the one who stands at the Queen's right hand. Say that I call upon the Queen's Own to join My service, and be a bridge between Our peoples.' *And so He left me, and so I have done. By my hand and seal, Solaris, Son of the Sun."*

The last words fell like pebbles into an abyss of silence as Alberich gave over any effort to keep his face expressionless. His mind was a total blank. If anyone had told him that these words would ever be spoken between Karsite and Valdemaran, he'd have sent for the Mind-Healers. Insane. Impossible.

"Gods don't ask for much," Myste said into the silence. "Do they?"

"I will leave this with you," Karchanek said solemnly, rerolling the near-transparent paper and inserting it in its metal tube, handing it to Alberich who took it numbly. "There are other sureties I have that I will bring to you later. I understand that you have a kind of magic that can determine if one is telling the truth, and I beg that you will tell your Queen that I submit to such willingly. This is no trivial thing we ask of you." He stood up, and Gerichen belatedly did the same. "You will know where to find me when you are ready."

Without asking leave—not that Alberich could have

given it at the moment—he and Gerichen walked out. Alberich stared at the metal cylinder in his hands.

"ForeSight—" Myste said firmly. "We need someone with ForeSight." She started to get to her feet, but Alberich shook his head at her.

"Eldan and Kero, these are who we need first of all," he countered. His own ForeSight, limited as it was, hadn't even warned him that *this* was coming.

Then again, would it? It only tells me about disaster looming, not if something good *is going to happen. . . .*

Small wonder he was a pessimist by nature. "I shall get them— if they are where I think, none other would be paid heed to," he continued, handing the cylinder to Myste. "If you so kind would be, would you with a scholar's eye look this over for tampering."

"I can try," Myste said dubiously. "But I don't exactly have a lot of Karsite documents to compare to it—or anything in Solaris' hand either."

But she unrolled the document and bent her lenses over it, much to Alberich's relief. He didn't want her haring off to the Collegium in search of someone with ForeSight and letting fall *any* hints of this evening's revelations. At least, not until she had gotten over her own shock and regained a Chronicler's necessary dispassion for the situation.

Herald-Captain Kerowyn was the logical choice to be informed, since she was practically in the Lord Marshal's back pocket. And as for Herald Eldan— well, that worthy was Alberich's source of information on Karse and the goings-on there. Not to put too fine a point upon it, Eldan was a spy, and but for a single slip, had never once alerted even the Priest-Mages to his true identity.

Kero wasn't in her quarters; neither she nor Eldan

were particularly pleased when Alberich interrupted them by pounding insistently in a coded knock on Eldan's door.

"I don't smell smoke and the Collegium isn't on fire, so this had better be *at least* that important, Alberich," Kero growled, cracking the door only enough so that Alberich caught a glimpse of tousled hair and an angry blue eye in the light of a hall candle.

"It is," he said. "A *friendly* visit I have had, from—Gerich's outKingdom visitor."

Kero blinked. "Friendly?" she said dubiously.

"*Very* friendly. *Unbelievably* friendly. This cannot wait until morning. I think it should not wait a candlemark."

"Right. I heard that," said Eldan's voice from deeper in the room. "Give us a little; we'll be right on your heels and meet you in your rooms at the salle. Outside of the Queen's suite, you've got the most secure quarters in the complex."

Alberich nodded and left them to put themselves back together in peace. Poor Kero! Eldan was only just back from his latest covert foray into Karse—which was how Alberich had known just who Karchanek really was—and already business had interrupted their time together.

But when had that not been the case with a Herald? Add to which, Kerowyn had been the Captain of her own Guild Mercenary Company, so she should be used to being interrupted by now. She might not like it, but she should be used to it. *She's been a mercenary for twice as long as she's been a Herald; Business always comes first for them,* he told himself. In fact, when they arrived at his door, he doubted there would be a single word said about what he'd just interrupted.

Nor was there, and the pair were, as Eldan had said,

just about on his heels; he wasn't more than half of the way back to the salle when he looked back and saw the two white-clad figures emerging from Heralds' Wing. He'd barely gotten inside his own door and heard from Myste that if there had been any tampering with the missive *she* couldn't find it, when they arrived at his door, as neatly turned-out as if they'd just come from standing guard at a Court ceremony.

Alberich explained the situation to them in a few terse sentences and handed over the letter and its tube. Kero examined the tube; Eldan, who was second only to Alberich and Myste in his mastery of Karsite, scanned it quickly and whistled.

"Well, that explains something—" he said, "—why on this last time, even the most reactionary of the old-guard were being v-e-r-y careful to be good little boys, and if they had any complaints about the new Son of the Sun, keeping them behind their own teeth."

Alberich shook his head. "Understand, I do not," he confessed.

"It's quite simple, and a bit scary, old man," Eldan replied, handing the letter on to Kero as they both took the seats so recently vacated by the visitors from Karse. "I'd heard all the stories about Solaris, but I hadn't talked to any eyewitnesses—not that it would be likely I could, since my contacts don't reside in such lofty circles. Still, the stories were all of a piece, and the Sun-priests were suddenly all acting like they'd put heart and soul into the reform movement. Karchanek's eyewitness account just clinches it." He glanced over at Kero. "Doesn't it, love?"

Kerowyn nodded. "No doubt in my mind. Wherever He's been for the last couple of hundred years, Vkandis is back now in Karse, and He's cracking heads and taking names. *Just like the Star-Eyed.*

Remember, I've seen this before, in my grandmother's Shin'a'in clan." She pursed her lips thoughtfully. "Mind, the Star-Eyed usually operates through Her spirit-riders and Avatars, but maybe that's what this Firecat is, a spirit-rider equivalent."

Alberich went very, very still. Of all the things he had hoped for to happen in Karse, this, if true, was the best and the least likely. It might be frightening for Valdemarans, who had no history of direct intervention by their gods, but for a Karsite this would be the return of things to their proper ways, ways long since lost beneath the centuries of rule by a corrupt and cruel priesthood. "You are certain?" he asked carefully.

"I've heard all of Kero's stories, and factoring in the atmosphere down there right now—well, I'm as certain as I can be without walking into the Temple there and demanding Solaris conjure up a miracle to prove it to me," Eldan said firmly. "Not that I'd give that approach a try. From what I've heard of the lady, she's got a pretty dry sense of humor, and might decide to ask Vkandis to teach me a little proper humility."

Alberich closed his eyes for a moment. *What, exactly, is one supposed to do when the prayers of a lifetime are so fully answered?*

:Be properly grateful,: said his Companion Kantor. *:And don't question why it has taken the God so long to act. That wouldn't be a good idea.:*

Kantor's reply startled him further. This statement, from a Companion, had a weight that went far beyond the simple words.

:There was probably something about Free Will involved,: Alberich replied, voicing the thoughts that had occurred to him in the dark of the night. *:And*

making our own mistakes.: Free Will figured largely in the theology of the older texts—the ones dating from before the Son of the Sun became the tacit ruler of all Karse and the priesthood began conjuring demons to enforce their will.

:And, just possibly, there was something about waiting to be properly asked to step in, prayers of the faithful and all that,: Kantor amended. *:Gods don't go where they aren't invited, not the ones we'd call "good," anyway. After all, as long as people seemed to be content to putting up with things as they were, there would be no reason for Vkandis to intervene.:*

:That would be the "Free Will" part,: Alberich reminded his Companion.

Kantor ignored the interruption. *:Vkandis, I suspect, has been dealing with wrongdoers on an individual basis once they died and were in His hands and in no position to dispute the error of their ways. I suppose even a God who intervenes regularly in the lives of His people cannot build a paradise in the world, since everyone would have a different idea of what paradise should be. But then again, I could be wrong.:*

Alberich found *that* last statement difficult to believe. Oh, perhaps another Companion could be wrong, but Kantor had never so much as missed a single hoof-step in all the time Alberich had known him. Kantor never spoke unless he had something of import to say.

And Companions were not unlike Firecats. . . .

Could they, as it was said of the Firecats, be able to pass the sincere prayer directly into the ear of a God?

His prayer? *His* God? What was it that Kantor had said—"the prayers of the faithful?" Was this, in part, due to him?

No. He would not even think that. Coincidence, merely, and he would confine himself to rejoicing that things had changed in his lifetime. Events had turned to the redemption of his land. A new Son of the Sun, more like in spirit to those of the old days, sat on the Sun Throne. And *if* he could trust this overture, then perhaps there would be peace between Valdemar and Karse as there had been, in the old days, the times he had read about in long-forgotten histories in the Queen's library.

If it wasn't all a cunning trap. If he could somehow convince Herald Talia, who had already been through more than anyone should have to endure, to walk into the wolf's mouth a second time.

:It isn't Talia you'll have to convince,: observed Kantor shrewdly, *:but her husband. And the Queen.:*

Oh, yes. There was Dirk to convince as well. And Selenay. Neither of whom were going to be as ready to agree to this as Talia.

"If you and Kantor are quite finished," Kerowyn said, with heavy irony, interrupting his thoughts, "the rest of us would like to actually discuss this."

"Out loud," Eldan added.

Alberich leveled a glance at them that would have made any of his pupils quiver where they stood. But of course, Eldan wasn't a Trainee anymore, and he'd faced worse than Alberich over his breakfast fire, day in and day out, for the past five years. And of course, Kerowyn never *had* been his pupil, so there went *that* particular hold out the window.

With a sigh, he sat down, and the discussion began in earnest. It as going to be more than a "discussion," when it finally got to the Queen—it was going to be a battle, and Alberich was not going to go to that battle less than fully armed.

In the end, it was Karchanek who won the battle, which was shorter than Alberich would have been willing to believe. Perhaps things were more desperate than he had thought, where Hardorn was concerned; he made his case to Selenay to hear Karchanek out, supported by Kero and Eldan, then didn't learn anything more until Karchanek himself came to tell him that Selenay had agreed. Alberich didn't hear as much of what went on in Council sessions anymore, now that Kerowyn (with young Herald Jeri as her assistant) was taking over many of the duties he had performed, but for Selenay and for her father.

That had only meant he hadn't needed to sit through the candlemarks of arguments, for and against the invitation. Rightly or wrongly, this had been one session that Selenay had decided *he* especially should not participate in.

No matter; Karchanek had been his own best advocate, once Selenay actually heard him out. Perhaps his two *most* persuasive points had been that he himself would remain in Selenay's hands as a hostage, and that Alberich himself and one other Herald should go with her. Kero had objected to that, putting herself up as Alberich's substitute. But this was one duty he had no intention of giving over to Kero—well, for one thing, as *she* assumed his role, he became more expendable and she, less so. For another, there was no one living in Valdemar who could read his fellow countrymen as well as he could.

He stood now beside Karchanek, who was arrayed in one of Gerichen's borrowed robes, beneath a slightly overcast summer sky, in, of all places, Companion's Field beside a hastily erected archway of brickwork. It lacked only two days to Midsummer, the longest day of the year and so the most auspicious for Vkandis, the day appointed for—

Well, Alberich didn't quite know *what*. Solaris

hadn't given anyone any indication of just what was going to happen, other than Talia being invested into the ranks of the Sun-priests. Maybe Solaris herself didn't know. But Midsummer was when it was going to happen, and somehow Karchanek was going to get them there for it. Talia had been here for a candlemark, Rolan beside her, both of them arrayed and packed for traveling. Kantor stood beside Rolan, calm and serene as usual, and in nowise intimidated by the presence of the King Stallion of the Companion herd. Beside him was Dirk's Companion, with Dirk fiddling nervously with girth and stirrups. There was also a crowd of Heralds, Companions, and interested parties surrounding them in a rough circle that was a prudent distance from the innocuous brick arch. No one knew what Karchanek was going to do. They only knew that it would be the first real demonstration of magic within the city of Haven for—centuries.

"—and when the Holy Firecat senses that I am reaching with my signature power toward him," Karchanek was explaining to Jeri, as he had already explained to Talia, Dirk, Selenay, and everyone else who was involved in making this decision, "he will open the Gate between us, exactly as if he was burning a tunnel through a mountain to avoid having to climb and descend to reach the other side."

"And you can't do that alone?" Jeri asked.

He shook his head. "Only one of Adept power can open a Gate alone, and then, well, it is better that it be done by two or more such Adepts, and *then* only to a place that has been prepared as I have prepared this archway. One cannot simply make a Gate into nothing, or into a place where one has never been. *And* the farther one is from the place where one wishes to Gate to, the more power it takes to make

the Gate. I cannot do that, no ten Adepts in Karse—
if we *had* ten, and not merely myself and Solaris—
could do it. *I* provide only an anchoring point. It will
be the Firecat who creates this Gate."

"I suppose," Jeri brooded, "that's the only reason
why you've never Gated in behind our lines with an
army."

Karchanek shrugged. "Power, lack of familiarity
with the place, and that there are very, very few Adepts. The Order as it was distrusted mages, and the
more power they had, the less they were trusted.
Those who manifested great power and demonstrated
an ability to think for themselves often met with unfortunate accidents, or fell victim to the White
Demons. So it was said."

"And Ancar?" Jeri asked soberly.

"Could learn this, has he those who will teach him,"
Karchenek replied grimly. "Never doubt it. *He,* as
were some of the worst of the Sun-priests of the past,
is not limited in power by what he can channel naturally—*he* can, and has, and will, channel blood-magic,
which has no limits other than the number of people
that one can kill. Yet another reason why this alliance
is so vital. Vital enough that I *will* remain here, whatever it costs me, hostage to the Son of the Sun's good
behavior, although . . ."

He didn't have to finish that statement; Karchanek
looked like a man haunted by his own personal set of
demons. In a way, apparently he was. According to
Kerowyn, who'd had mages in her Skybolts company
that hadn't been able to bear what happened to them
when they crossed into Valdemar, the reason why
there were no real mages in this land was because
they couldn't stand being here. The moment anyone
worked real magic here—something happened. Some-

thing—a *lot* of somethings, evidently—swarmed over the mage and gathered around him, night and day. And stared at him.

Now that didn't sound too dreadful to Alberich until he'd had a chance to see what the experience was doing to Karchanek's nerves and thought about it himself. What would it be like to have dozens, perhaps hundreds of people around you all the time, never taking their eyes off you, glaring at you by light and dark, sleeping or waking? Nerve-racking, that was what it was. And when the creatures were invisible to everyone else?

There was no equivalent to the Queen's Own in Solaris' "court," but Karchanek was close—lifelong friend and supporter, powerful mage, on whom she depended for able advice. That he pledged to remain as hostage was probably the *only* reason why, in the end, this plan had been agreed to. "And what do we do to keep you from spiriting yourself away?" Selenay had asked sharply when he first made the proposition himself.

He had shrugged. "Whatever you please. Bind me, blindfold me, keep in me a darkened room, drug me if no other solution presents itself. Whatever makes *you* certain of me."

Selenary had taken him at his word. There was a small cup of some drug or other waiting in a page's hands for the moment when the Gate came down again. Karchanek would be drugged until the morning of the ceremony, then watched like a hawk until the moment when the Firecat would call him and use him reopen the Gate to Valdemar, this time in the full presence of every important person in Karse at the High Temple itself, and send Talia and her escort home. He didn't seem at all unhappy about that—

"—the truth?" he said to Jeri, when she asked him about that herself. 'I will welcome it. To sleep, oblivious to all the *vrondi*-eyes upon me! I could ask no greater boon, at this moment. They do not just watch, you know. They talk, at me sometimes, but mostly among themselves. It is not just the eyes upon me, it is the chatter, the droning babble that never stills and never ends, that I cannot understand." He shuddered, and Alberich saw with an easing of his worries that a faint expression of sympathy flitted over Selenay's face.

Sympathy—for a Karsite other than Alberich. A good omen, but one he didn't have time to contemplate. Already Karchanek approached the brickwork archway, and he had warned Alberich that not even a Firecat could maintain a Gate at this distance for too long. They would barely have time to get through it.

As a lowly Captain of the Border Guard, he had never actually *seen* any priestly magic being performed, other than the simple act of kindling fire on Vkandis' altar; he'd only heard the howls of the spectral creatures conjured to harry "witches and evildoers" through the night. He couldn't bear to watch it now. Perhaps one day, when he'd had a chance to become accustomed to the idea of magic being used for anything other than harm, but not now. Not when his nerves were singing with the need to act, and he feared that if he watched Karchanek, a man he would like to think of as a friend one day, he might see the Priest-Mage calling a demon. . . .

So he busied himself with Kantor's tack, and when the signal came, he mounted in a rush, and drove through the Gate with his eyes closed, hard on Rolan's heels.

There was a long, long moment then of terrible

cold, then bone-shaking nausea, and the horrible sensation that he was falling through a starless, endless, bottomless night. It seemed to last forever, but Kantor's steady presence in his mind held him, as it had held him during the long, slow agony of healing from his terrible burns, when Kantor had rescued him and brought him here, to safety and a new life—

Then he was not *here,* anymore, but *there*—in Karse.

Sun blazed down upon him and the others, a sun fierce and kind at the same time. They stood, their Companions' bridle bells chiming softly as they fidgeted, in the middle of a bone-white courtyard surrounded on all four sides by enclosing walls. Before them waited a cat, and a woman.

The cat was the size of a large dog, with a brick-red mask, ears, paws, and tail shading to a handsome cream on the body, and piercing blue eyes. A Firecat—

:Indeed I am,: said a voice in his mind with a touch of satisfied purr behind it. *:My name is Hansa, and this, of course, is Solaris. Welcome home, Herald Alberich.:*

"I second that sentiment," echoed the woman.

She had presence that entirely eclipsed her appearance. If Alberich had not already known that her eyes were a golden-brown subject to changing as her mood changed, and her hair a darker golden-brown, he would not have been able to tell anyone that if he turned around and took his eyes off her. Yes, the Firecat was impressive—any feline that came up to his knee would be impressive, much less one like Hansa. And the faint golden glow that surrounded each hair certainly didn't hurt.

But Solaris had that same golden glow about *her.* And a great deal more. Measuring by eye, she was certainly no taller than Selenay and much shorter than Alberich—but she somehow loomed larger than that.

"You, I do hope, Herald Talia are," she said in slow and deliberate Valdemaran to Talia, who had dismounted. She held out her hand, and Talia stepped forward and took it. And both of them smiled identical, warm smiles that managed to humanize Solaris without diminishing her impressiveness by a whit. "And this the formidable Herald Dirk would be?" she inquired with a slight lift of one eyebrow that somehow had the effect of making Dirk flush.

There were no servants, no lesser priests, there was no one but Solaris and Hansa—Hansa, who Solaris scooped up with an effort and held draped over her arms, for despite the Firecat's aplomb, he seemed exhausted. It was Solaris who escorted them to their rooms, indicating with a simple nod of her head that the Companions should come also. She brought them down quiet, white corridors lit from above by skylights and ornamented at intervals with great Sun-In-Glory Disks on walls and inlaid in the floors.

The rooms were simple, probably priests' quarters; Dirk and Talia shared one, with Alberich in the next—and most interesting, a kind of rough box-stall hock-deep in fresh straw took up about half of each of the rooms. Kantor went directly to his with a shake of his head; after a long and searching look at *their* Chosen, Rolan and Dirk's little mare went to theirs.

"And here my own suite is," said Solaris, throwing open the next door, which differed not at all from theirs. "Some changes I made when they were mine. . . ."

Alberich could well imagine. Solaris' predecessor had been one of the worst in the long line of corrupt

and venial leaders. He could see that the plain door
was very new, and could only imagine the sort of
gilded monstrosity that had once stood in its place.
Something had certainly been scoured and sanded
from the wall now painted a plain pale wheat color.
Furnishings were just as simple as those in the rooms
he and the others had been given; two long couches,
three lounging chairs, and a desk and working chair.
Solaris put Hansa down on a low couch and straightened up again.

"We in the heart of our great Temple are," Solaris
said gravely. "My hand-picked servants, a brace of
trusted Priests, these all that know of your presence
are. Come here, none else shall."

"But—isn't there some preparation we should
make?" Talia asked. "What are we—am I—supposed
to be doing?"

"That, I know not myself," Solaris said ruefully, surprising all of them. "The Sunlord has not told me.
Here—come and sit, and tell you what I know, I
shall."

She took a seat on the couch beside Hansa, leaving
them to choose seats for themselves. Now, no longer
quite so dazzled by her presence, Alberich noted that
her robes were as simple as her rooms. . . .

And just as deceptive. For the chair he chose was
carved of tigerwood, comfortably cushioned with soft
doeskin tanned to a golden hue. And Solaris' robes
might be simple in cut, but they were a heavy golden
silk-twill, subtlety embroidered with the Sun In Glory
in a slightly darker shade. No matter what else she
was, Solaris was not ascetic.

"This much, I know," Solaris told them, one hand
on Hansa's back, stroking as she spoke. "At the Sol-

stice ceremony, some few chosen Novices made Priests are, here in the High Temple." She made a face. "Those with families of wealth and influence, most generally. *Some* times, of outstanding ability, one or two. Among them, you are to be. Last, you will be announced and made Priest. A simple ceremony, it is—repetition of vows, which I will show you, so that you know I do not bind you to more than I claim. More than that, I know not."

"But there will *be* more than that," Alberich stated, as Talia bit her lip.

Solaris traded a glance with Hansa. *:Of a complete certainty there will be more, much more than that,:* the Firecat said. *:But the Sunlord does not choose to impart to us precisely what He has in mind.:*

"Trust you must, to Him and to me," Solaris said.

It could be a trap. It could be something really horrible. Alberich knew without bothering to try and read his expression that all manner of grim possibilities were running through Dirk's mind. Whether Talia suffered the same concerns he couldn't say, but he rather thought not. Talia couldn't read thoughts, but she *could,* as an Empath, read emotions, and those often spoke more clearly and unambiguously than thoughts. Her expression showed no sign of worry; on the contrary, she seemed as comfortable as she could be with the news that a God had decided to spring some sort of surprise, not only on His own people and chiefest Priest, but on her. Whatever she read from Solaris, it gave her no concerns on that score.

Solaris sighed. "Inscrutable, the Sunlord is, and unknowable His mind . . . but a wish I have, in my weakness, that He be somewhat less so."

Hansa made a sound between a purr and a cough

that sounded like a laugh, and Solaris bent her golden gaze upon her Firecat. "And you, also," she added, with a touch, a bare touch, of sharpness.

:I am a cat,: Hansa reminded her with supreme dignity. *:And a cat is nothing if not mysterious. It is our charm.:*

To Alberich's surprise it was Dirk who chuckled weakly. "Well; Radiance," he said, having learned the proper forms of address from Alberich and Karchanek, "we're used to this sort of behavior out of our Companions. *They* seem to have a proper mania about keeping secrets from us mere mortals."

That relaxed Solaris; Alberich read it in the lessening of the tension of her shoulders. "When divine intervention requested is, and received it is, then churlish is must be to cavil at how it comes, one supposes," she offered.

Talia uttered a ladylike snort, and Solaris hid a smile behind her hand. "If God understandable becomes, need Him we no longer should," Solaris observed after a moment. "For we would be as He. . . ."

:An interesting observation, and an intelligent one,: Kantor said with approval, but no surprise.

Alberich could only wonder how this woman had managed to survive in the cutthroat world of Temple politics with a mind like that.

"Well, tell us about this ceremony," Talia said after a moment of silence, in lieu of any other comments, and Solaris hastened to tell them what she could.

When Talia and Dirk retired, Solaris motioned to Alberich to stay. "I would like to introduce you to my chief friends and supporters, aside from Karchanek," she said, switching to Karsite with obvious relief.

"And I wish to learn to know you, Alberich, and through you, the land I wish to make our ally."

He resumed his seat warily as she continued, after summoning a silent servant with a double clap of her hands and issuing orders for food and drink.

"You have been a Herald of Valdemar for longer now than you ever lived in Karse," she observed shrewdly. "Would you return to dwell here— permanently—if you could?"

He shook his head. He head already considered his from the moment that he was convinced Karchanek could be trusted. "No, Holiness," he replied with all respect. "Even if I were to be accepted by those who called me traitor. I am a Herald."

He half expected her to be insulted, but she smiled as if she understood. "Then from time to time, Karse will come to you," she said, and at that moment the servant entered with another, both bearing trays.

Now, scent—as Alberich well knew, since he had now and again used it as a weapon—is the sense that strikes the deepest and at the most primitive parts of a man. And he had not realized just how much he missed his homeland, until the scents of the foods of his childhood arose from the dishes that the servants uncovered, and briefly—briefly—he regretted giving the answer he had.

She must have read that in his expression, for she laughed. "Now you see how fair I am with you," she told him, and at that moment she showed her true age, which was less than this, and perhaps less than Selenay's. "For had I wished to have my will of you, I should have asked you that question with the scent of spiced sausage, dumplings and gravy, and apple cake in your nostrils!"

The servant handed him a filled plate, which he took eagerly. "This is not the fare I would have expected in the Palace of the Sun, Holiness," he said, prevaricating, for she had come *far* too close to the truth with that comment.

"Hmm. Larks' tongues and sturgeon roe, braised quail, and newborn calf stewed in milk?" She gave him a sardonic look. "My cook is appalled by my tastes, but my people know that *I* eat what *they* eat, and I have made it certain that they have heard this from the Palace servants. There has been far too much of larks' tongues on golden plates, while babies wail and children have the pinched faces of hunger on the other side of the Temple wall." She took the plate that the servant offered her; Alberich observed that both plates were of honest ceramic. "The golden plates went to replenish granaries; the furnishings and precious objects I found in these rooms bought new herd-beasts to strengthen bloodlines. Oh, I hardly gave *all* away," she admitted, and paused for a hungry mouthful herself. "Much has gone into the decoration of the Temple and I will not strip the Sunlord's sanctuary of its glory. But the wealth that I did was the loot of centuries come straight out of storehouses, and has restored, if not plenty, then at least sufficiency to my land. Plenty will come in time, Sunlord willing, and with the work of the people."

"And the border?" Alberich dared to ask. "There are still bandits there that prey on Karse and Valdemar alike."

She smiled grimly. "I have recalled the corrupt troops, put Guild mercenaries in their place until I can train young fighters who will serve and not exploit, *and*—" she paused significantly, "—I have distributed arms to the Border villages."

Alberich was in significant shock over the news that Karse had hired Guild mercenaries. He wondered how she had managed to convince the Guild that Karse was to be trusted, and had winced at the thought of the size of the bond she would have had to post. But to hear that she had distributed arms to the common people—

"I doubt that they will be effective; it is more a matter of improving their morale and bolstering their courage," she continued. "They'll likely be frightened of the Guild fighters until they realize that they are trustworthy, and being armed will make them feel more secure. Still, one never knows. They might surprise me, and take over their own defense."

Arming the villagers— If nothing else, *this* was the clearest indication that the Fires of Cleansing had been extinguished. No Red-robe Priest would *dare* to enter a village on a mission of Cleansing where the villagers were armed.

She ate in silence until she had cleaned her plate, then set it aside, accepted a cup of good—but common—wine from the servant and sat back. "Let me tell you the rest of my reforms, in brief. The village priests have been reassigned to new villages, unless *all*, or almost all, the villagers themselves protested and demanded that their priest remain with them. It might surprise you to learn that a good two thirds did just that."

Alberich shrugged; he hadn't seen that much widespread corruption among the village priests when he'd been a Captain. Those who abused their authority were attracted to the *real* seat of power in Sunhame.

"There are no more forays by troops and priests into the villages to Cleanse or to test and gather up children. If a parent *wants* a child tested, they must take the child to the village priest, who will call in a Black-robe Priest-Mage." She sipped her wine. "I surmise you already know that there are no more Redrobes, and no more demon-summoning."

"And you suppose these changes will endure past your lifetime?" *Which may be a short one,* he added mentally.

"Change is generational, but I intend to outlive all those who oppose me until there *are* no Sun-priests in Karse that *I* have not overseen the training of," she retorted. "I am young enough; Sunlord permitting, there should be no reason why I cannot do this."

If you survive assassins—he thought, when Hansa coughed politely, and he met the Firecat's sardonic gaze.

:That is why I am here,: the Firecat replied, with casual arrogance. *:I believe that the Sunlord plans to ensure that the Son of the Sun survives assassins—and everything else,:* Kantor observed.

Since he had quite left that consideration out of his calculations, he felt a wave of chagrin, which he covered by handing the servant his empty plate and cup. The servant left with the dishes and her orders to see that Talia and Dirk were also offered a meal.

With her attention no longer on her meal, Solaris proceeded to— "interrogate" him was too strong a word for what she did, since she was polite, interested, and deceptively offhand in her questions and remarks, but "interrogation" was what it amounted to. He had been prepared for it, and answered with all due caution, wondering if she, Hansa, or both might not consider putting the equivalent of a Truth-Spell on him.

They didn't, though, or at least not that he could tell, and Kantor didn't say anything about it.

She only broke it off when the servant returned with

three more Sun-priests, one older than Alberich, two young, all male. "Ah, good, you managed to get away," she said genially, as the three bowed to her before taking seats at her wave of invitation. 'This is Herald Alberich; I wanted you to meet him without the other two in attendance. Alberich, this is my dear friend and mentor Ulrich, and my fellows in the novitiate, Larschen and Grevenor."

The older man, Ulrich, smiled broadly and nodded; the one that Solaris had called Larschen widened his eyes and said, so seriously that it could only have been a joke, "I expected someone taller. With horns. And hooves."

Grevenor *tsk*ed. "What a disappointment! His teeth aren't even pointed!"

"And after I spent all that time filing them flat so I wouldn't alarm you!" Alberich replied, with the same mock-seriousness, and was rewarded by a smile from Solaris and a withering glance from Hansa.

:A typical feline,: Kantor observed. *:He only appreciates jokes when he makes them.:*

The atmosphere relaxed considerably now that Solaris' friends were here, and even though more questions came at him, he was able to ask as many as he answered, and within a candlemark or so, he had a very vivid picture in his mind of the first days when Solaris had come to power. It seemed that many of those in the temples outside of Sunhame had rallied to her after the miracle of her coronation. But before the miracle she had spent years in garnering the support of her contemporaries; Solaris was no Reulan, to come to the Sunthrone without opposition.

And that was intensely interesting. She had been prepared for this miracle, and when it came, she had everything in place to ensure that she simply wasn't

escorted off and quietly done away with so that the
running of Karse could go back to "business as usual."

Yes, that was interesting. *Very* interesting. So she
had known, for years, that she was going to be the
Chosen One, but instead of biding her time quietly,
she had created a support base that ensured she could
not be gotten quietly out of the way, and which gave
encouragement to others to fall in with them.

She was remarkably quiet about *how* she had
known, however, and Alberich could only wonder. For
all that she was amazingly down-to-earth among her
supporters, there was still something about her, a
sense that she probably *did* spend the hours in meditation and prayer that the Son of the Sun was popularly
supposed to do. And that she probably always had . . .
that here was a person for whom the service of
Vkandis truly *was* a vocation.

Alberich was not overly familiar with the aura of
sanctity, but he thought that it surrounded Solaris.

And therein lay her greatest difference from Selenay, although in many, many ways the two were very
much alike. Selenay was warmly and completely femi-
nine; Solaris was warmly and completely—neuter. It
was very much as if some cloak of power lay lightly
on her shoulders, and sent out a wordless message: *I
am for no man.*

In that, she was not unlike the Shin'a'in Sword-
sworn; Alberich had met one, some distant relative or
other of Kerowyn. Whether that was by choice, natural inclination, or necessity mattered not. That Solaris
would have cut her own breasts off if Vkandis had
required it of her was something that no one who sat
in the same room with her for a candlemark would
doubt.

And perhaps, after all, this was *why* she now sat in

the Sunthrone. Perhaps this was why Vkandis had taken so long to manifest Himself to His people. Someone like Solaris was rarer than someone with the special Gift that qualified her as Queen's Own.

Someone who had that much raw faith and still remained human and humane was rarer still.

Only a God would have the patience to wait for such a servant to be born—but a God could afford to take a very long view indeed.

Alberich and Dirk sat silently, side by side, high above the crowded sanctuary, in a concealed alcove that no one below would guess existed. The cunningly pierced carving gave them an excellent view without revealing that there was anything behind it. The air in here was cool and a little dank, enclosed entirely in stone as they were. Even the cunningly-pivoted door was stone. It was also dark; any light would show through the stone lacework of the panel behind which they sat. The Temple sanctuary beyond that screen was a blaze of white, red, yellow, and precious gold. Sun gems winked from the centers of carved Sunflowers, gilding was everywhere, and there were so many windows (besides the great skylight over the altar) that the place seemed as open as a meadow.

Down there, arrayed in a semicircle in front of the altar, were the Novices about to be made Priests. Only a few were ever endowed with their holy office standing before the Sun Throne. Fewer still were granted the honor of one of the major Festivals. And of hose few, only the highest took their vows on the Summer Solstice, the day when the sun-disk reigned longest in the sky. Four and twenty of those stood down there today; Talia was the last, and the others—who knew each other by sight at least—must surely be wondering

who she was and why she was among them. Censers
fuming incense—perfectly harmless, undrugged incense of a pleasant spice scent—stood at either end
of their semicircle. The incense drifted up to Alberich's hiding place, relieving the slightly stale scent of
the air.

One and all, the Novices wore simple robes of
black, without ornamentation. One by one by they
were summoned before Solaris, who administered
their vows—surprisingly simple vows—and arrayed
them in their black-and-gold vestments. Solaris herself
was a glory in her robes of office and crown, covered
with bullion, medallions, even plaques of gold, and
what wasn't sewn with gold was embroidered with Sun
gems. Alberich couldn't imagine how she could stand
under the weight of it, yet she moved effortlessly, calling each Priestly candidate forward, taking his—or
her, for half of the candidates were *women*—vows,
and with the aid of two acolytes, arraying them in
their new vestments. So far there was no sign that
Solaris had made any special announcement about
Talia—her core group of supporters knew, of course,
but no one else seemed to. Why was she keeping it
all so secret, if this was supposed to be the start of a
new alliance?

:Perhaps she's had—advice,: Kantor suggested. His
tone suggested that the advice might have come from
a higher authority.

Well, that was certainly possible, but Alberich worried that she had been left to her own devices to or-
chestrate this, and was playing her game too close.

Or perhaps she didn't intend to announce Talia's
origin at all.

That actually made him feel a lot less nervous
about this.

Perhaps she just intended to invest Talia without making any fuss about where she was from, and only after they'd gone home would she announce it. There would be no prospect of enraging anyone while the Heralds were still in Karse that way.

That plan would make Alberich a great deal happier than facing the possibility of a riot in the Temple when Solaris announced just what Talia was.

Dirk was equally edgy, actually fidgeting, peering through first one then another of the pierced holes in the stone screen that covered their hiding place. Alberich wished *he* could fidget, but discipline was habit now, and there was nothing he could do to relieve the tension that made him feel as if he vibrated in place. The narrow stone bench on which they sat bit into his thighs, and he wished devoutly that this was all over. . . .

One by one, the candidates approached, said their few words— and he was grateful that nothing in that vow interfered with Talia's pledges to Valdemar and its throne—were bedecked with their heavy trappings, and departed again.

And now, at last, it was Talia's turn.

The sun was at its zenith, and the rays poured down through the skylight above the altar. This was the holiest moment of the holiest day of the calendar and now—

"I summon the last candidate," Solaris called, in that peculiar, carrying voice of hers that sounded no louder than a simple conversation and yet could be heard in the last rank of worshipers at the rear of the Temple, even though there was a steady murmur of praying and talking. "I call Herald Talia of Valdemar."

Reaction rippled over the crowd like a wave. Dirk

went rigid, and Alberich gripped the stone with both hands. A silence fell that was as heavy as a blanket of lead. Hundreds of heads suddenly swiveled up and forward. Hundreds, thousands of wide, shocked eyes stared at Solaris, at Talia, as the latter bent her head calmly and accepted the vestments of a Priestess of Vkandis. Shock still held them, as Solaris took Talia's hand and turned her to face the crowd so that all of them could hear her take her vows—and could see the Firecat pace slowly down from behind the altar and place himself protectively at Talia's feet, purring, the sound being the only thing other than the two voices that pierced that silence. It did not escape Alberich that Hansa was between Talia and the crowd of worshipers.

Then Solaris spoke, and Hansa muted his purrs. Up until this moment, there had not been real *silence* in the Temple. Now there was, an empty, hollow silence, waiting to be filled. The few words of the vows, spoken in a tone hardly louder than a whisper, echoed at the farthest corners of the Temple.

Then, as the last of Talia's words died away in the awful silence, Solaris spoke again before the silence could be filled by any other.

"The time has come," Solaris said, in a voice like a clear, silvery trumpet call, addressing Talia, but also the crowd. "The time has come fo͏ the ancient enmity between our land and Valdemar to be burned away. It is time for hatred, death, and the taint of spilled blood to be burned away. Will you come with me, and trust to me and to the God to whom you made your vows, Herald Talia?"

"I will," Talia replied, in a voice as firm, if not with the same clarion sound. And she put her hand in the one Solaris stretched out to her. Together they turned to face the altar.

As they turned to the altar, flames sprang up upon it all in an eyeblink with a roaring sound; golden flames as high as a man and seemingly born of the rays of the sun falling on the white marble.

The crowd gasped, then stilled again.

No one had been there to kindle those flames. There was nothing there to feed it; no wood, no coal, no oil, and yet the flames leaped and danced and even from here Alberich could feel the heat of them, hear the crackle and roar. Solaris and Talia approached the altar, hand in hand, an Dirk shook like an aspen leaf.

There were stairs built onto the side of the altar. Had they always been there? Alberich hadn't noticed them before, but now Solaris led Talia toward them— toward the flames—

They were climbing the stairs.

They were standing in the flames!

The golden flames lapped around them, and Alberich stared, waiting for Talia to start screaming, waiting for their robes to burst into flame, waiting, with his throat closed with horror—

The flames enclosed them gently, like loving hands, or a shower of flower petals. The flames caressed them but did not consume them.

Talia was smiling.

Solaris was not smiling, but on her face was an expression that Alberich could not put a name to. Something ineffable—something beyond his understanding.

And the same stillness that filled the Temple entered Alberich's heart.

Wait. Watch. All will be well.

Feelings, not words; a peace deeper than anything

he had ever felt before, even when in profound communion with Kantor. From Talia? Perhaps; she *was* a
projective Empath, and strong enough to have sent
this out to the entire Temple if she thought it needful.

Or Talia might be the channel for something else.

His tension vanished, and something else took its
place. Out of the corner of his eye he saw Dirk's hands
drop from the stone screen, and knew that his fellow
Herald felt it, too.

Cradled lovingly in the heart of the flames, Solaris
remained unchanged in her golden robes, but something was happening to Talia.

No, not to Talia, but to her robes, he vestments.
They were changing.

He couldn't say they were *bleaching,* because there
was nothing in the transition to suggest the process of
bleaching. There was no fading to gray—no, Talia's
robes were *lightening,* not fading, they were becoming
full of light, growing lighter and lighter until they
glowed with a white intensity that outshone the flames.

Then, all at once, the flames were gone.

Solaris and Talia stood atop the altar, Talia looking
a little embarrassed, as if she had been given some
incredible honor all unlooked-for that she felt unwor-
thy of.

Talia's priestly vestments, the robes of a Sun-priest,
were no longer black and gold.

They were white and silver.

Heraldic colors.

"In the long ago," Solaris said, her voice floating
above the crowd like a subtle melody, "There was a
third order of Sun-priests. These were the White-
robes, whose duty was to serve as Healers, to solve
dissension, to keep the peace."

:Whose duty was also to serve the Goddess—but she

won't mention that at the moment,: said Kantor absently.

Goddess? What Goddess? When had there ever been a Goddess in Karse? *:What are you talking about?:* he demanded, but Kantor wasn't answering, and more than half of his attention was on the two women anyway. . . .

"Vkandis has chosen this woman to be the first of the new White-robes," Solaris continued, her voice stronger, as in a call to arms. "Vkandis has burned away all the hatred, all the death, all the evil that has passed between our lands! Vkandis has sent His purifying fire to show us the way, to give us this new, living bridge, of understanding between His land and Valdemar! I, Son of the Sun, now charge you—cry welcome to Talia, White-robe Priest of Vkandis!"

The cheering that erupted vibrated the very stone beneath Alberich's feet and left him momentarily deafened. But that was all right, for the cheers went on so long that no one would have been able to hear anything anyway.

The three Heralds and their Companions stood in front of the arched doorway into Solaris' private courtyard that would serve as the framework for the Gate. Hansa stared fixedly at the arch— presumably, in the little clearing in Companion's Field, Karchanek was doing likewise. Alberich was as tired as if he'd been running training exercises for a day and a night without a rest. Dirk looked stunned, as if all of this still hadn't quite sunk in yet. Well, Alberich didn't blame him. *He* didn't feel as if it had all quite sunk in yet either.

Talia's new vestments and robes were packed up into a saddlebag on Rolan's back; on the whole, given all of the bad blood between Karse and Valdemar, Solaris deemed it wise for them to leave now, before this first flush of good feeling faded and people began looking for the Demon-riders and their Hellhorses to have a few choice words with them. Few even among the Priest-Mages knew that a Gate was even possible, and those few were in Solaris' ranks; the arrival and departure. of the Queen's Own would seem miraculous, as miraculous as the transformation of Talia's robes from black to white.

Was it magic—or a miracle? Alberich knew which his heart wanted it to be. And he wished he could recapture a little of that wonderful stillness, that *peace,* that had come over him. But that was, after all, the nature of miracles. They were evanescent, and left little or nothing behind to prove where they had come from. It all could have been magic—illusory flames, and Talia projecting that stillness under Solaris' guidance. It could have been a well-orchestrated series of magic spells, set up by Priest-Mages in hiding just as Alberich had been. Who knew how many of those little niches overlooking the sanctuary there were.

Alberich didn't want to question it, though. His rational side said he should, and when he got home, Myste almost certainly would want to know why he hadn't. And he didn't have a good answer for her— *:And you will continue to believe in the face of her questions, even though at times doubt overcomes that belief,:* Kantor said. *:That, after all, is the nature of faith. And perhaps that is as it is intended to be, and the reason why miracles so seldom leave tangible evidence of their origin behind.:*

:What—: Alberich replied. *:So that we have nothing to rely on but belief?:*

:That would be the "free will" part, I think.: Kantor replied, with just a touch of impishness.

There was no time for further discussion. The Gate sprang into uncanny life. The stones of the archway began to glow; the brightness increased, and suddenly, instead of the room beyond the door, there was an empty blackness within the arch that made Alberich's eyes ache.

Then crawling tendrils like animate lightning crept across the blackness, tendrils that crisscrossed the darkness and multiplied with every heartbeat.

Then, with a jolt he felt somewhere in his chest, the blackness vanished, and the arch opened up on Companion's Field on the twilight, and his waiting friends, and Karchanek in front of them all.

"Time to go," said Dirk, and suited his action to his words, riding straight through without a backward glance. Poor Dirk! This had not been easy for him. . . .

"Thank you for your trust," Solaris said to Talia, and held her in a momentary embrace that Talia bent down from her saddle to share.

"And you for yours, Radiance," Talia replied, smiling, some of the peace that Alberich wistfully wished for still lingering in *her* gaze. Then it was her turn, and she rode through to the welcoming committee on the other side.

Alberich would have followed, but a restraining hand on his stirrup made him pause.

"Here—" Solaris said, handing him a basket that smelled of home. "I told you that Karse would come to you."

All of this—and she remembers sausages and herbbread for me?

She smiled up at him—once again, the ordinary-extraordinary woman that she was when she was not encased in the Sunlord's gold. "This could not have been done without *your* trust as well."

He coughed. "It was little enough, for so great a result, Radiance," he replied, shifting the basket uneasily.

"It was greater than you will admit," she retorted. "And I think you had better not say anything more that would indicate you disagree with your spiritual lord. I *might* arrest you for heresy."

"The day *you* arrest anyone for heresy will be the day that the sun turns black, Radiance," he responded, earning another smile from her. He hesitated a moment, poised on the brink of asking all those questions that quivered on the tip of his tongue.

But she was having none of it.

"Go!" she said, with a playful slap to Kantor's rump. "Hansa wearies and Karchanek cannot wait to quit your soil and its plague of *eyes!*"

Kantor leaped forward without any urging from Alberich, and as he fell through the arch in that moment of eternal darkness, he felt something brush past his leg—Karchanek, taking advantage of the fact that the Gate would not close immediately to escape back into his own land and place.

Then Kantor's four hooves thudded on solid turf, and he was surrounded by friends and fellow Heralds, and he realized that the basket he held did not smell of *home* after all. It smelled of childhood memories, yes, and of things he thought of as comforts that he had not enjoyed in a very long time. But not of *home*.

Home was here, in a land whose language had become his in dreams, among people who were dearer than blood-kin, who would gladly give him anything they had, including their lives.

As he would, for them.

And as for his God—well, Vkandis had shown more clearly than in words that a border was nothing more than an artificial boundary, and names were just as artificial. Vkandis had been here all along, cloaked in the hundred names for Deity that the Valdemarans had for Him; Alberich just hadn't known it in his heart until now.

'Welcome back!" said Eldan, relieving him of the basket so that he could dismount. The relief on his face said all that he would not say aloud—that despite all of the assurances, the guarantees, the others had been wound as tight with worry as *he* had been in the Temple. "I hope it all went all right?"

"Better, much, than all right," Alberich replied, the cadences of Valdemaran coming strangely—for just a moment—to his tongue. He looked around, and saw that all of the Council as well as Selenay and the Prince-Consort had surrounded Talia and Dirk to get *their* version of the story. His own friends, including Myste, surrounded *him*. "Many tales, have I to tell," he continued. "And tell them I shall, when we settled are, with good wine in hand."

"How arc you feeling?" Myste asked, taking his hand and looking into his eyes—perhaps looking for a sign that he regretted leaving.

"Well. Morc than well." He smiled down at her. "It is good to be home."

MERCEDES LACKEY

The Novels of Valdemar

Exile's Honor

He was once a captain in the army of Karse, a
kingdom that had been at war with Valdemar for
decades. But when Alberich took a stand for
what he believed in—and was betrayed—he was
Chosen by a Companion to be a Herald, and
serve the throne of Valdemar. But can Alberich
keep his honor in a war against his own people?

"A treat for Valdemar fans"
—Booklist

0-7564-0085-6

To Order Call: 1-800-788-6262

DAW 24

MERCEDES LACKEY

The Novels of Valdemar

To Order Call: 1-800-788-6262

Mercedes Lackey & Larry Dixon

The Novels of Valdemar

"Lackey and Dixon always offer a well-told tale"
—*Booklist*

To Order Call: 1-800-788-6262